The Fractal Melody

by

Frances M. Wood

Published by francesmwood books
Hillsborough NC
www.francesmwood.com
All rights reserved

ISBN 13 (paperback): 9798999343802
ISBN 13 (ebook): 9798999343819
Library of Congress Control Number: 2025915564

Cover art © Lesley W. Nelson 2025.
Portrait by Wilhelm Kreling 1855-1937 'German lady
playing piano', copyright expired.
Starry fractals (not its actual name) created by
insspirito (Garik Barseghyan), courtesy of pixabay.com.

Praise for Earlier Books Written by Frances M. Wood

Becoming Rosemary

Kirkus
'Wood debuts with a nearly flawless, always charming coming-of-age tale.'

Publisher's Weekly
'A hymn to the pains and joys of special gifts, magical and otherwise.'

Chinaberry Book Services
'Kind and compassionate...This is a lovely, lovely book.'

Daughter of Madrugada

VOYA
'Through the recounting of seemingly trivial happenings, Wood guides readers to an awareness of cultural differences and the effect of historical events on the lives of individual people.'

forbesbookclub.com
'A gracefully told and skillfully constructed tribute to family loyalty, love of the land and the resilience of the human spirit.'

Oneota Reading Journal: an e-journal from Decorah Public Library and Luther College
'This story shows the deep connections and love between people who continue to persevere through all of life's hardships.'

Booklist
'In the end, the question is about what it means to be American.'

When Molly Was A Harvey Girl

Booklist
'The values of education, courage, and simplicity all come together in this delightful tale.'

familyliteracyandyou.blogspot.com
'I thought this book was wonderful.'

CONTENTS

Chaos was the law of nature;

Order was the dream of man

Henry Adams

PRELUDE

> "Now, you and I don't have shells to crawl into like Bert the Turtle, so
> we have to cover up in our own way."
>
> From *Duck and Cover*, a school film teaching post–World War II
> children how to protect themselves against atom bombs.

1962

Moraga, California

Justa failed the IQ test in the third grade. She sat at her school desk, bending her head over the test booklet. But instead of doing what the teacher said—which was to carefully read each question and its answers before choosing—she moved her pencil over the answer sheet as if writing music. She turned upright ovals into eighth notes, quarter notes, and half notes. She penciled and erased, humming under her breath until what she heard began to make sense. When test time was over, she turned her answer sheet backside-up like everybody else.

She walked home beside Lowry who, being ten years old, had taken the test two years ago. They walked beneath plum trees, the pink flowers smelling like corn muffins. Up above—beyond the front yards, over the houses, at the very top of the hill—an oak-dotted meadow was noisy with birds. Justa wanted to be in that meadow, but she knew Lowry wouldn't go. So, instead, Justa sent her ears up high. She listened through the trilling of sparrows, the squabbling of woodpeckers, the announcements of jays. She waited for, and finally heard, the empty-room echoing of a dove.

"Come on!" Lowry grabbed Justa's hand and pulled.

When they reached the path to their front door, they saw Mommy waiting for them on the porch. "How did it go, pumpkin?" Mommy asked Justa.

"Okay," Justa answered.

"Did you finish early? Did you have time to go back and check your answers?"

"Yes," said Justa, her first and only-ever lie.

"Good." Mommy kissed Justa's cheek, then Lowry's. "You can tell Daddy all about it when he gets home." She shooed them into the foyer, then into the kitchen—a place of steam, the smell of beans, the metallic wobble of the pressure cooker. She opened the refrigerator door to pour out two glasses of milk.

Lowry slid, Justa climbed, into their usual counter stools.

"I think Mommy thinks you might be an almost-genius," Lowry said solemnly. "Like me."

Justa knew all about almost-geniuses. She knew how people poked and pried and made arrangements with their lives. Lowry's tap lessons, which she loved, had been cut because the teacher told Daddy that, while Lowry was certainly a very sweet girl, she didn't have the pizazz to be a dancer. Lowry's elocution lessons, which she hated, were doubled because that teacher said Lowry might someday want to debate.

Lowry didn't read fairy tales any longer. All the books she got for Christmas had titles like *How Machinery Works*. It made Justa sad when Aunt Edith visited, and Lowry had to prove—with science projects or test papers—that she was just as smart as Mommy and Daddy wanted her to be. Lowry looked so lonely—all alone—those times when she was smiling for the grown-ups.

Afterward, Aunt Edith always turned to Justa. "And what about Justie?" she would ask—a question that didn't exactly go to Mommy and Daddy, but seemed more aimed at Justa, herself.

"Noth-ing," Justa always answered. Two notes, descending.

If Mommy mentioned the word, 'piano', Justa ran for her room.

Daddy called Justa his little mouse. Mommy called her 'pumpkin' – maybe because she hoped one day Justa might turn into a carriage. But when Justa lay in bed at night, curled beneath her blankets with Raggedy Ann hugged against her chest, she was a bird. A sweet-singing swallow, sometimes. Or a blackbird, like the ones that lived in the hedge beyond the lawn and chorused before breakfast. Or a robin, coming and going, busily hopping, telling everything and everybody to 'cheery-up'. But the best bird of all—and the very best dream—was the thrush whose whistle looped like a ribbon of dark blue smoke, rising into nowhere. That bird, Justa knew, lived far, far away, and only came by to visit.

LEARNING

"The student now goes to college to proclaim rather than to learn. The lessons of the past are ignored and obliterated in a contemporary antagonism known as 'The Generation Gap'. A spirit of national masochism prevails, encouraged by an effete corps of impudent snobs who characterize themselves as intellectuals."

Vice President Spiro Agnew, October 19, 1969

Starting Autumn 1969

LLLLL

Lowry was at Stanford! She stood at her dorm room windows, looking down at the parking lot. Her family's brown station wagon was gone. She was on her own for the first time in her life. It felt...strange.

"Hi," said a voice.

Lowry whirled.

Two girls stood in the doorway, staring at her. One girl wore a long, hooded cloak. The other wore a granny-dress. Except the granny-dress girl wasn't a girl at all, she was a mom—old.

"Willa?" Lowry squeaked. Leaving home, she had felt pretty. Now she felt somehow displaced in her pale green dress with its Ladybug brand pin on the collar. And Justa's best tan sandals.

"Bilba," the girl-who-was-a-girl corrected. "Like in *The Hobbit*, but female." Bilba flipped her cloak back beyond her shoulders, revealing a violet mini-dress with long, medieval-looking sleeves. Lowry had never seen such clothing before, except maybe in plays. *A Midsummer Night's Dream* at Stern Grove in San Francisco.

Bilba reached into one of her sleeves as if it were a pocket and pulled something out. "I made this for you."

'This' was a brooch, a silver L in perfect cursive, the same cursive as the B clasp at Bilba's throat. Lowry couldn't imagine herself making something so beautiful to see, so rich to hold.

"And Mom wove this rug for our room."

Bilba's mother was unrolling a rug that had more colors in it than a crayon box: reds and greens and blues and yellows that blended, merged, and re-emerged in bursts of brightness.

"Wow!" Lowry breathed.

Bilba's mother suddenly looked young.

"So, do you say your name like 'Laurie'?" Bilba wondered.

"Or with 'L-o-w' like 'cow'? her mother asked.

"Like cow," Lowry answered. And somehow—even though she normally didn't like to use that word as a comparison—with these people, it felt okay to say out loud.

∽

For dinner, Lowry changed her clothes. She mixed separates—her dark purple mini skirt with the hot pink poor-boy sweater. She positioned a purple-and-green scarf around her neck, and fastened it with her silver L. She stayed in Justa's sandals. She wanted to remain—at least some—in her old world.

The other girls in the dining hall looked much as she had, pre-Bilba. In fact, two of the girls at her table wore Ladybug dresses. Both, it turned out, had been student body secretaries, like Lowry. Lowry listened to those two describe their home towns, their high schools, their boyfriends, until Bilba said, "Time for new boyfriends, ladies. With a ratio of three boys to every girl, we have our *pick* here."

It didn't matter what a girl wore, she could always talk about boys.

After dinner, Lowry stood in line at the hall phone. When it came her turn, she dialed 'O' for operator, and asked to make a collect call.

"Low!" Dad said, after agreeing to pay for the charges. 'L-o-w' as in 'go'. For the first time, Lowry took note of the discrepancy.

"Hi!" She was suddenly happy. So very happy.

"How's your roommate?" Mom asked from another phone, probably the kitchen one.

"Fun." Lowry didn't go into details. She didn't know how to translate Bilba into something that would make sense to Mom and Dad.

"Did you meet her parents?" Mom asked.

"Her mother." Lowry thought of the granny-dressed woman, her waist-length hair, the incredible rug she had left on the floor. "She's nice," was all Lowry decided to say. "Is Justie there?"

"Out on a walk," Mom said.

"I have to go," Lowry decided. Because it wasn't so easy, prevaricating.

Next morning Lowry awakened to girls everywhere. First a crowded bathroom with eight sinks, four showers, and four toilets. Then breakfast, where lines of girls waited to be served from cafeteria hot plates. Lowry didn't get in a line for orange juice, because Bilba was eager to get going.

"Eat with one hand," Bilba insisted. "Come on!"

Lowry carried her toast outside, to where her new ten-speed was locked against one of dozens of bike racks. Her Raleigh was a quick and nimble bike, but since Bilba rode an old three-speed—the fenders painted with peace signs and daisies—they lagged behind other departing girls.

That girl-flock, chrome glinting, sped toward Memorial Auditorium. From other dormitories, boys emerged on their bikes. The boys infiltrated until they outnumbered, crowded, raced against, the girls.

"Come on!" Bilba screeched, and finally they reached MemAud. Bilba first, Lowry after, they walked into the tiered hall, mostly filled. "Over here," Bilba hissed. And they stepped over the legs of boys until they could take two seats together.

"It's starting," a boy whispered as Lowry sat. Convocation.

The University President welcomed the class of 1973. A history professor—who wore a long, royal blue gown—started a slide show titled, 'Stanford, Then and Today'. 'Then' began with Governor Stanford in one of those old-fashioned photographs in which nobody smiled, followed by vistas of his ranch with sepia-tinted horses and cowboys. The ranch yielded to university construction. The Main Quad was pictured before, and just after, the 1906 earthquake. The Old Union looked new during World War I. Ex-servicemen filled the classrooms after World War II. 'Today' ended with a quick click-click-click: a collage of anti-Vietnam War posters. The collage seemed incongruous to Lowry, until the boy next to her said,

"My brother died in a place called Kham Duc."

Lowry turned to look at him. He was still staring at the now blank and silvered screen; a tear trickled down his left cheek.

That evening, Lowry thought long and carefully before she joined the phone queue. She put her money in the coin slot.

"Yes, yes, we'll accept the call." Dad was impatient. "How did it go today, Low?"

"I got my I.D.," Lowry told him. "We went on a library tour. We had Convocation this morning. The President talked. There was a slide show. Some of it was about the Vietnam War."

Dad's response was immediate: "Now, you be cautious. I don't want you getting involved in any of that. Professors sometimes live in an ivory tower..."

Lowry listened for Mom, for Justa. They had to be on the line, too, because Dad's voice was only half as loud as usual. To them, Lowry wanted to describe the boy, how he wore a red-plaid Pendleton shirt. Not Stanford red, not the color of the plush seats in the auditorium tiers. But a faded red, as if from many washings. He came from a family where they washed wool in the washing machine.

A silence snagged her attention.

Lowry took a guess, and mentioned, "The Dean told us we'd meet with our academic advisors on Wednesday."

"Good," Dad approved.

"We'll hear from you soon." Mom had entered the conversation only to say goodbye.

"Justie?" Lowry questioned.

"I'm here," Justa said.

And they all hung up.

⸺

In October Bilba came down with mono. The health center said she needed two weeks of recuperation. So her mother—wearing a long patchwork skirt this time—took Bilba back to La Honda in a dusty red truck.

That's why, on the evening of the 15th, Lowry sat by herself in Tresidder Union, nursing a cup of coffee. She could have stayed in FloMo after dinner, to hang out with the girls on her floor. Those girls were nice enough, but they weren't Bilba. They couldn't help her understand whatever was breaking open inside her.

In History 107—The American Revolution as a Social Revolution—Professor Stafford had said something important: that turning points in history were often weighted by small events or accidents. America was now in the midst of a war. Lowry only had to look around at Tresidder's walls, where a journalist alum had hung poster-sized combat photos. The photos told a story. A crew-cut boy, with a cocky grin, held a machine gun over his shoulder. That boy, in the midst of others, was pushing through jungle, knee-deep in mud. The group dispersed—some boys surging back, some turning to the side, one tipping over. The tipped-over boy, now face-up, was being pulled away by his legs. His once-cocky mouth was wide with terror and pain. Mud filled the cavity where his right eye and upper cheek had been.

At seven o'clock, Lowry left Tresidder to wind her way to Memorial Church. She fell into step with people she didn't know, some of whom were children. One tiny girl carried a Snoopy umbrella. Her father scooped the child up out of the thicket of legs, and perched her on his shoulders. The little girl opened her umbrella over her daddy's head as rain began to fall.

They arrived at MemChu too late to get pew seats. "Testing, testing," came from outdoor loudspeakers. Tight within a crowd, Lowry stood in the rain. She stared at MemChu's front, lit up with spotlights. Mrs. Stanford had gone all out, raising this church in memory of her dead son and dead husband. She had chosen arches, and stained-glass windows, and lots of gold paint. At the peak of the facade Jesus stood beneath a golden sky. Men, women and children in jewel-colored robes reached toward him. Mrs. Stanford had had the consolation of her faith.

The man whose voice came from the speakers, Professor Linus Pauling, never mentioned God. Instead he spoke about government: "Our presence in Vietnam has no rational or moral goal." His hope lay in citizen action: "This War will continue unless we, the people of the United States, say NO!"

The people in the courtyard shouted back his call, "NO!"

Lowry captured her own "No!" in her mouth. It rolled over her tongue, pressed against her lips. She carried it, confined, back to Tresidder where she had left her bike. She carried it, still unspoken, to Florence Moore Hall where the scent of Bilba's patchouli oil had faded to a hint of mint. She caught a glimpse of herself in the mirror, and turned face-on. Her rain-wet hair had become a long, limp frizz. And her face—it must have been rain; it might have been tears—was streaked black with mascara.

This is what she was right now.

She waited until her floor was quiet: the other girls noisily and finally shut into their rooms. Then she took a dime from her laundry jar and went downstairs. She could have used the hall phone—no one was standing there—but she wanted the privacy of a lobby booth. She pulled a bifold door shut, and pushed her dime into the slot.

"Yes?" It was Dad, as she expected. Her parents' bedroom phone was on his side. "Low? What's wrong?"

"I went to the Peace Moratorium tonight."

"Oh, Low." She knew exactly how that tone looked on his face: worry, betrayal, some anger. "I was trusting you wouldn't."

"Professor Pauling gave a speech. Anti-war."

"Sometimes war is *necessary*, Low. There's the communist threat..."

Lowry interrupted. She never interrupted her father, but she did so now. "Professor Pauling is one of the smartest men in the world. He won the Nobel Peace Prize and, before that, a Nobel for chemistry."

"Even smart men can be fools," Dad immediately countered.

"Maybe the Vietnam War was created by fools," Lowry cross-countered. Where had she had gotten that sentence from? It hadn't been in Pauling's speech. She didn't remember reading it anywhere. But the words flowed directly from her brain, out of her mouth.

Dad paused. When he spoke, it was with intense frustration: "I never thought I would be so disappointed in you, Low."

A year ago, even a month ago, that frustration would have made Lowry fall into guilt. But tonight she was a small person who had lent her weight to a big issue. "I know," she admitted. She added, because she meant it, "I'm sorry."

Afterward, upstairs, in the communal bathroom, she again examined her face. This time she saw something remarkable: more of herself.

JJJJJ

Justa crunched almonds in the blender, turning them into a crumble. Mom was making a cake, instead of pumpkin pie, for tomorrow's Thanksgiving dinner.

"Work it only until it's like cornmeal," Mom instructed. "We don't want a butter."

Justa pushed the stop button. She stirred with a chopstick. She pushed 'start' again. Crunch, crunch, stir, stir, crunch, crunch, stir, stir. The last stir was enough: like cornmeal.

When Mom made this cake for Lowry's birthday last year, Dad had been hugely complimentary. He called it a 'magical' cake.

That was then. This was now. Right now the family needed a big slice of magic. Dad had left three hours ago to pick Lowry up from college.

Mom finished creaming butter. She whipped egg whites. She blended in egg yolks, chocolate, the crumbly almonds, and a sprinkling of flour. This cake had so little flour, it was almost all chocolate. Both Dad and Lowry loved chocolate. No matter what happened, they would always have chocolate in common.

Mom put the cake pan in the oven. "We're having all-American everything else," she reminded Justa, reminding herself. "Turkey, stuffing, green beans, tomato aspic. Apple crisp for Edith. Do you think that will be enough to remind everybody of who we are, Justie?"

"I hope so." Justa wished she could offer something more. Mom was working so hard to make tomorrow a day in which to be grateful.

Justa wandered into the dining room where piles of good china lay next to clutches of sterling silver on the big table. Setting the holiday table was her annual task. But she could do that tomorrow. For now... She thumbed through her old John Thompson's lesson books. She chose Debussy's 'Rêverie', and set it on the piano stand. The piece opened slowly, longingly, lovingly.

"That's nice, Justie," Mom called from the kitchen.

The odor of baking chocolate filled the dining room. Justa was trying to reprise the past, too. Food and music were the only magics she and Mom possessed.

The front door thudded open, solid wood hitting the rubber-tipped bumper meant to protect the wall. Justa got to the foyer at almost the same time as Mom. There stood Dad, hanging his weekend jacket in the closet. There was Lowry, lifting a small suitcase over the threshold. They had angled their shoulders away from each other, as if they were entering the house without the other.

"Oh–h–h, dear," Mom exhaled worry. She forced cheer, "Low!" She grabbed Lowry before Lowry had a chance to shut the door. Lowry hugged in response, but it wasn't a tight hug.

Dad stalked out of the foyer and into the family room. "I need a drink," he announced.

Mom sighed. "Justie, why don't you help Low unpack. I'll take care of things here."

The only 'thing' Mom had to take care of was shutting the door. But things could be feelings as well as tasks. Lowry and Dad had brought a chill into the house that crackled: the ice cubes Dad extracted from their tray in the little refrigerator beneath the bar; Lowry's rapid sniffs as she snuffled back mucus the cold air had brought to the front of her nose.

Justa shivered.

In Lowry's room, Lowry released her fingers and dropped her suitcase. "What a ride, Justie!"

Justa listened. This was her job.

"Dad's a hawk."

Justa knew enough about politics to know Lowry wasn't talking about birds. There had been a telling hurt behind Lowry's statement—as if her disappointment in Dad's opinions cut deep. Lowry needed warmth. "Let me iron your hair," Justa offered. Ironing Lowry's hair had always calmed her in the past.

"Okay." Lowry carried the iron while Justa tugged the ironing board down the hallway. "We wouldn't be in Vietnam at all, except for the Cold War." Lowry knelt on her bedroom carpet. "You and I, we've never lived in peace, ever." She lifted her hair so Justa could fan it over the board. "We were born into the Cold War." Lowry's head was bent so low, her voice puddled to the floor. "I used to worry about the world blowing up. Now I can see us destroying each other bit by bit."

Justa knew of no way to ease such an enormous fear. She could only skim heat over Lowry's hair. She could only protect Lowry from burns by cupping a hand against Lowry's head.

On Thanksgiving afternoon, Aunt Edith blasted into the house—dropped off by one of the Yamada taxis that carried her everywhere. She lingered in the kitchen, mumbling and muttering with Mom, before tracking Justa down in the dining room.

"Well!" Aunt Edith barked. "How is the family barometer?"

"They can't back down." Justa knew what Aunt Edith wanted to hear. "They both believe too much."

"So they could go on like this forever." Aunt Edith was disgusted.

The prospect was dismaying—enough to make Justa want to skip dinner. But she was part of this day. She set out Mom's wedding china, Great-grandmother's silver. Earlier, she had arranged a centerpiece around the last bird of paradise from the garden. She had hoped the flower's colors—orange, red, blue and green—would make Lowry happy. That the brightness bursting from pinecones would cheer everybody up.

It didn't.

When everybody but Dad was seated, when Dad stood to carve the turkey, there was no 'My, that smells wonderful!' or 'Ooh, that's pretty!' Nobody seemed to care enough about the food or decoration to risk opening their mouth and saying something wrong. Last night's Round Table Pizza dinner had been ruined by Lowry's remark that soldiers in Vietnam had to make their pizzas with C-rations and tabasco sauce.

Aunt Edith hadn't gone with them for pizza. "So, Lowry." She waded into the breach with her usual lack of tact. "You've come home a radical."

"No," Lowry insisted.

"As good as," Dad growled.

"Lowry is experimenting with growing up." Mom sought for a milder explanation.

Lowry, incensed by this, protested. "I'm not an infant! I'm discovering the truth!"

"In lies!" was Dad's take on things.

Justa heard: Dad felt betrayed; Lowry was torn apart by this unveiling of her new self; Mom was anxious for their home.

Aunt Edith's style was not one to soothe. "None of you have been in war, I have."

"This is a different kind of war. A proxy war to prohibit Maoism, Stalinism, from ever reaching this continent." Dad preached to Lowry, not Aunt Edith.

"Fought in a far-off country filled with innocent people, as if those people aren't real, as if they don't deserve to exist." Lowry preached back.

"Would anybody like more stuffing?" Mom asked desperately.

Dad's focus was all on Lowry. "What can *you* do, anyway? You're not even old enough to vote!"

"I can believe in a future that's better than the one your generation screwed up for us," Lowry said fiercely.

Dad was hurt—as hurt as Lowry had been after their drive home. Justa could see Dad's hurt by the way his chest suddenly collapsed into itself. Aunt Edith must have noticed, too, because she held her palms out to signal, 'stop'.

"All right, that's enough from both of you. We're not going to talk about war any longer. Are you with me, Isobel?"

"Yes." Mom's concurrence held tears.

"Justa?"

Justa nodded—even though she knew silence wasn't a substitute for truth.

"All right then." Aunt Edith, who was really a pharmacist, appointed herself the judge at their table. "You, Dan, and you, Lowry, are going to hold it in. And, yes, Isobel, I would like more stuffing." She passed her plate to Lowry, for Lowry to hold while Mom wielded her serving spoon.

"I'd like more turkey, Dad." If this was the best the family could do, Justa would help.

Dad served her a slice of white meat. He had remembered, white meat was always her preference. "Thanks, Dad." She smiled gratitude at him.

It wasn't a meal of smiles, but at least there were no more tears. Dad and Lowry only picked at the chocolate cake. When dinner was finished—after Lowry disappeared, while Mom and Dad were working in the kitchen—Aunt Edith joined Justa in dismantling the centerpiece. Justa plucked away the bird of paradise: it had held as little magic as chocolate or Debussy.

Aunt Edith spoke in a low voice, with uncharacteristic hesitancy: "I don't know if I did the right thing."

Justa knew she hadn't.

"Your mother deserves the peace that neither the war-monger nor the anti-war-monger are willing to give." In that moment Aunt Edith looked fully her age, older than Dad by eight years. "During World War II, I saw American boys who quivered and shook, and couldn't tell me their own names. I saw the survivors who came in from Buchenwald. I don't know what is absolutely right. I only know that if we can have peace here in Moraga, it would be a good thing. Don't you think?"

"Yes." Justa certainly did think that.

Because Justa couldn't read Aunt Edith as well as she could read the others, because she hadn't known about these wounds in Aunt Edith's heart, Justa gave Aunt Edith the bird of paradise to take home.

～

Monday morning, at school, Justa stood in the outside corridor and closed her eyes to hear: the squeak and clang of locker doors being shut; the sliding thud of padlocks being pushed fast; the shrillness of girls, the loudness of boys. It was all such a relief after the Thanksgiving holiday.

Her first class of the day was choir. She wasn't a strong alto. But after class started, when the voices around her came together in a moment of perfection—as they rarely did—she felt a spurt of happiness. Beethoven's 'Ode to Joy' held all the thanksgiving and gratitude that had been missing at home. Futilely, Justa pushed her right-hand fingers against her open choir book, as if against piano keys, trying to round up the sounds and hold them forever in an extended D chord.

"Miss Matthews?" Mrs. Hudson's speaking voice intruded. Song trailed off. Justa flattened her hand over her book. "Would you like to do that on the piano? Leave me free to conduct?"

Justa had never played on the choir room piano before. The altos below her shifted aside to allow her to step down. She felt every eye on her back as she walked to, and sat on, the bench. With her fingers as light as possible, she played by ear the phrase they had just finished. The old upright was scratched and scarred, shedding varnish, but it held its tuning well.

"So that everybody can hear?" Mrs. Hudson encouraged.

The score on the rack was simple, uncomplicated by ornamentation. It would be easy. Justa nodded. She rested her hands on the keys. Her fingertips found shallow dips: these old ivories bore the imprint of generations of players. She looked at Mrs. Hudson, waiting for Mrs. Hudson's hand to come down. The signal came and everybody's attention shifted to their own roles. Justa played so all could hear. She became the invisible firmament that held their voices in the air.

When the end-of-class bell rang, people pounded from the risers, hurried out the door. Justa had to rush, too—take her purse from the cubby, get across campus to Algebra II.

"Would you like to do this again, Miss Matthews? Perhaps from now on?" Mrs. Hudson inquired.

Justa turned at the door. Mrs. Hudson's eyebrows were raised, awaiting an answer.

Justa said, "Yes," even though she didn't have time in which to think.

The invitation—the instruction?—was a surprise that she wore like a warm cardigan all day. This warmth didn't make up for the chill of last weekend, but it gave her something special to think about. Late that night, after Dad's snores had settled into their usual, irregular punctuation of the dark, she got out of bed and padded barefoot into the hallway. She passed through the kitchen, to the foyer. Carefully, quietly, she removed Mom's winter coat and Lowry's rubber boots from the closet. With equal care she unlocked and opened the front door. She stepped outside. She stood motionless on the flagstone path below the porch. She listened: to the eucalyptus trees creaking as they never did during the day; to the hoot of an owl; to the dribble and splash of a raccoon moistening its meal in the neighbor's koi pond. Justa held out her hands, curving her wrists and placing her fingers...on what? Moonbeams? The little finger of her left hand reached to find the owl's hoot. Her right hand moved higher to match the sound of water. The eucalyptus were both tone and percussion: her thumbs could be trees.

Only an unimaginable skill could play the sounds of nature. She was a girl who played 'Ode to Joy'.

But that was a start. It was something.

"All right," she whispered, putting a stamp of finality on the 'yes' she had given Mrs. Hudson. Her whisper added another layer to the music of the night.

LLLLL

Lowry fell in love on a cold, windy Tuesday in May. She didn't have any classes. Nobody did. Stanford was on strike. Last week President Nixon had announced he was sending U.S. troops into Cambodia, expanding the War. Yesterday, National Guardsmen shot and killed four student protestors in Ohio. Today almost every college and university in the country was on strike.

This afternoon Lowry was going to pass out anti-War pamphlets. She had just picked up the pamphlets at the bookstore printing office. The ones given to her were pink and titled *Don't Sacrifice Your Son*. "Because most of the people you're going to see will be ladies," the Crisis Pamphlet Coordinator told her. He was a graduate student from the Business School.

The box he gave her wasn't heavy, only awkward. She had plenty of time before meeting Bilba, so she decided to go to the post office to check for mail. When she got there, the door was blocked by students sitting on sleeping bags, wrapped in blankets. It took a moment for Lowry to figure out why: the post office was U. S. government real estate, there was a portrait of President Nixon inside. She began to turn away, but the boy closest to her stood, leaving his crumpled blanket like a marker to hold his spot on the ground. "Want some lunch?" he invited.

"Um..." Lowry had already eaten.

"A hamburger," the boy tempted. "Fries, too, if you want." He didn't smile, but his eyes were the color of moss against rocks.

Lowry had never seen eyes that color before. She found herself nodding.

"I'm Dennis Stillman."

"Lowry Matthews."

"I'm from Phoenix."

"Moraga."

Who, where-from: it was a standard college introduction, except for the fact that Dennis had not yet smiled. As he strode toward Tresidder his longer legs made Lowry reach with her own. Because of the people and bicycle traffic in White Plaza, he sometimes had to walk in front of her. She studied his back: his chestnut-brown ponytail was maybe half as long as her own; his faded jeans were tight, but not too tight. They were exactly tight enough. Dennis stopped at a terrace table, and said, with grave courtesy, "Wait here, I'll get everything. My treat."

A treat would be nice on this day of astonished grief and earnest anger. Lowry waited.

"Ta da!" When Dennis returned, his expression was still somber. He unloaded a tray of two hamburgers, two plates of fries, two chocolate milkshakes, two cups of coffee, and one piece of cherry pie. "You look like a cherry pie kind of girl to me," he said.

Lowry warmed her hands around her cup before she began to sip. Dennis dug right in. He ate both hamburgers, most of the fries—Lowry nibbled some—and one of the milkshakes. He talked through bites, he talked through gulps. "I'm almost twenty," he said. "Twenty! Do you know what my birthday pulled in the draft lottery?"

Of course Lowry didn't.

"Thirty five. When my student deferment ends, I'll be in group number thirty five of guys drafted for Vietnam." Dennis's face twisted in a way that had nothing to do with the food, his nose rising with disgust and his eyes tilting downward as if to channel tears that didn't fall. "I'm a poli sci major. That'll do me a lot of good in the jungle."

Thirty-five was a likely death sentence. Lowry put her hand on top his. Dennis looked directly at her. Those green eyes again: moss was tenacious, it grew without soil, it survived all weather. This boy's face wasn't a mask of tragedy, it was one of determination. She asked, quietly, "What will you do?"

"Fight," he said simply. "What else can I do? Fight for peace. I won't let them make me kill somebody."

It was then that Lowry fell not exactly in love, but in pre-love. When Dennis said, "They're giving me a birthday party tonight in Donner House lounge, you want to come?" She said, "Sure," because he was hurt, because she respected the plan he had chosen to go with. Because of those eyes. She asked, "What time?"

"Nine." He finally smiled. It was a half-smile with only one corner of his mouth crooking up. And Lowry fell more deeply. Because with that smile Dennis's eyes crinkled, and their color deepened to that of a forest floor at dawn.

∽

Lowry risked calling home because she knew Justa had a bad cold. She wasn't taking much of a risk because Dad was certainly at work, and Mom often shopped at this time of day. Phone calls home, ever since Thanksgiving, had become a dull recitation about classes and assignments—that was for Dad—and what the dining hall was currently serving—that was for Mom.

Justa answered with a croaking, "Hello."

"Mom out?"

"Safeway," Justa said through her snot. "Getting gigot. That's French for lamb. We're having lamb tonight."

"I met a guy," Lowry began.

"Cute?" Justa asked.

"Yes." Lowry considered: "Good looking. Not handsome."

"Nice?"

"I think so," said Lowry.

"You're not sure?"

"It's complicated." Lowry considered further. "He has a complicated life."

"Like what?"

"He knows he'll be drafted as soon as he graduates."

"Anti-War, then?"

"A pacifist."

"Okay." Justa blew her nose, fiercely. "I just heard the garage door open. Mom."

"Later, then," said Lowry. She hung up only half-satisfied. She had wanted to tell Justa about her plans for the afternoon. Justa never passed along information, but telling Justa that she was going out pamphleting was almost like telling the family that she was *doing* something, that she *could* do something. Part of Lowry wanted Dad to know that.

Bilba was in a paint splattered studio on the first floor of the art building. Under the direction of the Crisis Poster Coordinator she was making protest signs in advance of tomorrow's rally. The sign she worked on now read Old Enough to Die, Not Old Enough to Vote. She was filling in the sketched words, alternating letters in Day-Glo green and orange. "Is it already two o'clock?" she wondered.

"Yep. They told us to go Stanford Shopping Center," Lowry replied.

It turned out that Bilba's bike, with its broader, turned-up handlebars, held the pamphlet box more securely than Lowry's ten-speed did. They rode slowly on city streets, cautious of traffic they never found on campus. They chose a spot in front of Macy's where they could put the box down on a planter wall. They stood in front of a display of blue, pink, white and purple-red anemones, waiting for people to come up from the parking lot.

Some of the people, and the people were indeed mostly ladies, sought to avoid them. But Lowry discovered that if she caught a lady with her smile, that lady invariably smiled in return. Then Lowry could press a pink pamphlet into the lady's hand. "I hope you will read this," Lowry would say. She was better at pamphleting than Bilba, who hadn't spent her high school weekends cruising shopping centers. Bilba grew up in the Santa Cruz mountains; she didn't have a suburban smile.

"I met a guy named Dennis Stillman," Lowry told Bilba between ladies. "He asked me to his birthday party tonight at Donner."

"You should wear my violet dress!" Bilba was immediately enthusiastic. "Someone on our floor has shoes almost that color. Oh, and Mary Ellen's Mondrian tights!"

"Yeah," Lowry agreed. But she wasn't listening as hard as she might. She was wondering how many ladies they were influencing toward an anti-War position. The trash barrel outside the coffee shop, two storefronts down, was high with pink.

Bilba appointed herself Lowry's chief dresser. Probably half the girls on the floor stopped by to watch and comment. It turned out that 'Dennis Stillman' was a name some of them knew.

"He's pretty big in the Anti-War Movement," said one.

"He's their negotiator, even though he's only a Sophomore," said another. "Whenever the Movement needs someone to talk to University administration, they send in Stillman."

Lowry matched that information with the face of the boy who had brought her cherry pie. A negotiator for peace. She liked that.

"So what do you think?" Bilba had no interest at all in Dennis's Movement credentials. She moved Lowry away from their mirror so that Lowry could see herself in full. Bilba's dress—a softly draping polyester with an elastic neckline and abbess sleeves—covered Lowry's butt with three inches to spare. Mary Ellen's tights—right-angled geometry in primary colors—took her legs down to a pair of stack-heeled shoes. The shoes were size seven. Lowry wore a six-and-a-half. Bilba had stuffed the toes with Kleenex.

"I look like a J. Magnin hippie." A rich girl, playing wild. Lowry turned to see herself from the side. The dress's high elastic waist pushed her breasts into prominence.

"You look sexy." Bilba was proud of herself.

Sexy was good.

Riding a bike in those shoes was a challenge, though. Lowry ended up having to pedal with the balls of her feet. Once she got to Donner House, she had to figure out how to get off the bike without showing the whole world her Mondrian-covered buttocks. But when she walked into the lounge, she knew she was everything Bilba had dressed her to be because every boy looked her way—except for Dennis. He was so tightly sur-rounded—boys arguing with each other, boys appealing to "Stillman!", boys wanting his attention—that he didn't see her.

Lowry lingered uncertainly beside the refreshment table. A man some-what older than a graduate student poured wine into a plastic glass, and handed it to her. "Call me Russell." He refilled his own glass.

Lowry sipped. And nodded. And sometimes said, "Uh huh." Because Russell couldn't talk enough about himself. He was a lecturer in the politi-cal science department, and 'Stillman'—Russell never called him 'Den-nis'—was in two of Russell's classes.

Lowry's stomach began to roil. The wine the girls on her floor some-times shared never tasted like this. "Excuse me," she said abruptly, and she ran.

She couldn't find a Women's, so she ended up vomiting into a urinal in a Men's. She rinsed her mouth out over a sink caked with soap scum, tooth-paste, and little stubbles of hair. She felt better, but no longer sexy. Or even pretty. In this mirror smeared with shaving foam, her face was pasty.

She might as well go home to Florence Moore.

She trudged her violet shoes back down the hallway, bypassing the lounge. But this time, Dennis saw her. He beckoned and his gesture was like a pull at the neck of Bilba's dress. Lowry's step lightened; she followed that imaginary stretch of elastic. "Excuse me," she said, edging through the knot of boys. Dennis put his arm around her, touching her shoulder, run-ning his hand down her arm, cupping her elbow.

"...Selective Service..." "...Conscientious Objector..." "...War Resister's League..." After a brief, startled pause, the boys continued their multiple conversations. Lowry didn't join in. She had become too aware of her body. Her right shoulder was tucked beneath Dennis's arm. His left hip jutted into the right side of her waist. His jeans rubbed against her tights. Blue jeans, violet dress. She hooked her fingers into a far loop of his belt. Together, they made the color of midnight.

"Give the pigs what they gave. Shoot them all down." This boy was *loud*. He wore a Stanford Indians headband across his forehead.

"We can use our anger more productively, El Chico," Dennis advised. "Anger is a strength. It can be a tool."

"As is vengeance." El Chico punched one fist into the other palm.

"'There is a future for the man of peace.' Psalm 37:37," another boy said primly. He stood out as the only one in the group with clipped hair.

"'Religion is the opium of the people.' Karl Marx," El Chico shot back.

"Mahatma Gandhi. 'A small body of determined spirits fired by an unquenchable faith in their mission can alter the course of history,'" said Dennis. "That's what we are, El Chico. All of us. Determined spirits fired by unquenchable faith. All faiths." It was as if he held a boy in each hand, and was bringing them together.

Russell interrupted him—Russell interrupted all the conversations in the room—with what must have been his professor's voice. "Ten, nine, eight." Russell stood beneath a schoolroom clock fastened on a lounge wall. His audience captured, he flung his right arm up, his index finger pointing.

Lowry squinted. She only wore her glasses in big lecture halls. The second hand was ticking to midnight.

"Seven, six, five, four," the crowd joined the countdown. "Three, two, one," they roared. Then they sang:

"Happy birthday to you,

You'll be drafted, you're screwed.

Join the Army, you're barmy.

Join the Navy, you're fish food."

And Lowry laughed. She had never heard this version before. People were whistling, hooting, catcalling now—in a friendly manner, affectionate toward Dennis. A big sheet cake was plopped down onto the refreshment table. El Chico and the Christian headed that way, still arguing. Someone slapped Dennis's free shoulder. "Sorry, dude." This boy, darkly tanned with sun-bleached hair, also left them for cake.

Lowry turned her smile to Dennis. Then let that smile sink abruptly away, because Dennis's face was white. He looked as though he had been drained of all vitality, all life.

"Oh!" Lowry neither thought nor planned. She simply unhooked herself from his belt, faced him, and held out her arms.

Dennis came to her like someone who could see no other home. He buried his face in Lowry's neck, his head rested heavily on her shoulder. She knew she was holding up not just weight, but also a profound grief.

"They'll make me a killer," Dennis whispered.

She, of all the people in this room, was the only one giving Dennis what he needed. This was how she could promote the cause. Lowry would support a peace warrior with her love.

JJJJJ

1. *Leicht, zart* (light, delicate)

Justa loved summer mornings. She loved standing on top of a picnic table before the entire day camp, and lifting her arms like Mrs. Hudson before the choir. "You gotta get up, you gotta get up, you gotta get up in the morning. You gotta get up, you gotta get up, you gotta go to camp." Justa's choristers, being only eight to twelve years old, sang in a ragged, jumpy manner, ready to pop off to the next activity. Her own special group—a subset of the ten-year-olds—mobbed her at the end of today's song with questions and their own special news: "Miss Matthews, are we really going to make guitars out of Kleenex boxes?" "Miss Matthews, Jason shot a rubber band at me!"

By late afternoon all the children, as well as the counselors, were dragging. So Justa led taps. Hers wasn't a nighttime, go-to-bed, taps. Instead, she calmed the camp with a song of slow meandering that was filled with a satisfied weariness and ended with the promise 'home is nigh'. Because home should be a place of comfort. For everybody. Even though it wasn't that way at her house, not any more.

Back at her house Mom was creating a cold Provençal meal for a patio dinner. Justa washed her hands so she could help. She blended olives and anchovies and capers, while describing how she and the children had stretched and plucked rubber bands. Those empty Kleenex boxes created a resonance that made rubber bands sound as tangly and sharp as this tapenade tasted.

Sometimes Justa's world touched Mom's, and Mom's touched Justa's, in a way that made the sun shine.

But then six o'clock arrived, and the front door opened, and Lowry walked past the kitchen, her feet bare, holding Justa's old sandals in her hand. Dad followed after a pause, hefting his briefcase. They walked with the dourness of work—which is where they had been all day, Dad in Kaiser Permanente's actuarial offices, and Lowry at Oakland's downtown The Emporium department store. Each carried his or her own burden of discord.

Justa's heart lost its glow.

"A good commute?" Mom asked hopefully.

Neither Lowry nor Dad replied.

Mom addressed them separately. "Lowry, there are fresh towels in your bathroom." And, "Dan, I filled the ice trays in the bar refrigerator."

Last summer Lowry had come home bubbling over, eager to tell Mom and Justa about her day working in the various departments, the sorts of things people bought, what her fellow employees said and did. She would already have told Dad all her stories in the car. But, "Okay," was all she said today, this summer, this year. Her bare feet were more voluble, each step sticking with a little 'snick' on the linoleum floor.

"Dan?" Mom inquired.

Dad raised his eyebrows in silent self-defense. "I didn't say anything." He headed for the family room.

"A *niçoise* salad," Mom muttered determinedly. She picked up a jar of little pickles, as if cornichons might prove a unifying force.

They wouldn't. Justa knew that, for certain. She deserted Mom for the dining room, for the piano and an escape of her own immersion. She riffled through the stack of music Mrs. Hudson had given her for summer 'fun and work'. Some was choral, preparation for next year. Most were pieces Mrs. Hudson herself had played and enjoyed: more Debussy, lots of Satie, and some Schoenberg, who was new to Justa. She read through the first of Schoenberg's *Six Little Piano Pieces*. The instructions, *Leicht, zart,* meant light, delicate. She tried, but couldn't hear the notes in her mind. Certainly it didn't sound like *that*, with no tonal center. And the timing stopped and started as if confused, as if the music had been turned upside down—upset, sort of like the Matthews family.

Justa began to play. Her two hands, instead of meeting in harmony, clashed in opposition. Lowry and Dad.

"Justie, can't you play something pretty?" Mom called.

Justa couldn't. Not right now. This train wreck of sound was exquisitely planned. The tones that never resolved, but instead moved on to something startling. The meters were purposely out of step. Justa pushed on to the end. She had to, to find a conclusion.

The last two chords left her tingling.

She played the piece again. This time, her fingers found an oddly-shaped whole: these eighteen measures made an asymmetric kind of sense. She lifted her hands and looked around to what she couldn't see: Lowry in her bedroom, Dad in the family room, Mom in the kitchen. Justa, herself, was right here. All separate, each apart, all bound within the walls of their house.

"What about that nice piece that goes 'Tra la la. Tra la la?'" Mom called.

Six Little Piano Pieces became Justa's summer soundtrack.

2. *Langsam* (Slow)

The second piece was a natural accompaniment to the shopping bags Lowry began bringing home, filled with items she bought with her employee discount. If Justa went to Lowry's room to see, Mom—tentatively—would come, too. Then Lowry would reach into her bags, spread garments onto her bed, and wait. Bell bottomed jeans and trousers; close-fitting T-shirts of every color; thick socks of knitted gray yarn; sandals that were nothing but two leather straps over a cork sole.

The sandals were ugly. And expensive—Justa saw the price tag. Last year Lowry had brought home dresses and culottes.

At first Mom could find nothing to say—as if the sight of these clothes clogged up, rather than inspired, her brain. Then, with effort, she found comments. "The green shirt is a pretty color." "I would never have imagined bright purple pants, but I do think they will work. On you."

Justa agreed. No matter what Lowry bought, she still managed to make herself look pretty.

Despite its dissymmetry, piece number two ended on an ascending note.

3. Sehr langsam (Very slow)

If Schoenberg hadn't already been dead, he could have dedicated piece number three to the Vietnam War.

Every evening, before dinner, Lowry changed from her work clothes into last summer's pastel shorts and matching tops. Shorts and tops were what she wore to watch the news. Back in high school, she and Dad used to sit side by side on the family room sofa bed. This summer, Lowry got the sofa all to herself while Dad took the recliner bought for Aunt Edith's occasional use. Always, before, Dad switched channels to the Huntley-Brinkley Report. This summer—Justa didn't know when, perhaps during one of those tense commutes to or from Oakland—Dad and Lowry came to a compromise. Dad got The Huntley-Brinkley Report one night, Lowry got CBS Evening News With Walter Cronkite the next.

One day, passing by the family room, she heard Walter Cronkite tell the nation that the military draft lottery for men born in 1951 would be held later that evening. Justa paused. She held her breath so as to better hear reactions, Dad's and Lowry's, muttered or yelled. But she heard nothing. Except for a silence that deafened.

The next morning, Lowry got to the breakfast table early, before Dad had a chance to take possession of the *Chronicle*'s front section. As soon as he walked into the kitchen, she announced: "They've got the draft list here. If I'd been a boy, my birthday would have been number five. Fifth group to go to Vietnam, fifth group to be killed." She shoved the paper into Dad's hands, and asked, "Which side would you have been on, then?"

Dad's face had gone gray. "I never thought of it that way before," he admitted.

Maybe Lowry had won, on some level. But she wasn't triumphant. Her face had gone pale, too.

"We're just glad you're *not* a boy." Mom tried to cheer everybody up with her wealth of pancake odor, over at the stove.

Mom's voice wasn't part of piece number three. Dad's and Lowry's voices, sadly clashing, unhappily crashing, were.

4. *Rasch, aber leicht* (Brisk, but light)

The Fourth of July. As always, Mom planned a barbecue with chicken marinated in a special sauce. As always, Aunt Edith came for dinner. Today her driver was Tom Yamada, whose son, Fort, owned a landscaping business. Fort, like Dad, was a determined Enemy of Gophers. Fort had invented a new kind of trap Dad was eager to try out.

Dad exited as Aunt Edith came in through the front door.

"Hello, Edith!" Mom called from the kitchen.

"Isobel," Aunt Edith returned, but briefly. Two seconds later, she was in the dining room, standing beside Justa's piano.

Justa was working on Schoenberg's piece number four, which—though she could now play it perfectly well—she was still trying to figure out. She hit the last B natural, and stopped. Aunt Edith had brought a faint whiff of horse manure inside. Dad must have ordered fertilizer, too. Aunt Edith probably arrived in one of Fort's vans.

"Playing a lot of music nowadays?" From Aunt Edith, this was an atypical kind of question—a stalling sort of question.

"Yep," Justa answered.

"Hmm. I see." Aunt Edith stalled some more. Then she burst out, as she sometimes did, with a deeply accurate observation. "Music is your secret language, isn't it? Your father and I are tone deaf. Do you know that?"

Of course Justa did. Neither Dad nor Aunt Edith spoke with much inflection.

"I sometimes think you're saying things you don't want us to hear. Does your mother understand?"

Justa was honest. "Not entirely."

"Lowry?"

This was a harder question to answer. Lowry wasn't tone deaf, or unmusical, but she didn't always choose to hear. "Lowry has her own world to live in."

"You do know I'm keeping my eye on you, girl. Don't you?"

Justa hadn't known—and didn't know what Aunt Edith meant.

Aunt Edith abruptly changed the subject. "Is your mother still cooking from Julia Child like she does whenever she's feeling stressed?"

"We had ratatouille last night," Justa revealed.

Aunt Edith turned away from Justa's piano, and headed toward the kitchen. "Need any help, Isobel?"

Justa looked back at her music. She started at the beginning of piece number four and played it all the way through. She now had an inkling of what it was about. It was one question after another—a confession of confusion.

5. *Etwas rasch* (Somewhat brisk)

When Lowry talked, she talked only to Justa. And then mostly about a boy named Dennis Stillman. Lowry had met him near the end of her school year, when nobody was going to classes ("A damn waste of my money!" Dad had said when he read about it in the *Chronicle*), and Lowry was being a War Protestor. Lowry said protestors were often in conflict among themselves, unable to agree on how things should be done—except when Stillman stepped in. Stillman, Stillman, Stillman. In college, boys didn't use their first names.

As far as Justa could tell, all Stillman and Lowry did together was attend rallies and march for peace. Once, though, they went to a Joan Baez concert on the grass steps that were Stanford's amphitheater. Justa tried to smell the grass, she tried to hear Joan singing against a breeze. But Lowry couldn't remember any songs. She only remembered Stillman.

Toward the end of summer, the mailman brought a postcard from the Grand Canyon with a cryptic message on the back: *working here. see you Sept. ds.* As soon as Lowry got home and saw the postcard, she grabbed Justa to pull her into their bathroom—where Mom never followed.

"He wrote to me!" Lowry was so excited, as if Stillman hadn't written all summer, which—now that Justa came to think about it—he hadn't.

Justa began to wonder: was Stillman an unpredictable kind of person? The kind who reached out, only to pull away? Sort of like piece number five? Number five was her least favorite.

6. *Sehr langsam* (Very slow)

In September Lowry accepted a ride back to college from the friend of a friend. Dad and Justa helped her carry boxes, bags and suitcases to the car after the driver honked from the driveway. Mom came out to wave goodbye from the porch. "Well," Dad said, dispiritedly, as Lowry rode away. "I suppose I can go see how I'm doing with those gophers."

Mom and Justa went back inside. The house sounded so quiet without Lowry's added footsteps, something like it had sounded last year when Lowry first went away to school. But last year's quiet had been all absence. This year, silence held a distressing relief.

Justa wandered through the dining and living rooms, into the family room. She pushed aside the sliding glass doors. On the patio, sun beat hard upon Mom's herb pots, scenting the air with basil, chives, thyme. Dad sat on his haunches in the grass beyond, marking something on a clipboard with one of Justa's or Lowry's old school pencils. A Cost Plus wooden yardstick, placed in a gopher hole, stuck up into the air beside him.

Justa watched him for a few moments. She re-entered the sun. "Hi," she said.

"Hi, Justie." Dad kept on marking.

Justa counted more gopher holes—three that she could see. "There's the owl," she offered as a solution.

Dad looked up. "What?" he said, puzzled.

Justa pointed to the pine tree in the neighbor's back yard, which hung partly over their own. "An owl lives up there. He's gotta hunt. He probably likes to eat gophers."

Dad shaded his eyes to look upward. "I wonder," he considered. "I wonder if we could attract more owls? I'll ask Fort."

That evening, at the piano, Justa changed her mind. Before, she had thought piece number six was simply an unsettling sort of taps—a series of chimes Schoenberg had chosen to conclude his five preceding frenzies. Now she could hear the loneliness those last ten measures sighed out. Not an unredeemed loneliness—she picked through the piece with careful, tentative fingers; then with a dawning, increasing certainly—but a loneliness that somehow managed to end on a deep bass note of hope.

"Kids know the lines are drawn...protest and marches don't do it. Revolutionary violence is the only way."

From 'A Declaration of a State of War', the first of the Weather Underground Organization's nine communiqués.

Starting Autumn 1970

LLLLL

Lowry sat on the institutional carpet that covered the living room floor of Columbae House, Stanford's non-violence theme house. She sat with other pacifists, in a circle. Sometimes her mind sparked with something to say, but she didn't open her mouth. She was a girlfriend, and girlfriends never spoke. The boys in this circle were putting their futures on the line in order to end the War. Girlfriends didn't have so much to risk.

So she sat on dull gray carpet and listened to endless talk about draft laws. She curved her own side against Stillman's angular torso, and she let her mind wander. She would have to choose her major soon. Maybe history? Only this afternoon, her modern European history professor had said her paper 'possessed some insight into the human perspective'. She was still thinking about what that meant.

By ten o'clock she'd had enough. She patted Stillman's shoulder. He nodded acknowledgement, and she slipped away. Outside the nighttime air was cool and fresh. She filled her lungs, glad to be free of the stifling indoors. She rode her bike back to FloMo, and the moment she opened her dorm room door, Bilba announced,

"I'm changing my name again."

"Okay," Lowry said, bemused.

Bilba sat at her desk, she hadn't looked up from her botany textbook. "To Willow," she added that important detail. "What do you think?" She opened her arms into graceful branches. Her head was still bowed over what Lowry could now see was a diagram of a tree.

"It's pretty." Lowry mentally went from 'Willa' to 'Bilba' to 'Willow'. It made its own kind of sense. "Unusual."

But Bilba/Willow wasn't interested in further conversation. She was now entirely focused on a sketch of her future self, a dryad.

Lowry sat at her own desk. She gazed at a poster of Joan Baez and her two sisters. The Baez girls sat squished together, unsmiling, on a clawfoot loveseat, underneath the caption, *Girls say yes to boys who say no.* Joan's husband was in jail for refusing to be drafted.

"Well!" Bilba must have finished her drawing, because she was talking again. She turned in her chair, her eyebrows raised, waiting. "Have you done it yet?"

'It' was sex. Lowry, unlike Bilba, was still a virgin. Bilba was sleeping with a theater major whose draft number was three hundred and twenty-seven. Craig didn't have to worry about killing, or being killed, in Southeast Asia. He could amuse himself by dressing up like Richard the Third, by limping ostentatiously through White Plaza, by flailing a cane to both attract and avoid ten-speeds. Okay, so he was hilarious when he swore at speeding bikes in Shakespearean smut: "Thou beslubbering knotty-pated flirt-gill!" But Craig was safe.

Stillman had deep creases between his eyebrows. His worry never lifted. Even during kissing and petting he seemed one step away. Lowry couldn't tell Bilba all this, it was too private. "He's working on his Conscientious Objector appeal," was always a ready excuse. "I'm helping him."

Bilba shook her head, and went back to herself as a tree.

Lowry reached for the bookshelf, for a slender text from last year's Nineteenth Century English Literature class. Of all those books, only one—a long essay—had been written by a woman. There, Lowry found the sentence she wanted to remember, highlighted in yellow, with an inked star in the margin. She read the sentence three times, her lips forming silently around the words: 'The beauty of the world, which is so soon to perish, has two edges, one of laughter, one of anguish, cutting the heart asunder'.

She put the book down, and stared again at the poster—this time with wonderment. When Bilba was ready to listen, Lowry was going to tell her, "The human perspective in 1929 was hardly different from today."

⌒

On Saturday Lowry climbed into El Chico's gleaming red Pontiac Firebird. El Chico was really 'Alfredo Ruiz'; he was Stillman's hometown buddy. "You'll fit on the transmission hub," he told Lowry. The Firebird's narrow back seat was filled with stuff—boxes, bags—as if he had never fully moved into his dorm room.

It took some work for Lowry to fit herself on the hub. She ended up kneeling, with her back pushed as far as possible into the seat divide. When Stillman settled into the passenger seat, she held on to him for balance.

El Chico started the engine with a roar. "What the *inmigrantes* need is another Che Guevara." He was as loud as his car.

"The draft board wants to know what I can do to further American interests." Stillman grabbed the dashboard; Lowry clutched him harder; El Chico turned onto Junipero Serra Boulevard. "So I'm going to teach English to construction laborers, farmworkers, people who go on to apply for citizenship."

"All problems are one, and that problem is class," El Chico shouted. He tried to beat the red light where the boulevard changed names, couldn't, and slammed to a halt.

Lowry's stomach made a somersault.

Full green, El Chico gunned, and the street became the Alameda de las Pulgas. There were shops along the Alameda, a gas station, then small houses and a school. The houses got bigger, Moraga-sized. "Revolution, man, revolution!" El Chico boomed.

He was a Phoenix Country Day School revolutionary, a rich boy going wild. Lowry had to listen to him for four miles of red, yellow and green lights.

She almost fell out of the car when they got to Saint Fiacre Catholic Church—she was so grateful to be there. In the parking lot meant for hundreds, of the dozen vehicles present, El Chico's Pontiac shone like a candied apple. The other cars and pick-up trucks were dusty, patchworked with anti-rust paint. El Chico grabbed one of the bags from the back seat. "Come on," he said, even though Lowry was already stumbling, unkinking *her legs, heading toward the pink stucco school attached to the church.*

She was the first of the three to leave October sunlight, to open her eyes wide against the dimness of a school hallway. She was the first to step into the artificial brightness of an assembly room. Her entrance caused an instant hush. Thirty or so men—all small, all gaunt, all sitting around cafeteria tables—stared at her.

Reflexively, she smiled.

"*Hola!*" "*Qué linda!*" "*Buenos, señorita!*" She got thirty eager smiles in return, plus a rueful wave from a brown-robed priest that seemed to say 'Bear with them. They're Latin'.

Lowry grinned. Her own little wave said 'It's okay'.

Stillman and El Chico pushed in behind her, and the greetings stopped. The smiles modified down to a polite interestedness.

"Umm," Stillman was momentarily tongue-tied. "Hello there. I'm Dennis Stillman."

The Latinos, almost to a man, looked at their priest.

"*Mucho gusto, Señor Stillman,*" the priest replied.

"*...gusto...*" Soft repetitions filled the room.

"Tell them I'm here as a friend," Stillman instructed El Chico. "Start translating."

El Chico did.

Lowry sat down on one of the metal folding chairs that circled the room. She pulled a small notebook and Bik pen from her purse. She was here to take notes. The conversation went three ways—from Stillman to El Chico (or the priest) to the men, and back again. Lowry didn't have to record Stillman's intentions and hopes—she knew those by heart. The responses, while courteous, were always questions: Did Stillman have books to bring? Could he teach their wives, as well? Did he know a fast way to get a green card?

"Tell them I can help fill out forms," Stillman offered.

Immediately, the discussion coalesced into one subject: green cards. The questions became statements, the statements picked up speed. El Chico's translations shortened into nothing, the conversation becoming two-way, between him and the men. Lowry had taken Spanish in high school and for two terms at Stanford, but except for a few words here and there, she couldn't follow.

"Tell me what they're saying," Stillman hissed.

El Chico complied. "Employers take advantage," he said. "Work visas too short. *Salarios* go down."

He translated in bits and pieces. Lowry tried to take notes, but El Chico's translations lost sequence, then sense. She found more meaning in the men's gestures and facial expressions. The younger men were prematurely lined, their foreheads clenched in frustration. Their elders watched with eyes of frank sadness; they were exhausted. One of the young men rose to his feet, bowed with courtliness to Lowry's group, and then turned to address the grandfathers. This young man raised his shoulders high; he let his shoulders drop in the universal shrug of profound discouragement. He spoke with courtesy. "...*cedemos*..." Lowry understood that: we give up. "...*regresaremos*..." We will go back. "...*a México*." He spoke with regret.

"Oh no you don't!" El Chico jumped to his feet. "*Maricón! Puto!*", which were words Lowry had learned not in class, but from an AFS student in high school. Cowardly male whore.

The grandfathers bristled. Their juniors rose to challenge. The priest began to stand, too.

"Cool it!" Stillman tugged El Chico back into his chair.

"They need to hear about Marx!" El Chico snatched his bag from the floor. He pulled out a little red book. "They need to read Chairman Mao!"

"What they need," Stillman held El Chico's gaze, "is education."

The two boys were locked in a silent quarrel, the words of which Lowry could neither hear nor see. El Chico gave in first. "Oh, yeah," he muttered. "Right." He took a deep breath, and restrained his manner into regret. "*Discúlpenme*," he requested forgiveness of his hosts. He spoke on until the other side stood down.

The priest exchanged another rueful glance with Lowry.

At the end of the meeting, only Stillman was offered handshakes. The priest took both of Lowry's hands in his own, and said, "Your beauty gave something special to their day." El Chico left his bag of little red books on one of the chairs.

—

That evening, sitting in the usual Columbae House circle with her shoulder tucked beneath Stillman's arm, Lowry at first paid attention. But the topic was how best to aid and assist David Harris, a former Stanford student body president and Stanford's most famous draft resister. Lowry had heard this same discussion many times before. Harris was a test case for wider concerns: "How can draft resistance be a felony?" "Felonies are for murderers." "Draft resistance is, like, anti-murder!" Lowry didn't need to follow the arguments.

So tonight she attended to what she saw, more so than what she heard— just as she had done at Saint Fiacre. The visitor from the Revolutionary Front was another El Chico, with quick and angry slashes of his arms, censorious twists of his face. The moderates, who agreed with the Front's summary but were unwilling to support his solutions, criss-crossed their hands—rapidly, repeatedly, like railway signs—whenever they wished to interrupt. The countenances of the Christian Pacifists remained solidly and righteously implacable. Stillman waited until all three parties had a say, and then he held out his hands as if offering loaves and fishes. A loaf here, a fish there, and eventually the three divergent approaches angled toward those points on which everybody agreed: together, they opposed the Vietnam War; together, they opposed the draft of American men.

At last the meeting was over, and Lowry was alone with Stillman in his room. "The draft board can't refuse your appeal," she encouraged. "You're so good," by which she meant both well-intentioned and effective.

"I have to learn Spanish." Stillman's thoughts jumped over his success, landed on what had been missing in his day.

Lowry pulled off her shirt; she unhooked her bra. Stillman moved toward her. "Good," she repeated as he caressed her breasts. "Ohhh!" She traveled her fingers over the sharp edge of his belt buckle, down toward his zipper-covered penis.

But he stepped away. "I'll have to start with Spanish 1. And I'm a junior." He was working out a new difficulty.

Lowry watched him and considered: Stillman was an exceptional person. Exceptional people deserved special treatment. She gently pushed him onto the bed, where she lay beside him and kissed him into relaxation.

When she awoke, his open hand still curved over her left breast. Her nipple strained to meet the friction of Stillman's touch. An intense longing shot down some nerve that lead directly to her groin. Her other breast wanted to channel the same feeling: wanted to make her ache 'down there', but in a good way—exciting, compelling, opening while engulfing. She wriggled, temporarily, away from Stillman's hold. Quietly, hardly moving the blankets, she pulled off her jeans and panties. Wearing nothing but socks, she carefully unbuttoned Stillman's shirt, unhooked his belt, slid his zipper down. She cupped her hand over his half-erect penis.

Stillman awakened. "What?" he asked. But he shifted his weight so she could slide his jeans, his briefs, down his legs. When she pulled him on top of her, her own legs wide, she marveled at the expression on his face—still sleepy, not yet fully conscious—purely animal. With her hand, she helped his penis find its home. He pushed into her and she had to close her eyes because of the pain. But then the hurt faded, and she could look up: his eyelids were half-closed; the tender skin twitched until a final thrust. He collapsed with a sigh onto her chest.

Lowry gently rolled him off. She kissed his forehead; he fell back to sleep.

Not much later, she left his bed to ride her bike home to FloMo. She wriggled experimentally, testing the sweet soreness between her thighs. Dawn was in the air. Shortly the sun would rise, the day was new. Lowry was new—no longer a virgin. In a few minutes she would shake Bilba—now Willow—awake. Willow wouldn't mind. Willow would help her celebrate.

JJJJJ

Christmas Eve, and Justa was perched on the bathroom countertop watching Lowry rinse out a soap dish. Lowry had come home from college with pierced ears. She had also brought home, as her gift to Justa, two narrow bands of gold twisted into Möbius strips and mounted on gold posts. The earrings were lovely: pretty, small, delicate. Nothing unusual to see from a distance, but intriguing to touch.

Justa had said, "Yes."

But now, breathing in the rubbing alcohol with which Lowry filled the soap dish, watching Lowry drop in the two earrings—plus two sewing needles—Justa doubted. She caught her bottom lip between her teeth.

Lowry lined up other tools: a pen, cotton puffs, a matchbook from the Chinese restaurant that delivered dinner those rare times Mom took a break from cooking. And all along, Lowry talked. "I hardly ever see him," meaning Stillman. "He's at that draft counseling center in Redwood City all the time." A bewildered loneliness colored her voice. Lowry was sleeping with Stillman; she felt ignored by him. "Did you know that getting a green card exposes a man to the draft? Did you know that non-citizens are fighting and dying in Vietnam for the USA?"

Justa shook her head.

"Stillman spends most of his time with El Chico now. Put these rubber gloves on and hold an ice cube on both sides of your earlobe. It'll hurt at first, but then it'll go numb."

The ice cubes did hurt.

Lowry struck a match, running the flame over one of the needles, flaring off the alcohol. "Everything's sterile," she promised.

Justa hadn't thought about infections. She hadn't thought about the possibility of harm. She dropped her hand, the ice cubes. "Low—" she began.

"Good." Lowry leaned close, and,

'POP!' It sounded like ice breaking against Justa's molars, but smaller— a minuscule, empty chamber stuffed with air, suddenly squeezed.

Justa was too late.

"Yoo-hoo!"

Justa hadn't heard the taxi come up the driveway. She hadn't heard the front door open.

Lowry immediately reached for the doorknob but didn't get there in time. Aunt Edith filled the doorway. "I let myself in," Aunt Edith said unnecessarily. "Where are your parents?"

"Last minute shopping. You can put your gifts around the tree in the living room." Lowry was on the verge of being rude.

"Whatever are you girls doing?"

Lowry uttered a small, "shit."

Aunt Edith set her packages on the far end of the counter. She shifted Lowry aside as if Lowry were as easy to maneuver as a towel. "Weren't you going to mark Justa's other ear?"

"Oh!" Lowry was suddenly abashed. "I guess I forgot."

"You might have left your sister asymmetrical for life," Aunt Edith scolded. "Give me that pen," and she took over.

Justa could do nothing but trust. She allowed Aunt Edith to press the pen against her other earlobe. She held up ice cubes at Aunt Edith's instruction.

"We used to do this in the American Red Cross." Aunt Edith examined Lowry's ear-piercing tools; she nodded at them. "During World War II, we girls had to wear battle dress. It was cold there in England. Boots, heavy pants, heavy jacket. No jewelry because rings and necklaces could get in the way. Clip-on earrings might fall into... Well, cause problems. But one girl in our group was from New Mexico, and she'd had pierced ears since birth. We scrounged around, found old pierced earrings here and there, at pawn shops and such. They were the one way we could feel like women. Pretty. I still have my pair. Somewhere." She swabbed Justa's ear with a puff soaked in rubbing alcohol. She plucked the second needle out of the soap dish. "Sit up straight," she said, and stabbed.

This time Justa felt a prick, not a bee sting.

Lowry was immediately back at Justa's side, earrings in hand. Aunt Edith stopped her from helping: "Justa should learn how to do it herself."

Justa swiveled on her bottom, to see. Her punctures were even. Her earlobes were pink, but not bloody. Gingerly, she poked a gold post into the left earlobe. Then the right. It didn't hurt, much. The earrings were even prettier on than they had been in the box.

"I wasn't much older than you girls when I did this in England." Aunt Edith had gone back to reminiscing.

"How old were you?" Lowry was interested.

Justa paid no attention to their conversation. Instead, she used their voices and words as a test. She listened—really listened—into her two ears. First one ear, then the other. Both were fine.

∾

Christmas Eve Dinner was chicken consommé, Coquilles St. Jacques, pan-roasted Brussels sprouts, potatoes Anna, green salad with vinaigrette dressing, vanilla poached pears, and chocolate mousse. The chocolate mouse was for Dad and Lowry. Mom had adjusted the rest of the meal to fit Aunt Edith's food mantra of, "No salt, hypertension. No sugar, diabetes. No cholesterol because mine is sky high." That meant Mom had substituted halibut and white wine for the usual scallops, cream, and cheese of the Coquilles St. Jacques. She had made the potatoes Anna with olive oil instead of butter.

Aunt Edith began table conversation by picking on Lowry, their bathroom teamwork apparently forgotten. "So," Aunt Edith said. "You're going to major in history. Whatever for?"

"I want to get a sense of my own self in time." Perhaps because they were with Dad and Mom, Lowry sounded aloof. She sounded remote.

"What does that mean?"

"Coquilles St. Jaques, Edith?" Mom hovered at Aunt Edith's right shoulder, offering Aunt Edith a silver tray and two silver serving spoons. Mom had broiled each serving in an abalone shell. She had arranged the five shells to make an opalescent star.

"Oh!" Aunt Edith exclaimed. "How pretty, Isobel. And the fish exactly as I like it." Because she was looking to her right, her notice settled on Justa. "Why are you applying to a girls' college?" She was still interrogating—but Justa this time—as she moved a shell onto her plate.

"My choir teacher, Mrs. Hudson, went to Mills," Justa said. "She had a special professor, Dr. Weber. I went for an audition there, and he…" Justa worked to put the experience into terms Aunt Edith might understand. "He listened to me play." Justa had never been listened to with such care. "I played 'La Cathédrale Engloutie'." Dr. Weber had paced while she performed, moving around his office in such a manner that she could forget him—which was extraordinary whenever Justa thought about it. If he had sat beside her, or even behind her, her shoulders would have tensed, her fingers might have fumbled. But instead, he let her play.

"Debussy," Dad interjected knowledgeably.

Aunt Edith ignored Dad and his lack of knowledge. "Are you as good at music as your parents don't seem to understand?" she demanded.

Justa thought: Dr. Weber's office piano was a baby grand. The slightest push to the sustaining pedal had filled the room with vibrations. Forte was a thunder that Justa alone controlled; pianissimo was the slightest press of her hand. It was she, Justa, who had brought Debussy's cathedral up and out of the sea. She, Justa, who had sunk it again at her will. "Yes," she answered.

"Then why not go to Stanford, like your sister?"

"Oh, Edith!" Mom was now offering the tray of Coquilles St. Jacques to Lowry. "Justa isn't—"

"I don't have the grades." Justa helped Mom out.

"Grades, schrmades," Aunt Edith pooh-poohed. "Do you know what I think?"

They had no choice but to listen.

"I think you have your daughters all wrong."

Dad double-spooned his abalone shell off the tray with an air of resignation.

"How intelligent females handle their intelligence has always been a subject of great interest to me. Lowry's chosen one road, she'll always strive to be more intelligent than she really is."

Lowry sputtered incoherent indignation.

"While this one—" Aunt Edith jutted her chin at Justa. "Hiding in her music, learning a language that none of us can understand. I think this one might have what Lowry has, and more."

"Edith, please." Mom now held the tray for Justa.

"You're embarrassing our daughters, Edith." Dad tried to warn her off.

"Nonsense, I'm embarrassing *you*."

Which, Justa thought, was probably exactly right because Mom again, and abruptly, changed the course of conversation. "Why, Justie!" Mom scolded. She set the tray over Justa's empty plate so she could lift Justa's hair. "You, too?"

Justa hoped her earlobes weren't still pink, that they only glinted gold. But Lowry was sinking into her chair. Aunt Edith was rolling her eyes in a very Lowry-like manner. Dad was staring at Justa as if he couldn't identify what was wrong. His expression of bewilderment caused a bubble of humor to rise up Justa's throat like a burp. The bubble erupted as laughter when Lowry squeaked, "Aunt Edith did it!"

And then Aunt Edith was laughing, too—a surprisingly fresh noise, jolly and young. Lowry—at first hesitantly, then with more assurance—joined in. Their laughter combined in a sweetness of harmony, Aunt Edith carrying a free-spirited bottom note.

Mom, now as puzzled as Dad, smiled at him. He smiled, gamely, back.

Justa wondered what else inside Aunt Edith had been preserved from the ARC.

*

Because Aunt Edith told her to do so, after dinner Justa swabbed the fronts and backs of her earlobes with rubbing alcohol. She rotated the gold posts. It didn't exactly hurt; it was more like the soreness left over after being pinched by sharp fingernails. Justa hooked her hair over her ears, picked up a hand mirror, and examined herself from the side. She liked the way the flash of gold made her ear appear more significant.

She stopped by Lowry's room to say so. Lowry's resigned, "Okay," allowed Justa to look in. Lowry sat leaning against the headboard on her bed. She held a book on her lap but the book was still closed. She hadn't been reading.

"I like them." Justa pointed to her earrings. "Thanks."

"Sure." Lowry was a person deflated.

Justa made a stab at explaining something of which she, herself, wasn't certain. "When Aunt Edith tells us her stories—maybe that's how she sees her place in time."

This statement earned a sharp glance from Lowry.

"She has her own way of looking at things." Justa needed Lowry to remember that.

In the kitchen, Mom was setting up two after-dinner drink trays. The silver tray with the crystal brandy snifters was for Mom and Aunt Edith, who would now sit in the living room with their feet up, dozing before the Christmas tree. The plastic tray was for Dad and Hiro Yamada, who always drove Aunt Edith on Christmas Eve. "I'm sending the bottle out with you, Justie," Mom said. "Bring back the dirty dishes."

Justa laid the bottle down so it wouldn't topple. Outside, in the dark, she aimed toward the backs of two heads beneath the dim overhead light of…what wasn't a taxi, but instead the cab of a pick-up truck. Dad and Hiro sat angled toward each other, facing the same spot on the dashboard.

They were, as she expected, playing Scrabble with Dad's travel game board. When Justa knocked on the passenger window, Dad opened the door, then scooted far enough over so she could squeeze in beside him. "Armagnac," he told Hiro. "Delord, 1960. This one has an under-taste that's almost like chocolate."

"Triple letter score, 32 points," Hiro said.

"Damn." Dad studied his tiles.

Justa asked Hiro, "Were all the taxis busy?"

"Every single one," Hiro boasted. "Even the young guys"—which meant his grandsons and great-nephews—"are driving around tonight. Your aunt doesn't mind riding in a truck."

"You should have heard her at dinner," Dad grumbled over his tiles.

"That's why I never eat with you," Hiro congratulated himself. "I love your aunt, little girl. We all do. But that doesn't mean I have to sit with her at the table for a long meal. Christmas!" Hiro made a complaint of the word. "Sometimes I think my wife is a Nisei version of Edith. Relentless. Do you know what she's doing right now?"

"No," Justa and Dad said together.

"Well, maybe not at this minute. I don't know what she's doing exactly now. But when I left she was dressing that golden Buddha—you know, the one young Peter brought home from Takaoka—in a red, pointed hat with a pom-pom on top. Santa Buddha. For the great-grandchildren. Can you believe it?"

Justa giggled. She loved Hiro.

"As long as I get to eat your mom's food out here, little girl, and be away from Santa Buddha, I'm happy."

Dad finally chose: "Double word score, 28 points."

Justa left them to it. Back in the dark, she reached a hand over the truck's tailgate. She felt around until she touched the china plate and dessert bowl, the handful of silver, the wineglass—plus bottle—that she had brought out earlier. Dad would stay with Hiro, and the brandy, until Hiro decided he could no longer avoid Santa Buddha and drove home. Only then would Dad return to the house.

Justa aimed toward the porch light. Mom was already at her kitchen desk nook, reviewing tomorrow's menus. "Thanks, Justie." She didn't look up. "Would you take Aunt Edith's sheets into the family room? You're a dear."

The sofa bed sheets were in the bedroom hall closet, as were a pillow and spare blankets. Justa had to peer around the side of her bundle to walk it into the family room. She saw Aunt Edith, now settled into her recliner, a Christmas-motif throw over her legs. Lowry was sprawled on the yet-unopened sofa bed. Aunt Edith was saying, "I didn't decide upon pharmacy until afterwards, of course. I finished my degree when I got back."

"You mean you changed your major when you were a *senior*?" Lowry was amazed.

Justa left the bedding on the coffee table.

She went back down the hallway to her own room, to her favorite part of Christmas Eve. She tuned her little radio to WCPE's replay of Cambridge University's *Festival of Lessons and Carols.* She listened while she got ready for bed, as she settled onto her pillow, while she waited for the arrival of Christmas Day.

LLLLL

Stillman rarely laughed. And when he did, he looked like a person coughing—reluctant, as though the effort approached pain. Lowry believed at least part of his anxiety was caused by the poster he lived with. Above his bed he had placed a blown-up cover from *Time* magazine: a Buddhist monk, serene, straight-backed, meditating in the lotus position in the middle of a Saigon street, his body an inferno of self-set flames.

No wonder Stillman so often awakened with a cry of horror in the middle of the night.

Then Lowry would reach for him, hold on to him. He would feel for her breasts, her buttocks. But he seldom followed through. Instead he would roll away, smothering his... what? frustration? anguish? ...against his pillow. He wouldn't answer when she asked, when she tried to help. Lying at his side, Lowry continued to ache in body and in spirit for hours.

He was hardly going to classes anymore, except for Spanish. And that was because of El Chico. Lowry wished she liked El Chico better.

~

She had lots of time in which to study.

For her term paper in 20th Century American History she decided upon 'Women In Wartime'. So on this day she was scanning shelves in the undergraduate library, known as UGLY. She sampled books about the WACS, the WAVES, and the ARC. When she got to *Donut Dollies: The American Red Cross in Europe During World War II*, she slid that book from the shelf.

The photograph on the cover was a tinted black-and-white—a pretty girl riding a bicycle while wearing a slate blue military-style hat and jacket, matching knee-length skirt, and saddle shoes. Lowry carried the book to a table near the mezzanine railing, and began to read.

The girl pictured was Kathleen Kennedy, of *that* Kennedy family. While in England, Kathleen had organized fashion shows and benefits. She and her friends drove 'clubmobiles' blaring popular music—Tommy Dorsey's 'Marie', Glenn Miller's 'In the Mood'—to docks, hospitals, and train stations. There, they served coffee and donuts to servicemen. At the end of the day the girls scrubbed out their clubmobiles in preparation for tomorrow, and then they went dancing. Because they were all designated officers—so they would be treated as such if ever captured—they only danced with male officers. And so on to the next day.

Lowry snorted. "No way." She didn't have to be quiet, UGLY wasn't that kind of library. Noise traveled up the central atrium, bounced off the glass ceiling, and traveled back down. Lowry had overheard Aunt Edith discussing her ARC experiences with Dad, Mom, and the older Yamadas. Aunt Edith—at those docks, hospitals, and train stations—had helped transfer the wounded. The stink of smoke, unwashed bodies, and flesh rot permeated her clothes. Since her boarding house only allowed one shallow bath a week, the stink stayed in her hair. The girls resorted to cologne. 'We reeked like a whorehouse.'

In a state of supreme scorn, Lowry returned *Donut Dollies* to its shelf. She grabbed her bag and rode her bike away from UGLY. UGLY resembled a prison on stilts. The Main Library was Old Stanford. Lowry entered the building beneath sandstone depictions of Art, Philosophy, and Science. She stepped quietly beneath skylights, exploring until she found a vast card catalog with probably a hundred drawers devoted to A. She stood before the American R— drawers, and began writing down call numbers. When she had a bibliography that covered a full page in her notebook, she asked for directions. For those call numbers that were all digits, no letters, the librarian sent her to the basement.

A graduate student working at a counter underneath exposed, painted-over pipes, was more annoyed than helpful. He set his pen down with a tap of resentment. "Okay," he gave in. He disappeared, then reappeared with a cardboard box that he thumped down on the counter. "There are more," he conceded. "Six more, if you have to have them." He picked up his pen.

The box was filled with file folders. One held a black-and-white photograph, maybe five by nine inches, where seven young women stood at attention before a brick wall. Each wore a differently styled uniform. Somebody had written, in now-faded ink, an acronym below each girl: WAC, WAVE, WASP, ARC, SPARS, ANC, NNC.

Lowry angled her nose closer to the center of the photo.

The girl in the very middle, the ARC girl, looked something like Lowry herself. The hair was darker, the chin more rounded. What had Aunt Edith looked like when she was young? Now Aunt Edith's hair was graying, her chin widened by an extra fifty pounds or so. But could it be possible?

Lowry shot up from her chair. She demanded of the graduate student, "Would you make a copy of this?"

He released a fog of irritation in her direction. He jerked his head toward a corner of the room where a copier sat in shadows.

Lowry dug out all the nickels she had. She had to fuss and fiddle with the machine until she got something that was a fair, although not good, representation. Then she put the box on the graduate student's counter, and went in search of a telephone. She had to go outside and down steps to a kiosk. Justa answered, "Yes," to the operator's inevitable, "Will you accept charges?"

"I need Aunt Edith's phone number," Lowry blurted.

"She's on one of her cruises," Justa said. "She'll be gone a month."

"Oh-h-h." Lowry was so disappointed.

"Why?" Justa asked.

"I wanted to ask her some stuff about the Red Cross. For a paper."

"You can ask Dad."

Lowry thought. She thought some more. "Maybe," she told Justa. She put up the phone and gazed into the distance: at a fountain, at gates, at the sandstone beauty of Stanford.

When was the last time she and Dad talked—*really* talked? Lowry's mind tracked back to a year ago October, when she had called to tell Dad about the Peace Moratorium. That had not been a good conversation. They hadn't had a good conversation since. They hadn't had much to talk about; or maybe there was too much they didn't want to say.

Lowry turned around, slowly, and re-entered the Main Library. This time she took over a table in the sun-filled reading room. She laid the photocopy just above her notebook, and she began a list of questions. 'When did Aunt Edith join the ARC?' 'How long was she in England.' It would be great if Lowry could match up Aunt Edith's England dates with those of major battles. 'Did Aunt Edith ever mention any ships by name?'

She continued writing until the natural light above her dimmed. She glanced at her watch. She should hurry, she didn't want to miss dinner. But first, she had to stop by the bookstore to buy a manila envelope. To send to Dad.

⸺

On an otherwise unremarkable day in March, Lowry heard that Stillman's draft board had denied his appeal. Stillman could not, legally, be considered a Conscientious Objector to the War. Lowry got this news from the Columbae House baker who she met at the bike stands in front of Tresidder.

"We're giving him a 'hope' dinner tonight," the baker said. "You've gotta come. Seven o'clock?" And he rode away.

Lowry stood by her bike to calm her heart. Lots of boys emigrated to Canada or Sweden. Some, like Joan Baez's husband, went to jail. Lowry knew of one boy who starved himself until he was too thin to pass an army physical; he had been too weak to attend his graduation. She knew another who chopped off part of a finger so he could never hold gun. Lowry shuddered.

She walked her bike home. She spent her afternoon in FloMo not studying, but rather sitting at her desk and looking at the *Girls say yes to boys who say no* poster. At six thirty she was back on her bike, riding to Columbae House. Stillman wasn't there. He didn't come, and he didn't come. The baker kept the broccoli pie warm. The head gardener postponed putting dressing on the salad. When Stillman finally showed up at eight thirty, he had El Chico in tow.

"Dennis." Lowry purposely used his first name. She hugged him, tightly.

"*Lo chingaron.*" He's fucked. That was El Chico's succinct appraisal of Stillman's situation.

A Columbae girl grabbed Stillman's arm. "It's so unfair."

Everybody wanted their minute with him—or two, or five, or ten. Lowry ended up eating dinner standing next to the baker. The house dessert maker began passing out soft freeze ice cream in dixie cups.

"Hope and chocolate farts," El Chico mocked.

The baker watched El Chico appropriate as many dixie cups as he could hold. "Can't you do something about him?" the baker begged Lowry. "He's so wrong for what we are."

El Chico was absolutely wrong for what they were. But Lowry could do nothing about it.

⌒

Six weeks later, practicing her serve in the tennis courts behind the women's gym, Lowry sent her balls everywhere. She couldn't hold her mind to her task. Today was May 4th. El Chico had somehow inveigled himself onto the planning committee for tonight's vigil. Exactly one year ago four anti-War student protestors had been killed in Ohio.

"That's it, girls," the tennis instructor called.

Lowry stuck her racket into the cross-back holder she wore when riding her bike. Going down Santa Teresa Street, she heard a crowd's noise coming from White Plaza. It was too soon: the vigil wasn't supposed to start for three more hours. But when she got closer, Stillman was already standing on the steps to the music building. El Chico stood at his side. Russell, the poli sci lecturer, was lowering a megaphone.

Lowry used her bike as a wedge to force her way in among the crowd below the steps. "What's going on?" she asked a boy she vaguely knew.

"Russell's been telling us," the boy said excitedly. "There's Agent Orange research going on right here at Stanford! Agent Orange!"

Lowry doubted. She doubted to the bottom of her soul. If that were true, *The Stanford Daily* would have found out and reported long ago.

"So now we're going to march on the botany labs!"

Lowry had to get rid of her bike. The protestors began moving toward Serra Street before she got it locked up. The signs they were carrying—No AO at SU!—were carelessly constructed, like afterthoughts. She was the only person with a tennis racket. The density of bodies prevented her from getting around, through, to Stillman. But soon individuals, then small groups, began to break away. Lowry wondered if they doubted too. She finally reached Stillman's side.

He put his hand out for hers. "Lowry." She hadn't seen such brightness in his eyes since before the Columbae House hope party.

He let go. He had to. As one of the initiators, he held partial responsibility for this protest. He bounded up Herrin Hall's wide steps. Lowry waited for him to stop, to turn around, to address the abbreviated crowd. Marches always ended with speeches. But instead Stillman pushed open Herrin's entry door. He went in, followed by El Chico and Russell. Lowry was pushed up the steps by the people behind her until she, too, was inside. A guy with a tape recorder hanging around his neck shoved, wanting to get by. Lowry squeezed against a wall to let him pass.

"*Ya chingué!*"

El Chico had come up with another conjugation of the verb 'to fuck;' the soundman was getting that on his recorder. The soundman, El Chico,

Stillman and Russell disappeared through a doorway that only accommodated one person at a time. When it came Lowry's turn, she stepped into a laboratory far more sophisticated than her old bio lab back in high school. She recognized the tables and counters with microscopes, Bunsen burners and lots of specially shaped glassware. She could make sense of the plants suspended in some sort of preservation solution, the glass bottles set on long shelves against one wall. What she didn't understand was a bank of machinery, glass-fronted, with great tape-recorder-type wheels inside.

And then chaos began.

She saw who started it. El Chico, of course. He swept his hands against the glass bottles, toppling them to the floor. The room instantly stank of formaldehyde. Lowry coughed. But other people—mostly boys, some men—were copying El Chico. The room was loud with crashing glass, with a "Fuck them!" that became a chant. "Fuck them! Fuck them! Fuck them!" Stillman—Lowry had forgotten about Stillman, she looked for him now— stood in front of the weird machinery with his hands on his hips, studying it as if there were no mayhem around him. Then, his consideration completed, he picked up a lab stool and crashed it into a machine's glass fronting. He took another second to think, knelt to pull a plug from the wall, then stood to reach in through the hole he had made. He grappled with one of the great wheels, and tried to pull it out.

Lowry couldn't stand it: the destruction, the smell, the *craziness*. She had to get away. A man, also fleeing, reached the door first. He held the door open so she could pass through before him. "*Con permiso*," he said, before darting around her and racing down a hallway now totally devoid of people. From Herrin's front porch, Lowry could see him speeding across Serra Street.

Nobody lingered below the steps. That's when Lowry noticed what she hadn't heard before: the wailing of police sirens. All alone, standing before the front door of Herrin Hall, she felt suddenly unplugged from everything that had happened. It was as if time wrinkled back to the moment when she first rode her bike into White Plaza. She could think of nothing to do but go home to FloMo. She still had her tennis racket; it had stayed on her back. She walked down Herrin's steps like an ordinary person, and crossed the street herself.

She didn't turn around to see how many police cars came chasing down Serra Street. She simply continued walking until she got to her bike. Then she returned to FloMo. She burst in on Willow and Craig, cuddled on Willow's mother's rug, making out.

"Sorry!" She was startled.

"We thought you'd be with the protesters." Willow stood up, her new 'tree' garments of flowing pants, tunic, and gauzy scarf floating and drifting.

"I was," Lowry admitted.

"We heard about the march," Craig said. "A guy on KZSU was talking about fascist research at Herrin Hall." Craig's smile turned Shakespearean: "'Dream on, dream on, of bloody deeds and death: fainting, despair; despairing, yield thy breath!'"

"Richard the third," Willow provided the footnote for Lowry. "It's almost time for dinner. You want to go down with us?"

"No," Lowry answered.

Left alone, she curled up on her bed. Images of the afternoon forced themselves into her mind like slides being clicked around a carousel projector. Those plants—preserved for how long?—trampled into a muddy brown slickness on the laboratory floor. The glassware, once shaped so beautifully, now catching and reflecting the florescent light as shards. Stillman—but she wasn't going to go there. Instead, she concentrated on shapes and colors as she had first seen them. The silver-green of eucalyptus leaves, drifting in their bottle like kelp. The sand-drab of cactus, aswim. The pink of a plant that perhaps belonged in liquid, because it looked like coral. Lowry fought against recent memories with first glimpses until she fell into the calming, shapeless grayness of sleep.

She was awakened—hours? minutes?—later by the sounds of someone stumbling into her room. Lowry sat up and pulled her bedspread to her chin, even though she was fully clothed.

Stillman.

He was giddy, grinning, his ponytail pulled loose and drops of blood dribbling from his forehead to his left cheek. "I crashed a computer!" He was laughing. "Ruined ten years' worth of data!" His face was a portrait of unholy joy. "The pigs came after us." He tore off his jacket, his shirt. "El Chico and I got away." He kicked off his shoes. "I stole a bike." He discarded his jeans and stood with his erection pole-up, hard. "I'm here!" He opened his arms wide, a prize no draft resistor's girlfriend could resist.

Lowry only stared.

"What's wrong?" In an instant, Stillman plummeted down from his high. His penis softened. "Isn't this what you always wanted?"

A dozen responses attempted to sort themselves out in Lowry's mind. She could have asked: "What does destruction have to do with non-violence?" She could have accused: "You're supposed to be a pacifist!" She could have blamed: "What makes you so sure Russell was telling the truth?" But she said nothing, because a magma of heartbreak was pushing its way up her throat.

"Well?" Stillman insisted.

Lowry swallowed hard. She attempted to speak around the magma. All she managed to say was, "You laughed." Only two words, but they encompassed everything.

JJJJJ

When Lowry came home from Stanford, misery dragged behind her every step. Her body, neck to knees, sagged. Her posture, apparently, had seeped out with her happiness.

Mom made Lowry stop in the entryway; she put the back of her hand against Lowry's forehead. "You don't have a fever," Mom said worriedly.

"Just tired." Lowry spoke in a low and sunken voice.

Dad stepped into the house a few moments later. Even carrying two suitcases, he shrugged his shoulders at Mom. *I don't know*, he mouthed.

All by herself, Lowry dragged her belongings to her bedroom. She shut the door.

Mom and Dad turned, as one, to Justa. "What's going on?" Mom whispered.

Justa swiftly sorted through what she could and couldn't say. "A boy," seemed safest.

"A boy!" Mom repeated.

"A boy!" said Dad.

There was such relief in their voices, that Justa realized: she had given them a gift. 'A boy' was an entirely reasonable and not-to-be-unexpected explanation for such a depressed state.

"Was it serious?" Dad cautiously inquired.

Justa again felt her way through what she knew of Lowry's story. She concluded with what she believed to be the truth. A truth that would, coincidentally, allow her parents some hope. "Almost," she said. Not a 'yes'.

Mom sighed, a gentle exhalation before she spoke with purpose: "That means we should have macaroni and cheese for dinner tonight." One of Lowry's favorites.

"And strawberry shortcake." Dad added another of Lowry's favorites. "Do we need strawberries? Should I go to Safeway, Isobel?"

"Yes," Mom answered. "Please.

Later, when they sat to their meal, Dad announced, "I was able to pick up a copy of *The Pentagon Papers* in Safeway. Can you believe it? I think that book is everywhere. The true story of the Vietnam War. One day it's classified information. The next day it's leaked to the *New York Times*. And a week later it's in grocery stores."

Lowry rewarded him with the weakest of smiles.

Much later, deep into the night, when Justa got up to use the bathroom, she saw a light glowing from Mom's and Dad's room. She heard Dad's voice, outraged disillusionment disturbing the stillness: "How could the government have done this? *Our* government?"

"Go to sleep, Dan," Mom grumbled.

And so it began: Lowry brought home her own copy of *The Pentagon Papers*. She was again working at The Emporium, she was again commuting with Dad. They always traveled with one of their books. For reference, Justa imagined. Because when the two of them returned in the evening, their faces were often reddened from an argument that leaked over into dinner. It was a conversation that never seemed to end.

For her summer music, Justa chose songs she could play by ear and embellish at whim. Five decades worth: 1920 to 1970.

⌒

Justa waited on the front porch wearing a new, dark-red nubbly top, and new slacks that Lowry had described as 'this season's artichoke color'. Justa held a new, tailored jacket—'asparagus'—to protect her against the cool dampness of any seasonal fog.

Today Aunt Edith's cab was a large sedan, shiny black, with 'Yamada Taxi Service' in a discrete cursive beneath the driver's window. Today's driver was Ike, Hiro's older son.

As Justa got in, she asked the car's name. The Yamadas always named their cars.

"Mikey," Ike said proudly. "After my grandson."

Justa slid into the back seat. Aunt Edith was up front. "Bay Bridge," Ike announced. The back of his head had about as much gray hair as Aunt Edith's did, which wasn't very much. Aunt Edith, Ike, Dad, and a host of other Yamadas had gone to Acalanes High School together. The Yamadas and Aunt Edith still lived in Walnut Creek.

"Anybody ever tell you about the 'Edith'?" Ike asked over his shoulder.

People had, and many times, but Justa let Ike continue. She settled comfortably into a corner; she liked this story. Everybody did.

"It was during World War II," Ike began. "When they were just starting to send us Japanese to the internment camps. Edith saw the writing on the wall. She was a smart cookie even then."

"Smarter then than now," Aunt Edith remarked dryly.

"Smart enough to realize what we hadn't yet begun to imagine—that we were in danger of losing our cars, our business, our homes. Everything," Ike reminded her.

"I figured that with the country switching to war industry, there would be a shortage of vehicles, and soon," Aunt Edith told Justa.

"So she went to your grandfather," Ike picked up the story, "and she demanded—"

"I asked nicely," Aunt Edith corrected, primly.

"—that he buy up our fleet of taxis before we essentially had to give them away to profiteers."

"Those profiteers were buying up anything the Japanese had to sell for pennies on the dollar." Aunt Edith's tone was scathing. "The Japanese had no choice but to sell. They didn't know how long they'd be forced to live in those awful camps."

"It was twenty-seven months for us," Ike said as an aside. He went on: "Your aunt became our agent, and then she became our bank."

"I had Papa buy the taxis and the two houses for a dollar each. Far less than pennies on the dollar, but there had to be some exchange of money to effect legal change of ownership. And the new owner had to be Papa, not me. I wasn't old enough, only twenty-two, and besides I was a woman. But *I* held onto the titles."

"And then we," said Ike, "—my father, my brother, my uncle, my cousins and me—drove those taxis out to the country and stored them in that old horse barn your great-grandfather owned near the Sacramento River."

"They were safe there," said Aunt Edith. "Concealed. Grandpapa was totally gaga. Senile dementia."

"We put them up on blocks for the duration."

"And two and a half years later they were just fine." Aunt Edith was understandably proud.

"Not long after we were released from the camp, when Edith got home from the Red Cross, she gave us those very same one-dollar bills—"

"Which I had taken away from Papa when I took away the titles. I hid it all in a hat box in my closet."

"—so that we could buy our houses and taxis back. Edith stood over your grandfather while he signed it all over to us."

"I wouldn't let him ask for any more money." Aunt Edith was stern.

"And we got right back into business. Months and months before anybody else. We named the 1942 DeSoto 'Edith'."

"It was the prettiest," Aunt Edith revealed with unexpected vanity. "But"—and her voice returned to sternness—"as difficult as those days were, they were survivable. Which is why"—she was no longer sharing sentences with Ike, but had turned to pass wisdom over the back of her seat to

Justa—"I wanted you to start your adult life in a larger venue than Mills College. Difficulties are always easier to handle when you have enough space to lift your elbows before digging your hands into the necessary work."

"She'll do fine at Mills." Ike caught Justa's glance through the rear view mirror. He winked.

"But what if some day her life has to get smaller, like mine did?" Aunt Edith demanded. "Like after my first stroke when I had to move to an apartment because I could no longer take care of my house? Or after the second stroke, when the DMV told me I could no longer drive? Justa is at a point where her life should be enlarging, expanding. She should be grappling, reaching for what is beyond her normal areas of control. Not hiding in some cloistered shelter. She should be forging memories that, in the future, might end up being bigger than her life. Those are the kinds of memories that help to carry a person forward."

"I know that's how you feel, Edith," Ike gentled her. "But butt out." Justa wouldn't have dared such familiarity. "Justa's future is Dan's and Isobel's business, not yours."

Aunt Edith snorted dissent but, incredibly, stopped making points.

The Hills Bros Coffee sign was already visible from Justa's window; Ike and Aunt Edith's story had gotten them across the bridge. Ike took one-way streets into the City and stopped in front of Gump's. "I'll catch up with you," he told Aunt Edith before he drove away to park the car.

Aunt Edith knew exactly where she wanted to go. She knew the aisles, the departments. She got Justa to the jewelry section, and declared, "Edith Matthews." Her satisfaction, now, was entirely different than that which had warmed her voice during the telling of the story. This satisfaction was sparked by anticipation. "I have a special order."

"Of course, Miss Matthews." During the minutes the clerk was away, Justa closed her eyes and listened so she would remember. Gump's was a bubbling of quiet tones, people taking pleasure in the largeness of their time. Not words, not individual voices—more of a museum sound. Except for Aunt Edith. Justa opened her eyes. Aunt Edith's short intakes of breath were pops against the bubbles. Pops that became an "At last!" when the clerk said, simultaneously, "Here we are."

The clerk opened a small leather box for Aunt Edith's inspection. Justa leaned to see. Two drops of heart-red blood rested against black velvet. Ruby earrings, each stone the size of Justa's smallest fingernail.

"Lovely," Aunt Edith sighed out, and her breath evened. She carefully removed one of the earrings from the velvet. The ruby dangled from a sort of closed, golden hook. "European clasps," Aunt Edith told Justa. "When I found them a few weeks ago, they were in terrible shape. Got bent somehow. One of the levers was broken."

"All fixed now, Miss Matthews," the clerk said cheerfully. "And very fine rubies, too, I might add."

"Try them on," Aunt Edith told Justa.

"For me? Really?"

Aunt Edith nodded.

Justa removed her Möbius strips and put them in the now-empty leather box. Aunt Edith showed her how to slip the wires through her ears, how to push the levers so the clasps were secure. Aunt Edith pulled aside Justa's hair so Justa could see how the spots of red lined up with her lips. They made her lips look fuller, brighter, prettier.

"She looks beautiful," the clerk complimented.

The rubies nudged Justa's jaw when she turned her head—minuscule percussive taps that she realized were meant to accompany a brand-new life, her college life, adult life. "I love them," she said. She would have added, "I love you," if she had been bolder, if she hadn't been in a public place. Because in that moment she felt as special as a 1942 DeSoto.

'Buried Alive in the Blues',

on Janis Joplin's *Pearl*, was left an instrumental because she died
before completing the album.

Starting Autumn 1971

LLLLL

Sometimes, when Lowry was whizzing across campus, she encountered the Columbae House baker who always waved at her. Today he braked and yelled, "Hey!"

She pulled up before him. She tried to stay in place by wobbling, for a quick getaway. She gave up and put both feet to the ground.

She knew what he wanted, what so many people wanted from her nowadays: news about Stillman. Lowry had none. All she knew was what everybody already knew: that Stillman and El Chico had escaped consequences by fleeing to Mexico; that Augustus Russell was arrested, fined, and fired—in that order. Everybody suspected Stillman and El Chico were still in Mexico. Nobody knew where Russell ended up.

The baker raised his eyebrows at her in question.

"Nothing," Lowry told him.

"Did you see the *Daily* this morning?" he asked, almost happily.

Lowry had. The *Daily*'s prime War watcher reported evidence the War was winding down. Fewer men were being drafted. US troop levels were dropping.

"Maybe I'll be okay." Which explained his cautious happiness. If the War was fizzling he might be able to look forward to a future. He wrinkled his brow. "Such a waste." Meaning Stillman. "So many like him."

Lowry made her getaway.

She was returning to Grove House from FloMo where she had eaten dinner with friends. She didn't live there anymore; Willow had gone to Italy to study art. Left alone, Lowry wanted someplace smaller, more homey. Grove House was a former frat house turned coed dorm. Lowry's new roommate, Susan Inoue, was an engineering major who wasn't particularly interested in the Vietnam War. Lowry was glad of that.

Lowry turned the knob to their door. Susan looked up from a book with alarmingly few words. "Outrageous Paul is looking for you, looking for anybody," she said.

"Why?" Lowry asked.

"Bored, I suppose." Susan went back to her studies.

Shortly after Lowry moved into Grove House, when she still thought this boy was known as Paul Quimby, she had shared a kiss with him. The kiss was not a success, they both agreed on that point. Now she and Outrageous Paul were something like friends.

Making as little noise as possible, Lowry shrugged off her jacket and hung it in the closet. She regarded her own desk, pondering which homework to take up first.

"Good time?" Outrageous Paul was coiled around the door frame like a flexible lizard. Lowry must have left the door ajar.

Susan's shoulders, which had risen as if in attempt to cover her ears, dropped in exasperation. "Go away, O.P.," she ordered. "I have a test in Structural Analysis tomorrow morning."

Outrageous Paul remained glued in place. He scrutinized Susan's shoulders and spine. He scrutinized Lowry's face. "Such different needs," he mused. "But Dr. Paul can help! And no charge, either!"

"Will you close the door on him," Susan begged Lowry.

Lowry succeeded in shooing him away. She slammed. But only minutes later, while she was still prioritizing, the doorknob turned and Outrageous Paul let himself in. He entered like a butler, stalking majestically with one palm held flat and high as if balancing a tray. But all he carried was a small plastic box, the kind normally used for travel sewing kits. He bowed before Susan. "A little pep for you, Madam?" he offered.

Susan deigned to glance up from her studies. "If it's really free..." she considered.

"My treat," Outrageous Paul assured her.

Susan looked at her book, Outrageous Paul's hand, her book again. "Okay." She plucked a white tablet from the box's interior.

"For you, Madam." With a graceful swerve, Outrageous Paul stepped toward Lowry.

"I don't take drugs," she told him.

"Until now," Outrageous Paul qualified. "Maybe you need something now." He dropped his butler's posing. "When was the last time you were happy, Lowry?"

The question was so unexpected, Lowry's eyes dampened. She blinked. She couldn't remember.

"I don't think it will hurt you." Susan was now staring at Lowry too. She had postponed taking her tablet; she still held it between her fingers. "O.P. might be right," she allowed. "You're always so serious. You need a break." This coming from Susan, who never took a break. "What were you think-ing of?" Susan asked Paul.

"Half a tab of LSD."

Susan nodded. "You'll be okay," she assured Lowry. "You might even have fun. I'll keep an eye on you." To prove her word, she carried her book to her bed where she plumped up her pillow and sat with her back against the wall. Her eyes meeting Lowry's, she swallowed her tablet with no water.

Outrageous Paul frowned into his box. He pulled out a candy heart ex-actly like the hundreds Lowry had eaten in elementary school. "'Be True'." He read the heart's caption out loud. He broke the candy in half. "I think you should have 'True'." He held that portion out.

Lowry remembered precisely how the candy should taste: a dusty sweetness. Valentine's Day used to be so heady with expectation, with color. And now...

She looked down at the rug beneath her feet. This rug had been abso-lutely brilliant that first day of college, as if Willow's mother possessed a secret knowledge of the spectrum. Three years later the brightness had dimmed. Lowry didn't know when the rug was last vacuumed. But there had been a time when it was fresh and new. When she was fresh and new. When every moment was another chance at happiness.

"Okay." She decided abruptly. Her fingertips met Paul's. She popped 'True' into her mouth. She was expecting a somehow changed flavor, a chemical bitterness perhaps. But the dryness crumbling over her tongue was as sweet as what she remembered from the first grade, the third grade, the sixth grade. In those days she would have a Valentine's box on her desk at school. She would collect Sweethearts, Hershey's Kisses, punched-out gift cards. Mom had always insisted Lowry give every child in her class a card, regardless of how much Lowry might dislike that child. Regardless if the child was a boy—which was something that mattered in grammar school.

Boys mattered in a different way now. Outrageous Paul was smiling his success at her. Lowry smiled back. He was appealing in a puppy dog kind of way. Like a puppy dog, he was always wandering for love.

Lowry looked around. There was Susan—sweet Susan, surprising Susan—studying by the beam of her tensor lamp. Susan had curved the lamp's long neck so that light centered over her book before spilling into a circle of brightness over her bedspread. Her bedspread was red, right? But tonight it was gray. Not just any gray: a medium depth of darkness with ruby undertones.

"Who's the happiest person you know?" Outrageous Paul murmured. Somehow, sometime, Lowry had lowered herself to sit upon the floor. Outrageous Paul was lying beside her, half curled into a comma.

Lowry didn't have to think. "My sister." She shifted until Outrageous Paul became a comfortable cushion, a sort of on-floor wall, for her to lean against. Like Susan's wall up there above the cliff of her bedspread. Susan's wall was nearing white—not a blaze of lightness, but light subdued, compressed, touched with gray.

Lowry gazed at the line where bedspread met wall, where darkness met light. If she subtracted darkness from darkness, and light from light, she came to a line that had no dimension, that was a retreat into...nothingness.

Instantly, her innards froze. "No!" Her icy heart and lungs and liver warned her: do not fall into that which does not exist. With great effort, she pulled her eyes away from bedspread and wall to the rest of the room— which was likewise an amazing variation of the subtleties of gray. She peered, looking just far enough into each shade to see its undertones. Her own bedspread had hints of mallard green.

When she awoke it was morning, and she was lying on Willow's rug. Outrageous Paul snored softly at her side. Everything Lowry saw—beds, desks, chairs, walls—was back to its true color, washed by dawn.

"Hi," Susan whispered.

Lowry laid a hand flat against the rug. With her fingers barely touching the bumps of wool, she ran her hand along woof and warp. Willow's mother had known how colors became each other.

"How was it?" Susan asked.

Lowry's tongue had trouble finding words. 'I feel carved out' was most honest. She had tried so hard to find color within that world of gray. She hadn't been frightened then, but now... *I think I went into the underworld.* Did she say that out loud? She pressed her hand hard against the rug. Maybe the reason she hadn't gotten lost, left in that underworld, was because she was lying on top of love.

"Are you okay?" Susan asked, worried. "Are you all the way back?"

Lowry shook her head, then shook it harder, trying to loosen the dregs of last night's experience. Susan came down to sit beside her. Together they waited until the two halves of Lowry's world, colored and not, coalesced and became the slight dinginess of what her life was now.

When was the last time she was happy?

When she could finally articulate—after Susan evicted Outrageous Paul from their room, after Susan brought up a tray of coffee, eggs, and toast—Lowry said, "I know what I'm going to write about," meaning that open-topic paper her Social Change in America professor had assigned. She was going to write about loss. She was going to write about waste. She was going to write about the absenting boys of the Vietnam War.

JJJJJ

First Semester

Justa loved Mills. She loved the white-stuccoed buildings, and the little bridges over summer-shrunken streams. She loved the fullness of sound from the campanile bells that patterned her day. The bells had names: Hope, Peace, Joy. Their music reached as far as the campus wall and gate—

and then stopped, able to go no farther because of the cacophonous honking and screeching of Oakland traffic.

Within the range of bells, Justa lived in a forest. She loved the soughing of eucalyptus trees, swaying alongside campus roads and pathways. She loved how sycamore bark popped beneath her feet whenever she took a shortcut to the gym. She loved the splayed golden leaves which spiraled—the slightest disturbance of air—from the ginkgo tree beyond the President's House.

And she loved Dr. Weber who gave her private lessons twice a week.

Dr. Weber always arrived at his office a minute or two after Justa, his homburg on his head, his unbuttoned raincoat—not really necessary at this time of year—flapping against his hips like low-flying wings. He would unlock the door, sit down on a hard backed chair, and pant, "Now, begin." Sometime during the lesson, the raincoat would be hung neatly on a coat rack and the homburg would tilt rakishly from one of its spikes. Dr. Weber's quiet steps, as he walked about the room, were more directive to Justa than a metronome. She could hear his disapproval, feel his dismay, register his satisfaction before he approved, "Well, so!"

Her other courses that term were English, Music Theory, and Seeing History Through Architecture. To her surprise, she found herself getting A's in all her classes. "I think it's because people talk," she told Lowry on a rare occasion when they were both in their dorms at the same time, when both could use a phone. "It's not like high school when the girls would look at the boys before speaking. Nobody's afraid to talk here. And everybody listens."

"Do you talk?" Lowry asked.

"Sometimes," Justa affirmed.

But afterward, when she opened the door to her balcony, she only listened. She heard bats squeaking, katydids ticking off end-of-day, eucalyptus trees creaking in the wind. She listened close by, to the nighttime music that took the place of the daytime bells—Siu-Sing's chimes tingling permutations of a pentatonic scale.

She thought about crossing the balcony and knocking on Siu-Sing's door. They shared what had been built as a sleeping porch, linking two very small rooms originally intended for study and dressing. Nowadays girls with this setup used the balconies as a shared lounge, and crammed their beds into the little singles. Siu-Sing's room was especially crammed because she had a rosewood headboard and footboard. And a rosewood desk, chair, and dresser, all sent from Hong Kong. All shaped, carved and, in places, inlaid with mother-of-pearl.

Justa took six steps, and knocked.

"Come in."

Siu-Sing's room looked like a museum—or maybe one of those back rooms in a Chinatown store where Aunt Edith said all the really fine merchandise was kept safe from the casual hands of tourists. Siu-Sing's washing sink—the one in Justa's room dripped—was sheltered by an ornate dressing screen on which a dragon battled with a phoenix. Scrolls with more dragons, more phoenixes, hung on the walls. Dragons and phoenixes—those were the themes Siu-Sing's half brother had chosen, because it was he who had ordered the decoration of this room. His favorite color, persimmon, covered Siu-Sing's bed, window, and the tiny bit of glass in her balcony door. Justa knew every garment inside the closet had at least a touch of red-orange.

"Are you studying?" Justa asked.

"I am lying." Siu-Sing's English was almost perfect, except for an odd undulation resembling nothing Justa ever heard in Chinatown. It was a bleakness that settled Siu-Sing's voice like ashes. And yet also a light that brought her voice up, like renewal. Siu-Sing had a phoenix voice; she had the voice of an imaginary bird.

"I am writing to my half brother that it is impossible for me to have a personal telephone. That they are forbidden to freshmen. The truth is I do not want my half brother's voice in this room. Not now. Not ever." Siu-Sing sat in her carved chair at her carved desk. The characters on the persimmon-edged stationary she was using looked carved, too.

Justa sat on Siu-Sing's bed. On her own bed she would have sat cross-legged. But Siu-Sing's comforter was as slippery as silk. It probably was silk. Justa's bare feet felt dirty in this room.

"There." Siu-Sing completed her letter with a stamp from her 'chop', a hand-sized statue of a phoenix that had her own special characters carved into the bottom. That stamp became a small, square picture in red, a hash of lines in a damp paste that would dry in minutes. The picture meant *siu sing sing*, little stars. Siu-Sing had been named after the night sky. "It is the Moon Festival tonight, you know."

Justa didn't know what the moon festival was.

"Last year we went out onto the harbor in Zi-Wai's junk." Zi-Wai was Siu-Sing's half brother. "And we floated moon cakes and lanterns until they sank. We trailed a path of sweetness and light behind us until we docked at one of Zi-Wai's restaurants. I left the table for the toilet, and there I found my old nanny waiting. Zi-Wai had fired her eight years before, the day I achieved womanhood. He said since I was no longer a child, I no longer needed a child's protection. I was only nine. I wept for grief and for pain. My nanny told me I must always have this." Siu-Sing turned back to her desk. She filled a sheet of stationary with only one character. She held the sheet up for Justa to see. The character looked like a square-bodied stick figure, running.

"What does it mean?" Justa asked.

"Courage," Siu-Sing said simply. "My nanny told me I must have courage. From then on she searched me out and found me wherever she could. So that we could talk. So that we could plan. You will come with me to the fraternity party two weeks from now, Justa, will you not?"

The change of subject was distracting. Justa's mind was pulled from Hong Kong back to Mills. "I don't know." During her two months here she had not yet chosen to go beyond Mills' walls.

"Please?" Siu-Sing begged. "I would like to have you as witness."

"Witness?" Justa questioned. Sometimes, despite her perfection, Siu-Sing still missed a word, its precise meaning.

"As companion," Siu-Sing corrected.

Justa slid off the silk. She stood on the hand-knotted rug, another dragon battling another phoenix. She stretched up her arms to pull out the kinks in her back. She yawned; she considered. "All right," she said.

A Secret

During the next two weeks Siu-Sing was occupied with a 'secret'—the first syllable high, the second low—about which she would tell Justa only a little. "I am changing my room," she said. "Soon you will see." She kept the secret dark with the curtains pulled shut over her window and door. Justa could only imagine a redecoration because of the men who arrived in vans, who carried boxes upstairs under Siu-Sing's or the housemother's escort, and then brought boxes down. Justa was sorry: she had come to love Siu-Sing's room. Siu-Sing must have tired of dragons and phoenixes.

On fraternity Friday, Siu-Sing dressed in Justa's room. She brought over a persimmon silk dress, draped between her arms with jade jewelry puddled in the middle. She allowed the jewelry to slide onto Justa's bed, and Justa saw: some of the persimmon color was flowers. Every week Zi-Wai sent his sister orchids.

Justa's plan for herself had been to put on a nice sweater and fresh jeans. She decided instead to wear what Lowry had chosen for the Gump's expedition with Aunt Edith. "Can I help you?" Justa asked after pulling on pants, top, jacket.

"Thank you." Siu-Sing's dress was a traditional cheongsam which had to be lowered over her head and then buttoned down the side. It fit her body like water.

"Wow," Justa admired. Her Emporium finery suddenly felt baggy and shabby.

"The necklace clasp can be difficult," Siu-Sing warned.

Justa fastened the heavy necklace around Siu-Sing's neck. Still standing behind, she watched the mirrored Siu-Sing hang more heavy jade from her ears. Siu-Sing began to put a bracelet over her arm. "Will you wear no jewelry, Justa?" Siu-Sing asked.

"Oh!" And Justa remembered Aunt Edith's rubies. They were in her top drawer. When she returned to the mirror, Siu-Sing was fastening orchids to her hair with a jade and pearl comb.

                              ❧

Siu-Sing drove them to Berkeley. She owned a persimmon-painted, persimmon-upholstered car Zi-Wai had had delivered to the dormitory the second day of school. She drove carefully, cautiously—through Oakland, into Berkeley, past all the lights on College Avenue, toward fraternity row. She parked at a curb and, before getting out, said, "Justa, if you ever chance to meet my half brother you must tell him this." She repeated intonations until Justa could pronounce a phrase that sounded like 'mo gow nor'.

The car, while driving, had been wonderfully quiet. The fraternity was loud, very loud. Upstairs bedroom speakers faced outside, holding open sash windows. Other speakers—unseen, certainly much larger—poured music through downstairs windows, downstairs doors. Janis Joplin sang 'Me and Bobby McGee'. Led Zeppelin began 'Stairway to Heaven'. Ike & Tina Turner hit the last notes of 'Proud Mary'. It was clash of genres and keys.

Siu-Sing stepped through the wide-open front doorway. Justa wasn't allowed to follow because—"Hey, babe"—four or five boys were smoking tobacco and marijuana on the porch. One purposely blocked her passage. "You here for me?"

Justa grimaced annoyance at him. "I'm looking for Bob." Surely every fraternity had a 'Bob'.

"You mean Bobby Pullman?" The smoker exuded disappointment, but let her pass by.

Inside, Siu-Sing was nowhere visible. Loose hands found Justa's arms, her back—one brushed her butt. She wished she did indeed know a Bob. She picked out a tall, broad-shouldered boy who was weaving through the fraternity's living room, bumping into furniture and genially excusing himself whether or not the furniture was occupied. Justa's junior prom date had turned out to be a lush; lushes were maneuverable. She took the boy's arm, hoping he wasn't yet near the point when he would start vomiting. "Hello! Thanks for inviting me," she said cheerily.

Lush-boy blinked at her. "I did?"

"Oh, yes." She kept up the cheer. "Let's go find my friend, Siu-Sing." Lush-boy became her plow through the crowd of hands. Justa found Siu-Sing in the kitchen where a man far beyond university age was sliding the jade and pearl comb from Siu-Sing's hair.

"Do you want to go?" Justa asked hopefully.

Siu-Sing waved the man away. "We have done enough," she told Justa. Siu-Sing's normal smile showed no teeth, but this smile was open-lipped. She allowed Lush-boy to escort her, and Justa, back to the car. He did so with the same amiability he had shown the sofa cushions.

"That's it for me and fraternities," Justa sighed as Siu-Sing pulled away from the curb. It wasn't until they crossed into Oakland that Justa noticed— "Oh, Siu-Sing! I'm sorry!"—Siu-Sing's hair hung without flowers. "That guy must still have your comb!"

"It is fine," Siu-Sing said. "It is good." Her grin possessed teeth.

∾

The next morning Siu-Sing didn't get up for breakfast. When she also didn't appear for lunch, Justa wondered. Siu-Sing never slept so late. Afterward Justa tapped on Siu-Sing's hallway door. No response. Justa wasn't really worried, but when she went into her own room, something felt wrong. No, something *sounded* wrong. Siu-Sing's chimes were silent. Justa went out to the balcony: the chimes were gone. And the curtains had been removed from Siu-Sing's windows.

Justa pressed her nose against glass. Siu-Sing's room had lost color. The heavy wood furniture still stood in place, but the persimmon comforter and embroidered pillows were gone, as were the screen and the scrolls. The empty mattress, the walls, had returned to institutional white. The floor was bare oak. All the dragons and phoenixes had flown.

"Siu-Sing?" Justa asked herself a question for which she had no answer.

As if in echo, someone yelled, "Siu-Sing!" The hall phone must have rung: every girl on the floor allowed the half hour between one and one thirty for Zi-Wai's long-distance call from Hong Kong. "Siu-Sing!" the girl said insistently.

There was no one else to speak for Siu-Sing, so Justa went back through her own room and into the hallway where, reluctantly, she accepted the receiver. She heard the language of intonations in a male voice. "I'm Siu-Sing's roommate," she broke in.

Zi-Wai switched to English. "Where is she?"

"I don't know," Justa had to answer. "I haven't seen her all day."

Zi-Wai hissed, which gave Justa a moment in which to remember: "But she told me to tell you something." Justa tried to form the words exactly as Siu-Sing had taught her. "Mo gow nor."

"Mo gow nor?" Zi-Wai's voice was so furious, Justa dropped the receiver. And that's when she realized: she had failed to ask Siu-Sing what those words meant.

Another girl took hold of the receiver. That girl tried to listen. "I'll get Mrs. Cooper," she told Zi-Wai.

Throughout the hours that followed, after the housemother had been summoned and tried to reassure Zi-Wai, after campus and Oakland police arrived, Justa did her best to answer everybody's questions. She told Mrs. Cooper that Siu-Sing had not been ill. She told the police that she and Siu-Sing stayed for less than an hour at last night's party. She told the Director of Housing that, while she wasn't familiar with everything Siu-Sing owned, she could describe some items. She told the Dean of Students that, to her knowledge, Siu-Sing had been perfectly happy at school.

⌒

That was all Saturday afternoon and into the evening. On Sunday Dad picked Justa up to take her home for a pre-arranged cocktail hour with Aunt Edith. Aunt Edith had asked for a 'Justa report'. When Justa walked into the living room her heart felt like a mass of jagged edges.

"How's it going?" were Aunt Edith's first words. "Life in the cloister."

"Mills is not Catholic," Dad automatically contradicted.

Justa sat in a pale yellow chair across from Aunt Edith's matching sofa. "I have a friend," she began slowly. "I had a friend. Because she's gone. Her room is emptied out. Her car has disappeared. And nobody knows where or why."

The only responses Justa got were frowns: Dad's a lesser edition of Aunt Edith's, Mom's puzzled.

"I went to a party with her the night before, in Berkeley," Justa continued. "She lost some of her jewelry there."

"Oh, Justie!" Mom held out her arms, ready to comfort.

"Think, girl!" Aunt Edith's words curtailed Mom's attempt. "What else do you recall?"

Justa thought. But her thoughts were interrupted by the music of Siu-Sing's intonations, by the exotic cadences of Siu-Sing's memories. "Her chimes were major," was all Justa could find to say. "Her voice was minor."

Aunt Edith snorted disgust. "Look at me," she commanded, and Justa looked. Aunt Edith had dressed for this occasion in a suit the color of Justa's rubies.

"You. Must. Wake. Up," Aunt Edith spoke each word separately. "Child, sooner rather than later you're going to have to leave this fairyland of yours."

"What fairyland?" Now it was Dad who snorted disgust, but at Aunt Edith. "We're talking about a girl who has run away! Justie, did she leave any clues?"

"A message. It's in Chinese and I don't know what it means."

"What was it?" Aunt Edith, Dad and Mom all asked at once.

"Mo gow nor. She taught me how to say it."

Mom and Dad gazed perplexedly at each other.

Aunt Edith was figuring things out by herself: "So your friend had a plan. What have you seen or heard that seemed different?"

"The vans." Justa suddenly remembered. She hadn't seen all, but some had painted logos or words on their sides.

"Tell the police," Aunt Edith directed. "You will discover you know much more than you realize."

Aunt Edith's ruby suit was such a blaze of brightness in this buttercup-soft room, it made Justa's eyes well with tears.

"I know I'm not gentle." Aunt Edith sounded surprisingly so. "I know I don't always seem to be kind. But I do care for you on a level I don't think anybody else does."

Justa knew that. She had never doubted. But she didn't see how it could be of help now.

Zi-Wai

Mhhóu gáau ngóh meant 'leave me alone'. Justa learned this the following morning from another Chinese student who lived in the senior apartments. Leng Faa stood in Mrs. Cooper's office and pronounced Siu-Sing's message with tonal perfection, the *ngóh* making a little hill of sound. "I will assist in any way," she offered.

"Thank you." Mrs. Cooper was grateful. "Mr. Ngai, I mean Ngai Zi-Wai—is that correct?—will arrive sometime today."

"Oh!" Leng Faa gasped. It was mention of Zi-Wai's full name that had made her face go pale, then blank. "Except that I have a bio test on Friday," she backtracked. "I must study all day, all week." Her shoulders hunched with sudden desperation. "Bye-bye." And she fled.

"What did I say that was wrong?" Mrs. Cooper was bewildered.

Justa was, too. She waited for Zi-Wai all day. Even in classes she kept part of her attention toward the door, to the possibility of someone coming to fetch her. When she wasn't in class, she stayed in the dorm, her hallway door open.

She knew Zi-Wai had arrived when a girl whose balcony overlooked the back parking lot yelled out, "He drives a Maserati convertible." Only minutes later Mrs. Cooper sent a message up to Justa's room via the house intercom, requesting that Justa come downstairs.

Zi-Wai wasn't much taller than Siu-Sing, although his physique was square instead of slight. His gray suit was expertly tailored, as perfectly male as Siu-Sing's cheongsam had been beautifully female. He stood within the archway that led to the dormitory parlor, ignoring Mrs. Cooper's invitations to enter and sit, not responding to Mrs. Cooper's, "We're so sorry about this happening."

"Justa Matthews?" he said.

Justa nodded.

"We are all, of course, greatly upset," Mrs. Cooper continued.

Zi-Wai spoke only to Justa. "You knew her," he stated.

"I didn't." Because that was Justa's new truth.

"We kept her room for you, exactly," Mrs. Cooper contributed.

"Justa will show me."

Mrs. Cooper hesitated, but then pressed a key into Justa's palm. "Take him up, please."

It was like being followed by a tornado, a force of intent at Justa's back that was an inexorable shove. Up the stairs, down the hallway. After unlocking Siu-Sing's door, Justa stood aside. "Come," Zi-Wai commanded, and this time it was she who followed.

What she first noticed was the buzz of flies, which shouldn't have been there. So many flies. And then she saw what had not been visible through Siu-Sing's balcony window: the bare mattress was stained by juices from a persimmon. The persimmon was placed exactly where Siu-Sing's hips must have lain. The persimmon was pierced, broken open, by what looked to be a white stone shaft. Justa leaned forward. "That's her chop," she wondered.

She looked to Zi-Wai for an explanation, and saw that he had become ill. No. That twisting and shifting of his face was the manifestation of an unvocalized scream. Justa could not clear the sound of buzzing out of her head.

Zi-Wai re-established control over his lips. "You will tell me." His voice had lost all pitch.

Somehow, this intonality was more frightening than any vocal explosion would have been. Because Zi-Wai didn't tell Justa what he wanted to know, she started at the beginning. "I didn't hear the chimes." He shifted his focus to her, and only her, and she felt pinned—like the persimmon was to the mattress. She rushed, reciting the events that preceded Siu-Sing's disappearance. She dropped parts of the story, then scrambled the timeline. The buzz, the odor of rotten fruit, returned her gaze to Siu-Sing's bed, and she suddenly recognized what she hadn't before: the hand that forced the chop through the fruit, spraying juice onto the quilted mattress topping, had been a fist of rage. "Siu-Sing didn't want a telephone."

Zi-Wai snarled. Below the distortion of his face, his Adam's apple quivered.

Justa grabbed the doorknob and pulled. Mrs. Cooper waited in the hallway.

"Mr. Ngai—" Mrs. Cooper began. Zi-Wai pushed past her.

Justa waited until they both were gone downstairs. She then did something she hadn't dared to do in Zi-Wai's presence. She opened Siu-Sing's closet.

Siu-Sing had left some color in the room after all. She had pulled her beautiful silk garments off their hangers. She had cut and torn skirts and bodices; dismembered sleeves like body parts. She left a puddle of satin, brocade, and crepe de chine on the closet floor. Red-orange.

Justa sank into the small lake of destruction. She touched the sometimes soft, sometimes stiff, richness of the fabrics. She wept. She wept for Siu-Sing, for what Siu-Sing's life must have been. And she wept for herself, because she had acquired a new emotion on this day. Hatred.

⸏

On a day when rare snowflakes were predicted for Oakland, and the girls in Justa's dorm were continually running out onto their balconies to look up at the sky, Mrs. Cooper again requested that Justa come downstairs. Mrs. Cooper sent no further message, but Justa suspected.

Zi-Wai stood in the parlor. This time he had brought associates—two burly men, both Asian, each wearing a suit as richly severe as Zi-Wai's. They flanked him.

A middle-aged Anglo woman, seated on the sofa behind them, stared at Justa. "I have never seen her before," the woman said. Her words were a wind-gust of exasperation. "As I told you many times already, Mr. Ngai, my exchange with your sister was conducted entirely by mail. I do not know this girl."

"This is Dr. O'Malley. She's an expert in Asian art and antiquities," Mrs. Cooper told Justa as an aside.

"Is this your handwriting?" Zi-Wai held what looked to be an invoice in front of Justa's face. Somebody, on plain white bond paper, had written out the details of a sale—Siu-Sing's jade tree, the one that used to stand on her dresser. 'Solid gold stemmed; petaled with shavings of garnet and sapphire; leafed with drops of imperial jade.' According to this invoice, the jade tree was worth forty-seven thousand dollars.

Justa had loved that tree. At the slightest movement the leaves would rap a pattern of random perfection.

"Did you do this." Zi-Wai's question was a statement, an assumption.

Justa shook her head. In mute proof, she removed a scribbled note from her pocket. '16th C. ctrpoint, Secd species, 2-1 counter firmus.' Justa wrote in loops. Whoever wrote out the invoice must have gone to Catholic school; that person wrote in slants.

"Then I need no longer stay." Dr. O'Malley, even more deeply aggravated, stood. She brushed the creases out of the seat of her skirt.

"My sister did not act alone." Zi-Wai aimed his voice at her like a gun. "She had an intermediary."

"Who was not us." Dr. O'Malley underlined her words. She took a deep breath. She spoke more calmly. "And who was not this girl. I regret your distress, sir. But I think I have done all that kindness and courtesy demand. I repeat: in exchange for our check, we were sent the custom papers. We were given complete evidence of provenance. Our lawyers have checked and rechecked. The museum now owns the tree." With what Justa thought was admirable coolness, she moved into the archway.

Justa shifted into Dr. O'Malley's wake. Like a duckling at Dr. O'Malley's tail, she bypassed Zi-Wai's two men. She and Dr. O'Malley were almost at the front door.

"Siu-Sing turned your check into cash!" Zi-Wai bellowed.

Justa followed Dr. O'Malley's stride over the threshold, onto the porch. An Asian Art Museum van waited in the circular drive below. When Dr. O'Malley reached it, Justa broke away. The dampness that fell on her hair, that melted on her eyelashes as she cut through campus, might have been snow. She didn't care. She was grateful for a coldness she could gulp down to her core.

⌒

Three days passed by, and the same girl who lived over the parking lot knocked on Justa's door to say, "He's back."

Justa had to descend the stairs.

This time Mrs. Cooper had confined Zi-Wai, without his men, in her office. This time Mrs. Cooper was not urging Zi-Wai to sit. "I have told Mr. Ngai he may question you on *one* topic," Mrs. Cooper said tightly.

Zi-Wai immediately thrust a photograph before Justa's eyes.

Justa's expression must have displayed recognition, because Zi-Wai immediately asked, "Who is he?"

"He was at the frat party," Justa had to say. "He's the guy who took Siu-Sing's comb. I don't know his name."

"We will find him." With an expansive, almost friendly gesture, Zi-Wai removed a penciled note from his breast pocket. He held it up so Justa could read. He, or somebody, had listed in English Siu-Sing's scrolls, her screen, her jewelry, followed by their dollar amounts. "We will find them all."

"You may go now, Justa." Mrs. Cooper promptly dismissed her.

Once upstairs, Justa didn't stop at her own room. She continued down the hallway to the room over the parking lot. "Can I go out on your balcony?" She waited there, hidden from the ground, while her dorm-mate hung over the balustrade.

"He's getting in his car," the girl said.

Zi-Wai's Maserati started with a deep-throated growl that settled into a purr. Justa memorized those sounds. From now on she would stay attuned to that growl, to that purr. She lay awake deep into the following morning; with her ears permanently set to an automobile alert, her room had become too noisy for sleep.

Christmas Vacation

This Christmas was back to being what Christmases were like before Lowry went away to college and became political. Dad was constantly jovial, as if wearing a ho-ho-ho white beard he couldn't remove from his face. Mom laughed in the kitchen at everything. "Those are chunks, Low. I need *confetti*-sized pieces. You're cutting up green onions, not pineapples!" They were all so happy, so contented, their reassembled togetherness so precious, Justa couldn't speak out.

Christmas Eve dinner was squash soup, Cornish game hens with wild rice stuffing, Caesar salad, and an apple tart with almond cream. Mom baked a cinnamon apple for Aunt Edith. Afterward, when Lowry had trailed off to her bedroom, and Dad had gone out to join Hiro—*F. Yamada, Landscape Architect* stenciled on the van's side—and Mom was settled at her kitchen desk nook, Justa joined Aunt Edith.

Aunt Edith was still in the living room, sitting on the sofa with her brandy snifter still in her hand. She gazed at the Christmas tree. Her gaze was so wistful, so very different from her usual minute critical examination of everything, Justa hesitated to interrupt. "Aunt Edith?" Justa spoke quietly enough so Aunt Edith could choose to ignore if she wished. But Aunt Edith's expression snapped alert.

"Justa," she returned.

"I wanted to ask— No-o-o, I need to *tell* you," and finally Justa could talk about the pomegranate, the chop. "On the night we went to the fraternity party, Siu-Sing was wearing fifteen thousand dollars worth of jade. I saw that jewelry—the necklace, the earrings, the bracelet, the comb—on Zi-Wai's list." Justa ran out of story.

"He's hoping to find Siu-Sing through her treasures," Aunt Edith surmised.

"It's as though..." Justa shook her head. This was where her thoughts became tangled, where she couldn't parse logic out of horror.

"It's as though her value is only equal to the sum of all those expensive items?" Aunt Edith, as Justa had hoped, knew how to separate and subtract, how to voice what Justa had come to feel. "As though she is nothing but an object of art, herself?"

"Yes!" Justa agreed.

"Which means Siu-Sing's relationship with her brother was even less than a perversion of love," Aunt Edith went on. "Because it contained no love. It was only an ownership."

"Yes." As background, from the kitchen, Justa heard the toneless, sucking release of the refrigerator door—Mom, probably checking for ingredients. Lowry slammed the bathroom door, wood-against-wood. From outdoors, a firm metal creak meant either Dad or Hiro had opened the van up for extra air. This was what Justa knew of love.

"Life is too short," Aunt Edith said softly. She rose from the sofa and approached the picture window. She stood absolutely erect, absolutely still, now gazing into the dark.

Justa saw only reflections: Aunt Edith's rectitude, the horizontal sofa. "Do you think Zi-Wai will ever find her?" Justa asked.

"No." Aunt Edith continued to stare outward as if she could see into the night. "Your friend is a young woman of exceptional determination. She recognized her resources. She has made use of them to pattern her future." Aunt Edith stepped close up to the glass. She placed her hand against the hard, flat barrier. Her hand shone pink and pale against the shadows. She spoke toward the window, but to Justa. "Do you ever read poetry?"

"In my English class." Justa, puzzled by this turn of discussion, wiped away tears she hadn't noticed before.

"A very famous poem urges us to not accept the inevitability of darkness." Aunt Edith still spoke toward the glass. "It shows how anger can be a source of strength, even comfort. Your friend is an example: she used her anger for her own good."

"I don't understand," because Justa didn't.

Aunt Edith took her hand from the window. She turned away from the glass. She placed her night-cooled palm on Justa's still-damp cheek, a caress from somebody who never made such gestures. "Learn from your friend, Justa. Realize your powers. Make use of them. That is my Christmas wish for you."

Second Semester

Justa unpacked her Christmas gifts in her room at Mills—sweaters, books, and the framed print of a 19th century pianist that Dad had seen in an antique shop window and bought on a rare impulse. "Because she reminds me of you, Justie. It's her profile. Not exactly your nose, but still..." The girl wore a casual dress, apron, and loose kerchief around her neck. She sat, fully relaxed, in a room that looked as though it had never been touched by anything angrier than a Beethoven sonata.

Justa couldn't decided where to hang the print, not right off. She held it up over her desk. She tried it beside her balcony door. She knelt on her bed, positioning it various places there. She did not consider the closet wall; that was the wall she shared with Siu-Sing's room. She ended up with the print temporarily, and precariously, angled on her desk, leaning against her class books like a fragile bookend.

She was marking her calendar for the new year when she heard the familiar intercom buzz. Mrs. Cooper wanted her.

Justa had made her way down these stairs so many times, hundreds of times, before. But today her feet could only pattern the three times she had descended to meet Zi-Wai. Because she dreaded, she trudged. She tentatively tapped her fingernails against Mrs. Cooper's closed office door.

"Come in."

The invitation was upbeat, even cheery. Not a Zi-Wai-in-the-room voice. Still, Justa turned the knob cautiously. He wasn't there.

"I have two things I must tell you, Justa," Mrs. Cooper began. "First, and most important, the Dean has informed Mr. Ngai that he may not come onto campus without prior authorization, and that even with authorization he must always be accompanied by a senior member of college administration. All the guards at Richards gate have been informed." Mrs. Cooper then gave Justa the kind of smile that belonged to the months before Siu-Sing's disappearance. "Second, a sophomore girl will be moving into Siu-Sing's room. Her name is Lisa Papadakis."

"Okay," Justa said.

"Life is back to normal," Mrs. Cooper promised.

Maybe. Even after Lisa moved in and proved quiet, studious, and disinclined for conversation, Justa avoided looking at their shared wall. She never stopped listening for the growls and purrs of Zi-Wai's car.

⌒

On a piano lesson day, Justa ran through a mist that was turning to rain. Her plan was to grab a rain jacket from her room before going to Dr. Weber's office. When she saw Mom's car parked below the dorm's front steps, she supposed Mom had dropped by with a box of cookies or éclairs. Justa pulled open the passenger-side door, and slipped in. "Hi!"

It was that half-second pause before Mom responded that told Justa most of what she needed to know—the world had changed again. Mom's hesitation was a catch of grief. "Dad?" Justa panicked. "Low?"

"Edith." Mom's face was set into those angles and planes Justa remembered from when grandparents died. Stoicism. The unexpected countered by long expectation. "A big stroke, this time. She was probably gone in an instant."

An instant was a measure of time. Time was so important to life. It was important to sound. Time provided a beginning and an end. But right now time was folding inward, shrinking, becoming a spot. An instant wasn't long enough. There had to be more between 'to be' and 'not to be'. More for Justa to hear. She needed to listen into that instant. She needed to stretch it out for forever—or at least long enough to say goodbye.

Only then did she notice Mom was weeping; there was rain inside the car as well as out. "Your father is taking care of everything. He'll pick you up on Saturday. We don't yet know when. Edith left a will. She mentioned you. Do you think you'll be okay?"

"No." Justa didn't have to think to produce that word. One clipped note. One discrete moment of time. She left the car to stand in what had become a downpour. Mom got out of the driver's seat to walk around, to hug her. Rain bounced off the car's hood, a disordered metallic contrast to the slow, matching rhythm of their heartbeats. They stood together for many minutes.

"I'm so sorry," Mom said. "So very, very sorry." By the time she drove away, Justa's bangs were dripping into her eyes.

Justa ascended the porch steps half-blindly. She was stopped by somebody seizing her arm. Justa didn't recognize the touch, but she remembered all too well that hot and grasping breath. Zi-Wai.

She shook hair and water out of her eyes. Zi-Wai was dressed in what must have been camouflage—a worker's overalls instead of a bespoke suit. Justa wrenched his hand away from her sweater. "Leave." She pushed him so hard, Zi-Wai stumbled to a lower step. "Me." Anger made her taller than he: Zi-Wai had shrunk in threat, if not in stature. "Alone." She grabbed the railing to lean forward, the better to shout fury down onto his face: "I mean it!"

She gave him a final shove, then turned to stalk up the remaining steps, not bothering to watch what was happening behind. She could hear, though: Zi-Wai had tumbled. She hoped into hell. Her first task, after entering the dorm, was to chalk a note on the board that hung on Mrs. Cooper's closed door. *He's back.* She retrieved her jacket, and by the time she was outdoors again, Zi-Wai was gone.

She didn't practice her assignment on the way to Dr. Weber's office, as she usually did. She didn't move her fingers to inaudible sound. Instead she gathered all the surrounding rain noises, and bound them tightly around a solid core she hadn't known she possessed. Not until she was seated on the piano bench did she realize: when she played, her music was going to go beyond printed notes. She was going to release the chaotic as well as the inevitable. She put her fingers to the keyboard.

Dr. Weber padded around—listening from the far corner; choosing a spot near the window; stopping by the coat rack—as he always did. When she finished: "Finally," he said, "You play."

"I've always played." Justa was suddenly weary. So very, very weary.

"No, child. Before you almost played. Today you met Herr Beethoven."

It was a compliment that hurt.

The lesson over, Justa stepped outside into what had diminished into a drizzle. She closed her eyes and strained, opening her ears to their greatest distance. She heard the whistle of an ocean liner at the Oakland port, but no further. She could not hear into forever.

Aunt Edith had left a will.

Justa ran to the nearest phone booth, across the street. She inserted her dime and, when Dad answered, she went straight to her question. "What did Aunt Edith say about me?"

Dad harrumphed. It was such an unlikely response, neither grief nor an attempt at consolation. It was the same harrumph that had so often accompanied his dealings with Aunt Edith. When she was alive. "Your aunt left you enough money for the rest of your college education. But with a stipulation attached." He was reluctant to tell more.

Justa waited.

"She wants you to attend Stanford or another, and I quote," now Dad spoke resignedly, "'sensibly sized and variegated institution—coed, multi-programed, with ample opportunities both on and off campus—in which Justa may spread her wings'."

Justa's throat and mouth produced her own unlikely response. She found herself snorting; then heard herself laughing.

"Don't worry about it, Justie," Dad's concern was evident. "If the money doesn't go to you, it will go to me, which means it will pay for your education wherever you go. Edith knew that. She just wanted to make her opinion known to the end." He paused, and his voice collapsed into sorrow: "That's who she was."

When Justa hung up her chest was still light with laughter. She needed to think. She needed to walk. She ended up circling the entire inside perimeter of the Mills campus, almost two miles. Wherever possible, she dragged her hand along the barrier wall, sometimes stone, sometimes wire. She heard, and often saw, the bustle and heartbreak that was the city of Oakland: a man with a stolen grocery cart containing his sleeping bag and other bundles, scolding himself on a street corner; ill-tuned cars with smoking tail pipes that passed him by. Justa laughed again, but this time without merriment. It was a sound that encapsulated everything she felt, everything she had ever known about Aunt Edith. It was a sound as full and true—and limited—as the campanile bells with which Mills measured time. Hope. Peace. Joy. Aunt Edith had been so much more.

Justa cut back into the center of campus. She made her way to the library. She called Dad from there.

"All right," she told him. "I'll do it."

"Do what?" Dad was momentarily mystified.

"Go to Stanford. If I can get in. If not, maybe Berkeley or SF State." The words sounded foreign, coming from her mouth. They sounded bigger than she was.

"Oh, Justie, that's not necessary." Dad's voice was so sincere, so melancholy.

Justa was sincere, too. Also determined: "Aunt Edith wanted me to find my powers."

LLLLL

On the way to Aunt Edith's memorial service, Lowry was peevish. She didn't say anything about it because this certainly was not the time or place to make her feelings known. But she sat in the back seat of Dad's car as far away from Justa as she could get. Aunt Edith had left bequests to Dad, Justa, and UCSF medical school—which, creepily, got Aunt Edith's body. But there had been no mention of Lowry or Mom.

Lowry wanted something, anything, to get her out of this ill humor. She couldn't discuss the will right now with Dad because he had his own stuff to deal with. Or with Mom, whose focus was all on on Dad. Or with Justie, who sat silently in her corner looking like someone who had been beaten up.

This worried Lowry. She could understand Justa being sadder than herself because Justie had always been Aunt Edith's favorite. Those ruby earrings! Lowry, on the other hand, had always known herself to be Dad's special girl. People said Aunt Edith had been too young to die. Dad was WAY too young. Wasn't he?

Lowry only succeeded in scaring herself.

They rarely attended the Unitarian Universalist Church in Walnut Creek. That was Aunt Edith's thing. Today Dr. Trojak asked them to wait in his office until they heard piano music. Then they were to walk into the sanctuary and go down the center aisle to the first row of chairs. They were to sit on the right-hand side.

So they waited, nobody saying anything. The piano music started and Justa didn't flinch. Lowry wasn't a musician, but she could tell: the pianist was making a lot of mistakes. Lowry sidled close to Justa, exactly like Mom was staying close to Dad. In two groups of two, they entered the sanctuary.

Everybody they passed by was a Yamada; most held a white flower. Once seated, Lowry leaned forward so she could glance around to the left. The four mourners who sat immediately across the aisle were Aito, the patriarch of the Yamada family who had immigrated from Japan; Hiro, born a U.S. citizen; and Hiro's wife and widowed sister-in-law. They all wore black kimonos.

Dr. Trojak began speaking. "When I first met Edith, all those years ago, she described herself to me as an Albigensian Christian. Nobody was going to split her God into a trinity. Goodness should be the guiding principle of the world. The Albigensians called each other Good Man and Good Woman. I am here today to tell you about a Good Woman."

Lowry would look up 'Albigensian' later, at school. But for now she allowed her thoughts to wander. She left enough of her mind with Dr. Trojak so she would catch anything new she didn't already know about Aunt Edith—such as, "When we were raising money to buy this site, Edith somehow convinced Pete Seeger to perform at a fund-raising hootenanny. I think we attracted all the young and disaffected within a fifty mile radius."

Lowry tucked this fact into the space in her brain reserved for Aunt Edith. She studied the photograph that had been placed on a small table. The photo must have been taken on one of Aunt Edith's cruises: her smile was more relaxed than Lowry had ever seen; her short hair was ruffled by wind. On each side of the photo stood a large, empty, clear-glass vase.

"And so we mourn her," Dr. Trojak finished. Almost finished, because he and Mrs. Trojak moved to stand, one each, behind a vase. Hiro's wife and sister-in-law helped old Aito rise from his chair. Aito shuffled to the table. The women grasped his elbows, and Aito bowed to Aunt Edith's portrait. Then the women took their turns bowing. Hiro, who had been walking behind the three, bowed before placing two long-stemmed white orchids before each vase. Dr. and Mrs. Trojak arranged the flowers within the vases. The oldest Yamadas returned to their chairs.

Another rustle, and the entire row behind Lowry—both sides of the aisle—stood. Lowry glanced over at Dad and Mom. They didn't seem to know what was happening, either. Justa was now gazing at the photo, her expression somehow smoothed.

This queue of mourners was led by Ike, the oldest of his generation. He wore a black suit and dark tie. The women wore black kimonos or dresses. Yamada plus spouse, or single Yamada, each carried a white flower. It took time for the fourteen or so couples-or-individuals to arrive at the table, bow, and offer a flower. This gave Lowry time in which to distinguish: roses, lilies, tulips. The new flowers joined Hiro's four orchids. Every flower was pristine, pure, perfect. They satisfied Lowry, deeply.

She resisted looking over her shoulder when she heard more people, many more people, stand up. The new group was led by Ike's oldest child, Mari O'Brien, and her husband, Sam. They were trailed by their twins, auburn-haired with mischievous eyes. Lowry couldn't resist: she winked at the boys. They grinned back. Aito had never forgiven Mari for marrying a non-Japanese. Even Hiro didn't talk to his granddaughter until after the twins were born; then he relented.

The twins wore already muddied navy-blue sweaters and slacks. Some of the adults in this group were in modern-day black mourning; others had outfitted themselves in a somberness of alternative dark colors. The adults carried carnations and mums. The children all brought baby's breath to the altar. Even the smallest, Fort's three-year-old daughter, bowed.

There was a catch of breath to Lowry's right. Justie was half-smiling as Fort's little girl gazed solemnly down at her patent leather shoes.

While Mari's group returned to their seats, Dr. and Mrs. Trojak tweaked until the flower arrangements became unidentical—but perfect—complements beside Aunt Edith's windswept happiness. The last Yamadas settled, becoming silent except for the sounds of one baby babbling and another beginning to wail. With a graceful sweep of his hand, Dr. Trojak motioned for Lowry's family to rise and to leave.

$\backsim$

Not much later, Lowry stood in the fellowship hall where church ladies were serving tea and cookies. She watched Dad greet and thank people for attending. She saw Mom talking to the Mrs. Yamada who had written a cookbook. Hiro patted Justa's arm.

One of the people who had lined the walls of the sanctuary made her way toward Lowry. She told Lowry her name, which Lowry didn't retain. Lowry did, however, hold on to what the woman said. "We're going to miss Edith. She was an important part of our travel adventures. Those cruises are the only time women like us"—the woman gestured at a small group over by the refreshment table—"can be ourselves."

Women like us. Lowry and Justa had discussed this before, but Mom and Dad wouldn't say 'Aunt Edith is a Lesbian'. Now Lowry knew; now she could tell Justie. Lowry shook the woman's hand as if helping to cradle a secret.

The woman rejoined her friends, and Lowry scanned the gathering for other people she didn't know. Co-workers? Neighbors? Lowry's mind began to sort the entire company into tiers. The first tier was Dad, chief mourner and most greatly grieved. Lowry, Justa, Mom and the Yamadas were all second tier, sharing the loss. The third tier—all those unknowns— had filled in the weave of Aunt Edith's life.

After another hour or so, in the car, while Mom was quietly talking to Dad, Lowry reached across the back seat to take Justa's hand. Lowry held on while Justa's fingers relaxed. She was satisfied when Justa squeezed back. She held on to Justa's hand all the way home.

LOVING

Starting Autumn 1972

JJJJJ

Stanford. Justa was at Stanford. She stood in the middle of her new dormitory room while her family busied themselves around her. Dad was hanging the print he gave her last Christmas. Mom had chosen a bed to be Justa's, and was spreading sheets—a new color, sky blue this year—for Justa's new start. Lowry was at the sink closet, hanging Justa's sky-blue towels.

"I think it's great you got Lagunita Court." Lowry, chatty, still sounded mystified. She had been astonished when Justa got an acceptance letter. They had all been astonished. Back in high school, when Justa's SAT scores turned out to be in the high percentiles—that had been a pleasant surprise for them. Her Mills grades were mostly A's—which pleased them all. But even Lowry hadn't put those SAT scores and grades together and realized that, bolstered by a letter from Dr. Weber, they might mean Stanford.

"Now that I'm in Grove, I think these older dorms really have it over FloMo." Lowry's intent was to be welcoming.

"Casa Granada." Mom pronounced the Spanish words carefully, as if each vowel were a hoop through which she had to throw her breath. The other Lagunita casas were called Eucalipto, Adelfa, Naranja, Olivo, Magnolia. All trees. *Granada* meant 'pomegranate'.

"What do you think, Justie?" Dad stood to the side of the print.

One unhappy evening, back at Mills, Justa had curved her hands to imitate the 19th century girl. Justa had placed her own hands over her desktop and imagined: the girl was preparing to play an E minor chord with her right hand, an arpeggio with her left. Justa decided: the girl was playing Corelli's Sarabande in E Minor.

"It looks great, Dad," she now said. She squatted beside the orange crate that held her music and pushed its heavy weight against a wall.

A tall girl with white-blonde hair opened the door without knocking. She stood perfectly still. Only her eyes moved, from one of Justa's family to another.

"Hello?" Mom said tentatively.

Justa rose from her squat.

"Hello." The girl's voice was a measured one, with undertones of crispness. She reached back into the hall; she tugged a trunk-sized suitcase into the room. She complained to the suitcase, to the hallway, "I don't need half of this. And there's more."

Mom immediately waved Dad, Lowry, and Justa into action. They helped, sometimes squeezing past each other, bringing in four more suitcases, a large tote and a small train case— all pale green with little brass labels near the clasps. They lifted and carried until luggage covered the floor beside the unmade bed.

"It was piled so high, I couldn't see out my rearview mirror." The girl was aggrieved. "It was my mother who chose. She did all the packing."

"Perhaps we should have introductions," Mom suggested.

The girl blinked. "Oh!" Her exclamation rose like a balloon. "How do you do?" She shot out her right hand as if it had been trained. "I'm Christine Kelsey. Please call me Crystal."

Justa couldn't help spurting laughter as she held out her own hand, Christine/Crystal was such an odd combination of self-absorption and perfect manners.

"Did you choose 'Crystal' for yourself?" Lowry was interested.

"No. My father did. When I was born he said I was the crystal reflection of his smiles." Crystal's inflections were those of simply conveying information.

But—"Oh!"—Mom melted. "How lovely, dear! We're Justa's parents. I'm Isobel, this is Dan. And this is our older daughter, Lowry."

"We should go, Mom, Dad." Lowry stopped Mom from saying anything more. Lowry sent Justa a grin, followed by a discrete rolling of the eyes. The grin meant 'I'm here, you can call me any time'. The eyes meant 'Good luck' and 'can you believe your roommate'. Lowry shepherded Mom and Dad into the hallway, shutting the door on bodies but not on sound.

"Why couldn't we stay?" Mom's voice, muffled by solid wood, was as aggrieved as Crystal's had been.

"They have to get to know each other on their own." Lowry loaded her voice with experience.

"We can get a cup of coffee, or something, somewhere. Can't we?" Dad said.

Their footsteps faded away over thin carpet. Crystal must also have been listening, because she waited until the family sounds were gone before she asked, "Why Lowry? Why Justa?"

"We were named after our grandmother." Justa guessed this was what Crystal wanted to know. "She was Justa Lowry. Then Justa Lowry Matthews."

"Huh. An ancestor split in two."

It was such an absurd statement, but so apt, that Justa laughed again—this time fully, nothing held back. "Do you want me to help you unpack?" she offered.

Dresses, skirts, slacks and jeans, blouses, tops, and shoes. Crystal only wanted everything dumped on her bed so she could toss most of it onto the floor. "I'll have to repack," she said crossly. Her discard pile grew high. The dresses, the skirts, two coats. Flats, heels, and an elegant pair of leather boots. "It can go in the basement," she muttered. Her real life turned out to be what she carried in the green tote and an unmatching Olivetti typewriter case. The tote held maybe a half dozen leotards. The typewriter flattened a paper file of, "Poems," Crystal said. "I write poems."

"I play the piano," Justa informed in return.

Crystal stopped sorting. "What do you play?"

"Beethoven, the Beatles, Brahms—" Justa began listing composers.

Crystal interrupted. "I dance them all!"

⁓

It was Crystal who noticed the baby grand pushed into a corner when they went into the dining hall that evening. "If we come back tonight," she said over herb crusted chicken and sweet potato casserole, "you can play and I can dance."

Justa would never have done such a thing on her own. Certainly not on the first day of school. But hours later—when the food service people were long gone; after Crystal changed into a leotard and urged "Come on!"— Justa did.

The dining hall was spooky with shadows. Crystal found and flicked on lights. Justa helped push aside tables before she sat on a chipped wooden bench to examine the piano. It was a Baldwin, the case battered, but the keys nicely even.

"I'm ready." Crystal stood in the center of the makeshift dance floor, again perfectly still. But this time raised up on bare toes, poised as if ready to fly.

Justa put down a finger. Middle C vibrated with decent accuracy. She ran a C scale. The instrument was in tune, its voice American—full and deep. She ran a G scale, then E minor. She shaped her right hand into an E minor chord and began to play.

She had chosen the Corelli Sarabande that long ago evening at Mills because it began not so much as a dance, but as a dirge. That had been her mood. Tonight, when she reached the key change in the middle, she glanced at Crystal. Crystal had cupped the plaintiveness in her hands, and was fashioning it into a globe before her face. Justa began the lighter, brighter B minor, and Crystal's hands fell apart as if she were Pandora offering good as well as evil into the world. Her hips shifted to the side; her left foot crossed behind the right; her body became a sort of arrow encouraging her dance into the possibility of cheer. That possibility loosened into a certainty. When the key returned to E minor, Crystal returned to her cupping and fashioning, once again serious but no longer somber. Justa held the last chord to signal the end, and Crystal froze. She looked like a pause in being.

"Again?" she said. "I want to change the footing in the middle."

"Okay." This time Justa played the Sarabande as a dance. Then she experimented by turning it into a scamper. Whether she speeded up or slowed down, even when she began to extemporize, Crystal adjusted. In her leotard—her feet flying, landing, *percussing*—Crystal became another sort of instrument. Crystal became part of the music.

CCCCC

Before Justa, Crystal wasn't lucky in her roommates. She hadn't made friends at Stanford. Mother said the problem was that Crystal had chosen a college with no sororities. Mother had been a Tri Delta at the University of Southern California.

This autumn, Crystal signed up for a course titled 'Women: Realities; Constrictions; Comprehensions'—partly because she hoped for ammunition to use in her endless quarrels with Mother. The course instructor, Tillie, was a former union organizer who had become a published author. She was *not* the kind of woman who had a standing appointment at the hairdresser's. Tillie's every class was a quotable event. 'Find your own movement. Don't allow others to force you into their rhythms.' Crystal categorized these quotes as 'Tillieisms'.

Sometimes she heard a sort-of Tillieism at the dinner table, because Justa collected a chain of friends. Betsy, who lived in one of the singles on their floor, began to wait for Justa before going downstairs. Betsy sang in the Stanford Chorus and liked to talk music. Betsy and a graduate student named Farhad were a couple, although they never touched. Where Betsy sat, Farhad sat. He didn't say much, but was occasionally fascinating. "In my country, historically, women wore the veil. I think there will soon be a new-old—the past magnified and made more severe." To Crystal, this sounded like a Tillieism from the Middle East.

But, "Nonsense!" Betsy disagreed, her Southern USA accent an interesting contrast to Farhad's Iranian one. "Your Empress is working hard to *enhance* the role of women in Iran. Also, she's gorgeous," which mattered to Betsy. "Feminism"—this last, sternly, addressed to Crystal—"does not preclude beauty."

It was Betsy who found a boyfriend for Justa. One day, while Crystal was eating lettuce, she felt Betsy's elbow in her ribs and heard Betsy's whisper in her ear, "Look!"

Crystal looked, but all she saw was a boy hovering nearby who was staring at Justa through John Lennon eyeglasses.

"What do you think?" Betsy whispered. "He was doing that a few days ago, too."

Crystal thought. There was nothing remarkable about the boy in appearance, but Justa didn't come across as being extra-special at first, either. Crystal looked back and forth, the boy to Justa, Justa to the boy. She shrugged.

Stymied, Betsy wrinkled her nose at Crystal. Then, her Gone-With-the-Wind style cranked up high, she urged the boy, "Now you just sit right down here!"

The boy immediately sat. Then he didn't seem to know what to do with himself. Shyly, he pointed at Justa's ear—no, her earring. "Möbius strips," he said. "They're why I wanted to meet you."

Justa smiled.

His name was Gil, and for a math major he wasn't totally nerdy-looking. He actually had muscles. He lived, as part of his work-study job, in the Stanford fire station. He said he sometimes came to Lagunita Court to meet up with his freshman roommate. The old roommate belonged to one of the fraternities behind Lagunita, across the lake.

Crystal, on principle, deplored the Greeks—all of them, Alpha to Omega. The frat boy, Scott, located Gil and took over a chair. It turned out he was majoring in economics. "'The Dismal Science,'" Crystal was glad to say. She didn't know who had coined the phrase, but she relished the quote.

Scott raised his eyebrows. He informed Justa, not Crystal, "Gil helps me with the math."

It was those supercilious eyebrows—or more exactly, the sun-streaked hair combed down close above them—that made Crystal blurt out, "Are you Mormon?"

"What?" everybody asked, more or less in unison.

"His hair." Crystal pointed with her nose at the mop covering Scott's forehead. "He looks like that singing teenybopper, Donny Osmond."

"Crystal!" Betsy was aghast at her bad manners.

"He's got a reason." Gil grinned at his friend.

Scott exhaled, dramatically, in Crystal's direction. He brushed back his bangs to reveal a hairline receded an inch past normal. "My dad was bald by forty. And no, we're not Mormon."

"Oh." Crystal didn't have a clue as to how to gracefully extract her foot from her mouth.

"And that is why we eat here, Gil," Scott remarked. "Because brotherhood—the firehouse, the fraternity—lacks the female touch."

⸜

Betsy called Justa's collection of friends 'The Table'. It was a repeating group of six, sometimes seven if Justa's sister, Lowry, happened to be around. Seven people leaning over plates, grabbing rolls from the basket, talking about music, mathematics, economics, social change, whatever. Lowry was a real plus, Crystal thought, because Lowry brought an historian's insight to Women: Realities; Constrictions; Comprehensions.

"For my term paper I'm going to write about how women's shoes can be a form of bondage," Crystal announced one evening.

"Great topic," Lowry approved. "You can start with the Chinese and keep on going. Shoes can free us or cripple us." Lowry was excellent for Tillieisms.

Scott, fraternity man, economics major, scoffed, "Sounds downright frivolous to me."

"Frivolous!" Betsy exclaimed. "How can you say that? We are women; we love our shoes. At my debutante ball all of us wore silver shoes. It was so pretty—thirty white dresses and, below them, sixty silver shoes. They hurt horribly, but I wouldn't have worn anything else. I'll keep them forever."

"Totally unnecessary." Scott raised both hands in emphasis.

He was so certain he had finalized the conversation, so complacent, that Crystal came out with her own Tillieism: "We often love what we hate, just as we hate what we love."

But, "Oh, no!" Betsy scolded. "You can't cut it down as small as that. You're making it so hard and cold." Betsy sighed one of her Southern sighs. "You know, Crystal, sometimes I worry you might be as cold as the substance that gave you its name."

Dinner over, Scott and Lowry joined the economics, history, and political science majors in the TV lounge. Crystal stopped to watch them watch the CBS Evening News. A great cheer rose when Walter Cronkite's face appeared on the screen. The group settled in, as if to listen to a favorite uncle. The top news of the day: National Security Advisor Henry Kissinger, discussing treaty negotiations to end the Vietnam War, had announced 'Peace is at hand'. Tears began to descend Lowry's cheeks.

Tears were the opposite of 'cold'. 'Cold' was a word Crystal often heard from Mother. It was a judgment that made her feel perennially sidelined from the rest of the world. But she didn't cry, hardly ever.

She could barely wait, though, for the next two hours to pass, for the dining hall to empty of students, for the food service people to put on their coats and leave, for Justa to help her push aside tables. Then she took her spot on the cleared floor and stood, her feet gripping the wooden floorboards, her body clenching itself into a tense uprightness. Justa took forever to settle into practice, to became intent on her piece. But finally Crystal could pull music over her head like a tunic. The notes descended down her torso and extended through her limbs. Her muscles eased, her back became supple. She translated Justa's arpeggio into her own arabesque. And with that, she stopped being Crystal. She became nothing more than a shape blending movement to movement. That shape was not a cold person, or an untearful one, or even Mother's deplored societal misfit. That shape was nothing but Crystal, herself.

Anger is a dragon
Trailing grief
In its wake

I am that tail,
At the mercy of
Temper

JJJJJ

Justa sat in a soundproofed practice room in the basement of Dinkel-spiel Auditorium. The walls were beige, the ceiling was beige. The piano had a bright, almost-sparkly sound that was swallowed by beige. Kath, Justa's new piano teacher, possessed a sunny disposition that matched the instrument. Kath hummed, she sang, to direct Justa. Since Kath had gotten her master's at Mills under Dr. Weber, she shared much of his technique. But she hadn't mastered his gift of a teaching silence. Perhaps that was because the practice room was too small for Kath to walk around, for her to express an opinion with a step or a pause. For whatever reason, Kath made noise.

Justa didn't like that.

Neither did she like what Kath was making her learn: Ravel's Sonatine. The composition was twitchy and difficult, with tricky fingering and crossing hands. It turned Justa's arms into pretzels. When Justa listened to Ruth Laredo play the same piece—she found a recording in UGLY—she heard the chords falling from the pianist's hands like water.

"I can't do it," Justa told Kath.

"Bum ba... bumba bum... ba," Kath sang the first two phrases of the second movement, the minuet, before encouraging, "Yes, you can!" Kath's voice dropped into momentary seriousness, "You must."

"Must?" Kath had made it sound like Justa's life depended upon conquering the Sonatine.

"Dr. Weber said so." Kath, no longer dire, was halfway back to smiles. "He said to start with the Sonatine because it would make you angry. Which it has. Because it is technically difficult. Which it is. Because you know it should be beautiful, and you'll fight with yourself until you find that beauty. He said you'd need that fight, that energy, to start well here at Stanford. He also said—and you won't like to hear this—that we should spend all term on the Sonatine if necessary."

"You've got to be kidding me." Justa felt betrayed by someone she loved.

"We'll intersperse with other things. Give your hands, mind, psyche a break. But in the meantime"—Kath brushed a finger over the sheet music—"back to Ravel."

Justa glared at those pages until notes became stamped like inked dots over her vision. After she left the lesson, the notes were still there. Outside on the porch, through black floaters, she recognized rain. The rainy season had started early this year. Before Mills she had rejoiced in the pattern of raindrops. At Stanford what she heard was interrupted by what she saw. Ravel.

"Shit," she said.

⋖

Tresidder was across the widened concrete pathway. Justa needed to wash the failure of music from her hands. Before grabbing a cup and standing in line for coffee, she went into the ladies' room. Lowry was there, standing at the mirror, attempting to pat frizz out of her hair.

"Hi," Justa said.

"Hi!" Lowry always looked so surprised when Justa chanced upon her. Lowry turned away from the mirror. "I just got back. I took the train up to San Francisco to see Emi Yamada."

Justa did a quick run-through of the Yamada family tree. Emi was Hiro's only daughter, Ike's younger sister. Emi managed the Marimekko store in San Francisco.

Lowry leaned against the wall beside the sinks. Now that Justa could see her properly, Lowry looked tired.

"You know how I'm writing about the Japanese internment for my honors thesis? Emi went through most of high school while interned at Manzanar. She and Dad had been in the same eighth grade class. Did you know he kissed her before she left?"

"No." What a strange thought: Dad, young; Dad kissing somebody other than Mom.

"It was Emi's first kiss." Lowry slid down the wall until she sat on the floor, a lump of humanity around which other girls had to walk.

Justa took over the space of wall next to Lowry. She also sat, pulling up her knees with her music bag against her chest so as to take up as little room as possible.

"Emi wouldn't talk about Manzanar," Lowry continued. "She doesn't want to remember any of it. She wouldn't talk about the place, the people, her school. What she did say was that Manzanar was the dividing line in her life between when she felt safe, and when she never felt safe again. She thinks that's why she never married—even though the Yamadas have pretty good marriages—because she made the conscious decision, when she was fourteen years old, that the only person she could ever fully rely on was herself. Later, she went to art school in Oakland, studied design. She gave me a wall hanging." Lowry's voice was flattened.

"We had lunch and then I came back to Stanford. The wall hanging is really pretty. And this is what I figured out on the train. I have never, ever, felt not-safe. Not like you did at Mills, with that crazy brother. Not like Stillman, who truly feared for the lives of other people, as well as his own. Do you know how many guys from Stillman's year, from my year, dropped out?"

Justa shook her head.

"I can see the empty spaces they left behind. I can see those empty spaces in my classes, in the dorms and houses. I had never thought of safety as being something special. Now all I can think about is the people who are forced to lose it." Lowry had sunken into herself. She was smaller on the floor.

Justa ventured: "Maybe the only way out of not-safe is to trust." As she had given her trust to Aunt Edith. "And to take a risk." Which she hadn't fully done, not yet.

Lowry began to straighten up. She did so with obvious emotional effort. "People might step on us," she said, as if only now realizing how much they were in the way. "I guess we should leave."

"Okay," Justa agreed.

She walked Lowry to the bike racks. She hugged Lowry before seeing her off toward Grove House. Justa mounted her own bike, thinking: this first term at Stanford, she had found new friends, a possible boyfriend—and was given another year to spend with Lowry.

If she had been who she used to be, she would think her life had opened up into new opportunities for joy.

She dismounted. Instead of pedaling, she pushed her bike into the rain. She pushed herself, beside it, trying to hear—as well as see—the Sonatine.

Dots of music, dots of rain. Patterns upon patterns. She became awed by the multiplicity of juxtapositions. By complexity, by depth.

That evening, sitting at the Baldwin, she felt like a selkie returning to the sea: wondering if she might still find her breath in salt water. Slowly, carefully, she walked into the waves.

"So," Crystal said when their time together was finished, "it sounds like you're finally ready to make friends with Ravel."

LLLLL

Originally, last year, Lowry had planned to write her honors thesis on how American wars in the 20th century were links in a chain. But the flowers at Aunt Edith's memorial service changed her mind. She couldn't help remembering each orchid, tulip, and spray of baby's breath. That's why she was knocking on the door of Professor Delton's office. She didn't know him well. She had never taken one of his classes. But when she switched topics she had no choice but to switch advisors.

"Enter."

"I'm here for my appointment." She had to wait while he blinked her into recognition.

"Ah, Miss Matthews." He finally remembered. He poked at the stacks of papers on his desk, eventually pulling out and opening the green folder containing her draft. His brow lifted. Lowry tried, but couldn't read his reaction. Condemnation? Tepid approval? Praise?

He looked from the draft to her, back to the thesis again. "Japanese Americans before, during, and after World War II." His recognition, of her paper, was now keen. "I must say I was intrigued."

Praise! It made Lowry relax to her toes. She had gathered facts, lots of facts. She had spent hours interviewing the Yamada family. She spent even more hours weaving the larger historical facts in with the Yamadas' unique story, showing how national history could be seen as an amplification of the personal.

"I've made a few edits." Professor Delton rapidly scanned pages. "Showing where you need to dig into statistics."

Lowry scanned with him, upside-down, from across the desk. He had lined out entire paragraphs, even pages. She couldn't help but protest. "I don't want to bury the Yamadas in numbers," she said timidly. An overload of numbers would obscure her purpose: a story about real people, real lives.

"The Yamadas are merely a springboard to your true disquisition." Professor Delton's statement was categorical. "Your most interesting point is that the First Amendment Petition Clause is sufficient basis for reparation. Use *that* as your focus." He finally looked up. He beamed enthusiasm at her. "If this thesis ends up being what I think it can be, I will feel confident about recommending you to Stanford's PhD program."

Lowry was stunned. In early October she had talked to Professor Delton about getting a master's degree. Back then his encouragement had been meager.

"The Faculty Senate has recommended active recruitment of women." Professor Delton shook his head ruefully. "Quite a debate, last meeting. We, here in History, have never had a tenured female professor. If we must, I'd feel more confident about somebody trained in our own department."

"You mean me?" Lowry was trying to keep up. In ten minutes her advisor had jumped from tearing apart her draft, to entering her into a PhD Program, to granting her faculty tenure.

"Well, it all starts with an excellent thesis and my letter of recommendation. But"—Professor Delton tapped the green folder—"I do think you have a talent for research."

An hour later, the green folder tucked in her bag, Lowry's mind spun in a whirligig of red, black, and white—the colors of Stanford's doctoral regalia. Lowry Matthews, PhD. Professor Lowry Matthews. Speeding through campus, she waved to acquaintances who didn't know she had a talent for research. A-Talent-For-Research. Each word was a push down with her right or left foot.

She got to Grove House in record time. She was again rooming with Susan, Willow having chosen to continue her studies in Italy. Lowry ran upstairs where Susan, as always, was working on a problem set. Lowry interrupted Susan's work with a "Listen!"

Susan put down her mechanical pencil; she listened carefully. She mulled, "Academics isn't just research, it's also teaching. Is that something you want to do?"

Lowry's whirligig slowed. She had never taught anybody anything before in her life. Except Justa. She had taught Justa how to play Monopoly.

Outrageous Paul was now leaning against their door frame. "You'll end up poor if you stay in academia," he opined. "Not to mention that getting a PhD can take *forever*. You should come to law school with me. Three years, in and out, and you're set to do pretty much anything. Arbitrator, negotiator, legislator. All-around change maker. You can even lead a non-profit." He patted his stomach as a change in subject. "Coming to dinner? Lasagna tonight."

"No." Lowry was scheduled to meet up with The Table at Lagunita Court. She grabbed for a hairbrush, and her eyes were caught and held by Emi's wall hanging. Silhouetted trees and birds printed on heavy white cotton. A photograph taken by someone who lay on the ground pointing a camera upward. Black and white with no grays. Emi had described the Marimekko as 'Finish-Japanese art; starkness heavy with emotion'. To Lowry, Emi's gift looked more like a yearning for freedom, for the openness of the sky.

Back outside, Lowry merged into the freshness of a winter dusk. She took the long route to Lagunita, weaving her bike around other housing units. She passed through the odors of various dinners: Sigma Chi was having roast beef; the Columbae cooks were preparing some sort of cabbage. A Benihana catering van stood parked in front of Storey House. Storey House girls were always watching their figures.

Lowry coasted. Wasn't food equal to, if not more important than, statistics when attempting to record the truth of history? Susan's family, in Hawaii, went without soy sauce those first weeks after the bombing of Pearl Harbor. They were afraid buying soy sauce would be seen as a seditious act. Lowry had included this example in her thesis.

Professor Delton wanted her to delete such details.

By the time she got to Lagunita and told The Table, "My advisor thinks I have a talent for research," Lowry found she could no longer muster the enthusiasm such an announcement deserved. She picked at her fish and chips. "He thinks I should become a professor."

"A professor!" Justa's surprise peaked, then dropped as she became thoughtful: "A professor..."

"Do you really like history so much you want to spend the rest of your life thinking about it?" Crystal asked.

"Maybe," Lowry allowed.

Dinner over, she rode her bike through the half-darkness that was Stanford at night. Street lights gave way to shadows, gave way to security lamps. Tresidder was its usual flood of electric glare.

To her left, pinpricks of light moved at a walking pace down the avenue in front of the School of Education. The Office of Religious Life had scheduled an ecumenical march in support of the Paris Peace Accords. Earlier that day Lowry had intended to march, to hold a candle and shed light on the hoped-for ending of the Vietnam War. But after meeting with Professor Delton, she had forgotten. She wasn't too late to join in, though. She caught up with the straggling end of the crowd. She walked her bike awkwardly with one hand, using the other to hold aloft the candle someone gave to her. A gentle night breeze pushed the flame toward her face. Hot wax dripped down her fingers. There was never hope without pain; there was often pain without hope.

Statistics were only a sketch of reality.

By the time she returned to Grove House and the quietude that was life with Susan, the afternoon whirligig was long gone. For the second time that day, Lowry interrupted Susan's studies. "I've been thinking about what O.P. said. About how lawyers can do things. Advocate. Negotiate. Make changes. Sometimes he talks sense."

Susan considered, nodded, and added, "Lawyers have to be talented at research, too."

Lowry's LSAT score was respectably high. Outrageous Paul's was stratospheric. He was kind. "You're a legal eaglet, Lowry." He dumped applications on her bed from those law schools he now deemed beneath his consideration. Georgetown, Northwestern, Duke. Lowry looked through the Duke application. Only four pages: Personal Data, Education, Family, Letters of Recommendation. And a blank space on the last page where the applicant was encouraged to write about pretty much anything that made him stand out. All the schools asked for a similar essay.

That became her concern. Lowry couldn't think of any way in which she stood out. When she told Professor Delton she wanted to stick with the Yamada angle in her thesis, his gleam of interest in her extinguished with a click.

"All they're asking is who you are," O.P. encouraged. "Me: I come from six generations of attorneys. The first one became Maryland's attorney general."

He was no help at all.

⌒

Then, at breakfast one morning, Lowry picked up *The Stanford Daily*. She read a headline, 'Phi Delts At It Again', and sputtered scrambled egg onto the paper.

"What's wrong?" Susan asked.

"A topless dancer at one of their parties." Lowry condensed the story to its essentials. "They raffled her off!" Lowry tried to picture the girl, whoever she was, peekaboo clad in feathers, spangles, lace. Desperate for income. Dependent on the whims of frat boys. Never safe.

"She must have agreed," Outrageous Paul said.

"That doesn't matter. They used her like chattel. What they did was practically slave trade." Lowry scanned further down the page. "And here's an ad: 'Stanford Women Unite! Banish Brazen, Baleful, Brotherly 'Love'.' Somebody's scheduled a meeting."

"English majors," O.P. guessed. "English majors against the Phi Delts?" He sniggered. "My money's on the frat boys."

"It's people like you who allow things like this to happen," Lowry scolded.

She had to reschedule a consult with Professor Delton—no loss to either of them, there. At two o-clock she tapped on the door of one of the trailers that the housing office rented out to upperclassmen. The girl who opened the door was delighted to see Lowry. "You came because of what we wrote?" the girl asked.

They were four roommates gathered around an orange crate coffee table: talking, talking, talking; finding different ways to express their horror; going nowhere. Seven newcomers arrived who were as little organized—and appeared as little capable of organizing—as the trailer residents. If Lowry had learned nothing else during her year of sitting silently beside Stillman, she had learned strategy and tactics. "The Phi Delts won't hear us, the administration won't hear us, the Stanford community won't hear us unless we *do* something," she told them all. "We have to make a statement that's physical as well as verbal."

"Yes!" One of the newcomers sounded relieved to finally hear sense.

"You mean like a protest march?" someone questioned.

"A protest march," Lowry agreed, and she began handing out assignments.

The English majors were to write a second ad, this one announcing that Stanford Women Unite! would hold a planning meeting the following afternoon, all women invited. The sensible newcomer would wait for copy and then turn the ad into 8.5 x 11 Xeroxes. The remaining students promised to post the flyers around campus.

The next day when Lowry looked over the girls crowded in—and even out through the doorway of—the trailer, her adrenaline jumped to where she could feel her pulse in her eyebrows. She launched, as if into forgotten country, into leadership.

"Okay!" she said. "We need poster board and markers for signs." She sent a group of sophomores to the bookstore with money culled from everybody's purses. "And someone has to call *The Daily* and KZSU." An English major volunteered. "We need to figure out the most visible and public route to the Phi Delt house." Susan and a civil engineering buddy were on that immediately. "And a spy." A hand shot up from beyond the shallow front porch. The hand raised a few inches as its owner went up on her toes. Crystal. "Go find out what time the Phi Delts start dinner," Lowry laughed.

By six o'clock Stanford Women Unite! was ready. Twenty-seven women strong, they marched through campus and up Mayfield Avenue and Campus Drive, gathering recruits along the way. Now numbering thirty-six, they circled in front of the Phi Delts' dining room windows, stamping round and round, their feet sinking into a lawn made soft by recent rains. "Bros of the flesh, detumesce!" That was the English majors' chant. "Two, four, six, eight, Phi Delt is worse than second rate!" was the engineering coalition's favorite. Lowry insisted on an occasional, unified, "Close Phi Delt Down!" Something prosaic enough to make their intention absolutely clear.

A KZSU soundman showed up with his recorder, microphone, and a *Daily* cameraman. The *Daily* reporter arrived with a Taco Bell bag in hand, still munching. He knocked, loudly, on the Phi Delts' front door. An angrily reddened face stuck itself out on the stalk of an even redder neck.

"What do you think about women, now?" the reporter questioned. The soundman's microphone was in position. The cameraman flashed away.

"Women's libbers." The face hastily withdrew.

The next morning Lowry's picture and name were on the front page of *The Stanford Daily*. The article concluded with a statement from Stanford's housing office. 'We are considering the suspension of Phi Delta Theta.' Which, if it wasn't an *active* statement, was a step in the right direction.

"The Phi Delts are in trouble." Susan congratulated both Lowry and herself over pancakes.

"I lost my bet." O.P. was magnanimous in defeat.

Yesterday's excitement now over, Lowry's usual, quieter mind began assembling thoughts. She poured a final cup of coffee to carry upstairs. Placing the cup on her desk, she again studied the Duke application. 'What makes you stand out?' all the admissions committees wanted to know.

She sat down and uncapped a pen. She articulated the great lesson she had learned over these last four years. 'As an historian I have been trained to look at the big picture. But what I have seen, what I know to be true, is that it is the accumulation of small differences that changes the world. I am a person who makes small differences. That means I am important to time.'

JJJJJ

His name was Gil Musicant and long ago, before pogroms, one of his ancestors had been fiddler to the czar. Gil, himself, made no pretenses to music, except for the clarinet he still owned, left over from his days as a member of his high school band. But he listened with a kind of ear Justa had never encountered before: Gil heard numbers; he vibrated to progressions. He used the dining room piano to show The Table how a chromatic scale, octave note to octave note, consisted of thirteen keys—of which eight were white and five were black, split into groups of three and two. Only Justa saw: those were the Fibonacci numbers, backwards. She had learned about Fibonacci at Mills.

"And when you set them up as ratios," Gil told her, so intense as he did so, so intent that she understand, which she did, "three over two, five over three, eight over five, and so on, you approach the Golden Mean."

"Which is an irrational number," Justa remembered.

"The *most* irrational," Gil said, "and an expression of perfection."

Irrational perfection: Justa found the concept a contradiction until she saw how Gil responded to a piece composed by Erik Satie. Gil often, and Scott sometimes, studied in the Lagunita dining hall while she practiced and Crystal danced. This week's piece, 'Air de l'ordre', was another challenge. "We'll give it a whirl," Kath had said when she assigned it. "I know you like chords."

These chords were written with no time signature, no bar lines. Justa felt she was swimming in a sea with no horizon. Nearing the end of a long, almost song-like section, she forced herself to consciously inhale so as to relax her body. With one of those breaths, she happened to glance up and over.

Gil's eyes were shut as if he couldn't listen otherwise, as if the only oxygen he was capable of inhaling were her chords.

Justa's eyes slid back to her music. She was at the bottom of page two. Two pages out of three. She finished, and started again. Page one. Page two.

Grab a breath and start three. It was then that it occurred to her: two over three was the inverse of Gil's first approximation toward the Golden Mean. For the rest of that evening, she experimented with playing in anticipation of the two-thirds point. She discovered a sense of fullness there that thrust her, inexorably, on to the final notes.

Irrational perfection.

"It was sort of like sex." Justa held on to her amazement until she and Crystal were alone in their room, the day now over, not yet ready for bed. "I think." Justa didn't know for sure. Up until now boyfriends had been simple affairs of kissing and necking.

Crystal—her back flat on the floor, her hands propping up her hips, her feet pedaling in the air—inquired, "Do you want find out? With Gil?"

"I want to get to know him better." Justa was firmly decided. She didn't want to make a big mistake and give her heart away to sorrow, as Lowry had done.

"The first boy I ever slept with," said Crystal, and somehow she could speak languidly even while pedaling fiercely, "made love like he ate dinner. He always started with whatever was in front of him, and then he rotated his plate to the left. He always ate clockwise, right around. It didn't matter what he started with—bread, vegetable, meat or potato. I was just another dinner plate."

"Maybe he'd read the rules for making love in a book. Maybe he was nervous. Maybe it was too soon for him." Justa could find excuses for such a boy.

"It was only high school," Crystal admitted. She had stopped in her pedaling. She folded her legs and lowered them so her knees hovered over her nose. "Gil's older. He's a lot smarter. He's obviously crazy for you. I know you like him."

Justa did.

When The Table lingered after dinner, Gil's hand always held hers. His fingers were long, strong, and surprisingly thin. Sometimes his thumb traced a pattern on Justa's palm—a squiggle, a turn, a line. When he told Lowry, "My draft number was 85," he drew two circles, two lines, and a final curve. He responded to the uncertainty beneath one of Crystal's most definite statements by saying, "Crystal, I count you as a friend, too," and wrote a number 2. His friendship with Scott, a loyalty that bridged the distance between his own position as a student employee of the university fire department, and Scott's as a resident brother of Zeta Psi, was Greek symbols translated—6 for Zeta, 23 for Psi.

On the evening before the Big Game, when the traditional bonfire was lit in the dry bed of the vernal lake behind Lagunita Court, Justa got to see Gil for the first time in his role of fireman. He and other work-study students were being paid to keep both conflagration and celebration under control. Gil worked while the rest of The Table enjoyed. Scott clapped his hands high for the pom-pom Dollies, five prancing and dancing girls wearing short red dresses and shiny red boots. Crystal, Lowry, and Betsy shouted encouragement for The Incomparables, Stanford's ragtag marching band. The Incomparables—tubas to piccolos to snare drums—played 'Onward, Christian Soldiers' while marching backwards. Even Farhad, normally so somber, so silent, cheered, "Give 'em the axe!"

It was a din against which Justa didn't mind closing her ears. She funneled all of her awareness into watching. Gil knew how to contain a fire. He shoveled and tossed embers back into flames that were two storeys high. He knew how to calm exuberance. With no more authority than a bright red T-shirt—Firemen Kick Ash—he waded into the bonfire's great heat to stop some guy who wanted to throw a dining chair in as fuel. The guy argued, pushing his head pugnaciously forward, his face oranged by flames. Gil turned so Justa could only see his back—a red spot of responsibility amid all the planned chaos. The guy dropped his shoulders, let fall the chair, and reluctantly grinned. They retreated together from a warmth so excessive their skin must have been hurting.

"I wonder what Gil said." Crystal had come back to Justa's side, lowering her own noise to a normal level in order to penetrate Justa's temporary deafness. "I would have punched that guy." Crystal's voice suddenly deepened with worry. "Do you think Gil might be too steady? Maybe sort of dull?"

"No," said Justa. "Not at all."

Gil wasn't the least bit dull. He was immensely alive, but in a considering way that perhaps only Justa, being a listener, could understand. Scott was a louder talker at The Table. Crystal, and sometimes Lowry, were even louder than that. But Gil perceived what they didn't. He discerned patterns that quicksilver people like Crystal so often danced over. For Gil, the world was a vast expression of possibilities, linkages that provided opportunities up ahead and then disappeared once a path was chosen. "Take football, that game of rules." He once attempted to explain his thoughts to the others. "Every moment is a choice. Every choice leads to a surprise."

"So?" said Crystal.

She couldn't see what Justa intuitively understood: the world was over-lain, and perhaps created, by an intricate mesh of music that was of unde-finable origin. Every song came from somewhere. No song was ever ex-actly replicated.

For the December game at the University of Oregon, Gil took time off to pile into Crystal's Chevy Nova with the rest of The Table. They drove up Highway 5 to Eugene where…Stanford won! On the way home, Justa heard Gil sing for the first time. Betsy had started The Incomparables' new theme song of 'All Right Now'. Justa loosened her grip on the steering wheel because that uncertain baritone—as it scooped its way into the notes that Farhad's surprisingly accurate tenor held constant—was as tender as the half-moon lighting their way home.

How could such an unprepossessing boy—highly myopic, of angular build—own a sound that was so elemental? No, the truth was the reverse: a person like Gil couldn't help but belong to the unfathomability of sound. Justa tried to emulate the dips of Gil's song on the piano, but couldn't. She experimented with every piano she encountered—in practice rooms, dor-mitories, function halls—and was defeated. Gil's was not the music of strings, but rather breath from a heart.

She thought about this one winter evening as she walked around the lakebed, which she did most days now before dinner. Once dry, the lake was filling up from the rains. Creatures were moving in—birds, insects, frogs—small beings whose musical range extended for only a few notes. The tree frogs combined into a chorus, each individual contributing two pitches, a down and an up. But every frog's voice was tuned slightly differently, a minuscule semi-semi-semitone away from its neighbor. The resulting chord—almost-the-same but intensely variable notes sung by a thousand frogs—was one of the earth's most densely packed statements of desire.

Perhaps Justa's intensifying feelings for Gil—and his for her—were simple biology, too. Two.

But she didn't think so, not when her own song was changing so profoundly. Not when at night, playing for Crystal, she couldn't help but respond to the rain on the roof. She would veer from Haydn's notation, or Kabalevsky's, or whoever Kath had assigned for that week, and instead follow the incorporeal conductor high up in the storm. The percussive beat he/she/it created was a pattern of chaos that should have been beyond Justa's fingers. Except that it wasn't. Crystal, trying to keep pace, always collapsed, laughing. But Justa wouldn't stop, because for that space of time she knew herself, her life, her music, to be magical. She was achieving a near-impossible height and breadth of music—and all because a boy named Gil Musicant had looked her way, then zeroed in as though she were the resolution note in the composition of his life.

LLLLL

Moraga: Ten days until departure

Lowry was supposed to be transferring folded clothes and other items from her bed to Aunt Edith's old Red Cross steamer trunk. The trunk still had Aunt Edith's initials stenciled beside the lock: *EKM*. Dad had offered, but Lowry didn't want, to have those initials changed. Lowry was taking bits of everybody to North Carolina.

Like Willow. Willow's rug was the bottommost layer in the trunk. Mom had had the rug professionally cleaned so once again it was as bright as a box of crayons. Lowry was sole owner now because Willow was staying in Italy for good. Instead of coming home for graduation she had married one of her Italian art professors. Willow. Married. Lowry still had trouble putting those two words together. When, in her initial shock, she went trolling the Stanford bookstore for a gift, and the clerk asked what Willow was interested in, she had blurted, "Hobbits." That was how she came to buy the most expensive book she ever hoped to purchase. Because the clerk, instantly excited, tracked down—in San Francisco—a hardback copy of *The Hobbit* published in 1951, the year Willow and Lowry were born. The rare book dealer wrapped it specially for posting to Europe.

Too much was happening, had happened, for Lowry to absorb. Standing here, doing nothing, electric sparks shot lightning to her stomach, chest and throat. Why was packing so hard?

She hefted up her new Adler typewriter. Even its weight didn't settle her body.

Dad had been so proud when he presented the typewriter to her. "For our very own esquire," he said. He was calling her 'Lowry Jeanne Matthews, Esquire' every chance he got, ever since she was accepted by Duke Law School.

She could have chosen Hastings Law School in San Francisco instead. Or Davis. Then she wouldn't have needed a trunk. She could have just put boxes in a car. But Outrageous Paul claimed that in the legal world prestige mattered, big-time. And last term, before graduation, Lowry had been thinking herself eager for an adventure—like a hobbit.

"Low?" Mom was standing in the doorway as if she needed special permission to enter the room of an esquire. "Do you have a moment?"

Lowry had a whole afternoon's worth of moments before Fort and his little brother arrived to put Aunt Edith's trunk into one of Fort's landscaping vans, before they drove Dad down to the Oakland freight terminal. "Sure," she said. She laid the typewriter on top of the rug.

Mom closed the door before speaking quietly. "I know you haven't had a real boyfriend since that boy." Mom had never spoken Stillman's name; Lowry had never told it to her. "But whatever you do—law school, attorney—I want you to always remember that you're a woman." Mom placed a small, gold-wrapped package into Lowry's hands. Within the gold paper was a gilded box. Inside the gilded box was one golden ounce of Miss Dior perfume.

Lowry unscrewed the cap and inhaled: spring iris, winter jasmine, a whiff of patchouli.

"It's a promise," Mom said, "that someday you will fall in love again."

That made Lowry cry. Which made Mom shed a few tears, too. Together, they protected the perfume by sliding the gilded box into a wool knee sock; folding that sock against its mate; and fitting the socks into a boot. Then Mom tucked bedding around the sides of the typewriter case. She refolded a quilt to be the next layer. Lowry set the boot on top.

"Next, your clothes," Mom directed. She stood back. She smiled at Lowry with such love, Lowry wanted to stay home forever. But Mom reopened the door, and walked away.

Lowry smelled baking chocolate now. Mom was making double-chocolate brownies for the Yamada brothers.

Lowry had to continue on her own.

The other boot. Pairs of shoes. Jeans and pants and skirts. Before putting down shirts and sweaters, Lowry established a layer of books. She wasn't taking many. The most important was *The Courage to Remain Japanese in America*, which Dad had had professionally xeroxed and bound, three copies. One for her, one for him to display on the coffee table in the living room, and one to give to the Yamadas.

Earlier this summer she had driven to Hiro's house in Walnut Creek. There, after performing the correct bow, after carefully pronouncing the few Japanese words she knew, "*Ohayō gozaimasu Yamada-sama*," she offered the volume to Aito—father, grandfather, great-grandfather, great-great grandfather. Aito solemnly lifted the buckram cover. He examined the title page, the table of contents. He said something in his never clear English, made incomprehensible with age. Hiro translated: "He says it's about us."

For graduation the Yamadas had given Lowry a pearl necklace. On the cover of the accompanying card, Dorothy of Oz clicked her ruby red heels together. The message inside read, 'May your journeys through life always bring you home'.

Right now, Lowry wanted to see that necklace. She needed to, badly. She lifted the top of the small cedar jewelry box that held the pearls, several pairs of earrings, the silver L that Willow—at the time, Bilba—had given her the first day of college. Lowry reached in. It was the L that she fisted against her palm. The pokes of the letter were a reminder: she had changed; Willow had certainly changed. They had become what they never would have guessed.

Somewhere, stuck into a book, Lowry had a photo of herself with Susan and O.P., their arms circling each other's shoulders, all wearing purple orchid leis over their graduation gowns. All grinning broadly. All had plans: Susan had a job lined up in Hawaii; O.P. had chosen Harvard Law; Lowry was going to North Carolina.

Abruptly, she sat down on the floor. She dropped the L onto her lap. She clasped her face in her hands. How could she be so homesick, when she hadn't even left home yet?

Nine days until departure

Mid-afternoon, Justa called Lowry to the phone. Lowry's ear was blasted by two little boys bellowing their version of 'I Fought the Law'. Lowry laughed. Somewhere in the background Mari Yamada O'Brian was shouting, "That's enough, guys. Okay, that's enough!" Mari appropriated a telephone receiver from one of her twins; the other twin, on another line, again crooned out the word, "la-a-aw," but this time in a deep-voiced, TV Western mode.

"Put down the phone, Mikey!"

Click.

"Hi, Lowry."

"What's going on?" Lowry had never spoken to Mari over the phone before.

"Nothing. Well, everything." Mari made the contradiction sound absolutely normal. "I just wanted to let you how much I enjoyed reading your thesis. Well, enjoyed isn't the right word, because it wasn't fun. But I learned things I hadn't known. I was so little when we lived in those horse stalls in Tanforan, before they sent us to Manzanar. I don't remember when my great-grandmother died there. Nobody ever told me she died of sepsis, that she'd had a kidney infection, that she could have lived with proper care. Those people—Americans!— made us helpless, then didn't let us argue for ourselves."

"I know." Lowry, after having written her thesis, did know.

Mari kept on: "I only have one more thing to say, and then I've got to get back to my little devils. It's about time women went to law school. They're bound to be smarter than the men."

"Oh." Lowry was nonplused, the topic had changed so quickly. "Okay."

That evening during dinner, when she told everybody about talking to Mari, none of them seemed surprised. By the fact of the call. By what Mari had said. By anything. Dad only proclaimed, from the cloud of pride upon which he floated nowadays, "You're going to do great things, Low."

Which somehow wasn't nearly as encouraging as Mari's rushed approval.

Eight days until departure

Nearing bedtime, Pete Yamada called.

Lowry hardly knew him. She rarely saw him. Pete worked for Bechtel, and designed bridges all over the world. He could be almost anywhere, at any time. "About your thesis," he started right in with an explanation for his call. "What grabbed me was what happened to those guys, our guys, the Japanese-Americans who signed up and *fought* in World War II. How they almost didn't get the GI Bill. Put your life on line for your country; don't get anything in return. It's an American theme, isn't it?"

It was.

"I wonder who'll call you tomorrow?" Pete mused.

"What?" Lowry was again nonplused by a Yamada turn of conversation.

"Oh, poop. I've spilled the beans."

"Beans?" Lowry was down to one word responses.

"I guess I have to tell you, now. Granddad Hiro asked your family what more we could do for you, and Justa came up with the idea of a countdown before you left. Granddad Hiro made us send him written applications, letting him know what we wanted to say. He picked and chose, and put us on a roster. I got tonight."

Afterward, Lowry went in search of Mom, Dad, and Justa. She found them conspicuously gathered in the family room, all in bathrobes, all pretending they weren't waiting for a report on this latest phone call.

"You!" Lowry burst out, her laughter bringing down tears.

The next day, the evening after that—a week's worth of Yamadas. Some, Lowry already knew and got to know better: like Fort, whose real name turned out to be Fortitude because he was born in the camps. She deepened her acquaintance with Yamadas less familiar: like Fort's younger brother, who was named Victor because he had been born after internment. Each Yamada had his or her own take on the thesis.

Lowry loved it.

On the afternoon before departure

Willow called.

"Willow!" Lowry screamed into the phone.

"How are you?" Willow screamed back. "I mean, I know how you are—scared, right? That's what Justa said."

"Justa seems to have discussed me with the world." But Lowry wasn't upset by the fact; she had been made happy. "You're married!"

"Talk about being scared. By the way, *The Hobbit* you sent me? I've never had a gift that touched me more."

"It's your totem."

"You're right about that. I've certainly been on an adventure. Wait a moment, I have to look at my notes."

"Notes?"

"Justa sent a telegram. 'Remind her of who she is, and what she wants to do.' Okay. Well, you're the girl a professor said had insight into the human perspective."

"You remember?" Lowry was amazed.

"Nobody ever said anything like that about *me*," Willow replied. "You care about people. I only care about paints."

"That's not fair," Lowry countered. "You have friends."

"Sure, I have friends. And a husband. A really handsome, sexy husband." Willow and Lowry giggled together. "But I don't love the world at large," Willow continued. "I don't want to step into the mess of human problems. You do."

Lowry did.

"To do so, you must leave your shire." Willow was firm.

The truth of Willow's statement sent those electric sparks flashing—again—throughout Lowry's body.

"Go," Willow ordered her. "Go."

That night

Lowry dozed more so than slept. Her traveling outfit hung on her closet door. Her purse hung from the back of a chair. Her book bag with airplane reading sat on her desk. She had a new bag this year, a canvas Danish schoolbag that expanded to hold a sweater, a thermos bottle, a folded umbrella, anything she might need for a day at the law school.

"Low." Justa opened her door so quietly, Lowry scarcely heard the susurrus over carpet.

"What?" Lowry whispered back.

"Will you come with me? Right now?"

Lowry slid out of bed. Wearing only a nightgown—no slippers, no robe—she followed Justa outside to the darkest corner of their backyard. "Look," Justa said. Because it was a full-moon night, Lowry could watch Justa's arm rise like a blackboard pointer. Her gaze was guided up to the stars. Stars were much brighter here in Moraga than they were in Palo Alto. Justa's arm described a half circle, and Lowry saw—or blinked until she was certain of what she was seeing. A rainbow stretched across the sky. Not an ordinary rainbow—this one was shades of gray. Or maybe grayish hints of the faintest colors. It was an arch of paleness against darkness, opposing the moon. It was the most magical phenomenon Lowry had ever witnessed.

"It's something for you to remember," Justa said simply.

Justa is everybody's hope, Lowry thought. *She's what we come home to.*

‘To Everything There Is a Season’
is a song Judy Collins retitled as ‘Turn! Turn! Turn!’ on her third album.

Starting Autumn 1973

LLLLL

Week One

The South isn't a foreign land. Southern speech isn't a foreign language. That was Lowry's mantra those first days in North Carolina. She didn't entirely believe herself. Standing in the Duke Law School courtyard, sipping a Pepsi, she found herself entangled in extended vowels and unusual verbiage. The first boy she spoke with looked like Southern California—sun-streaked hair, summer tan. But when she began a conversation by remarking, "I saw you moving into the Graduate Center. Did they ever get that elevator working?" he responded with, "No-o. Ah ma-ash the button but it wo-ont git to the fi-ith floor."

Lowry didn't fully understand. Mash? Why 'mash'?

Passing around and through other clumps of new students, she overheard other variations of 'getting to know you', and was relieved. The accents spread the continent. She guessed: Boston? New York? Maybe Texas? Most, like Lowry, spoke in a Walter Cronkite blend.

She glanced down at her plate. The food was purely Southern. Barbecue that was not ribs, but rather shredded meat seasoned with vinegar. A cole-slaw made not with mayonnaise, but with vinegar. So much vinegar.

She could either eat or converse: those were her only choices here. Maybe the reason she wasn't feeling sociable was because of the weather: she could practically drink this air. She would try to be friendly again, tomorrow. But for now, what she really wanted was a shower. If she cut across campus, the graduate women's dormitory was only about a mile away. She had a Duke map; there were pathways.

She set out. She walked in the sandals she had worn her first day at Stanford, her good-luck sandals. By the time she neared the dormitory all the Pepsi was sweated from her body; her sundress had become pasted against her back, her breasts, her bottom, her thighs.

And here was a bus. She should have waited.

The girl emerging—Lowry had overheard her talking about study groups at the orientation party. Despite the discomfort of her clinging dress, Lowry quickened her pace so as to catch up. "Hi. I'm Lowry Matthews," she introduced herself. "I'm interested in a study group, too."

The girl stopped. She stared, as if in disbelief. She shook her head—once to the right, once to the left—in an obvious gesture of dismissal. Detaching herself from Lowry's presence, she walked away.

Lowry, left in a haze of diesel fumes from the departing bus, stood disconcerted.

"You blew that," said a voice from behind her, maybe Midwestern.

Lowry turned. Another girl from the party. This one had a bosom that so overtopped her slim figure, it seemed a breath of wind might unbalance her.

"Don't you know any better?" the bosomy girl asked Lowry. "Black," she pointed to the retreating girl. "White," she pointed to Lowry. "The key word is R-E-S-P-E-C-T. Not friendliness. And respect means always staying one step away, unless you are invited into the fold. Where are you from that you don't know this?"

Lowry didn't bother to answer. Now there was a second girl at the law school she knew she would never like.

That was it, for getting to know people. The next day she didn't have the energy to experiment with friendliness, because classes started and she was overwhelmed. The professors moved through their material too quickly. She didn't know how to respond to the socratic method. Worst of all, anything she read for one class muddled her recollection of all her other classes. In desperation, she began outlining each class as immediately as possible, before she forgot. That meant three hours of outlining every day, in addition to the six hours of reading she had to do.

She received a postcard from Outrageous Paul at Harvard. It held only one comment: 'For the first time in my life, I must study'.

Week Two

In the mornings, before heat boiled the oxygen out of the humid air, Lowry walked to the law school. It was the only exercise she got all day.

More importantly, it was a time to recite sotto voce what she had memorized the night before; a time to practice theoretical responses so that if a professor cold-called her she wouldn't choke or lose her voice. On this particular morning she felt especially prepared for Criminal Law. Last night, in addition to the assigned cases, she had read a hornbook and a commercial outline.

But Professor Henley surprised them all by announcing, "John Dean. Obstruction of justice." This wasn't the beginning of a case. This was current events. Lowry hadn't looked at a newspaper since leaving California.

The usual hands shot up. All boys. The class was almost entirely boys. Professor Henley called on them in rapid succession, allowing each to add one sentence to a summarization of the facts:

"Last January seven men were convicted of conspiracy, burglary, and wiretapping the Democratic National headquarters," said the first. He pointed to his chest, "None of those men went to Princeton." It was an unheard-of personalization.

But this wasn't a normal class. Professor Henley laughed.

"Prior to sentencing, one of the convicted men informed the judge that he and the others had committed perjury under the orders of White House Counsel Mr. John Dean." The second boy also pointed to his chest, adding, "Mr. Dean did not attend Dartmouth."

Professor Henley seemed to be enjoying the exhibition.

"Dean began cooperating with a Senate investigating committee headed by our very own Senator Sam Erwin"—this boy proudly snapped his bright red suspenders—"who got his undergraduate degree from the University of North Carolina."

"President Nixon quickly fired Mr. Dean, who did not go to Davidson," said the next student.

"Then, this past summer, Dean testified that President Nixon, himself, has been personally involved in trying to contain and cover-up the so-called Watergate affair. As my famous fellow Yalie, Mike Doonesbury, has adjudged, 'Guilty, guilty, guilty'." This last was said with relish.

"An accusation is not an indictment," Professor Henley chided, but he was also chortling. He wound up the summarization by contributing his own statement: "The Senate Committee's special prosecutor, Mr. Archibald Cox, has promised Mr. Dean that, by pleading guilty to one count of conspiracy to obstruct justice, he will be immune from further charges."

Obstruction of justice. Lowry flipped pages in her casebook. One of the assigned cases had been about obstruction of justice. She didn't listen while a student, who deplored that Nixon was a Duke law grad, recited a legal definition of 'conspiracy'. She heard her own name only dimly. The boy to her left jabbed his elbow into her arm. Lowry looked up. Professor Henley was frowning at his seating chart. "Do we not have a Miss Matthews here?" he inquired.

"Me," Lowry squeaked. She immediately hated herself for squeaking.

"Well?" Professor Henley raised his eyebrows.

"Would you mind repeating?"

"What does 'obstruction of justice' mean in the case of Mr. Dean?"

Last night, in the library, Lowry had memorized all twenty-one ways in which a person might commit obstruction of justice. Right now, she could only remember the first. "He assaulted a process server?" she ventured weakly.

Professor Henley frowned. "Mr. Chambliss!" he called.

One of the hand wavers responded promptly. "Whoever endeavors to influence, obstruct, or impede the due administration of justice shall be punished. Title 18 of the Federal Criminal Statues, section 1503." This boy spoke in a deceptively lazy Southern drawl. "We from Emory read statutes."

Lowry had never felt the need to slink before, but that's what she did when class ended and she could finally leave the lecture hall. She stuck to corridor walls like a lizard. She had planned to hide in a toilet cubicle for a while. But when she entered the restroom she heard a flush, and who should come out of a stall but Big Tits herself.

Big Tits noticed Lowry, looked thoughtful for a moment, then grinned and stuck her ample chest even further into the air. "Ms. Nancy Salinsky," she declaimed sonorously, emphasizing the Ms., "from the University of Chicago, where we have our own share of jack-asses."

Lowry gaped, caught on, and stuck her own far-less-impressive chest forward. "Lowry Matthews. From Stanford, where we do not grow larger than a C cup."

"Ha!" Ms. Nancy Salinsky's laugh was as generous as her bosom.

It felt so good to weep while laughing. Those tears almost substituted for a cry.

That evening, Lowry called home.

"Nonsense!" Dad said bracingly, after she described her CrimLaw debacle. "I'm sure you're doing just fine."

"Have you seen *The Paper Chase* yet, Low?" Mom asked anxiously. "We saw it last weekend. Is law school really like that?"

Lowry couldn't say. Movies, like newspapers, were pastimes of another life. "Law school is... Well, it's words." Finding the precise words now, with which to explain herself, was proving surprisingly difficult: what she had previously assumed she knew perfectly well, law school had complicated by adding new and greater depths. "Words like 'promise,'" she attempted. "Webster's only gives it three meanings, but my law dictionary gives it seven."

"Really?" Dad's response was polite and easy.

Nothing in Lowry life was easy anymore. She couldn't even convey to her parents what in her eyes had become a daily reality: in the universe of law, words expanded like nova events.

Week Three

The outside temperature was no longer so hot, the humidity no longer so drenching. When Lowry's last highlighter gave out, when she had to walk to the Union in mid afternoon, the air was as pleasant as back home.

She allowed herself a half hour of recreation in the bookstore. She wandered the aisles. She picked up a T-shirt with Duke's Blue Devil emblem on the back—why not? She found pink highlighters as well as yellow. She had never seen pink highlighters before. For a moment, she wished for more colors—wouldn't it be great if she had enough to highlight a case according to topics? Make all the facts yellow. Make critical reasoning pink. She would need at least three more colors for the history of a case, dissenting remarks, the ruling.

She continued on to pens. While putting a bag of Bics into her basket, she saw a number of those big-barreled, multicolored ballpoint pens that allowed a person to click down red, blue, or green ink.

She bought two.

Back at the law school, in the library, she sat at a carrel rather than a table. She didn't want any interruptions. She opened her CrimLaw case book, and proceeded to highlight and underline. It would only take a glance, and she would find what she needed to know if she was cold-called again.

She felt brilliant.

She wanted to share her discovery, her technique. But the only more-than-acquaintance she had made so far was Ms. Nancy Salinsky. Nancy was at a table, sitting elbow-to-elbow with a black-haired, blue-eyed boy who looked more and more familiar the closer Lowry approached. She finally realized: he was the boy who sat next to her in every class; who had nudged her; who must also have a last name starting with 'M'.

"Hi," Lowry whispered.

"Hi." The boy had a bit of a drawl. A Southerner.

"Can I show you something?" Lowry asked.

"Well..." Nancy didn't exactly refuse.

"Sure," the boy was willing.

"Look at this." Lowry sat at his side and began to explain. The more she told, the more interested the others became—until Nancy was borrowing Lowry's second multicolored pen to experiment with; and James McElroy, from Vanderbilt, was saying, "This is terrific."

Lowry was proud of herself for the first time in law school.

"But we shouldn't tell anybody," Nancy warned. "This could give us an edge."

"I need an edge," James confessed.

"A study group"—with a circular wave, Nancy lassoed the three of them together—"that's what we'll be."

At last, Lowry belonged to a study group.

The next morning, in CrimLaw, they took their assigned seats and opened their books to matching colored markings. After class they compared black-inked margin notes. The outline they produced, together, was Lowry's most comprehensive yet. At the end of the day, they continued: reading, underlining, discussing. Even laughing at times.

It turned out the law school wasn't impervious to friendliness, after all.

Week Four

When Professor Pacelli in Constitutional Law announced, "We must not forget that we are living in an era of historic events," Lowry was instantly suspicious. He sounded too much like CrimLaw Professor Henley on her John Dean debacle day. Professor Pacelli's inspiration was even worse. He created an oversized moot court with students on the right side of the lecture hall representing the US Senate, and students on the left representing President Richard Nixon. "We'll call our case *Senate Watergate Committee v. Nixon*," Professor Pacelli cheerfully rolled out his made-up title. "Bound to reach the Supreme Court, eventually. I'll hand out a list of citations you might use. Our court will hear this case tomorrow, this time exactly. I'm giving you twenty-four hours."

Seventy people groaned.

After class Nancy nabbed Lowry and James, saying, "Thank god, we're all on *Senate Committee*. Forget about today's outline, we'll do it tomorrow. We have to be first in the library. Lowry, you pull cases. James, you start xeroxing them. I'll run to the Union and get nickels."

Lowry and James weren't first in the library. They were third and fourth. The girl who had left Lowry in a diesel haze—Miss Brightwell—and one of the few Black guys were first and second. By the time Nancy got back with the nickels, James had used up most of the change they already had, and eight ConLaw students stood behind him. After Torts, twenty-one stood at the two copy machines. The library didn't become a war zone until the rest of the class had eaten their dinners and ambled in. By then, Lowry's group—finished xeroxing; having divided up the cases—was highlighting, underlining, taking notes on the xerox sheets.

James' stomach growled. Nancy directed: "Go get food, James. Lowry and I will move all this into the lounge." And James brought back a bag of hamburgers.

They didn't leave the law school until after midnight. They passed by a boy who was carrying a bed pillow into the library. The following morning CrimLaw was dotted with empty seats. "Where is everybody?" Professor Henley wondered.

Three hours later Lowry, James and Nancy huddled for a brief review: President Nixon possessed audio tapes in which he and his aides reportedly discussed the Watergate affair; the Senate Watergate Committee had subpoenaed those tapes; President Nixon refused. Lowry's group took their places in ConLaw with stacks of color-coded cases ready for reference.

"Let's hear from *Nixon*!" Professor Pacelli said, with high expectation.

It was like watching, listening to, a tennis match.

The left side of the room, *Nixon*: "Ever since George Washington, Presidents have been invoking executive privilege."

The right side of the room, *Senate*: "Executive privilege is nowhere explicitly mentioned in the Constitution."

Nixon: "Executive privilege is a long-understood element of the separation of powers doctrine."

"Miss Matthews!" Professor Pacelli called, because Lowry's hand was up for the first time ever, in any class.

"In *Marbury v. Madison*, 1803, the Supreme Court disallowed President Thomas Jefferson's assumption of executive privilege"—underlined in red. Lowry next quoted the Supreme Court's reasoning, bold in pink: "'It is emphatically the province and duty of the judicial department to say what the law is'."

"Thank you, Miss Matthews." Professor Pacelli gave the floor back to *Nixon*.

"Oh, my God," James exhaled at Lowry's side. "You did it. You *talked*."

Lowry had not only talked, she had earned a 'thank you'.

She helped *Watergate Senate Committee* win.

Later, leaving class, congratulations came from all sides. "Good job in ConLaw today, Matthews," people said—even the inveterate hand-wavers.

Lowry thought they sounded sincere. Miss Brightwell passed by; she gave Lowry a considered nod. Lowry gave a considered nod back. On impulse, she bought three cupcakes from a law school wives bake sale. "My treat, a party!" she invited her study group friends.

It wasn't until that evening, returned to the dorm, she remembered: today was her birthday. She was twenty-two years old. She only remembered because two packages lay before her door. The largest was as big as a hat box, and stamped 'fragile'. Mom had baked and mailed a cake from California. The smaller package, from Justa, was a cassette marked 'The Table'.

"Hi, Low!" That was Justa's voice. "We're in the dining hall. All except for Crystal, of course. We want to say..." Justa struck a chord. The ensuing chorus of 'Happy Birthday' was ragged, but reasonably tuneful.

"Okay, Lowry." That was Gil's voice, followed by a clunk as he, or someone else, resettled the tape recorder on a hard surface.

Justa played 'Happy Birthday' again, a solo ornamented with grace notes and arpeggios. She riffed. She toyed with variations. She segued into 'Twinkle, Twinkle Little Star', part Mozart but mostly Justa. She closed with a long, upward glissando that ended in the highest high note. She held the pedal to maintain the sound of starlight, and whispered—more breath than tone, the faintest solar breeze—"Good night, Low."

Click. It was over.

CCCCC

Crystal was in France with seventy-six other Stanford students. On the bus from the Orly airport to Tours, her seatmate was a boy with hazel eyes and a reddish afro six inches deep. His skin was the color of beach sand washed brown, then tinted red with sunlight.

"Kendall Soames." He settled himself with a bounce. Crystal hadn't experienced any give in these seat cushions.

"Crystal Kelsey," she informed him loftily, before telling him what she had already told other boys on the plane, what she hoped would be known throughout the group by the end of the day. "I'm not looking for a boyfriend here in France. I have other things to do." When their six months in

France were over, Crystal planned to be able to read—to understand—Baudelaire's poems in French.

Kendall raised his eyebrows; he shrugged; he offered, "Want a comic book?"

Crystal accepted a *Tintin* with polite scorn—comics!—which dissolved as she began to read. She didn't know the vocabulary. She couldn't follow the grammar. She needed the bright pictures to fathom the story. It was a time travel adventure—maybe? With Tintin ending up in medieval Paris?

She pulled a dictionary out of her green tote, and started again. She was on her third reading when they arrived at the old hotel that was Stanford in France. She handed back the *Tintin*, then bumped her luggage up two flights of stairs to a door with her name on it. As well as the usual furniture, she had a private sink and bidet. She would have to learn how to use a bidet.

She left her room to wander and investigate. On the floor below she found classrooms, a dining room, offices. She opened the big front door, but stopped on the very top front step. She watched all the human movement—French movement—on a highway, a river, a bridge.

That was enough for today. Exhausted, she returned to her room.

The following morning she slept through breakfast, but not her first class, *L'Art et L'Architecture*. Listening to nothing but French for an hour—and understanding maybe half of what she heard—made her very hungry. This time, when she exited the front door, she walked around the corner to a sort of main street. She went into a bank where she turned a traveler's check into francs without having to say anything.

In the café next door, she pointed at something that looked half pastry, half bread roll. She spoke her first words to a native, *"Un café, s'il vous plaît,"* and left the counter feeling confident. The confidence lasted only long enough for her to discover that the pastry-roll was delicious, and the coffee too strong—because men began crowding around her little table. They talked all at once; they talked over each other. She tried being polite—*"Bonjour;" "Comment allez-vous?"*—and shaking hands. But when one of the men kept hold and began to stroke her palm with his thumb, she pulled away. *"Au revoir,"* she said with finality. She didn't mind leaving her coffee; she took her roll.

But they followed her. Other men, from the sidewalk, joined in. By the time she reached a cathedral square, her escort had invented a French equivalent of double dog dare, darting forward one-by-one to touch her arm, her shoulder, her back, once her breast, and laugh when she slapped them away. They acted out the meaning of *j'ai envie de toi* by cupping and caressing their groins.

She sought sanctuary inside the cathedral.

As she paused to start up the stone steps, an especially bold suitor pressed his erection into the crack of her butt. "Get off!" Crystal turned, and furiously shoved. The man stumbled back, and crash-landed into the arms of another tourist. Kendall Soames.

"Ugh!" Kendall gulped breath back into his lungs. "What the hell?" he expostulated to Crystal.

All of her retinue, every one, backed away. Crystal's men stared at Kendall. Ordinary citizens carrying purses, books, bread, or briefcases stared at Kendall. The people of Tours were a homogeneous crowd: short of stature with brown hair and sallow complexions. Crystal and Kendall stood out like another species.

"*C'est un esclave,*" an old man lifted his cane to point at Kendall. "*En vérité.*" He is a slave. Truly.

His decrepit female companion squinted from Kendall to Crystal, back to Kendall—as if she had just that moment understood something important. "*C'est l'esclave de cette femme!*" He belongs to that woman.

This time Crystal understood it all. And it was *unbelievable*.

Kendall simply looked defeated.

"Are they following you, too?" Crystal asked.

Kendall didn't answer. Instead, his hazel eyes slitted for a considering moment, then cut to Crystal. With no warning, whatsoever, he became an entirely different person. He lifted his feet and pranced—actually pranced—behind her. Crystal turned her head to see him drop to one knee. He pretended to lift an invisible something that was heavy and long, and somehow attached to Crystal's back.

"What?" He was confusing her, as if this morning hadn't already been confusing enough.

Kendall glared, as if to say, *Catch on!*

And after a breath or two, she caught on. Yesterday she had seen a cartoon boy strike this exact pose, but with the trailing end of a lady's gown. Tintin masquerading as a page boy in medieval Paris.

Crystal lifted her nose with élan. She clutched the front of her jacket, now yards and yards of medieval fabric, and entered the cathedral as she imagined a grande dame of great position and authority might do. She paraded from painting to statue to reliquary, regally disregarding those *Tourangeaux* who had left the square to scramble after. When she came to a life-sized sculpture of Saint Sebastian, she stuck one hand back to Kendall. "Give me a ruler, oh slave," she said—in French when she could find the words, in English when she couldn't—"so that I might measure this man's penis." She hoped the word was the same in both languages. She cracked up. Kendall's eyes and mouth began as big Os, but then he was laughing with her.

"*Arrêtez de rire!*" Stop laughing. The decrepit old woman made the sign of the cross.

"In inches or centimeters?" Kendall snickered.

"Centimeters," Crystal wheezed, "because it's so small."

⌒

Dear Justa,

I went out on bikes yesterday with a sophomore boy named Kendall. He's from Darien, Connecticut. I borrowed one of the school's old three-speeds, and Kendall rode the fancy ten-speed he bought as soon as we got here.

We went to visit a man his high school French teacher knows. We didn't have to go far. M. Guérard lives in a cave that has balconies and window boxes. M. Guérard and Kendall talked really fast, but after our second bottle of wine I was understanding a lot.

M. Guérard is missing the tops of his ring and pinky fingers, both hands. The Nazis cut them off during World War II, when he was part of the French Resistance. He was an upholsterer,

and he hid messages in chairs that he took through Nazi barricades
into Tours. When they caught him, they wanted to know something about which he knew nothing. They never asked him about
the chairs.

Crystal had run out of space. She had to crunch her name in after
'chairs'. She folded the aerogram in thirds, licked the seal, and wrote Justa's
Stanford box number on the front. When she began this letter, she thought
she was going to write about Kendall. But M. Guérard took over.

She flipped the aerogram. She added a message to the outside back
where any postman could read it, assuming the postman read English. 'I
have a new friend.'

The windowsill in Crystal's room was wide enough, and long enough,
for her to sit sideways with her feet up and a notebook, dictionary, and
both French and English editions of Baudelaire's *Les Fleurs du Mal/The
Flowers of Evil* stored beneath the tented angle of her knees. But instead of
studying, she was watching winter rain fall into the Loire river. She was
eating a French apple that tasted exactly like an American Golden Delicious. When somebody knocked on her door, she called out, "*Entrez,*" expecting to see the maid who daily cleaned out the sink and bidet. Crystal
mostly used the bidet to soak her hand washables.

But, "Hey," it was Kendall, carrying two pastry boxes tied together with
string.

"Oh, good!" Crystal put her apple down. Kendall had a goal: he was going to visit every patisserie within a thirty kilometer radius from Tours.
Mostly he rode his bike, sometimes he had to ride a train. He always
shared. Now he opened his boxes to show off a raspberry tart the size of
Crystal's palm, and a creamier confection with chocolate on top. "Your
choice," he offered.

"*Framboise.*" The sight of raspberries made Crystal greedy. Raspberries
in France were not the same as raspberries in the United States. In France
they were sugary with a hint of tartness, as deeply flavored as wine. Crystal
didn't quite grab.

Kendall ate slowly, consideringly. He licked the little flecks of chocolate from his lips after each bite. "The patisserie in Villandry is the best so far," he proclaimed. "I got these in Rochecarbon. Too miserable to bike any farther today. I need a hat. Do you have a hat?"

"Nope." Crystal only owned scarves. But she had an idea: "Want to try out some patisseries in Paris tomorrow?"

"Why?" Kendall was suspicious.

"I want to see the unicorn tapestries at Cluny."

"Ummm," Kendall's enthusiasm ebbed even further.

"I'll buy you lunch," Crystal wheedled. "A hamburger." Hamburgers didn't exist in Tours. The closest hamburger restaurant anybody knew about was in Paris.

Kendall thought. "Well, all right," he assented. "If I can find a hat."

He borrowed somebody's railroader cap that crested, that could not confine, his afro. But it kept him somewhat dry when they were walking to the train station the following morning. "Maybe it'll stop raining by the time we get there," Crystal hoped. The rain fell even harder as they trained northward.

In Paris, they metroed, they walked. Nobody followed them. Partly because it was Paris. But also because—and this was true even in Tours—being a male with a female companion meant they were usually left alone. They dripped into the Hôtel de Cluny with sodden, squeaking shoes, leaving big, American-sized footprints behind them on the floor. Crystal stood before the tapestries: unicorns, virgins, flowers. For hour after hour, year after year, people had pierced canvas with bronze needles, painting non-perspective, two-dimensional pictures backwards, creating visions of eerie romance. Four hundred and fifty years later, their art still enthralled. "It says here that the unicorn loves her. The virgin." Crystal scanned a guidebook. "But I don't know if she loves him back."

Kendall wasn't listening. He had wandered off to chat with the guard. "A great guy," he told Crystal when she gathered him up to take him back to the Métro. "I learned a new joke. What is a Belgian fondue?"

"I don't know. What's a Belgian fondue?"

"French fries and mashed potatoes!" Kendall snorted, he howled. He shot laughter down a Métro tunnel lined with grimy movie posters.

Crystal didn't and couldn't comprehend French humor. But what did it matter when she was with Kendall? At the Franklin D. Roosevelt station, she took his arm and pulled him upstairs to the street. "First we'll buy an umbrella," she planned, "and then we'll get our hamburgers."

"*Avec des* French fries," he insisted.

She was sharing Paris with a friend. Justa sometimes played a Gershwin melody: movement catching on light; the beat pounding like heels on a boulevard. A hint of spring; the breath of fall. Americans in Paris. Alongside Kendall Soames, Crystal Kelsey danced down the Champs-Élysées in the rain.

Each breath out is a grâce
That pierces the sky.
Who knew life could be
So simple.

JJJJJ

Justa remembered: Aunt Edith saying, "You. Must. Wake. Up." Emphasizing each word so Justa couldn't fail to hear.

Gil

She and Gil were squashed, two bodies in her narrow bed. As a junior, Justa had ranked a single room, but the bed was still a long twin. She and Gil had just begun—those first touches, those initial kisses—when the Stanford firehouse horn whonked.

Gil's hands stilled. "Gotta go." He pulled away, his erection shrinking. He donned pants, shirt, shoes as he fled Justa's room. The door slammed. Justa stretched. She sighed. She had might as well go to the dining room and practice.

But from the dining room windows, she saw a second sunset tingeing the eastern sky. The earlier, western, sunset had been pink and orange. This eastern one was a dulled and cloudy red. She went out into the courtyard where people had stopped to look up and over the roofs. They, she, sniffed the smoke drifting overhead. Fire engines—many more than Stanford's two—wailed from far away.

"Let's go see," somebody said, which became a mass call to bicycles. Students began unlocking, mounting their bikes.

Now Justa could tell: the wailing was approaching from the north and west as well as east, a triangulation around campus. This had to be more than a stove fire in a dorm kitchen, or a roach left smoldering on somebody's mattress. She ran for her own bike.

Her bike merged with others until she couldn't choose her own speed, she was so crowded in. She became a part of a parade. The other students seemed to be in a holiday mood; their excitement heightened by the uncanny sky, sharpened by the increasingly bitter air. Fenced by their racing wheels, Justa pedaled, she pumped. Her breathing shortened into determined gasps. Her heart raced before her as if she would never catch it up. The crowd turned, an angling flock, onto Serra Street.

Justa's first thought was, *Encina Hall*. Her second was, *It's beautiful*, because the fire was. Yellow-red flares licked, hinted, enticed from top-storey windows. Yellow-gold flames danced—a whoring, exposing, laughing reel—along the roof. Fire sang: roars, sighs and sibilances that matched no other pitches in nature. Justa, helplessly enraptured, witnessed a fierce wildness at the peak of its glory.

And then she heard Gil. She wouldn't have found him otherwise—so many firemen had gathered, maybe a hundred, maybe two hundred. Black helmets, yellow helmets. Stanford helmets were red. When Gil shouted, "Okay!", her ears picked him out him from the other yelling, calling, helmeted men. Gil was the figure to the left front of the conflagration, aiming his hose at a second-story window. "Turn it on!" She could hear him even though the fire hissed, even though other men were shouting the same or similar words, even though students were telling, "Christ!" "Fuck it!" "What the hell!"

Her eyes rose from Gil, up and up, following a ladder that reached five stories high. One lone firefighter clung to the top rungs, spraying from one long hose. If he fell, he would become a marshmallow dropping into a bonfire. Defenseless. Roasted.

Only then did Justa feel the fire's great heat on her own skin—and she was safely distant. Fever forced the throbbing in her throat to slow. Her heart returned with a sick 'thud' to her chest. She spoke a prayer that was immediately buried beneath the clamor: "Gil can't go up there."

She focused her hearing and vision, as if her concentration alone could keep him unharmed through the next three hours. Gil remained grounded. When he, along with other red helmets, finally climbed onto a Stanford engine—last to leave—she allowed herself to break away. Her ride back to Lagunita was a solo journey. She returned to her room and waited.

Gil came to her around three in the morning. When she heard a scatter of gravel against her window, she ran down the hall and down the back stairs to open the security door.

Gil was still revved up. He said, "The fire was so hot, the nozzle of my hose began to melt!" He showed her his heat-blistered palms. "And this is through gloves!" Protected by adrenaline, he didn't feel any pain.

Justa tugged him by the elbow up the stairs, up the hall, to her bed. They lay as close as they had been before the alarm, but this time Justa smelled lingering ashes through the overlaying scent of firehouse shampoo. She tasted the salt of sweat behind Gil's ear.

"I couldn't wear my glasses, but that didn't matter. I wouldn't have been able to see a damn thing anyway through all the smoke and the steam and the water!"

She kissed his singed eyebrow. She held him close until he talked himself down from his fireman high and fell asleep.

Then she slipped from his side, dressed, and went outdoors to her bike and the dawn. The eastern horizon was now sweetly pink. She pedaled grimly, determined to extinguish the embers of wildness that still entranced her mind. She smelled the ruins before she saw them: stale smoke. Then she observed: blackened sandstone; fallen roof tiles that lay broken and smashed; the empty-eyed blankness of blown-out windows. Encina Hall had been one of Stanford's earliest constructions, with extra arches, medallions and columns. Victorian exuberance. Venerable. Vulnerable.

At The Table that night, Scott looked Gil over—although not as thoroughly as Justa had done—and said, "Man, I can't believe that at Stanford firefighting is a work-study job."

Beethoven

Justa got one credit for being an accompanist with the Stanford Chorus. When the San Francisco Symphony invited the Chorus to provide voices for a performance of Beethoven's Ninth, she was almost as thrilled as the singers. On performance day, riding in a Chorus bus, she sat next to Betsy. Betsy massaged her throat. Betsy spoke with preserved breath: "Where will you be sitting?"

Justa sat in the first balcony of the Opera House. She picked out Betsy's face from the dark embankment above the orchestra. The faces held silent until deep into the fourth movement, and then song welled out in wonder. When Stanford's first sopranos sustained a high A for eight long, glorious, unimaginably infinite bars, Justa began to cry. She wept through the conclusion of the symphony—Beethoven's last composed, and the first symphony, ever, to include human voices. Justa held her tears back, barely, during the boarding of the midnight busses home to Palo Alto. Once again seated beside Betsy, she let her tears flow.

"What?" Betsy's voice was loud now, pitched over the din of people recently freed from stage fright.

"He never heard it," Justa said, saltily.

"Heard what?" Betsy cupped a hand behind the ear closest to Justa.

"He never heard his own music," Justa said.

In his deafness, Beethoven had created glory.

A Famous Pianist

At the master class with Lorin Hollander, Justa was so excited she clasped her hands to keep her fingers from moving. She wanted to hear only Hollander's notes, none of her imaginary own, when he played Bach's 'Jesu, Joy of Man's Desiring'. His rendition was perfect.

Afterward, when he stood and held his hands up and open in display, she gazed like everybody else. And saw nothing special, except for length of fingers.

Hollander told them: "I played with unerring instinct until I was seventeen. Then, inexplicably, I lost the freedom and control in my right hand." He wiggled those fingers. "My confidence faltered. My music became curtailed." He allowed his arms to fall. He looked from student to student, meeting everybody's eyes. "What had been absolutely natural, I had to learn again. It was an effort of many years." His glance caught Justa, moved on. "I had to delve to the very source of my musical gift. But once there, I discovered the unexpected." Hollander smiled with a beatific calmness that matched the perfection of his *Jesu*, not the agony of his story. "I discovered whole worlds of creative possibility."

Justa loosened the grip of her fingers. She couldn't imagine being betrayed by her hands. She couldn't imagine surviving, far less thriving, beyond such a loss.

Beethoven, Again

Nowadays Justa didn't always practice in the dining room. Often, instead, she rode her bike to the Knoll—once the university's presidential mansion and now home to the music department. The ride was a pretty one, around the eastern edge of the lake and up a little hill. The Knoll pianos were finer than the dormitory pianos. And if Justa was lucky, she could practice in a room with superior acoustics. This month she was working on a piece that Kath had chosen from one of the yellow 'Schnabel' books. Herr Schnabel had edited and published all of Beethoven's sonatas. Justa was working on No. 25 in G major. It was a short piece, only three movements, but it required thought as well as skill. Deep within the presto movement there was a voice that yearned, sometimes with spots of anger. In the andante movement the yearning became so stretched and spun, woven into a gossamer so fine, that Justa was draped in anguish. The vivace movement demanded optimism—although the previous anger occasionally emerged from the bass notes. There was a balance in this last movement that Justa had to work hard to maintain. That was the movement where she should have been spending her time. But what she wanted— what she couldn't help but do—was to sit at the Steinway grand with her soul as open as her hands, and send the andante movement spinning its heart toward the ceiling, toward the walls, through every square inch of architecturally wonderful air.

She felt so enlarged then, achingly complete.

If she left the Knoll late, and if the moon was full or the stars unclouded, she would ride her bike through campus, skimming past the Main Quad and ending up at the Stanford family tomb. In the dark light of night, the tomb was overshadowed—no, embraced—by an enormous old oak tree. Justa would stop beneath the branches, not completely dismounting, and wait. If she waited long enough, she could almost hear the deep and rumbling echoes of time that were this tree's ancient soul—experience, heartache, endurance, completion.

It was only at these moments, and only in this position—balanced with one foot grounded, one foot on a pedal, always prepared for a moment's flight—that Justa allowed her personal yearnings to become andante. Then, and only then, did she put what she had been learning into words. Love = Risk.

Betsy

Betsy was graduating early and leaving Stanford in mid March. Before then, she had exams to take and papers to finish. She had to pack up her Stanford life. She also had to prepare for two weddings, one in Atlanta, and one in Tehran.

"It will all be Mama's acquaintances," she told Justa about the Atlanta wedding. "Mama's inviting everybody who is anybody—even those people she doesn't like—and promising them a show. General Lee's great-great-great granddaughter is marrying a man whose grandfather was a prince. Being a prince is supposed to make the color of Farhad's face disappear."

"He's not that dark," Justa protested.

"He's on the other side of a divide; Mama's playing Old Atlanta society politics to fudge it." Betsy shrugged her shoulders and sighed. "In Tehran, Farhad and I will switch places. I'll be the blonde foreigner who exudes the West. I don't know what Farhad's mother is going to do about that. But"—with obvious effort Betsy hefted her spirits—"I'm going to join the Women's Organization of Iran, maybe teach while I learn Farsi. Did you know that the Empress's high school biology teacher became a physician, a parliamentarian, and then the country's Minister of Education? Eventually I might go to medical school."

"Where?" came out of Justa before she realized that of course there were medical schools in the Middle East.

"I...I don't know," Betsy faltered.

Justa asked—she had to, Betsy was that close of a friend—"Are you sure you want to do this? Get married? Go so far away?"

"Why, yes!" Betsy seemed repelled by Justa's doubt. "Of course! Don't you see? I'm so happy!"

"Okay," Justa soothed.

Betsy calmed. "I know you don't know Farhad all that well, he's so quiet. But he's a brilliant engineer. He's going to do wonderful things for his country."

Justa had no reason to disagree.

"He's done wonderful things for me." Betsy's voice now held the smoothness and purity that characterized her singing. "I never knew I had so many possibilities inside of myself until I met him." Betsy was holding her final human biology text. When she pressed her hands against her heart, she squeezed the book between fingers and chest. "If I have to give up the 'me' I was in order to experience my own courage, then I will. I'm ready."

Kendall

Six thirty a.m., the beginning of Spring term. The bird chorus, this morning started by a goldfinch, was gaining voices. When Justa opened the lake-facing security door and stepped outside, she startled goldfinch and all into a temporary hush. Then a blackbird trilled, rough-edged and challenging. Another blackbird answered. The chorus exploded.

Justa passed through their music, walking up the dirt path to the vernal lake. Last winter's rains had been long and heavy, making this year's lake deep and reflective. The water now mirrored the lifting sun. She followed the perimeter path counterclockwise, her focus the sometimes rising, sometimes flat, bank at her right hand. Wherever the oak trees and bay laurels grew densely tangled, where thickets of manzanitas and madrones filled the understory, she stopped and peered. Finally, she saw it—a dark green line that clashed against the softer curves of vegetation. The top fold of Kendall Soames' REI pup tent.

She approached, but was stopped short by a barrier of poison oak. She studied the tangle of brush and tree and vine until she saw an incongruous bamboo pole, cut eighteen inches high and stuck vertically into the ground. A clue.

When she set a foot on each side of the pole, she saw what to do. If she ducked under that madrone, and used the available forked stick to shift aside vines, she would avoid the worst of the poison oak. She did so, and crawled into a small, natural clearing—sandy and soft, nice enough for a bed. She sat down on an exposed root and waited. A pair of pants and a T-shirt hung over the low-hanging branch of an oak tree, a pair of boots below. She turned the boots upside down, shaking them to dislodge any spiders, announcing herself with the slap of laces against leather.

A hand unzipped the tent's fly screen. A reddish head of hair poked out. "Who's that?" yawned Kendall Soames.

"I'm Justa," she answered.

His eyes popped open. Greenish-brown eyes, as Crystal had described. "How do you do?" he inquired.

"I'm fine."

Kendal blinked—not so much at her, as to wake up his eyes. "Would you mind handing me my pants? And my shirt?"

"Not at all."

He pulled back his head like a pond turtle.

Justa lifted her face to slanting sunlight, filtered through overhanging oaks. That high D was a wren-tit—three sharp chirps followed by a rapid pulse of five.

Again the fly screen opened. Kendall scooted out.

"Do you want to go to breakfast?" Justa invited.

"Okay." He reached for his boots.

Justa led him through the madrone tunnel, over the bamboo pole, back around the lake, to Lagunita Court. In her aerograms Crystal had described Kendall as an early riser, which he wasn't today. His T-shirt was inside out. He tried to put on his boots as he walked, hopping dazedly, pausing, tying, hopping again. By the time they got to the dining hall he was shod, but still yawning. Justa pointed him toward the coffee.

She made herself a cup of tea. When she next looked for Kendall, he was more alert, tipping his coffee cup against his lips, examining the breakfast offerings of lukewarm fried eggs, glutinous oatmeal, and shredded potatoes baked in oil to resemble fried. He turned a half circle, saw the table where bowls of granola, pitchers of milk, packaged bread, day old sweet rolls, and an enormous jar of peanut butter had been deposited, and headed that way. With one hand, and great consideration, he began making himself a peanut butter and sweet roll sandwich.

Justa set her tea on an empty table. Early morning students were few. Scientists, mostly, with eight a.m. classes and labs. Most of them boys. White boys; also Asians. Kendall was the only Black person there, student or server. Justa watched as he gathered and balanced—on the crooked elbow of his left arm—two apples, three slices of bread, and a saucer on which he had spooned a half cup or so of peanut butter. He searched for her, and she waved. She helped him unload his elbow.

"I guess this is a sub-table of The Table," she welcomed him. "Crystal's friends."

"Her two best friends, that's what she says," he clarified. With a dull knife, he sawed, rather than sliced, his two apples. He glued apples onto bread with peanut butter, creating a double-decker apple and peanut butter sandwich that he wrapped in paper napkins and set aside, as if for a snack. "I don't think Crystal's ever had many friends."

"No," Justa confirmed. "She hasn't." And because Justa wondered: "Why didn't you want to live in Toyon Hall?"

Kendall wrinkled his nose. "Too far away."

Too far from what? From Crystal? "I can show you Crystal's window when we leave," Justa offered. "She got the single next to mine."

"Thank you."

His sincerity possessed enough depth to make Justa's heart twist a little. "What Crystal wants is friends," she cautioned. "We're special."

"Not special." Kendall shook his head at that word. "We're..." He thought while chewing through a big bite of sweet roll. He swallowed. "Special," he defined, "is when you're the only Black kid in a high school of fifteen hundred. It's not so great." And he changed the subject. "I play the recorder. Did Crystal tell you?"

Crystal had, in one of her aerograms. What Justa wanted to ask was 'Are you special here, too?'— even though the answer was all around her. Instead, she followed Kendall's lead of topic: "What do you like to play?"

In answer, Kendall pursed his lips into a whistle and blew the calls of that morning's goldfinch. He reformed his mouth, added his hands, and emulated the lapping of lake water against its bank. With a wide mouth and pulsing Adam's apple, he copied the whistle of a train coming into the Palo Alto station three miles away.

Everybody in the dining hall stopped talking. The servers stopped clacking spoons against their hot trays.

Kendall subsided to quieter tones: the whip of wind around lakeside trees; last night's tenor hoots of a screech owl. The individual hoots melded and molded themselves into a tune—human music, gentle and desiring.

The dining hall applauded.

Justa remembered: she had heard this particular theme in her dreams the night before: a dryad's flute playing from far beyond her open window; an exquisite expression of loneliness; a gorgeous rendering of unrequited love.

CCCCC

Crystal was excited. She was proud. She was going to introduce Kendall to The Table. Well, what was left of The Table. Too bad Betsy got married and was already away in Iraq or Iran or wherever in the Middle East Farhad was from. And Lowry was gone, too. And of course Justa had already met Kendall on her own.

But still, there were Gil and Scott. They, Justa and Crystal were already seated for dinner. Why was Kendall so late? The others were digging into their salads.

"Kendall!" Crystal stood to beckon. As soon as he was close enough, she grabbed his sweater, pulled him even closer, and announced, "This is Kendall, everybody. Kendall Soames."

Kendall selected a chair.

Crystal kept on going: "This is Gil Musicant, he's Justa's boyfriend. And this is Scott…" She had to pause. In fact, she had to stop. She didn't know Scott's last name.

"Hanson." He reached around her to shake Kendall's hand. "But we've met, right?"

"I was mostly benched freshman year." Kendall was opening his napkin, doing all the normal things. But he was using 'bench' as a verb. Crystal had never heard anybody use 'bench' as a verb before.

Scott had. He became almost as excited as Crystal was moments before. "I remember!" he said. "You have a *great* arm. What happened?"

"UCL," Kendall acronymed.

"Oh, man!" Scott commiserated.

What were they talking about?

"I have other appendages," Kendall continued his conversation with Scott, across Crystal's plate. "Once, in Le Mans—Crystal wasn't there; I don't know where you were, Crystal—I got some coaching from Pelé. Just a street game. Some kid started it. I was there. Pelé appeared. We all practiced headers. It was great."

"Wow!" Scott was sincerely impressed.

"Whoa," Gil was impressed, too.

Even Justa asked a truly honest, "Really?"

Crystal sought for something to say. She remembered Le Mans very well: the Roman wall, some Roman baths, a cathedral, a big race track. She had seen race cars there, and slender drivers wearing tight fitting jump suits. She hadn't met anybody named Pelé. Where had she been at the time? No matter. "Yeah!" she agreed. "Those drivers were incredible."

Silence. Kendall, Gil, Scott—even Justa—all stared at her with various expressions of puzzlement, blank wonder, concern, and in Scott's case, hilarity.

"Crystal," Justa said after everybody had been quiet for much too long. "What are you talking about?"

Crystal saw her hands, felt her face, heating up. "I don't know," she admitted.

She only opened her mouth to eat for the rest of the meal. Kendall and Justa used their silverware, dishes, chairs and the table to make sounds together—clicks, clinks, tappety taps. Gil, after Kendall said he was a geology major, asked about the fire resistance of sandstone. Scott listed all the athletes in his fraternity, name and sport, many of whom Kendall knew. Those two left the table together as soon as they'd finished their multiple pieces of cake. The table, lower-case 't', was now littered with white dessert plates. Justa was still making the heavy china go *ping* with the tines of her fork.

"I've got Chorus tonight." Justa stood.

"I can walk with you as far as the firehouse." Gil was leaving, too.

Crystal was abandoned.

She went up to her room, changed into leotard and tights, and crossed the street to the women's gym. Nobody was in the large dance studio, so she switched on the lights. In an hour or so, when night fell, the mullioned windows would reflect like broken mirrors. She plopped herself down near an electric outlet, and upended her gym sack. She sorted through multiple cassettes, chose a tape, and plugged in her player. Then, with conscious grace, pulling herself up from the floor as if by a string attached to the top of her head, she began to dance. She danced out everything she had felt during dinner—an anticipation which was blocked by irritated frustration before being sunk by embarrassment. 'American Pie' ended with a chorus of tragedy, and Crystal collapsed. Once again she was a heap on the floor— but this time with her limbs positioned exactly so. She held her posture— one leg extended, the other bent, her head touching her knees, and her arms shrouding her head.

"Hey," Gil said, and Crystal got herself all twisted up in her sudden untangling. Gil stood in one of the doorways, his right hand resting on the frame as though he'd been there a while. "Justa said you might be here. I brought you a Coke."

"You did?" For the last five minutes Crystal had been sweating out a turbulence of emotions. Now something resembling pathetic gratitude surged upward from her chest, like another blush.

"Sure." Gil rolled a can in her direction. He opened one of his own. "I thought maybe you should know," he said kindly, "that Pelé is one of the greatest soccer players, ever. And that Scott and Kendall were talking about baseball first, before they moved on to soccer."

"Oh, yeah. *Le football*," Crystal sighed.

Gil slid down the door frame until he, too, was sitting. "Why did you go all silent?" he asked. "I mean, after the Pelé thing. It's not like we haven't heard weird things from you before."

Dancing created clarity. Dancing demanded truth. "Because dinner didn't go like I planned," Crystal had to confess. "I thought I was bringing someone to The Table who was all my own. Like Justa brought you and Lowry and Betsy, and you brought Scott, and Betsy brought Farhad."

"What do you mean, 'all your own'?" Gil's normally mild expression, behind his eyeglasses, turned incredulous. "Did you think Kendall had no life before you? You didn't invent him, you know!"

That, Crystal realized, was exactly what she had thought.

"I'm sorry," Gil apologized immediately. "I shouldn't have said that. Not when you're so down. But you're acting like he's Schrödinger's cat."

Crystal didn't know anybody of that name, far less anybody of that name who owned a cat.

"You're acting like it's you who gets to determine reality," Gil explained. "Don't you ever think about who Kendall is when you aren't around?"

"No." Crystal's voice came out tiny. Gil had just layered another definition onto her own, particular, original sin—thoughtlessness. Mother used the 'th' word so often, it had practically become Crystal's middle name.

"When you think about it, that's what makes us strangers to each other," Gil was musing now, disappearing behind his thoughts. "Because we continue to exist when the other person isn't around."

Crystal wasn't in the mood for philosophy, not when she felt so ashamed.

Gil reappeared to the present. He frowned down at his coke can, then crushed it. "I didn't make things any better, did I? I should stick to math."

"No," Crystal countered. "You helped." Because he had shown her where she needed to make amends.

She waited until he was well gone before she returned to Lagunita and her room. She put off a shower until later. For now, she pulled jeans, socks, and a long-sleeved shirt over her leotard. Then, using the illegally cut key Justa had given her, she got into Justa's room from where she borrowed a candle. Downstairs, she propped open the security door with a brick. Her hand cupping flame—the backs of her fingers shielding against wind, her palm scorching—she swiftly walked up to, and followed, the lakeside path.

She found Kendall easily, his flame was so much brighter than hers. A Coleman lantern throwing out brilliance as though it had plenty to waste; turning a depth of branches and twigs into a maze of black bars; making Kendall look like bits and pieces of a person behind those bars. A person sitting on the ground, his head bent over a book.

"Kendall." She didn't dare come any closer. Justa had told her about the poison oak.

Kendall squinted in her direction. "Crystal?"

Crystal told him, "I'm allergic."

"There's a way in. I'll show you." Kendall put down his book, patting it as though to tell it to stay right there. He stood, stepped, ducked, stood again, circled something, and came to take Crystal's arm and lead her, carefully, into his camp.

She sat on the bare earth that was his floor, on the other side of *Carbonate Sedimentary Rocks of Europe*. "Dinner didn't go the way I planned," she began.

"I had a good time," Kendall assured her.

"I know. That's why." Dance was always honest. "It made me jealous."

"Jealous?" Kendall was amazed. "Why?"

"Because you already knew Scott. Because you had already met Justa. I wanted you to be my friend, alone. I'm sorry."

"Oh. Wow." Kendall did something he had never done before. He touched Crystal's cheek. "I am most definitely your friend, Crystal," he assured her. "And I always will be." He withdrew his hand. He turned so he could crawl into his tent. He came out a minute later with another black branch—no, his recorder. "Listen," he said, "this is you."

And while Crystal was figuring out how she could feel both humbled and cherished at the same time, Kendall blew. He blew shining sounds that grasped and grabbed at the lantern's white light, that sent an opalescent fullness into a night crowded with stars. He finished by lowering his recorder and trailing his song with speech. "That's what the word means: 'crystal'." She heard the small 'c', distinctly. "It's what I think, Crystal,"— a big 'C', clearly—"whenever I think about you."

Haloed by the light
   He brings
Warmth into my bones

Flying music like a kite
   He sings
A path to bring me home

LLLLL

June was as hot in North Carolina as September had been. Lowry discovered this because she didn't go home for the summer. She told Dad she was staying because of the job she got at Duke law library. But really, she was staying because of 'Skywatch'—an apartment built on top of an old slave cabin, the cabin having been remodeled time and again since 1865. Women law students had been passing Skywatch from a newly-graduated to a second-year for over a decade. Lowry was the latest lucky legatee. The property owners were a Peace Corps couple who lived downstairs during their rare furloughs home. Their only request—other than rent—was that their tenant keep the property occupied so that it never appeared vacant and open for vandalism.

Skywatch had two skylights: one in the sitting room ceiling; the other making a canopy of night over Lowry's bed. Every other window, even the small bathroom one, looked out onto treetops. In the mornings Lowry could watch the sun rising pink over the sweet gums to the east. In the evenings the sun set in orange behind loblolly pines to the west. Sometimes in the middle of the night, awakening to stars, Lowry would rise from her bed and go out to her balcony/porch. Descending a cedar-slabbed staircase to the driveway, she would walk around to the front of the slave cabin and let herself in. Standing on the red-pine floorboards, breathing in the odor of red clay that rose from beneath, she tried to enter the cabin's depth of human history. She never succeeded.

Her rent included use of the owners' beat-up Corolla. When she drove to the law school at seven thirty in the morning, the air was already becoming heavy. She always had to park a block or two away, which meant that by the time she opened the law school's front doors, the first blast of air-conditioning felt desert dry.

She spent nine hours there. During the first four, she helped other people—mostly professors or their assistants—by checking out books and loaning pens. During the last four, she shelved the materials those same people either returned, or left scattered on tables and carrels. Her favorite hour was the time she took for lunch: sitting in the lounge; eating a sandwich; reading one of the paperbacks Pamela Brightwell had given her when they both left the graduate women's dormitory. Curled up in a faded upholstered armchair, reading *The Princess Bride*—it turned out Pamela had a romantic streak—Lowry's body and brain slowly began to relax from the grip of first year law.

⌒

One day, her noontime reading stuck with her too long. She had been deep into *I Know Why the Caged Bird Sings*—the autobiography of a woman who understood all too well the scent of old red clay. Lowry was holding an image in her mind—Maya's grandmother shoving Uncle Billie into a vegetable bin to hid him from the Ku Klux Klan—when she realized she was lost. She was shelving State Codes, which should have been easy because each state had a distinctive color. But, somehow, she had gotten through the As and the Bs and was now gazing at Delaware, maroon. How had she skipped the Cs? Where *were* the Cs. She was momentarily confused.

"One stack over. Blue," advised a very Southern male voice. Lowry turned to see a face she recognized. She didn't recall his name, but she knew she didn't much like him. He was a hand waver, one whose brilliance sometimes turned other people's arguments into sputters.

"I can find it myself," she said brusquely.

"Of course you can," the boy replied. "You're a California girl, and you're heading Westward." It was a clever mix of truth and puns. Lowry was indeed a California girl. The West company was a major publisher of legal codes. She couldn't help but crack a smile.

The boy used her smile like a hook, pulling her with him one stack over, placing her before a shelf of volumes whose color exactly matched the book she held in her hands.

"Thanks." She shelved blue with blue.

"Dinner?" he promptly suggested. "I get off at six."

"No," she replied. But added as an afterthought, "thank you."

Which should have ended it. But Trey—she had never known anybody called 'Trey' before—sent a formal invitation in the mail. The invitation had been set by a printer: the words bumped beneath her fingertip. And the invitation wasn't deposited in her law school mailbox; it arrived at Sky-watch, four miles away. Lowry hadn't thought anybody at the school, other than administration, knew her residential address. She was amazed. She was annoyed. She didn't respond.

But when someone tied a big pink bow on the windshield wipers of the Corolla—and somehow got through the locked door to leave a bouquet of mixed flowers on the driver's seat—she was incensed. She stormed back to the law school, thundering from floor to floor, seeking Trey Chambliss. She found him in the development office. He was on the phone, feet up on a desk. He put up one finger to pause her, and said, "Your gift will ensure the matriculation of a deserving student."

Lowry hissed: "What you did was illegal! Breaking and entering!"

Trey tilted the receiver up, blocked the mouthpiece with his other hand, and whispered, "What I did was use a coat hanger. Star Laundry." He tipped the receiver back down. "Thanks, John. Bye."

"You had no right!" Lowry seethed.

"I had no right," Trey agreed, uncharacteristically humble—like a little boy in trouble. "But," and he brightened up, "will you have dinner with me?"

"NO!"

From then on she didn't know if she was suffering a persecution or en-during a courtship. Sometimes she felt one way, sometimes the other. No more break ins, though. Trey was always scrupulously respectful. But he began bringing his lunch and his own book to the lounge. And every day it seemed his armchair shifted a little closer to hers.

"All right," she conceded after a month of this. "What are you reading?"

"*In Cold Blood.*" He showed her the cover. "Truman Capote."

"Yes," she said shortly, which ended that conversation.

But somehow, some weeks later, when he was reading another true crime book, they got into a conversation about goals. Trey's was criminal law.

"Community law for me," Lowry told him.

"Soft law," he opined.

She opined right back: "The law is power. A well-trained attorney, lucky enough to be in the right place at the right time, can direct society toward a better future."

"Changing the world for the better." Trey rolled the words so the phrase sound like the cliché it was.

Lowry narrowed her eyes. "What was your draft lottery number?"

"360," he bragged. "Free and clear."

"Smug enough to feel impervious to harm," Lowry scorned, and she made a show of shifting her interest back to her book. But even as her shoulder turned away from Trey, she wondered: why did she have to be so nasty?

That evening, in Skywatch, she stood in the breeze that ran through her opened sitting room windows, and looked up through the skylight to see an anvil-shaped cloud. Another Southern skill to learn—like getting used to being called ma'am—was accepting thunderstorms. Earlier in the summer Lowry had thought lightning might come through the bedroom skylight to fry her in her bed. She had spent that night on the sitting room floor, soothed into sleep by Willow's rug.

Who was she to determine, in her overall ignorance of the world, what was always good and right and what was always bad and wrong? She really should be fair enough, kind enough, to allow people like Trey their time.

The following morning, when she discovered another formal invitation—this time in her law school mail box—she checked 'I accept' on the response card, and stuck the card into the enclosed, already-stamped, envelope. She sent the envelope to be delivered via US Mail to a box somewhere to the left of her own.

She had forgotten how much fun it was to dress up. School had been jeans, casual tops and sweaters, with the occasional pair of nice slacks for when she felt the need to boost her confidence. Work was linen drawstring pants with cotton peasant blouses. Tonight, though, was girl time. She riffled through the dresses and skirts hanging in her closet. She hadn't yet worn any. She hadn't even snipped the tags off a flowered wraparound skirt made from a soft, drapey fabric. She remembered buying a top to go with the skirt, which was now...where? She burrowed through drawers until she found a clingy tank the exact color to match the leaves on the flowers. Among the scarves she never wore, she found a scarf/shawl in a complimentary shade; she could use it to protect her shoulders from any overly-cold air conditioning.

She looked at herself in the bathroom mirror, stepping up on the bathtub rim to see if the skirt still fit her waist and hips. It did, very well. And even though she didn't have a tan, her arms and neck and face were rosy. That was one good thing about all this heat. Although it did mean she must be careful about odor. Lowry sniffed her underarms, then remembered the perfume Mom had given her last summer. Lowry dabbed her wrists, behind her ears. She regarded herself for a last time and felt downright dainty.

Because she didn't want Trey to go to the wrong door—and because she wasn't yet ready to allow an intruder into Skywatch—she waited in the driveway. She stood in the westward-sliding rays of early evening, her back warming, the iris and jasmine scents of Miss Dior deepening. She knew sunlight made her hair glint copper; she felt surrounded by a nimbus. When Trey arrived, she laughed at the admiration sparking his face.

He looked good, too.

He wasn't a particularly handsome boy, but he stood and walked well as he got out of his car (sunset orange) and escorted her around to the passenger seat. He wore a lightweight summer blazer that matched his eyes, soft brown. His hair was dark brown, not as long as Lowry would have liked, but not so short as to make him look unequivocally Republican. And his tie, well his tie was the exact green of her tank top.

He opened the door and helped her in, a quaint bit of courtesy to which she responded by sliding her legs in properly, in unison. She settled, feeling the black leather cushions sink and mold themselves around her weight. "What kind of car is this?" she asked when he was again behind the wheel.

"A 240Z," he told her. And then, because the question must have stayed on her face, "A Datsun."

This Datsun was nothing like her borrowed Corolla. It could have been another species of vehicle, it was so comfortable. And quiet. Even with the engine turned on, Lowry could hear Trey speak without straining her ears.

She waited for him to begin talking about himself. But instead he asked about her life: her Duke experience, her undergraduate career, her home in California. He drove through a forest, the westering sun whipping like a strobe between tree trunks. He kept his eyes on the road, only rarely glancing at Lowry, as if giving her space to expand her story. So she did.

"My sister's name is Justa. She's a musician, and I think she's pretty good. She's special. What I mean is, she has a special way of being. And being with things. And being with you. Her boyfriend's best friend calls her a 'magical mystery girl'. Which sort of captures what she is, but not exactly. I sometimes feel clumsy around her." Lowry had never confessed this before. She didn't know why it was coming out now. But since she had started, she had to finish. "Not physically, but mentally. It's like I'm going in a straight line and bumping into things, while Justa's seeing everything that's around the edges."

She stopped. He couldn't possibly understand. She was certainly incapable of explaining herself further.

"Sometimes it's the people who walk in the straightest line that carry the brightest light," Trey remarked.

She stared at him. He still watched the road ahead. He had an excellent profile. He wasn't plain looking, not at all.

"Thank you." Her gratitude was sincere.

He pulled in before an old farmhouse that was now a restaurant. Lowry sat and waited while he came around to open her door. He ushered her onto a porch lined with rocking chairs, and into a dining room filled with antiques and sunflowers. The maitre d' seated her at a table that had been scratched and shined, scratched and shined, until it was deep with history.

"To California girls." Trey lifted his wine glass.

Lowry didn't have to order. Trey had done all that when he made the reservation. The plates simply appeared. Lowry only had to lift her fork and taste. Trey had chosen dishes she'd never heard of before: first a mussel soup; then apples fried with mushrooms; then grits topped by caramelized onions and shrimp; and finally a coconut cake filled with oranges and rum.

Lowry ate. She indulged. She drank three different wines. By the time only coffee remained on the table, she had surreptitiously loosened her skirt. "That was amazing!" she groaned.

Trey escorted her back to the 240Z, gently cupping one of his hands beneath her elbow. Once again cradled by leather cushions, she snuggled against the headrest. She was ready—eager now—to hear the story of Trey's life.

But to her surprise he didn't talk while driving home. Instead he sang to her in a lovely tenor that was nothing at all like his law school voice. He chose a song as old-fashioned as the farmhouse, as old-fashioned as the table. "'Tell me, pretty maiden, are there any more at home like you?'"

Lowry felt her eyelids begin to flutter shut. She tried to hold them open.

"'There are a few, kind sir, but simple girls and proper, too.'"

She was so calm... So contented...

"'If I loved you would you promise to remain forever true?'"

She couldn't help herself. Quite simply, and not at all properly, Lowry drifted away into a lullaby sleep.

LOSING

Everything changes.

A basic tenet of Buddhist philosophy.

Starting Autumn 1974

LLLLL

The school year began, and they no longer had days together. But sometimes they had nights. They met at Trey's apartment, always: a utilitarian studio with only the basics—a bed, a table, two chairs. The kitchen was a square of cracked linoleum. The bathroom had water rust in both sink and shower. Lowry thought it ugly. But the building bordered the university and, "I just sleep here; it works." Trey had signed the lease.

Lowry didn't like the apartment, but she loved the sex. With Stillman she had had to instigate, to make certain Stillman could follow through. With Trey she only had to slide between the sheets and enter into pleasure. Pleasure became relaxation. While Trey talked himself down into sleep, she dozed.

On this night, after Chinese takeout and sex, lullabied by a neighbor's stereo, Lowry's doze slid into a half-dream. Fleetwood Mac was singing 'Green Manalishi'. Trey was saying, "As a starting solo practitioner, I'll have to be flexible." And the part of Lowry's mind that was still attentive envisioned a highly bendable...Gumby!

"...referrals that build my reputation..." Wearing Trey's brown sports jacket, Gumby was surrounded by interested admirers.

"...impressed that I got on the *Law Journal*... In Lowry's last glimpse of Gumby, he stood on the steps of a white-columned, white-pedimented courthouse, accepting an award from a six-foot-tall white rabbit. Grace Slick, of the Jefferson Airplane, sang background.

The next morning, early, Lowry recalled the dream as a bedtime story. No, a story*book* because of the pictures. Trey still slept, so she had to stop herself from chuckling. She dressed in near silence, shut the door with a soft click, and stepped into a morning that was as moist as summer. Her Corolla had dew on its windows. As she drove back to Skywatch, the sun began drying out the day.

She had been almost twenty-four hours away from Skywatch. So her first task on entering was to open a window. Her second task was to check that everything was as it should be. The bright red beanbag chair she bought last June still sat on Willow's rug. Emi's wall hanging, stretched over its wooden frame, remained properly parallel to the floor. Emi had once described the black-and-white photograph on fabric as 'Japanese-Finish art, starkness heavy with emotion'. But in Skywatch it was a reiteration of the view from Lowry's windows, a benign interpretation of treetops.

She plopped down onto her beanbag. In an hour she had to be back at the law school. She must shower, dress, make breakfast from supplies she kept in the refrigerator. But for a minute—for maybe five—she would simply allow herself to be at home.

⮰

She and Nancy and James were still a study group. This year they were teaching themselves how to interview clients. Nancy invented their first case: "An alliance of tenants is suing a landlord who has refused to take measures against an infestation of bedbugs."

"Ick," said Lowry.

"I'm an old woman living on Social Security." Nancy assigned them each a personality. James, you're a disabled Vietnam vet. Lowry, you're an immigrant with poor English who's working in a minimum wage job."

"Okay," Lowry and James agreed.

"Okeydokey." Nancy made her voice sound frail and helpless.

In their other role—as the team of attorneys working to help the alliance—they trooped into the library to research statutes and ordinances. That was the easy part. That was Monday.

Off and on, throughout Tuesday and Wednesday, Lowry tried to think of herself as somebody else. Aito Yamada? He had been an immigrant with no English. But that was in 1894, another century. Although...only five years ago, Lowry—with Stillman and El Chico—had joined a priest-led meeting in Redwood City. One of the men attending—a gentleman in bearing, wearing housepaint spattered overalls—had been exceptionally expressive in face, hands, and body. Lowry hadn't needed Spanish to understand him.

In the dark of Wednesday night, she abruptly passed from sound asleep to wide awake—in her own bed, not Trey's—with the loud thought in her mind: 'I need pictures.'

Thursday afternoon she left the Law School for Perkins Library, Duke's main library. She stayed there until midnight, collecting enough xeroxed photographs to create a story. She was the father in a family of peasants in Mexico. She was the boy rolling beneath barbed wire to get into the United States. She was the mother standing in front of a windowless, cement block house near the lettuce fields. She was the tiny girl clutching her mother's skirt while gazing at the world through wide, anxious eyes. She was a family sitting on a dumpster-saved sofa in a room where the wallpaper was peeling in strips. She was a baby whose torso and face were blotchy with bites. She was the mother whose own blotchy chest looked too withered with illness for nursing her child.

The next morning, showering, Lowry discovered an itchy bump on her throat. Probably a spider bite, she assured herself. She hadn't vacuumed for months. Yet... For the rest of the day she couldn't help touching the bump—as if its shape and degree of itchiness might reveal a bedbug origin.

Friday evening, in an unused classroom, Nancy and James wore costumes. James wore a Goodwill T-shirt, jungle camouflage with 'Nam's the Bomb' in lurid orange letters. Nancy took her identity all the way with support hose, a faded chenille robe, and a bubble cut wig.

Lowry only had her manila folder, and a bump.

She was the first client up, interviewed by Nancy, then James, then both together. Even though Lowry had planned this, she was amazed at how many questions she could answer by pointing to a photo and saying, "Me," and, "Mine." She transferred the mild anxiety of her bump to something much greater. Her hands shook when she displayed the baby. "*Sick*," she insisted.

"I wish"—Nancy gagged in an old-lady like manner—"that I had chosen something less nauseating than bedbugs."

When it came Lowry's turn to be interviewer, she listened with a heightened attention to the concerns of the disabled veteran, and to those of the aging woman with meager income. For a short while, she had been their neighbor.

Late that night—only evening, West Coast time—she called Justa. Lowry no longer had to dial the dorm number, because Crystal's mother had given Crystal a Princess telephone—the one encumbrance Crystal deigned to employ. Crystal fetched Justa from across the hall.

Lowry sat on her red beanbag chair in her perfect Skywatch. She gazed at Emi's wall hanging: in the artificial light it was an accurate, and stark, representation of reality. She spoke with the person who would best understand: "Aito's wife died in Tanforan because the Yamadas were treated like animals."

A moment of silence from Justa. Then, "But Aunt Edith saved their homes."

It was an offer of something Lowry had not yet considered. She hung up so she could search through her board-and-brick bookshelves for *The Courage to Be Japanese in America*. Dad had had her thesis bound so beautifully. At the back, as a special coda, Lowry had included a small, square passport photo of a young woman wearing a peaked, army-style Red Cross cap. The young woman's smile was wide, excited. She had used bobby pins to attach the cap firmly to her short, permed hair.

Aunt Edith had been twenty-two years old when she first went abroad. Exactly the age Lowry was now.

⁓

Lowry's favorite course this semester was Anthropology of Law. Because Professor Guildford's area of research was the Eastern Band of the Cherokee Nation, that's where he found most of his teaching examples. Today, while discussing the Band's Qualla Housing Authority, he drew a vertical line down the middle of the blackboard. He titled one half as '10 years ago', and the other half as 'now'. Beneath '10 years ago', he wrote '90%'; and beneath 'now', he wrote '50%'. Then he darkened the room to begin showing slides. Ten years ago, 90% of the Band's housing had been huts made of wattle and daub, or cabins with broken siding and tumbling-down chimneys. No power, no running water, no indoor toilet. Now 50%

of the homes were modest brick buildings with firm roofs and sashed windows. Professor Guildford switched the lights back on; he returned to the blackboard. He began listing statistics for then and now—on health, family stability, high school graduation, and so on.

The statistics told a story.

"It all starts from the floor up," he informed the class.

Afterward, when Lowry stopped at one of the law school's three restrooms for women, she was still musing. She pushed opened a stall door and noticed what she had seen countless times before: scars of old urinal plumbing on the wall, left over from the days when the law school taught only men. Back then—ten years ago—the rare female student had had to use the secretary's lounge. This restroom was a concession against the norm.

'It all starts from the floor up.'

From then on she spotted housing concerns almost everywhere. In Law and Poverty, she found herself thinking about how living situations factored into disadvantage or crime. In State and Local Government, she took special note of those laws and ordinances that reflected age-old prejudices. She began to see cases through a special lens—what did housing have to do with the particular issue or offense?

On a nonprofit day—when such employers came on campus to interview prospectives for summer jobs—the group that intrigued her most was The Housing Initiative in Raleigh. That was because the director, five years graduated from Duke Law, described his mission with a degree of passion she hadn't seen since Anti-War Movement days. His face gripped with intensity when he said, "Our clients are minimum wage earners, fixed income people. People who are getting by—just. And find themselves up against a gamut of infinitely superior powers—landlords, banks, the tax man."

When, a week later, the director of The Housing Initiative called to offer Lowry a summer fellowship—"Not a lot of money, but enough to pay your expenses with something left over"—she accepted.

Because Trey's grandfather had to have hip surgery, Trey couldn't spend Christmas in California as they had planned. Instead, the day before Lowry left, he had her unwrap two boxes, one large and one small. The big box held a Coach briefcase, caramel-colored, silken smooth to touch, and smelling like the leather jacket Lowry had coveted, but been unable to buy, as a teenager. "So that when you start at The Housing Initiative they'll know you're from Duke," Trey told her.

The smaller box was the size of a package of tea bags. "Ta da!" Trey said as she took out a toy car—white like her Corolla, but with little flowers painted all over. "Flowers on, not in, your car," he explained.

With the tips of her fingers, Lowry felt the bumps of flowers: on the doors, the trunk, the hood, even the hubcaps. "You can paint!" Her touch found the hook fastened to the roof. "It's a Christmas ornament!"

"I used to put together models when I was a kid," Trey boasted.

On Christmas Eve he called Moraga. He asked to speak with everybody there. Lowry heard reports as people moved away from the phone.

"He told me you played my tape for him," said Justa.

"Apparently he ate half of this year's birthday cake." Mom smiled.

"He called me 'Sir'," was all Hiro revealed.

Lowry had to wait fifteen minutes while Trey and Dad conversed. She sat on a kitchen counter stool, hearing one side of the conversation, watching Dad's face for signs of...anything.

At last, Dad winked at her. He grinned. After hanging up, he complimented: "Quite a young man! Studying with a prosector; going to intern with a judge; and come January, he'll be cruising with the police!"

                                           ~

It was called the Night Rider Program, and one evening Lowry rode along.

She waited at the law school's front door, watching out for Trey. Her eyes tracked every headlight that swept by. When a lightbar flashed red, she stepped out into the cold where Trey held open the rear door to a police cruiser. Lowry slid into the back seat, and while Trey was making introductions, she saw that the back seat doors had no handles; she was separated from Trey and Officer Ruffin by a Plexiglas screen.

"Nice to meet ya, Ma'am." Through the holes in the Plexiglas, Ruffin's accent was Southern strong. "There's a thermos back there with coffee for you. If you want it. We got our own up front." He pulled away from the law school, and Trey continued their conversation about basketball, his accent gradually thickening—as if Southernness was catching.

Ruffin drove them through campus: men's dormitories on the left blazing lights from every window; the playing fields to the right lost to darkness. When they got to the border of campus and community, lit windows became occasional, street lamps marched ahead.

Beyond the Plexiglas, Trey and Ruffin stopped talking. They bent their heads toward the radio. "Hold on, Ma'am," Ruffin called over his shoulder, and he executed a quick U-turn. He sped up, although with no siren or lights.

Trey turned so Lowry could better hear him: "Somethin's up at the ER."

A few minutes later Ruffin came to a stop at the entrance to Duke Hospital's emergency room. Trey immediately hopped out to open Lowry's door. The moment she was on pavement, Ruffin drove off.

"He's gotta park in the lot back there," Trey explained.

The interior of the emergency room was blue. Pale blue walls. Darker blue linoleum floor. Rows of bucket chairs in Duke's signature royal blue. "The restrooms are that way." Trey pointed down a blue-walled corridor.

When Lowry came back up the corridor to rejoin him, she stopped before getting too close. She didn't want to intrude. Trey was crouched before a chair that supported a small woman dressed in the blue garb of a Duke janitor. One of her arms was plaster-white from the base of her thumb to her elbow. Small as she was, Trey looked up to address her. Officer Ruffin stood behind Trey, listening.

Lowry moved near enough to eavesdrop. Night Riders were supposed to be observers, nothing more. But for some reason, Ruffin was allowing Trey to take the lead.

"We can help," Trey was saying. His accent had switched back. He was, again, an authoritatively educated gentleman from Georgia. "We can make him stay away."

"He brought me here." The woman's freckled face was pinched in an anguish that might have been physical, that might have meant more. "He's not all bad."

"He broke your arm," Trey said with courteous sympathy.

"And then brought me here 'cause he's worried about me missin' work." The woman smiled wryly, with bitter acceptance. "He's worried 'bout me havin' my pay docked."

"If you report him, he'll have a record," Trey advised.

Trey was conducting a client interview.

"First offense might not get him much of a sentence," Trey continued. "But if he tries to hurt you again..."

"There's a shelter," Ruffin cut in.

The woman swung her face sharply toward the officer. "You don't know what I got." Toward him, she was scornful: Southern White woman to Southern Black man. "I own my house."

Ruffin sucked air in through his teeth, but backed off. He gestured at Trey to continue.

"All the more reason to report him," Trey coaxed. "We don't want someone like that hanging around your property, maybe damaging it."

The woman wilted, as if the possibility of a broken house meant more to her than her broken body.

"We'll get a restraining order," Trey assured. "It'll scare him."

The woman stayed shrunken, hesitating. "Alright," she finally whispered.

Trey shot a glance back to Ruffin. In doing so, he noticed Lowry. Trey blinked several times, rapidly, as if he had forgotten that Lowry was part of this night, too. "I have to call a taxi for my friend," he told the woman, "and then I'm going to help you make your report." He stood, waving Lowry toward the pay phones.

While shepherding her there, he quietly exulted, "I'm going to call Jack Pomeranz." That was the prosecutor with whom Trey had arranged his individual study course. "He'll let me in on it, I'm sure. The start of my career, Lowry!"

After the phone call, from the distance of the automatic front door, Lowry watched Trey comfort, cajole, and encourage the woman. A set of headlights swept Lowry's way. Dodd's Taxi. An ordinary sedan; not a Yamada vehicle. Riding back to the law school, Lowry reviewed what she had witnessed; she searched her memory to see more. Trey had been skillful, confident. A solo practitioner in the making. Lowry had been right to not butt in. She had her own question, though: why was the woman was more willing to risk her body than her home? The answer to that would take careful probing, but it might reveal the backbone of the case. Lowry would tell Trey this, tomorrow.

CCCCC

Before

Mid-January, already. A break in the seasonal rains. A crisp, dry Friday. The Table at dinner.

Kendall, who now had a room in close-by Roble Hall, invited Gil and Scott to camp out with him at his old site beside the lake. "We'll lay a tarp down. Can you guys get sleeping bags?"

He didn't invite Crystal or Justa, which made Crystal feel left out. She told Justa so.

"Do you really want to drink that much beer?" Justa asked, which wasn't the point.

To work out what the point was, Crystal joined Justa in Justa's room. Justa sat cross-legged on her bed, with sheet music all around and a stack of blank music paper on her lap.

"I'll bet it was Scott's idea." Crystal aimed blame in the direction she wanted it to go.

"Nope." Justa was marking and unmarking her music paper with pencil and eraser. "Kendall talked to me earlier, when he was beginning to think about it."

"He wouldn't have thought about it if Scott hadn't boasted about being an Eagle Scout yesterday," Crystal said darkly.

"He wasn't boasting, and you're forgetting that Gil's an outdoor guy, too. Think about how Gil spends his summers." Which was working in a logging camp near his family's home in Idaho. Neither you nor I is a camper," Justa was unkind enough to add. She carefully penciled dots on her paper, erased them, put them in again. Gently, she suggested, "You could invite Kendall to spend the night with you sometime."

"No," Crystal said abruptly; she left Justa to her incomprehensible musical notation. She went into the hallway between their two doors. Sex could ruin a friendship, *destroy* a friendship. It had happened to her before.

What she needed was something to do.

She could write a letter to that agency Kendall had located in Paris! The one that placed American girls as au pairs in French homes. She and Kendall had a plan: she would take care of French kids for a year, become fluent; then, after Kendall graduated, they would get back to traveling together.

Gil was applying to PhD programs for next year. Scott was applying to business schools. Justa hadn't decided on anything yet, but Crystal was an applicant, too.

She scrunched her face, assembling vocabulary. She needed her French dictionaries. This letter was going to take work, but after she had a draft she would ask Kendall to look it over.

～

The following morning, way too early, somebody knocked on her door. Totally grumpy, Crystal pulled the door open—and was shocked awake by the fact that she was displaying tide pool pajamas to Kendall and Scott. Anthropomorphized crabs and sea anemones crawled over her torso and limbs.

"Hi!" Kendall said brightly. He wasn't disturbed by her deshabille.

"Crabby today?" Scott chortled.

Kendall ignored him. "Can we borrow your car?"

"What for?" Crystal growled.

"A surprise!" Kendall promised.

Crystal scooped up keys from her bureau and tossed them over. She went back to bed. She slept until lunch, where she only found Justa.

Justa reported the little she knew: "They've got lumber, nails, a saw, a hammer. They're building something at the campsite. We're not supposed to snoop."

Crystal was *not* the kind of person who snooped. Normally. She certainly wasn't going to snoop today. But the afternoon was a long time going by. She couldn't keep her mind on her letter. She couldn't grip her thoughts to a poem. Finally, she pulled sweats over leotard and tights and went across the street to the Women's Gym. She was setting up in the dance studio when Kendall rushed in, saying, "Here you are!" as if *she* was the one who went missing. "You've got to see it! Come on!"

He charged back across the street to where Justa was waiting. "If you ladies will follow me..." He sparked excitement as he led them around the lake, through the poison oak. "Ta-da!"

And there it was: a shoulder-high platform in the lower branches of the oak tree. Some boards looked more broken than sawed. Those had the sharpest splinters. There were gaps between the boards, and the platform tilted upward toward the trunk. "My table," Kendall said proudly. He pointed to a sign nailed to a branch: *La Table Sur L'Arbre*.

"*Our* table," Scott corrected.

"Ours," Gil agreed.

Justa simply laughed.

"This is your surprise?" Crystal doubted. The platform was too high for a meal unless people were standing. If it was meant to be a deck, three people might manage perching on it—if they didn't slide off.

"It's a boy thing," Justa informed her. Justa gave Gil a bird-like peck on the cheek. "How about a picnic?" she offered. "Our treat."

Crystal drove Justa to Chef Chu's. She helped select six boxes of take-out, plus fried rice. She drove back to Stanford; she followed Justa through the poison oak. And all the while, Crystal considered 'It's a boy thing' in depth. She didn't like the inevitability of that explanation: it implied that against some forces of nature she was merely a spineless objection.

At *La Table*, she studied the sight before her as if examining a painting in the Louvre. The three boys were now sitting on three edges of their weekend masterpiece. Three butts, with six legs dangling. Above those legs and butts, three faces with totally dissimilar features. At the moment, all wore the same expression. Self-congratulation.

Crystal sighed with reluctant acceptance. She sought in her bag for General Tso's chicken to give to Kendall. She found prawns in lobster sauce for Scott. Justa was handing something to Gil. Crystal distributed chop sticks all around. She sat on the ground beneath Kendall's legs to open her remaining box—Ma Po's hot bean curd. "Anybody want to switch?" she asked.

She ended the meal with spinach noodles in her hair.

⁓

Scott's fraternity was famous for its legendary Valentine Night Bashes. Crystal, on impulse, decided the entire Table should attend.

"You want to go to a *fraternity*?" Justa questioned.

"Were we invited?" Gil asked, confused.

"Okay." Kendall was agreeable—although mostly interested in the red velvet cake that was the dining hall's concession to the holiday.

Scott was not agreeable. "Crystal, I have a date."

"We won't interfere," Crystal promised. "She won't know that we're there. But this is our senior year—except for Kendall. And there'll be *dancing*."

"You're supposed to wear costumes," Scott let her know.

"I can take care of that"—Crystal immediately had a plan. She didn't finish her cake; instead she dashed upstairs to grab her keys and wallet. She sped to Macy's where she bought four red polo shirts, all grabbed from the same rack. That took forty-five minutes. She spent the next half hour cutting large white hearts out of construction paper. She wasn't handy with scissors, but the intended shape was recognizable. When she joined Justa, Gil and Kendall in Justa's room, they greeted her with various degrees of hilarity.

"Here's Crystal, the pod person!" Gil announced as she came through the doorway.

"The *Greek* pod person," Justa amplified.

Kendall dropped his shoulders with an exaggerated sigh. "We have to crash the bash," he said lugubriously.

Crystal clipped off shirt tags with Justa's scissors. She dropped a shirt in each lap. When Gil held his up, she saw: it was wide enough that both he and Justa could fit inside. Crystal had unwittingly bought extra extra large. Hilarity rose higher, but she soldiered on. She gave them each a paper heart. She gave them each a red marker. She instructed, "Write your love's name on your heart, and I'll pin it to your back."

Having a task settled them down some.

Gil surrounded 'Justa' with a heart shape made of numbers. "The golden mean," he explained.

Justa surrounded 'Gil' with a heart of quarter notes.

Crystal wrote *La Table Sur L'Arbre*.

Kendall found a black marker on Justa's desk, and with red and black drew something that looked like a square-shaped bracelet made of dots. "Rhombohedral SiO_2," he lectured. "Alpha-quartz silicon dioxide to those of you who never got past Geo 1."

They had become Crystal's red polo-shirted, white-hearted team—which was never her intention, but she appreciated their forbearance. She chivvied them around the lake to Zeta Psi, where they showed themselves off to Scott. His only costume was an Abraham Lincoln stovepipe hat; he pretended to be envious of their shirts. The band, Kingfish, had set up in the fraternity dining hall. With all windows and doors opened wide, music flowed down the lawn to the lake. Scott danced with the team before he left them for Dorothy of Oz. Then Crystal danced a medley of Kendall, Gil, and Justa. She danced with the three together. She danced by herself. The nip in the air didn't matter, only the dancing. Just before the moon rose, Kendall took a breather to stand on a bench and point out the stars: Betelgeuse, the Hunter, Orion's belt. "I will sleep on *La Table Sur L'Arbre* tonight and dream of infinity," he declared.

> *To those friends four*
> *I wish to make it clear:*
> *Each holds my heart—*
> *All ineffably dear.*

After

When Crystal woke with a jerk the day after, she felt oddly bereft—of melody, of the touch of cool light. Those were her last memories: the sound of Kendall's recorder traveling at the speed of moonlight, her curtains turning silver.

"C-C-C-Crystal." It was Justa's voice that had awakened her.

Crystal blinked her eyes open. Justa's face, above her own, was unnaturally white. The light was dim, but still... Justa's complexion had somehow become bleached to the color of a daybreak ghost.

"Are you okay?" Crystal was immediately concerned.

Justa's head shivered. From neck down, though, she was tight and still—frozen solid. Crystal pushed herself up. The front of Justa's blue jacket was dark and heavy. Justa's arm loosened; she put a hand on Crystal's Princess phone; where Justa touched, the white plastic turned red.

Crystal pushed to her knees. "You're hurt!"

Justa dialed three numbers. "Help." She spoke the word into the phone, not to Crystal. "Stanford. The lake. Behind Lagunita."

Crystal reached out her own arms. "Show me!"

But Justa didn't display her wound. Instead, she whipped around and darted through Crystal's still-open doorway.

Crystal pulled on her slippers. She grabbed her robe, snatched her car keys—just in case—and ran. Justa was no longer in the hallway. But from downstairs, at the bottom of the enclosed stairway, the security door creaked. Crystal took those stairs two steps at a time. She pushed open the door, heavy steel. Outside, her Nova sparkled with dew. She looked left and right before looking upward. Justa stood beyond the unofficial parking lot, on the rising path that led to the lake.

A police siren dopplered, coming closer, arriving fast.

"Justa?" Crystal called, terrified.

A university police car rounded the side of the dorm. It bumped over rutted dirt to a stop. A uniformed policewoman hopped out, toward Crystal. "Did you call?" she asked.

"She did." Crystal pointed to Justa.

A firehouse emergency vehicle rounded, bumped, and slammed to a stop. Gil burst out. Two other men followed. Gil sighted up Crystal's finger. "Justie?" Gil was running up the path, reaching for Justa exactly as Crystal had done. But exactly as before, Justa turned away. She fled, pushing her head forward and spearing herself into the air—as if cutting a direction for the others to follow.

So they did, all of them—Gil, two men, the cop, and Crystal. They rushed around the lake. All but Crystal crashed through the poison oak at Kendall's campground. Crystal automatically stopped. How many times— dozens?—had she stood in this same spot, waiting for somebody to lead her safely in? She was allergic; her feet held her back. She heard clips of speech from competing voices. She smelled something musty-sweet, like wet metal. She heard a ripping noise, as if a seam was being torn.

And then Justa screamed—anguish metamorphosed into molten sound.

"Catch her." That was the cop's voice. There was a crackling, some static, and the woman enunciated—as if to make her message especially clear— "PC 187. Black male. Early twenties. Apparently bludgeoned."

Bludgeoned? For some reason, Crystal couldn't define that word.

"Crystal." Gil was half carrying, half pushing, Justa through the poison oak. Crystal took Justa into her arms. Justa's face was all circles and holes: emptiness for a mouth, darkness for eyes.

"Kendall?" Crystal dared, but was afraid to ask.

But Gil was gone again, and Justa not answering.

As if Justa were a child, Crystal eased them both down to a sit. She wrapped Justa within her own quilted bathrobe. Justa's blood—no, not Justa's, but Crystal did want to think any further—stained the pink nylon.

The cop said "...sedative..." and Gil re-emerged.

"Let's go," he ordered. He was all grim purpose and hardened neutrality. This must be what he was like as a fireman. He urged Justa back onto her feet. He propelled her down the path to the parking area. Crystal stumbled behind. Gil stopped at the Nova. "Where are your keys?"

They were in the red-sticky pocket of Crystal's bathrobe. She was now anointed with blood, too.

Gil plucked the keys from her hand. "We're going to the hospital. Get in."

Crystal got in.

They couldn't yet leave; they had to wait for two screaming police cars to come to their own jolting stops. Sheriff's cars from Santa Clara County. Crystal read the words on the cars very carefully. She needed to be careful right now. Extremely.

Gil was taking too much care. He drove too slowly. He should rush, hurry, so they would be out of the way when an emergency team sped Kendall to the hospital. But...

"Justie," he murmured. "Justie."

Outside the windows, Stanford was waking up. That was a laundry service van going by. Groundsmen were mowing. The hospital loomed ahead. Gil was taking an ordinary route to the emergency room, not the ambulance road. He was parking.

Crystal had to help get Justa out of the car and into the hospital waiting room. She had to sit in an airport-style chair, designed so people wouldn't touch each other. She sat all alone. Gil was beside her, and Justa beyond that, but Crystal was lonelier than she had ever been. The loneliness was an aching that started in her toes. It moved up through her feet, her calves, her knees. It pushed higher: up her thighs, into her stomach, toward her chest. It scooped out her innards, thrust her organs up her throat.

Crystal dropped her face into her hands. If she couldn't see, she wouldn't have to know. She wouldn't have to taste the searing reflux.

She halted all knowing.

❧

"Justa Matthews? We'll take her."

❧

"Can you tell us..."

❧

"I'm Detective John Stevens."

❧

"What exactly did you see?"

Somehow, time jumped and Crystal stood at the entrance to Lagunita Court. She stood beside forsythia bushes thick with blooms, wearing—she didn't want to look down—her nightgown, robe and slippers. What she wanted, more than anything else, was a long, LONG shower. She ran with her eyes averted from human contact. Upstairs, her hallway was blessedly quiet. Her door still stood open.

She skidded into the shower room. Without watching her hands, she removed nightgown, robe and slippers, and shoved them into a waste bin. She stepped into a stall, turned on the water, and waited to become clean.

The hallway slowly awakened; girls came into the shower room chatting and laughing, starting their days. Nobody spoke to Crystal, because she was protected by water. She stood beneath that protection until her skin felt tight enough to split. Then she waited longer, until all the girl noise was gone. When she shut off the flow, she stood dripping. She had no towel. She shed drops behind her as she sped down the empty hallway to her open door.

Once she was dry, she didn't know what to do. In her mirror's reflection, she was naked. She pulled on a leotard; it held her body together. Leotards were comfort. Leotards meant dance. She picked up her gym sack.

She ran across the street to the dance studio. There she switched on lights to make the bell-shaped windows dim, pushing away that world beyond with electric brightness. She grabbed a tape and shoved it into her recorder. Crosby, Stills, Nash and Young's *Déjà Vu*. She danced against beat, drive, emotion. She danced while her hair almost dried, and then again slapped wet against her cheeks. She danced her way to the edge of an abyss and there, on the precipice, she kickturned, staying in place, spinning up courage. Like Orpheus, she would descend. Like Orpheus, she would try.

She stopped—she had to. Her throat was as raw as strep. She needed rest and fuel before continuing. She looked for water and saw Scott sitting on the floor before the mirrors. She hadn't heard him come in. She had forgotten he existed.

Again time jumped. Or maybe it was she who leapt. She found herself sitting cross-legged on Scott's lap, with the top of her head burrowing into his chest. His arms were tight around her. The water that dripped from her hair onto the back of her neck was partly her sweat, partly his tears. They mingled.

> *I didn't see your inner elbow,*
> *the tender back of knee,*
> *the intricate fold of cerebellum*
> *thrown out upon the leaves*
> *like a scattering of meat*
> *to tempt the shy and hungry fox,*
> *the lost and wandering hound,*
> *the friend-forsaken coyote*
> *now clawing at the heart strings*
> *that forever noose its neck.*

JJJJJ

Deposition

Justa sat in a windowless room in the fire station. She had work to do: important work. She was busy wrapping herself, surrounding her body—her ears—with something to block out sound. That something was nothing, no-thing, a non-existent batting like whatever was in the walls around the music building practice rooms. Nobody saw what Justa was doing, not even Gil who persisted in holding her hand. He didn't know that layers of nothing had begun to separate his fingers from hers.

"Describe it, please," the detective said. "The disarray." Because of the batting, his voice had no cadence. No up, no down. Only moving forward. One word stepping after another. That is what the no-thing did: it erased the depth of sound. Justa only had to hear the surface.

She could reply. "There was Kendall's sweater. His books." Interestingly, her voice likewise held no music. All she pronounced was a linear array of words. That was good. "They were thrown into the dirt, tangled with leaves."

"What else did you notice?"

"His recorder. I didn't see his recorder." In that moment—for that one, single instant—Justa felt her feet pushing down on the softness of decades-deep mulch; she smelled a stench that made her think of menstrual periods.

She gasped. Her body jerked. The detective shoved a plastic basin between her feet. Justa bent until her head was level with her knees. She opened her mouth and let flow sour bile, chunky with last night's carrots. When the push into her throat subsided, she sat up again.

Gil was holding a glass of water, but there was more she had to say. "I saw a pool of darkness on the ground." Her stomach turned over; another push, but she held it down. "I called his name." She couldn't risk saying the name. Not out loud. "He was asleep. He was in his bag."

"Justie..."

Why was Gil saying *her* name. And this was something else interesting: Gil's voice, her voice, the detective's voice, were all in the same key. Which was to say, no key. The nature of sound, what made it expand beyond life, was the infinity of variability. Now all that was erased.

"Let her talk," the detective told Gil.

"I stood on tiptoes so I could shake his shoulder." Justa had only meant to wake him up. "His shoulder was both sticky and slippery. My hand slid down into some..." Her hand of memory too easily touched what had been spongy and soft. What felt like... "Meat!"

"You've asked enough." Gil was putting his arms around her.

"Just a few more," the detective insisted. "Miss Matthews, did you hear anything."

"No." This was a point she hadn't appreciated until now: there was no sound track to her memories—not even the rhythm of breathing. Not her breathing, not...

"And then you..." The detective wanted her to fill in a blank.

"Ran. I ran for help." Not for hopelessness. She needed to make that fact clear. "I didn't know until the firemen ripped his bag open. Then I... It was his arm." The arm that protruded from the rip in the sleeping bag. An arm that was stiff, not limp like a body being rescued. That's when Justa had screamed.

She screamed again now, tonelessly.

Gil was shaking. He made her body shake.

"Okay, okay." The detective was obviously trying to turn the sound down. "Take her back to her dorm. We'll need to talk to her again. But not until later."

Gil could hardly stand.

Justa could re-wrap herself against the world.

She supported him up.

Facts

Kendall died on February 15, 1975, between one and two a.m.

He was killed by a depressed fracture of the left temporal bone, causing fragments of skull to penetrate the brain, causing massive bleeding into the brain.

Also:

The left side of his face was lacerated and contused.

His right shoulder was fractured and contused.

His neck was lacerated and contused with a cervical fracture at C4.

He was killed by a piece of 2x4 lumber that had been left over from the building of the table.

He had been found on his stomach, head turned to the left, away from the assailant. He suffered no injury to the right side of his head, or the front of his body. He had likely been asleep when the battering began. He had likely never woken up.

On February 16, a twenty-nine year old White male named Mark Cunningham went to the Free Clinic in Palo Alto with a massive case of poison oak. His T-shirt was illegible because of blood. He wore an Eddie Bauer down jacket similar to Kendall's now missing one. Cunningham claimed he remembered nothing from the night of February 14-15 because he had been on a really bad LSD trip. His worst ever. He was held for questioning.

Memorial

A week and a day later, on Sunday afternoon, Justa, Gil and Crystal took over the end of a side pew in MemChu. Justa hadn't wanted to be here, but the others thought it important they attend. So here Justa was.

The Kendall Soames Memorial Committee—who were those people?—were assigning seats up near the dais. They assigned a pew seat to Scott, who was wearing a suit.

A pounding of feet, and the Black Student Union surged into the chapel—dozens of them. Justa knew some from the chorus. Most of the guys wore a black glove on one hand. The BSU poured down the center aisle, then divided to take over the pews behind Scott.

More footsteps, more people, and the church was filling. Warmth exuded from the bodies behind Justa's back. "I think all of Roble and Lagunita are here," Crystal whispered. A man wearing the white-throated robe of a preacher entered from a side door beside the pulpit; he ushered two people to the very front row. A Black woman; a White man. Surely Mrs. and Mr. Soames. Justa couldn't see their faces, only their sides and backs. Mr. Soames walked like an automaton.

Crystal passed Justa a program. First, the man with the preacher's collar—the Dean for Religious Life—climbed up to the pulpit and read a poem. Then the University President mounted the lectern, from where he described a university in grief. Afterward, five people arranged themselves on the dais. Justa knew the soprano, the alto, the bass. The other two proved to be second soprano and tenor. They sang three movements from Bach's Mass in B Minor. By the time the first kyrie hit Justa, it had become a warpage of sound waves traveling down the nave of the church.

Next, the chairman of the Geology department spoke. He tried to make a mild joke about how difficult it was to find a well-rounded engineering type: Kendall had been the exception. Nobody laughed.

Scott was the final speaker. He too stood at the lectern—which was really a statue of an angel holding a reading board over its head. He told the Pelé story, and how Kendall had loved that spot by the lake. Scott spoke slowly and steadily. He took a cloth handkerchief from his breast pocket and used it to wipe his eyes, his cheeks. After he finished, he blew his nose, the sound of which became amplified. When he left the angel's embrace and walked down the aisle to take a place beside Justa, his steps echoed in a respectful hush.

Then Cheryl stood up from where the BSU sat, and began singing acapella.

Her contralto arrived like a sword of truth and life; it pierced Justa's eardrums. All that was left of Justa's ears were jagged corners that hurt, hurt, hurt. "'And grace will lead me home'," Cheryl sang. Justa tried to shove Cheryl's voice down into a spot of nothingness, like where the Mass had ended. But the voice consumed too big a space. It ascended, rising above the church's stained-glass windows.

Justa started to rise, to flee. Crystal grabbed the back of her coat. "Sit," Crystal hissed.

"'Will be forever mine.'" Cheryl had ended, but her voice still hung beneath the timbered ceiling—as if waiting.

"Mrs. Soames asked especially for you," Scott whispered.

Justa had to sit through the Dean's closing poem. She had to stand for the recessional. Then she had to go to another historic building—the President's house, designed by Mrs. Herbert Hoover. The exterior of the Hoover House was no more ugly, no less beautiful than Mrs. Stanford's Mem-Chu.

Inside, trays of cookies, fruit, and small sandwiches had been set out in a large dining room. A student server poured punch into glass cups. Crystal and the boys helped themselves to refreshments, but Justa only wanted to do what she had been forced to wait to do. Alone, she entered an enormous living room where she joined a small crowd. Mr. and Mrs. Soames sat on a sofa in the crowd's midst. Mr. Soames' voice was loud. Mrs. Soames' was a murmur during his silences. Justa moved forward as people in front of her moved away, and other people pushed from behind. When she finally got to the sofa, she held out her hand to shake, and said, "Hello. I'm Justa Matthews."

Mrs. Soames covered Justa's hand in both her own. "Justa. Thank you," she said, and Justa couldn't help but listen for Kendall. He was in the cadence. He was in the kindness. "Kendall once told me that you were the center of everybody's heart."

Justa stopped breathing. She couldn't bear the responsibility.

"My dear Mrs. Soames." A woman elbowed herself around Justa; Mrs. Soames loosened her hold; Justa was jostled backward, expelled from the crowd. The living room opened into the front hall; she looked longingly to where her coat hung. But if she left now her friends wouldn't know she had done so. They would search for her. They might make a fuss.

So instead she hid in one of the curves of a circular staircase. She chose a spot from where she could see down, but where no one would see her unless they looked straight up. She crouched. She had once seen a squirrel crouch exactly this way, moments before being hit by a car.

"Hi."

She didn't know the voice.

"You okay?"

She didn't have to answer.

"Can I get you something?"

One of the BSU guys was staring up at her. She didn't know him. She had never seen him before the memorial.

"It's crap, isn't it." He sighed and took a seat below her feet. "The university is trying to show how inclusive it is. Show they support Black Americans. Hah! That's why they're making such a deal out of that poor guy's death. I wonder if it's what he would have wanted."

"No." Justa was so certain, the word escaped from her mouth.

The BSU guy nodded agreement. "We were there out of respect. Cheryl didn't know him, either, but it was her idea to sing."

Justa closed her ears against the memory; she clutched her body around her soul. Even so, she heard the BSU guy stand, descend a step. A few seconds passed before he mentioned, "Somebody said you're the music one."

Justa couldn't bear to answer.

"Okay, then," he said gently. And left.

Sounds

Three months later, Justa was preparing for her senior recital. Last September, when she and Kath chose this day, Justa had been excited—already nervous. Today she felt numb.

She stood unmoving while Crystal walked a circle around her. Weeks ago, Lowry had sent Justa a special recital dress. Justa had only now tried it on.

"Pretty," Crystal judged. "But too big."

The dress was Justa's correct size. She must have lost weight.

"And way too long." Crystal clucked at the wrongness. "Wait here." She left, then returned with two dictionaries of matching size: French-English, English-French. "Stand on these." She crouched and upended a small box of safety pins onto the floor. "Don't move." She started pinning up the hem.

Justa remained still. Her sink closet door was open. In the mirror she could see the high-waisted, dark red velvet bodice; creamy lace sleeves; the beginning of a long, cream-colored muslin skirt.

Crystal, at the bottom of the skirt, scooted herself around, hemming every few inches or so. "If I even it out about right here," Crystal muttered to herself.

Justa had more gifts to wear. Mom and Dad had stopped by earlier, on their way to the Knoll where Mom was setting out food for a reception. Mom had given Justa a shoebox wrapped in pink paper and tied with a bright red velvet ribbon. The dark red leather pumps inside exactly matched the bodice of Lowry's dress. "Lowry told me what to buy." Mom was as excited as Justa should have been. "And where to buy them. Aren't they gorgeous!"

Dad had handed Justa a palm-sized, black velvet box. He cleared his voice. "Gumps keeps records." It was he whose nerves were jangled today. "Color's the same as Edith's gems." Inside, beneath the black velvet top, lay a ruby pendant and gold chain.

Now Crystal was finishing up at Justa's feet. "Perfect!" Crystal congratulated herself. She pushed her unused pins back into their box. She rose, stepped back for a fuller view. "Next, jewelry."

Everybody was trying so hard.

Up at the Knoll, Gil stood on the sidewalk like a signboard, gesturing for people to drive around to the side of the building. Scott, in charge of the parking lot, pointed Crystal to a spot near the door.

Kath waited for Justa in the entry. "Finally!" Kath sighed out, even though Justa wasn't late. But Kath was bouncing on her heels; her freckles were practically popping on her face. Justa had never seen her so wound up.

A touch of cool air reached Justa's back, and Kath called out "Hello!" as if rescue had arrived. Justa turned to see Dr. Weber blowing in. Exactly like four years ago, his unbuttoned raincoat flapped like wings. He was a memory, unbidden.

"My dears." He leaned over the bouquet he held to kiss Justa's cheek, then Kath's.

Mrs. Hudson, from high school, entered next. "I'm so proud," she caroled. Another memory.

"Go, go!" Kath shooed Justa and the teachers into the recital hall.

Hiro was already there. He stood up from an audience chair. "Little girl," he said, and the warmth of his voice almost breached Justa's numbness.

But—"Go!"—Kath motioned Justa toward the piano.

The piano teachers sat themselves down like triplets. Mom and Dad left the adjoining parlor to sit beside Hiro. Gil, Crystal, and Scott, who had saved seats in the front row, came in breathless and last. Scott reached for Crystal's hand; Crystal put her other hand on Gil's arm.

"Are you ready?" Justa's page turner, a junior music major, whispered.

"Beethoven's Piano Sonata Number Twenty-Five in G Major," Justa informed her audience. She took the bench, lifted her hands above the keys, and began. Last year No. 25 had been her favorite piece. Today, it was three short movements that she sped through.

People applauded.

"Franz Liszt, *Bénédiction de Dieu Dans la Solitude,*" she announced in Crystal-coached French.

She and Kath had chosen this piece together. Last September the *Bé-nédiction* had been one step above Justa's playing level. She worked on it all autumn, through the first half of winter, until it made her feel as though she were lying in a wildflower meadow, watching the sky. Or sometimes dancing around a waterfall.

There was no waterfall, no meadow now. In substitute, the piece had become easier to play since last February. It turned out that when Justa stopped channeling emotion, her fingers found technical challenges to be less difficult: the abundance of sharps; the rapidity of the rolling chords; the extra stretching of her hands. Without the intrusion of feeling, she could speed through this piece, too. She finished the *Bénédiction* in seventeen minutes.

It was over. Finished. She could finally bow to mark an end. Kath looked crushed; the two other piano teachers looked worried. Gil, Crystal and Scott remained connected, tense, not loosening. Hiro put his hands together in a slow, compassionate beat. Mom and Dad clapped wildly.

Six presentation bouquets from six different people. Crystal carried them away so Justa could be kissed more easily. As soon as was possible, she excused herself for the restroom. There she created noise by flushing the toilet and opening a faucet. There she allowed herself to breathe deeply, heavily—her torso finally filling out her dress with air. When she left the restroom she overheard—she didn't see—Dad talking to Dr. Weber.

Dad, with worry, "What happened? Did she miss a lot of notes?"

Dr. Weber, kindly, "Not enough to matter."

Dad, "Then what?"

A pause, during which Justa's bodice again collapsed against her body.

Dr. Weber, carefully, "I think that every piece asks a question. Every piece seeks to find the answer. This is what your daughter failed to do."

Dad, bewildered, "What question?"

Dr. Weber, simply, "What is the name of God?"

It was a sucker punch. Justa bent over her stomach.

But then she was being grabbed by Crystal, pulled into the parlor, handed a drink by Scott, pushed into conversation with guests to whom she had previously paid no attention: other music students, people from the chorus, residents from Lagunita Hall. The social part of her recital—perhaps because Mom had provided so much food—lasted forever.

∾

She didn't want to be taken out to dinner. "I'm already full," she told Mom and Dad, although she hadn't eaten much. She negated Crystal's assumption that she would return to Lagunita in the Nova, "No." Something about the way she said that word made even Gil back off.

She walked alone to the lake. Disguised in gifted finery, she stood on the shore. She looked across the evaporating lake bed to where Kendall had died.

The name of God. Is that what music was? She listened: to everything she had ever heard, to everything she had ever played. Her fingers refound their now-trained movements of the *Bénédiction*.

In silence, she could ask. In silence, she might find the answer.

In silence, she found a naught.

She wept.

LLLLL

What Lowry Found

Lowry's first glimpse of Dad, as she emerged from the jet bridge in San Francisco, told her that things at home were far worse than she had known. Dad grinned, of course. He waved his hand. But his features looked like hills and craters on his face. And when he hugged her, he grasped—as if she were a life preserver.

"Dad?" She wriggled out of his arms so she could see his face again. "What's wrong?"

"Justie." He swallowed, a massive movement of his Adam's apple. And then he began to talk. He talked non-stop as they found Lowry's luggage, got to the car, while they drove home. He told how he and Mom had learned about Kendall: Crystal, barely comprehensible through tears, had called them. Justa, through Crystal, had said she didn't want them to come to Stanford. Justa, through Crystal, had said she didn't want to go home. That first week they called every evening, but Justa wouldn't speak with them directly. They didn't hear her voice until the evening after the memorial. And then, Mom said, it sounded as if someone had squashed it flat.

None of this was new to Lowry. But when Dad began telling her things that hadn't passed over the phone line to Skywatch, she became incensed, and then cautious: "All Mom told me about the recital was that the dress I sent was 'elegant'." In retrospect, that information was so blatantly meager.

"What with your exams and everything, we didn't want to worry you," Dad confessed.

"Did Justie blow it?"

"Something went wrong with the music. 'Technically fine, emotionally absent.'" Dad sounded as if he were quoting somebody.

"Is Justie going to graduate?"

"Yes," Dad clutched the steering wheel as tightly as he had clutched Lowry.

"Then why," Lowry had never, *ever*, thought she would ask Dad this question, "are you scared?" Because that's what she felt from her father—fear.

Dad slowed, he stared straight ahead while other cars passed him. One honked. Dad stayed glued to his lane. "Your mother and I," he told the windshield, "we don't know what to do."

⌒

The next day, Sunday, was Justa's graduation day. In the car, all the way to Stanford, Dad told anecdotes about Lowry. "When we went to *your* graduation..." The stories seemed to cheer him. Mom didn't say anything more than "Oh, my" and "Do you remember, Low?"—as if she were holding herself together with a paste made of flour and water.

Lowry was spooked.

It wasn't until they had parked and climbed up the football stadium bleachers that she began to relax. Here, beneath all the sun and air, endless possibilities awaited. Lowry had been too excited, at her own graduation, to listen to the commencement address. But today Professor Moynihan, from Harvard, spoke on 'Can the System Work?' Trey had once said that he and Lowry were legal bookends: profit, nonprofit. He was working within the system, she trying to change it. It was a picture of their relationship that she liked.

Mom and Dad looked better in the outside freshness, too. After the speeches ended Lowry said, "Why don't you wait up here while I go get Justie? It's a madhouse down there." On the field, graduates were out of their chairs and flinging their caps as hundreds of attendees converged toward them. Lowry converged by going down a few dozen steps, sliding under a railing, dropping over a barrier, and landing on the track. She zigzagged through a maze of empty folding chairs. She pushed through groups of happy families. She finally stood, precariously, on a chair so as to look out over heads. She eventually spotted Crystal's hair, glowing platinum in the unrelenting sunlight. Once Lowry located Crystal, it was easy: that was Gil's profile; that was Scott with his mortarboard still on; and that was the crown of Justa's head.

"Hey!" Lowry shouted. She waved. They neither heard nor saw her. She carefully got off the chair. She resumed pushing through clumps of people. "Justie!" she called.

Justa turned.

What Lowry had seen on Dad's face at the airport was a pale reproduction of this: sallow skin that yellowed in shadow and bleached gray in the sunlight; sunken cheeks; a mouth falling downward at the corners, as if pulled by gravity; big circles beneath the eyes; eyes that were frighteningly dim.

Finally Lowry understood. "Oh, Justie." She put her hands on Justa's shoulders—so thin. She moved her hands upward to gently cup Justa's face. To do so she had to brush away hair that seemed at once unwashed and too dry.

"It's going to be okay," Lowry promised.

What Lowry Decided

Lowry closed the door to Mom's and Dad's bedroom, ensuring solitude. The first person she called was Trey. Their conversation went something like this:

Lowry (anguished): Things are so much worse than I knew. I have to help.

Trey: Okay. How long will it take?

Lowry (because she fears it to be true): The rest of the summer.

Trey: You've gotta be kidding.

Lowry (immediately and unaccountably incensed): You didn't come for Christmas because of your grandfather!

Trey: That's different!

Lowry (still furious): How?

Trey: Whoa. Let's think this through.

Lowry (dropping her chest over her knees, suddenly despondent): I already have.

Trey: No, I don't think so. What will you be doing in California? I mean, other than helping your family?

Lowry (resigned): I'm going back to my old job at The Emporium and I'm taking Justa with me. I have to get her doing something.

Trey (putting on his best lawyer voice, so compelling): You're making a *huge* mistake. When future employers see that you spent your summer working at a department store, they're going to think you couldn't cut it in law school—that you're a lightweight, a flake. That you're not serious about the law.

Lowry (desperate, but determined): I have to, Trey. Justie's nightmares—they're ghastly. They wake us all up. And she isn't playing music. Not on the piano. Not even on her radio.

Trey: It's your parents who should be doing something.

Lowry (sitting up again to better share her perturbation): They're as stuck as she is. They're pathetic, Trey.

Trey: Let them get help from somebody who's qualified. Like a psychiatrist.

Lowry (echoing a position statement she has heard her entire life from Dad, Mom, even Aunt Edith): Our family doesn't need psychiatrists.

Trey: Make them start!

Lowry (deciding to not reveal the second part of the position statement—'We take care of our own problems'): It's not that easy.

Trey (his voice swooping into the pleading tones of a lover): And what am I supposed to do? Go a whole summer without seeing you?

Lowry (weeping, choking): You can ask for a long weekend, come out for a quick visit.

Trey: I'll try.

Lowry hung up the phone. She didn't have any tissues. She used the front of her T-shirt to mop and blow. She had ended the conversation sitting perched on the very edge of the bed. Her arms, shoulders and back were rigid, her leg muscles tensed as if preparing escape. Escape to where? She was stuck.

She must make two more calls. Another hard one, to the Housing Initiative, telling them she would not be returning. A much easier call to Pamela Brightwell, who was going to be thrilled. Pamela was working at Durham Legal Aid this summer, and unfortunately stuck between the June termination of an apartment lease and a September move into a group house with other members of the Black American Law Students Association. Now, instead of bunking with friend after friend, she could sublet Lowry's Skywatch.

Lowry would solve *one* housing problem this summer.

She would have to make a list of things to ask Pamela to send to California.

Oh, shit.

What Lowry Did

Lowry hadn't seen Victor Yamada for ages. When, that summer before Duke, he and Fort came by the house to pick up her trunk, she had had other things on her mind. She hadn't been social. So when he showed up today as they had agreed, in The Emporium's menswear department, she squinted to make certain. Victor was the youngest of his generation—the 'tree Yongsai' as Hiro called them for being so tall. Victor was four or five inches taller than Lowry, and four or five years older. She didn't know him well at all. He had started college when she was in junior high.

Nowadays he was a nice-looking guy whose hair appeared more ignored than tended. He shoved it from his face with an exasperated gesture, and said, "This is totally irregular." He had told Lowry the same last Thursday when she called to ask a favor. Victor was a resident at Langley Porter Psychiatric Institute; it turned out he had no spare time. But Lowry begged long enough to make him agree to change his schedule. Today he insisted, "Your sister knows why I'm here?" Because on this point he had been definite: he would not offer an opinion—diagnosis, treatment, anything—unless Justa consented.

Lowry didn't tell him about Thursday evening when she stood over Justa—trapped her in the bathtub—until the water went cold and Justa agreed to comply. It was the biggest fight they'd had since Justa let Lowry's gerbil loose in grade school.

Lowry simply said, "Yes. Justie's waiting for you. Here's a tie." She had bought the tie so Victor would have something to take to the gift wrapping station where Justa worked. "You'll come back right after, okay?"

"If you weren't Edith's own..." Victor grumbled. But he sighed; he accepted the bag containing both tie and the receipt he would need to get free gift wrapping. "Which way do I go?"

Lowry showed him. Then she spent the next half hour giving people the wrong shirt sizes, ringing up purchases incorrectly, and forgetting to say "Come back and see us soon!"

When Victor returned, she tugged him to the book department which was usually ignored by staff and customers alike. "What happened?"

Victor spoke quietly, and seriously. "Justa was alone. Not doing anything—well, reading a book—but not working. She didn't recognize me at first, but she knew who I was. What on earth did you say about me?" He waited, his eyebrows raised.

Lowry chose her words carefully: "That you're a Yamada. That you're a doctor now. Enough to make her agree." Lowry hadn't told Justa that Victor was a psychiatrist-in-training.

Victor let his eyebrows fall. "Well, we talked. She wrapped my tie." Again he went silent.

Lowry had neither the time, nor the willingness, to share his stops. "So? What did Justie say? What's wrong with her? What am I supposed to do?"

"Supposed to do?" Victor frowned. "I didn't come here to assess you. I came to assess Justa. I can only convey to you what she allows." He continued with almost lawyerly care: "Your sister is suffering from shock and a severe depression. She's willing to take an antidepressant I've recommended. It should help with the nightmares. For talking therapy, I can refer her to a psychiatric social worker in Walnut Creek who I think is very good. Justa says she'll think about the talk therapy."

"I'll convince her," Lowry vowed. "Did you give her the prescription?"

"She said you can take care of it."

Lowry accepted the slip of paper. "Thank you." She wished she could give him something more than a Ralph Lauren tie. "I've been really worried."

"I understand." When Victor smiled he looked briefly like Hiro—except much younger, much taller, and with messy hair.

✐

On the silent ride home that evening, after Dad picked them up from The Emporium, Lowry pulled down the vanity mirror above the shotgun seat to observe Justa. Justa was a sinkhole of depression back there. Lowry put together a to-do list.

Before dinner she called the psychiatric social worker. Check. After dinner she borrowed Mom's car and drove the prescription to Aunt Edith's old pharmacy. Check. Back home, vial in hand, she knocked on Justa's door. "May I come in?" she asked. She took the heavy sigh she heard as a 'Yes' and entered. "I got the pills."

Justa was sitting on her floor, cross-legged, looking out the window and doing nothing else.

"Victor said you agreed to take them."

Justa lifted her arm. Without looking, she pointed to the top of her bureau.

"You promised a doctor who's a *Yamada*."

"All *right*." It was anger and frustration that pushed out Justa's sigh, this time. Which was maybe a good sign.

Lowry relaxed. A little. "And the social worker will see you on Saturday, two o'clock."

"I'm not going." Justa's answer was as flat and certain as a wall.

"We won't tell the parents. I'll drive you." Lowry wasn't above some big-sister bullying.

But, "No." Justa was obdurate.

∾

In the ensuing days, as Justa's nightmares became less noisy, something began to change. It was as if the sinkhole had begun to churn. Rather than being detached and distant, Justa became a constant fug of blame and resentment that rose and fell, and most often wafted Lowry's way.

"No," Justa said when Lowry suggested she take advantage of her employee discount to purchase a pair of shoes to replace those with run-down heels.

"Leave me alone!" Justa said when Lowry offered to plug in Justa's still-unplugged radio.

But, "Thank you," Justa once said to Mom, when Mom poured her a glass of orange juice.

Three weeks into the pill regime, during the drive home, Justa actually offered a statement—to Dad—that she'd had to figure out how to wrap an ironing board for a wedding shower that day. Afterward Dad held Lowry in the garage for a moment to say, "I think your sister's getting better. Do you think so, too, Low?"

Lowry did think so. She also thought this summer was the most frustratingly difficult in her life. And she *still* had to get Justa in to see the social worker. She began making hints coded just enough to exclude their parents. "Let's check out the new Victoria's Secret in Walnut Creek tomorrow, around seven. Okay?"

"No."

"We could go buy candy at Mrs. See's on Saturday, at four."

"No."

"How about a movie. Any movie. Thursday at six."

Mom thought Lowry was sweet for trying to entice Justa into some fun. Lowry was busy developing her own fug. She held it contained until the night Trey said he wouldn't be coming to California because, "We have a full docket, Lowry"—then all she wanted to do was to cry. But she couldn't hide her tears in a pillow because she wasn't yet in bed. Before getting into bed she had to use the bathroom. It was one of those nights when Justa was taking one of her long, long baths. Lowry grabbed what she needed, and flung herself into the bathroom anyway.

"You could knock." Justa slid the shower curtain down its rail so nothing but her feet were visible.

Lowry squeezed way too much toothpaste onto her toothbrush. "You could stop ruining my life." The words spat themselves out alongside the white foam from her mouth. Lowry was aghast.

"*You're* having a miserable summer?" Justa's hand yanked the shower curtain away to reveal her face. "I'm not going to take care of you."

"No, because it's become *my* job to take care of *you*." Lowry couldn't seem to stop.

Justa's face turned sunburn red—which had to be passion, because there couldn't have been much heat left in her bathwater. "I never asked you to!"

"You wanted me to let you crash and burn?" Lowry found she didn't know who she was angrier at: herself or Justa.

"What I wanted—" Justa flung the shower curtain aside and stood, water streaming from her shoulders, breasts, hips. She stamped—once, twice, three times—as hard as she could, sending spray up over the bathtub rim. She reached down and, with hands that hadn't touched a piano for months, scooped up a sprinkle of water to throw in Lowry's direction.

"Here," Lowry's mood somehow reached an inexplicable level of sardonic pity. "I'll help you." She filled her toothbrush tumbler with water from the sink and upended it over her own head. Her cheeks puffed; she blew out, "God, it's cold!" When she opened her eyes, Justa was staring at her.

During that minute of wet darkness, Justa's shoulders had relaxed into mildness. Justa's shoulders had begun to quiver. "All I was going to say"—and Lowry saw Justa was shaking with mirth—"is that I want you to give me some time."

Time. Time in which to change? Or time for the world to change around her? For a moment of confusion, Lowry was stopped still.

"I'll be finished in five minutes," Justa promised.

"Right," Lowry agreed. She rubbed a towel over her head. The floor was a skiddy mess. Leaving the bathroom, her damp feet marked the hallway carpet. Once again she took over Mom's and Dad's bedroom. This time she called a number she had committed to memory in case of emergencies.

"Langley Porter Institute," a woman announced.

"Could you please page Victor Yamada?" Lowry requested.

Victor came to the phone sounding out of breath. "Lowry?" Sounding worried: "Is it Justa?"

"I think Justie's going to be okay, Victor." Lowry had never felt so expansive—relief made buoyant by gratitude. "She laughed!"

What Lowry Arranged

On a Sunday morning in early August, Gil showed up on the Matthews' doorstep. He'd pedaled his bicycle all the way from Berkeley, up and over the hills, coasting down to Moraga. Mom, after opening the door, dragged him inside to start filling him up with water, gazpacho, and a sandwich that featured last night's London broil.

"Justie!" Mom called Justa from her room. Lowry, from her vantage point on top a kitchen stool, got to see how Justa greeted her boyfriend after two months apart.

Justa's smile, while not twinkling, was warm. Gil reached for her, grabbed her, hugged her. Justa hugged back—although not with the desire with which Lowry intended to meet Trey after a summer apart.

"I told my folks I needed to come early, to find an apartment. Want to help?" Gil was hopeful.

Justa nodded.

"We'll both come," Lowry decided suddenly.

"Okay." Gil might have been puzzled by Lowry's entrance into his plans, but he was game. "I'm staying with a guy from the math department until then."

Justa put Gil's food and drink on a tray. She led him out to the patio. Lowry watched all this, and her sudden fraction of an idea expanded into a 'what next for Justa' campaign.

She headed to the garage where Dad was tinkering with his lawnmower. "Gil's here," she announced.

"Oh?" Dad was pleased. "I'll go say hello." With a rag that had been the sleeve of an old Lanz nightgown, he wiped oil from his fingers.

"No." Lowry stopped him. "He's with Justie. Let them have time alone. I thought I'd offer to take him back to Berkeley. Can I borrow your car?"

Dad helped Lowry load Gil's bike into the trunk of the car. They secured it with a bungee cord. All finished, Lowry saw Dad back into the garage and then did exactly what she had forbidden him to do. She walked around the house to the patio. Approaching the umbrellaed table, she announced, "Justie, I need to talk with Gil for a while. Privately."

"Oh!" Justa's surprise was piqued. But—"Okay"—she blew away like something that could have been picked up by a breeze.

When she was beyond sight and hearing, Gil sighed. "It's one of those days when she's hardly here, isn't it?"

"No." Lowry was happy to contradict. "Justie's getting better. Slowly, but it's happening." Lowry took a deep breath; she was about to put her campaign into action. "I think for Justie to continue getting better she needs a change of place. I've got to go back to law school. My parents don't know how to cope. I'm afraid they'll fuss and fret and try to turn her back into a child. I think Justie should go to Berkeley and move in with you."

Gil was gobsmacked.

Lowry gave him a minute. She studied him: thick-lensed eyeglasses; muscles that pushed against a limp linen shirt that was undoubtably L.L.Bean. Gil had spent another summer in a logging camp. Lowry conceived of a wrinkle: "How was Idaho?"

Gil obediently followed her non sequitur. "I killed a lot of trees," he answered. Then, "It helped."

"All cleared out now?" Lowry had to know before going any further. "Not just the trees."

Gil nodded. "Pretty much. Lot of anger in a logging camp. Good place to leave it behind."

Lowry was assured. She pressed: "Justa needs help."

"I know. But"—Gil began to count out objections—"I'm going to be really busy. I don't know how much time I'll have to spend with her."

"Which is perfect," Lowry interrupted. "Justie needs time alone to figure stuff out. That's what she told me. That's what I believe." There was a sadness in Gil's eyes that seemed to go nowhere and everywhere, both at once—where he had been, Lowry prayed never to be. But she didn't stop, she couldn't stop. She was her sister's advocate. "Living on her own—with you—Justie will have to try. Every day getting up, going to work. Coming home to someone who cares about her but won't interfere." Lowry begged: "Do it for her, Gil, please."

"What if it doesn't work out?" he worried.

Lowry understood. Justa could prove disastrous for him. Gil was starting a Ph.D. program. This wasn't a time when his mind should be divided.

So she told him what she believed: "Justie has to learn that she's still got herself. That she still *is* herself. That what she has to do is put herself back together." Lowry paused, regrouped. She asked, "Do you love her enough to try?"

Behind those thick lenses, Gil's eyelids twitched. "Yes," he finally assented.

⸎

Driving home from Berkeley, after a tour directed by Gil's friend, Justa was uselessly silent.

That turned Lowry into a cheerleader: "You'll like Berkeley!"

"Hmmm." Justa was an unimpressed audience.

"You'll be around other kids, not out in the suburbs. Lots going on there!" They were entering Caldecott Tunnel; Lowry risked a glance to her right. Justa wasn't giving a clue as to what she felt. "Oh, come on!" Lowry said, exasperated. "Tell me!"

"All right." And Justa sounded equally exasperated. "Fixing is not something you can do with a screwdriver."

"What's *that* supposed to mean," Lowry demanded.

Justa sort of explained her cryptic remark: "You seem to have appointed yourself to be the screwdriver of my life."

"Well, somebody's got to do something," Lowry shot back.

"Then you can be the one who talks to Mom and Dad." Justa was pert.

⸎

After dinner Lowry cornered Mom in the laundry room. Lowry shut the door, even though there was plenty of white noise from washer and dryer to cover any conversation Dad might hear. Lowry needed to get Mom on board, first.

Mom was folding clothes at the long work counter. Lowry put her hands down flat on the dryer and then pushed herself up, with a twist, to sit. She and Justa used to do this all the time when they were young. It wasn't so easy now. But still, Lowry managed to perch herself where she could enjoy a nice warmth beneath her bottom. Where she could experience the shake and wiggle that made her... That made her miss Trey even more.

Had she felt like *this* when she was young?

Lowry slid down from the warmth and whatever to help Mom. Safer on the floor, she could keep her mind focused. "We saw some nice neighborhoods in Berkeley today," she began. "Safe ones, not wild." She knew how important this information was.

"Really?" Mom was lining up Dad's socks, counting them. "Thirteen," she muttered.

Lowry shook out shirts and trousers—anything a sock might stick to. She found a streak of black against a yellow polo shirt, and handed it over. She considered: how best to penetrate Mom's preoccupation? Lowry decided to go directly to her point. The shock factor might help her case. "I want Justie to live with Gil. I think she should be someplace where she has to take care of herself, do her own laundry."

Mom's abstraction vanished. Lowry had gained her full attention. "Live with Gil?" Mom rolled the words in her mouth as if they came from a foreign language. "You mean, together?"

"Together," Lowry asserted. She said nothing more, but her argument was prepared and ready.

Mom placed her two hands on the counter and leaned forward, as if she needed support to continue this discussion. She didn't look at Lowry when she said, "I have to confess, I've sometimes wondered the same."

Lowry was floored. Her argument sputtered and died. *Butter my butt and call me a biscuit*, she thought. This summer had changed Mom, too. Profoundly. And Lowry hadn't noticed.

After a long minute, Mom nodded her head decisively. "But Low?" She worried, "How on earth are we going to convince your dad?"

Ever since always, one of Dad's favorite jokes had been, "My women are ganging up on me." Today it was no joke.

Lowry entered the living room where Dad was working on a crossword puzzle. He looked up at her, smiled, went back to his fun. Mom, following Lowry, began to busily rearrange magazines on the coffee table. Lowry stood before Dad until he looked up again.

"Low?" he questioned.

"We have to talk about Justie," she told him.

"You've helped." Dad was pleased. He was proud. "She's so much better."

"But she still has a ways to go," Lowry warned.

"We want Justie to return to being Justie," Mom put in.

"What she needs now"—Lowry provided the details—"is independence. But with a friend. I want her to go live in Berkeley. With Gil."

"No. Absolutely not!" Dad was horrified.

"Dan, we think it's necessary." Mom was surprisingly firm.

Dad's expression of horror turned into betrayal. He would never, ever, have expected this. From Mom. Of all people. "But they're not married," he fought back, as if the equation of 'Justie plus Gil plus Berkeley' could only be possible if 'wedding' was stuck in there, too. "Yet"—he sparked some hope.

"No." Lowry immediately squashed that hope. They mustn't lay any more burdens on top of Gil's wounds. "And I don't want you to put any pressure on them."

"People will think..." Dad started.

"This isn't about sex," Lowry interrupted. Although honestly, she hoped—very much—that 'Justa plus Gil plus Berkeley' would naturally evolve into lots of comforting, reassuring, sharing sex. "This is about helping Justie. Gil is still grieving Kendall's death, too. Justie needs to share."

At the reminder of Kendall, Dad's insistence on propriety fizzled down. "Oh, my."

"We don't care what other people think." Lowry gave him a new position statement to mull over—one that might help him rebuild the family identity along another line of pride. "We only care about Justa."

"I don't know, Lowry. I don't know." Dad bowed his head over his worry.

His hair was thinning on top. For a moment Lowry was washed through by a wave of love and sympathy that almost made her want to sit on his lap. She let the feeling pass. But it was with gentleness that she said, "Dad, if we love Justie, we have to let her go. Now."

Dad's face paled with distress.

That's when Lowry realized how much law school had changed her. It was a change that went deeper than an ability to lay out facts, to use those facts as tools of persuasion. It went all the way into how her spine felt standing before Dad, presenting her case. Lowry was an equal, not a petitioner. She was an adult, not Dad's smart girl.

Maybe she was too big for Dad's lap, but she wasn't too grown up to lean down, say, "Thanks, Dad," and kiss that tender bald spot.

~

She couldn't wait to get on a plane and return to North Carolina.

Starting Autumn 1975

CCCCC

"Education is a gift, not a right, Crystal." Mother enunciated, crisply. She stalked up the front steps and through the open front door, her perfectly combed hair, perfectly ironed blouse, and perfectly creased slacks disappearing.

Crystal, by definition, was not perfect. She glared at the scattering of boxes and items on the front lawn. Then at her father. "I don't need any of this stuff." She pointed to the box that held a citrus presser, newly purchased. And the box that held a wok, newly purchased. Mother had whirlwinded through Robinson's Department Store, furnishing an apartment that neither she nor Crystal had ever seen.

"It's how she worries," Far explained.

"It's how she controls," Crystal seethed.

"She came around to the idea of you returning to Stanford." Far pushed his glasses up so he could scratch the bridge of his nose. He sighed. He was so often the middleman in these arguments. "We did agree to pay," he mildly—and fairly—reminded.

For his sake, Crystal tried—but didn't entirely succeed—to be gracious. "Thank you."

Far reached down for one of the bigger boxes. He hefted it. "How about you take this TV as a compromise? It can ride shotgun. I can fit it in your car."

Crystal could manage a concession. "Okay."

Far positioned the TV. Crystal secured her bike to the rack behind the trunk. A few adjustments, and it was time to go. Far kissed Crystal's cheek.

And she drove.

How many times had she taken this route? Highway 55 to Interstate 5. Through LA, and then hours spent in the Central Valley. Enough Central Valley tedium to allow Crystal to wonder: what the hell was she doing?

Just over two weeks ago, the professor with whom she had studied poetry for four years called to ask if Crystal might want to go for a master's degree. Somebody had changed his mind about enrolling in this autumn's creative writing program. "There's a space," Professor Seacat said. "And you can take over his apartment lease, too."

Crystal hadn't known what to reply.

Professor Seacat helped her out: "I know it's last minute. But it will give you a purpose. And a place to put your grief."

Crystal arrived in Palo Alto late in the afternoon. Her new address, Dartmouth Street, was one of a cluster of cottage-lined streets, all named after colleges. A hand-written sign on the door of number 2258 read: 'Drive around back. Upstairs. Key on table.' Around back, up a set of red-painted stairs, a small apartment sat over a carport. Flower baskets filled with fuchsias hung before the apartment's windows. The entry stood open.

Getting out of Crystal's car was a creaky affair; once out, she had to unkink her back. Before unloading anything, she detached her bike from its rack. On bicycle wheels, she rode east. Holding her heart constant against her ribs, she rode onto the Stanford campus. She had to dodge eighteen-year-olds on brand-new bikes. Freshman Week was ending. Tresidder exuded the odor of French fries. *Frites.*

Crystal clutched her heart closer.

Her first stop was Lagunita Court. She remained astride her bike, outside the walls. She breathed in the muskiness of marigolds, the grayness of dust. She didn't go look, but she knew: the lake behind the dorm was always dry this time of year.

The second stop on her pilgrimage was the geology building. There she took an elevator up to the library level. She stepped no further than into the lobby. The library was showing off its collection of maps. One map was a modern mockery: the Atlantic ocean filled with monsters; a caption over an oddly shaped Australia reading 'Here Be Dragons'. The bicycling map of California—1895—showed the state surrounded by sketches of waist-coated gents atop bikes that didn't look so different from Crystal's. And then there was 'The Land of Make Believe'. The cow jumped over the moon. A turbaned figure rode atop a carpet. The dragon, here, looked like a phoenix.

Kendall had once told Crystal that he thought heaven was a make-believe. When had he told her that? In France? At Stanford? Crystal tried to hear him now, but she couldn't remember which language he had spoken in. She didn't think she'd offered an opinion then.

She wished she had an opinion now.

⁓

Back in Dartmouth Street, she remembered to lock her bike up to the post of her new, red staircase. She hadn't locked her car before. She thought to do it now because she removed a package of sheets. The entry still stood open. She only glanced around enough to locate a double bed. Then she lay down, pulling her knees to her chest. She didn't open the package. She didn't shower or change. She closed her eyes.

In the morning her eyes were gritty. Her mouth felt foul. She went down to her car for her suitcases, and because she didn't know which held useful stuff she had to bring them all upstairs. After she brushed her teeth, she took stock of where she was: the bathroom had all that was needed; the bedroom was cramped around the bed; in the front room, a breeze blew in through the windows. She changed clothes before going in search of a grocery. She found a Safeway. Carrying those over-filled paper bags up the red steps wasn't easy. She had to be aware of where she placed her feet.

She had to be aware for the rest of the morning, carrying up boxes and packages. Most of Mother's items she could shove into kitchen cabinets. The TV was, of course, a problem: the only horizontal surfaces available were the desk, the bed, the bookcase, the table, and the minuscule kitchen counter.

Poets used desks; they slept in beds; the bookcase was only deep enough for books, not the protruding end of a picture tube; poets used tables for the overflow from their desks; they did not always cook.

Far had asked for a compromise. Crystal deposited the television on the counter. She did not plug it in. It sat like an unattractive piece of electronic sculpture: one black eye, nine inches in diagonal, reflecting back her face. She scowled; it scowled.

"Mrs. Soames asked for Justa, not for me." Crystal had never said this out loud before, but she could say it to a TV. "Why? Why wouldn't Justa tell me? Justa became a black hole. That recital was awful. Not so much the music... Well, yes, the music. Kendall: ever since, I've been empty too."

Crystal looked back into the eye. At some point she had cast her sight down, probably when she sat at the table. She didn't remember sitting at the table.

"Justa won't share. Scott did. Isn't grief something you're supposed to share? Professor Seacat thinks I need a place to put my grief. Where is that supposed to be? I'm not going to put my grief into Kendall: he's going to stay with me just as he is. He's my memory. I don't have a future."

Crystal was gazing at the table again. Resolutely, she stared at the TV.

"Do you want to hear how I spent my summer? I was the family chauffeur. Driving Bee and Sean around. They're my little sister and brother. Do you know how loud a gaggle of fourteen-year-old girls can be? They like to window shop and eat Balboa bars."

For a moment, Crystal's mouth remembered: chocolate-dipped ice cream on a stick. The imaginary sweetness melted back to nothing.

"Bee's a good kid. She has so many friends. Sean went to Little League, Boy Scouts, birthday parties. *Destination* birthday parties. Mother volunteered me as a chaperone for Disneyland three times. I don't know what she was thinking: that Disneyland would cheer me up? Sean has lots of friends, too."

Crystal squeezed her eyes shut so she would no longer see the mirror image. This was what she was discovering grief to be: an endless reflection of miseries. The bottom of it all was loneliness.

⌒

Crystal's second morning in her apartment, she awakened wearing a nightgown. Her old college alarm clock told her the time was 11:33—which couldn't be right. In the other room, a rental phone took up what was left of the counter, next to the TV. Crystal picked up the telephone earpiece and heard the familiar buzz: Pacific Bell had gotten her deposit. They had given her a new number, pasted on the rotary dial. She dialed the prefix plus 1212, and heard a canned voice say, "At the sound of the tone, the time will be 11:39 a.m." Crystal had slept in for the first time in months. On impulse, she called Justa's number in Berkeley.

No answer.

She had a lot to do. First, figure out where to put her suitcases. The half-coat-half-linen closet might work. It did, pretty much. Yesterday she had simply piled all desk stuff on the desk, shoved her books willy-nilly into the bookcase, and heaped any article of clothing that wasn't already on a hanger into her laundry basket. Today she would organize. She worked hard, employing both body and mind, thinking of nothing else, until four o'clock when she realized that she was holding a book inherited from Lowry. She had Lowry's telephone number, somewhere. She called.

Lowry picked up on the eighth ring. "Hi!" She sounded rushed. "Hold on."

Crystal held on.

"I'm back." Now Lowry sounded like she was mumbling through food. "Mind if I eat?"

"No." And Crystal remembered: she had missed lunch. "What are you eating?"

"Dinner. Pizza. Still warm. I just picked it up."

"I have pizza!" Half of last night's pizza sat in Crystal's fridge. Yesterday she had taken it from the freezer, plopped it on an oven rack, and forgotten about it until cheese dripped onto the burner and sent out smoke. "We'll have dinner together!"

They did. Three thousand miles and three time zones apart.

"What do you have on your pizza?" Crystal asked.

"Anchovies, among other things. I only get to eat anchovies if I have a pizza all to myself."

"All I have is sauce, cheese, and round slices of meat that I think might be pepperoni." Crystal hadn't read the box before she threw it away.

"I think I have the better pizza," Lowry gloated.

Crystal chuckled. She hadn't had so much fun in ages. She said so before realizing how pathetic that statement must sound.

Lowry immediately became serious. "Have you seen Justie yet?"

It was a plummet like on the Matterhorn in Disneyland. "I only got to Stanford day before yesterday. Called this morning. Nobody there. Or nobody answering," Crystal had to say.

"You wouldn't believe what this summer was like," Lowry complained. "I'm still exhausted from it. All I want now is an easy life without anybody asking too much of me. Except for the law. I like digging into the law. Total escape. Sounds weird, I know."

"No," Crystal assured her. "I had a crappy summer, too."

They chewed.

"I miss her." And Crystal revealed her greatest fear: "Sometimes I think she doesn't like me any more."

"Oh, Crystal." Lowry's voice was kind. "It isn't you. It isn't even me. It really isn't anybody. I think Justie's stopped liking herself. I can't explain why, because I don't understand."

"What should I do?" Crystal entreated.

"What she told me," Lowry said dryly, "is that I have to wait. She didn't say for how long."

"Wait for what?"

"I'm not sure about that, either. Everybody wants Justie to return to being what she was before. But I don't know. What happened was really big."

"Really big," Crystal agreed, her throat choking with sadness.

"I'm sorry about Kendall," Lowry said softly. "I mean, for you. I'm sorry for your loss."

Crystal gulped. "Thank you."

"Just wait," Lowry encouraged. "Like me."

> *To J -*
> *Thinking about you,*
> *Hoping you are well.*
> *Wishing you were whole,*
> *And not so grieved.*

I worry about your grief,
Do you know that?
Do you feel my love across miles
Of hope and estrangement?

JJJJJ

And what becomes of harmony, if there is hell?
The Brothers Karamazov

The apartment was near the northwestern corner of the Berkeley campus, easy walking for Gil to get to Evans Hall at all times of day and night, and less than a half mile from the BART station. Justa's salary of $450 a month, plus Gil's graduate fellowship, was only enough to rent a studio that had been remodeled from a much larger apartment's kitchen and dining room. Gil's folding foam mattress, when unfolded, took up most of the dining room floor. The kitchen accommodated a card table. But when the two matching chairs were opened, the stove became inaccessible.

Walking to the station before ten in the morning, or leaving it after four in the afternoon, Justa normally walked in fog. She was glad that Berkeley was a foggy city: fog muted sound. She could gather fog like cotton with which to block her ears. When she descended into the slick-walled station, her ears stuffed full of nothing, the noise that bounced off those walls didn't spear into her brain.

Berkeley's main public library was only a block or so away from the station; once or twice a week she stopped by. Pushing open the library doors, she entered a space made weightless by air and made heavy by marble. White marble floors, marble walls, a marble staircase that went up four stories high. The many-windowed room through the archway to her left was lit by fog. None of the people at those tables ever looked up at her. She was alone. She browsed.

She had begun reading books at her desk in The Emporium the summer before, filling time between customers. Then she borrowed books that were supposed to be sold; she returned them with the spines barely creased. After moving to Berkeley, she no longer had to be concerned about spines. At first she borrowed Jane Austen. Then she read the Brontës. She went up, in alphabetical order, to Colette. Today she was in the D stacks. She chose *The Brothers Karamazov* by Dostoevsky. She had never read a Russian novel before.

She carried the Dostoevsky home where she was surprised to find Gil. He wasn't often in the apartment. Sometimes they were awakened in the middle of the night by a call that said Gil could use the university's mainframe computer. Sometimes he didn't return until ten o'clock the following evening.

On this evening he was preparing toasted cheese sandwiches. He was in one of his the-world-is-so-exciting moods, which Justa found herself closing up against, always. "Professor Sung is trying to see chaos!" he exclaimed as soon as she walked in. Her mind chugged into all the possibilities inherent in that statement. Unrhythmic disharmony? She wrinkled her face into a knot; she tried to squeeze the thought out of her brain.

When she opened her eyes, Gil was studying her with the expression she hated most: the one that spiraled her deepest hurt into fear. It was as if he was learning how to dislike her.

"You weren't the only one who lost Kendall," he said sternly. "I lost him, too."

She had learned, recently, how to comfort Gil in bed. Tonight, after sandwiches, she did so. Their two bodies still fit together with the perfection they had created at Stanford. She allowed her hands to play over his skin. She tried, she really did. Her efforts almost worked—but not completely. She knew where the fault lay: she had stopped hearing the pulsebeat of Gil's song.

⌁

After asking what Justa's work schedule would be for the month of October, Lowry sent a short letter: 'Be ready for Hiro to come get you on the morning of the 28th between 9 and 10. Do Not Stand Him Up! Hiro will be giving up paying jobs so he can take care of you.'

Today was the twenty-eighth, and it was almost nine o'clock. Justa stepped out into one of Berkeley's rare fog-free mornings. Sunlight sparkled off Hiro's windows—he was driving Mikey, the black town car. "There you are, little girl." Hiro stopped, but didn't park. There was no parking anywhere nearby, ever. He leaned toward the passenger side window, speaking loudly enough to cover the sounds of other cars on the road. "Hop in."

Justa hopped.

"Lowry told me to give this to you in private." Hiro tapped an envelope resting on the gray leather between them. Justa didn't recognize the penmanship that spelled out her name. "Wouldn't tell me what it's about. Asked me to take you to the nearest pharmacy. Which is where?"

"That way," Justa pointed.

Hiro grumbled with pride while she tore the envelope open. "As if I wouldn't guess it has something to do with Victor. Something to do with medicine. I mean, my great-nephew is a doctor." His pride segued into concern: "What's Victor got to do with you, little girl?"

"He's giving me something to help me sleep." A half-truth.

Hiro gusted out a relieved smile.

Sunlight blew in through Justa's window. It turned the whipping fronds of her hair copper, gold, chestnut brown.

"That's not so bad," Hiro declared. "I've had to take a little something now and then. Once in a while. I'm glad Victor could help. But you know who I think could really help?"

"Who?" Justa was forced to ask.

"That professor of yours I met at your concert. Not the young woman. That German man. Not that we talked much. But I felt we had something in common: German Jew, California Nisei. Different histories with similarities. And he's a musician, too." Hiro's eyes widened, as if he were catching a thought out of the air. "How about—after we go to the drugstore—I take you to him? He's in Oakland, right? Not down in Stanford."

It was as though a cannon ball punched through Justa's chest. "No," she found the breath to say. "No," this second time, firmly.

"Why not?" Hiro was inspired. "You think your professor doesn't know anything about tragedy? Think again, little girl."

An army—because by now Hiro had become an entire army—was circling, tightening. Had Lowry planned this?

"No," Justa insisted, for the third time.

They were in sight of Compton's drug store—thank god, at last. Along this street, as along most Berkeley streets, cars were parked nose-to-tail.

"Want me to drive around and find parking?" Hiro offered. "Go in with you?" But,

"*No*," Justa said for the fourth and final time. "I can walk back." She managed a tardy, "Thanks, Hiro." She got out and pushed the heavy car door until it thudded shut. Hiro couldn't pause for long in this traffic; he immediately moved ahead. Justa waved at his rear window. She waved him away.

But she felt him—well, really Lowry—at her back all the time she was in the drugstore: while she handed over Victor's refill prescription; while she waited in the chair that had been courteously placed near the magazine stand; while she paid at the counter. Lowry was a wind without breeze, a pressure between her shoulder blades, a force that pushed against Justa's back all the way to the apartment.

⌒

Because she volunteered to work on Black Friday, Justa was allowed to take a vacation day on the fifth of November. She drove Mom's car down Highway 680. Her destination was the Old Courthouse in San Jose. She hadn't told Mom where she was going. Gil, likewise, knew nothing of her plans. Nobody did. Justa had to do this for herself, by herself.

The courtroom she was directed to was small and wood-paneled. Only five people sat on the wooden pews. Justa had wondered if others from Stanford might show up. Kendall's professors? The Black Student Union? None of the five was Black. The only person Justa recognized was Detective Stevens, and she didn't want any conversation with *him*. She chose a pew near the exit, where the detective was unlikely to see her unless he turned all the way around.

When the judge entered the courtroom, Justa shot to her feet along with everybody else.

"Let's get going," the judge instructed the bailiff.

The five other observers sat down, but Justa still stood. She had to see everything perfectly.

What she saw was:

1) A door opening to the judge's left, through which two armed guards brought the collapsed figure of a man.

2) A White man, a small man, whose head was sunk to his chest, whose chest was sunk between his shoulders making him even smaller. Mark Cunningham had bent his neck so deeply his face was almost hidden. As if he was trying to roll himself into nothingness within the blare of his orange jumpsuit. As if he were trying to minimize himself against hate.

"Your honor, if I may approach the bench?" asked a suited man sitting at Cunningham's table.

Justa didn't bother trying to listen in. She tried to see into, through, past the exposed part of Cunningham's neck. His viciousness: where did he keep it hidden?

Her attention was disturbed. Someone was coming into the courtroom late. Justa automatically turned her head to disapprove. A middle-aged woman was arranging herself in the pew opposite Justa's own. A Black woman, the only nonwhite person here. Mrs. Soames? It couldn't be.

"Mr. Cunningham, do you understand?"

Justa whipped to face front. The judge's voice had entered her ears like rolling thunder. He was still frowning his question at Cunningham. Cunningham's attorney, returned to their table, gave Cunningham's arm a push. Cunningham stood.

Now Justa did listen.

"Yes, sir."

It was a doleful voice. Baritone.

"I understand you have pleaded guilty to aggravated assault and voluntary manslaughter. Do you still stand by this plea?"

Cunningham's lawyer said, "We do."

The judge gestured with his hand, as if to wave the attorney away. "I want to hear the accused's reasoning in his own words."

"I remember me." Cunningham's words became thick, as if with tears. "I remember being covered with that kid's blood. He didn't deserve it, that jacket. Why did he have it, and not me?"

The back of Justa's throat seized her stomach. Or maybe it was the other way around. She couldn't tolerate the continued sight of Cunningham's quivering shoulders. He had no right to sadness. He had no right to *any-thing*. To share her anger, Justa glanced toward the latecomer.

Who was, indeed, Mrs. Soames. Justa couldn't mistake the curve of the nose, the firmness of the chin. Justa stared: Mrs. Soames was pressing her hands together, as if in supplication; the tips of her fingers touched her lips. But then her profile crumpled, she bowed her head. And Justa saw an agony ineffably greater than her own.

The judge boomed, subwoofer, "Mr. Prosecutor? This was a particularly heinous crime."

Justa couldn't help but cross the aisle, toward Kendall's mother. From somewhere on the outskirts of Justa's attention, another man spoke in staccato: "Mr. Cunningham has acute hepatic and alcoholic cirrhosis of the liver. His chances of surviving a manslaughter sentence are nil. The victim's family wishes to avoid the ongoing heartache of a trial."

"What?" Justa said aloud. She hadn't yet sat down. The staccato man, now that she looked at him, was a person she had previously thought of as simply another suit.

"All right then." The judge nodded. "Mr. Cunningham, I'm ordering that you be committed to the custody of the California Department of Corrections. You will serve eleven years for voluntary manslaughter and four years for aggravated assault, with the terms of imprisonment to run consecutively."

"That's all?" Justa spoke loudly enough to make people—Detective Stevens—look around at her.

"Come here." Mrs. Soames' soft, clear tones pulled at Justa. Mrs. Soames—still watching the judge, Cunningham, the attorneys—held out her hand.

Justa obeyed. "Are they saying he's not so guilty?" she hissed.

"Shh." Mrs. Soames rubbed Justa's hand with both her own.

The proceedings continued. Justa listened for a while. But the men up front were conferring about details that did not matter. Not to Justa. Mrs. Soames, though, focused on speaker after speaker. Not until the end—not until the judge announced, "This case is adjourned," and exited through his private door; not until the bailiff held the side door open for the attorneys, for Cunningham and his guards—did Mrs. Soames turn her full face to Justa.

Her eyes were brown, not hazel like Kendall's. But the shape of her eyes was exactly his: it was the shape of kindness. "After the prosecutor called to explain what a trial might entail," Mrs. Soames said, "and described the citizens likely to form the jury, I spoke with the defense attorney. I told him a plea bargain was okay." Her voice was a viola to Kendall's cello, her cadence the same.

"Why? Justa keened.

"Because I think forgiveness is the only way to get through all of this. Because I think it's only through our response that we can find any meaning. Don't you agree?"

The question was an impossibility. It was chaos.

Mrs. Soames continued: "Kendall's father feels like you do. He believes in President Johnson's Hate Crime Act. He thinks those laws will guide courts like this one. His hope has never been measured down to the reality that I do, and Kendall did, continually experience. My husband remains naive in that way. And he's furious with me. I don't think our marriage will survive." Mrs. Soames pressed Justa's hand, lightly. "Kendall told us so much about you and Crystal, Scott and Gil. Thank you for being his friends." With that, she let Justa go. She gathered up her purse. Stepping around Justa's knees, she entered the aisle and walked out of the room.

"Miss Matthews?" Now Detective Stevens was coming up the aisle. When Justa didn't respond, he also left.

She stayed put in Mrs. Soames' pew. She waited until only her breath filled the echo of this otherwise empty chamber. With each exhalation, she sorted: even a minimal sentence would ensure death; even a demon could inspire empathy; she had the choice of different directions, beyond blame.

The last was too much for her. She tried to close her ears against that particular exhalation. She couldn't. She halted breathing, and was deafened by her heart. She let her head fall, and saw: her palm was still curved into the shape that Mrs. Soames had pressed it. An arc, perfect for the piano.

**Is there in the whole world a being who would have the
right to forgive and could forgive?**
The Brothers Karamazov

LLLLL

Lowry sat in her favorite spot in Skywatch—beneath a skylight, and in the bright red beanbag chair surrounded by Willow's rug. She had turned the rug into a kind of desktop with law books stacked here, the paper she was writing there, the phone at her side. On her way to her chair, through the desktop, she had to be careful not to trip on the phone line. Right now, she was regarding the ring on her hand. She liked it. No, she loved it! A star sapphire surrounded by tiny diamonds, and with more tiny diamonds continuing partway around the band.

Trey loved her, and this was his proof.

She loved him back. She did. She had said 'Yes' last night after he got down onto one knee, held out a little velvet box, and let his voice fill the library as though it were a courtroom. "Will you do me the honor of becoming my wife?"

The students around them began whooping, shouting. "Do it, Lowry!" "Figure out his income potential!" "Are we all invited?"

Lowry cracked up. She laughed so hard, she almost peed her pants. With all that commotion around her, she had to say yes—just to shut everyone up. She didn't get to say 'Let's discuss this'. Afterward, she and Trey had spent the night together at his place, celebrating. Their celebration was *wonderful.*

She did love him. And she loved him even more when she showed Nancy the ring this morning. Nancy hadn't done all the girl stuff, jumping up and down with congratulations. No. Nancy asked, "Do you know him that well?" Which was a stupid thing to say, given that Lowry had been dating Trey, and Trey alone, since the first summer of law school. Later, when Lowry was having a discussion with Trey—for only an hour, but that was enough—Trey said Nancy was still sore at not having made the *Duke Law Journal.* That was partly right. The only woman to make the *Journal* was Pamela, and all the men students thought it was because Pamela had an advantage for being Black. They conveniently forgot she was brilliant in class.

But back to love. Lowry had always known Nancy wasn't romantic. Look what she was doing to James! Making all her career plans without considering his, and he so in love with her. Who knew how, and where, those two would end up?

Lowry was going to end up in Atlanta, where she had never been. That's where Trey wanted to build his career. Lowry could make friends with his sister, and Trey would help her find a job. Finding a job wasn't going to be as easy as it should be, since Lowry hadn't gotten any legal experience last summer.

The ring was gorgeous. A star on her hand, and—Lowry looked up to the skylight—stars in the nighttime sky.

The sun was beginning to set in California. Lowry should call Mom and Dad. She would, soon. But first she wanted to practice this phone call. It was such a big one. Before Kendall happened, she would have tried the call out on Justa.

Lowry let her engagement ring finger brush against the rug. She and Willow had shared everything with each other from day one. Tomorrow Lowry would mailed off a quick letter to Italy. Willow would surely respond promptly—and maybe in bright colors. Maybe a hand painted note? Lowry felt a catch of homesickness for Willow.

Lowry's other college friendships hadn't continued. Susan disappeared home to Hawaii after dropping a graduation lei around Lowry's neck, smacking a kiss on Lowry's cheek for good luck. And Paul: was he still at Harvard? Harvard had made him work; it would have been like him to give it all up.

A blip of light crossed the skylight. A satellite. Here, then gone.

Justa still had Crystal, despite everything Justa had become. Justa, Justa, Justa. Maybe Lowry's brain was working so slowly because she, herself, hadn't yet recovered from last summer. Lowry needed to tell Mom and Dad about her engagement in exactly the right words so they would rejoice, instead of worry. They were in a habit of worry now. She wanted to give them something to *not* worry about.

What if she called Crystal? Did she even have Crystal's phone number? She could get it from directory assistance. 411. Lowry dialed. She eventually heard Crystal say,

"Oh, my god!"

                                  Frances M. Wood

"Hello to you, too." It felt good to talk to Crystal. Crystal could be fun.

"Okay," Crystal said, as if she were continuing a conversation that had never started. "I took Justa up to Strawberry Canyon last weekend, and she was different. It was like someone had stuck an egg beater inside her, and was turning the handle, fast. She couldn't seem to stand in any one place, or stay on any one topic. I've never seen her like this before. She was talking about her work, and the BART system, about the house across the street from her apartment. And then it all stopped. We heard a rooster call—and you know it was mid-afternoon by that time—and Justa stood stock still, and she said, 'It's calling the day moon out of the fog.'"

Lowry heard her own sigh matched by a sigh from Crystal's end of the phone line. They were in unison. "Before I left for law school," Lowry revealed, "Justie gave me a rainbow. As a going away present."

"Oh–h–h." Crystal exhaled like someone whose heart was soaring from her chest.

"I have something else that will cheer you up," Lowry offered. She really, really, really wanted to talk about herself. Just once.

"Okay."

"I'm getting married!"

"Oh, my god! That's great, Lowry! When?"

Which was exactly what Lowry had wanted to hear. "Next summer, after graduation." Lowry was finally beginning to feel happy. She hadn't realized this, but she must have needed a girl-to-girl reaction. "I'm trying to figure out how to tell my parents."

"'I'm getting married' won't do?"

"I have to say it in such a way that they don't have any doubts. That they can't be anything but happy."

"Oh, right. Justa." Crystal understood, perfectly. "Let me think. This is a big step. Especially since your last guy was Dennis Stillman. Whatever happened to him?"

"Still an outlaw in Mexico, as far as I know."

"Uh-huh," Crystal seemed to be settling something in her mind. Finally, "My thoughts are this: you've finally met *the* guy."

"Yes," Lowry concurred, firmly.

"He's number one in your law school class?"

"Top five."

"Comes from a good family?"

"I'm going to meet them at Thanksgiving."

"We'll take they're a good family as a given," Crystal decided. "He's Emory and Duke, after all. Decent looking?"

"More than decent!" Lowry was briefly offended.

Crystal continued to create her own picture of Trey: "With career aspirations that fit into the bourgeoisie or upper middle class?"

"Well, yes." Lowry couldn't figure where that question had come from.

"The reason I ask is because your last is an outlaw in Mexico."

"Oh, yeah."

"So there you have it," Crystal said, as if punctuating the end of a brief. "You have found an 'eminently eligible man.' That's what my mother calls them. Mothers *love* eminently eligible men. Just get your parents high on Trey's accomplishments, and I think you'll do fine."

This was the boosting that Lowry had hoped for.

⌒

Mom reacted exactly as Crystal had predicted: "Oh, Low, he sounds perfect." Mom's was another girly response.

Lowry laughed. "I used that perfume to good purpose."

"Huh?" said Dad. "What perfume?" He got back into the conversation with "You make us proud." Which filled Lowry's soul with contentment. "It's so good to hear something fine for a change."

"Justie borrowed my car the week before last," Mom excitedly interjected.

And they were back to Justa.

Conversation etiquette required Lowry to ask, "What did she want it for?"

"She said she had to do something for Kendall. Put flowers, maybe, on that...spot? A good sign, don't you think?"

"Yep." Although Lowry didn't have a clue as to what was going on.

"Life is looking up," Dad contributed, merging Justa's success with Lowry's.

When she hung up, Lowry was totally wiped out. She had work to do: she was writing a paper for Professor Guilford. Her pens, a legal pad, were all within reach. She could start reading that book, over there.

Or she could spend the evening watching for a falling star.

A star on her hand. Stars in the sky. She was an engaged woman. She was happy.

Lowry met Trey's parents, Chuck and Elaine, at the restaurant where she and Trey had gone on their first date. Lowry wore one of the two interviewing suits she bought last summer. Elaine was also dressed up, in a navy and yellow wrap dress. Elaine did not shake hands. Perhaps she was one of those women who never shook hands. She had a sweet face. Chuck had a red face, and looked like a dad pulled from his work.

They gathered an hour before their dinner reservation so as to become acquainted. Chuck bought drinks for them in the restaurant's anteroom. Lowry asked for sherry, because that's what Elaine did. And somehow—Lowry didn't know how this happened—she and Elaine ended up sharing one small two-person table while the men took over another table nearby.

To eavesdrop, Lowry had to listen in stereo. While Trey and his dad talked about Trey's future law office in Atlanta, Elaine was all about the wedding.

"Don't worry about a thing, dear," Elaine assured her. "Trey's told us you have to work especially hard this year to make up for last summer. I'm so sorry about your sister. Is she doing better?"

Trey wanted a bungalow office. Lowry would have to get a map of Atlanta. To Elaine's mention of Justa, she replied with what was safest, "Yes."

"And he's told us you want to have a simple wedding during the week before graduation, in Duke gardens."

"Yes," Lowry agreed. Chuck began extolling the benefits of renting in a high-rise.

"I hope your mother won't mind if we barge in here," Elaine's gentle voice flowed like an underground river beneath Chuck's insistence of the convenience of having rent, janitorial, and utility bills all rolled into one monthly check. "But since we live so much closer we thought we might help out."

Lowry's attention spun to Elaine. Whenever Lowry thought about planning a wedding she had a small panic attack.

"That's why I brought these." Elaine reached into a tote bag she had placed on the floor beside her chair. She pulled out three thick magazines. She set them in a pile between the two sherry glasses. The cover of the top magazine showed a gorgeous bride kissing a stunning groom.

"They're all the same." Elaine beamed. "One for us, one for your mother, one for you. I thought you could look through your copy, decide what you want, and then either your mother or we can make it happen."

Gratitude swelled within Lowry—like being pumped with helium. "Thank you! Mom will be mostly interested in the food."

"Does this restaurant cater?" Elaine wondered. She asked the waiter who led them to their table. The restaurant did.

Lowry found she and Elaine had lots to discuss throughout dinner: dresses, flowers, attendants. They talked while eating curried peanut soup, soft-shelled crab salad, roast turkey with pecan-cornbread stuffing, sweet potato patties, green beans flavored with Virginia ham. Elaine winked at Lowry, and mimicked loosening the tie of her wrap dress. Lowry discretely unfastened her skirt button.

"What do you think?" Elaine inquired.

"I'll tell Mom!" Lowry replied happily.

For desert, there was a choice of red velvet cake or chess pie.

This was turning out to be Lowry's favorite year of law school for so many reasons. Trey, of course. But also because she and four other like-minded students had created not one, but *two* ad hoc seminars. The first they titled Utopias from Nauvoo to The Farm (With a Stop at Levittown In Between), for which Lowry got to study history again. She saw history differently now: back at Stanford she had thought of social movements and trends as being happenstances. Now, with a legal mind, she saw such changes as pivots—less chance, more determination—based on choice or policy.

She picked three gowns out of Brides, on pages 37, 106, and 322. Mom approved. Mrs. Grant (Trey's sister, CeeCee) had the gowns sent to Montaldo's Dress Shop in Durham. Ladies with heavy Southern accents surrounded Lowry with comments and measuring tapes. She chose, and was out of there in two hours.

The second seminar they created was Designing the Ideal Planned Community. This class was pure fun. Lots of talk, and lots of sketching on big pieces of butcher's paper. Lowry got to buy art supplies—charcoal pencils, a protractor, compass, and triangles—that felt wonderful in her hands after years and years of punching typewriter keys.

On her next phone call to Elaine, Lowry had page numbers for invitations (only thirty in total, for immediate family and law school friends), announcements (up to two hundred and fifty for everybody else), a cake topper, a cake stand, a cake knife, and a guestbook. Twenty minutes and done.

The seminars were on-campus courses. She loved them. But the course that meant the most to her was the independent study she developed with Professor Guilford. Every other week she drove the Corolla up into the Blue Ridge Mountains to interview members of the Eastern Band of the Cherokee Nation. She was to be a contributing author for Professor Guilford's forthcoming article: 'Incorporating the Rights and Issues of Real Property and Housing into the Qualla Boundary Legal Code'. She was becoming a person who made a difference.

Since she was so short of time, Elaine (or CeeCee) would handle all the arrangements with Duke Gardens regarding chairs, etc.

The problem was, she didn't yet know how to use her studies to launch herself into the perfect job. Her counselor at the Career Center briefly lamented that she was geographically limited to Atlanta. But then he put together a list of nonprofits that looked possible, some of them interesting, none exactly on spot.

She showed the counselor's results to Trey.

A few days later he presented her with a new compilation that included three large legal firms mixed in with the nonprofits. "We think these firms might have sympathy with your interests," he explained.

'We', Lowry understood, meant Trey's grandfather, Clarence, as well as Chuck. Prominent in the construction industry, lifelong Atlanta residents, they had contacts.

Two of the Chambliss contacts offered interviews; three of the nonprofits did the same. Lowry scheduled all five interviews for the week between Christmas and New Year. Trey booked them into the Atlanta Hyatt Regency for five days of sightseeing, love, and tension.

To prep Lowry, to help ease the tension, they roll played. Trey acted the part of a prospective employer.

Trey: "Your second summer experience looks, well, empty to us, Miss Matthews."

Lowry: "I was offered an excellent job with the The Housing Initiative in Raleigh, but had to decline because of a family emergency. My younger sister became very ill and my family was afraid for her. I had to go home. It was I who worked with the medical system. My sister is past danger now." All Trey's words. Maybe speaking of Justa as if she had cancer was marginally dishonest, but this margin did allow Lowry to smoothly avoid follow-up questions that could take her down a rabbit hole of family mental illness. That was a taint Trey said she must avoid.

Trey: "Why are you interested in us? Why Atlanta?"

Lowry: "My fiancé will be starting his own private law firm here. Atlanta is where I plan to make my home."

On the afternoon of Christmas day, Dad drove Lowry to the San Francisco airport. Trey picked her up in Atlanta.

"We'll try a different restaurant every night," he promised.

Their week took on a pattern: half work, half play. One interview per day. If the employer was a nonprofit, the interview never lasted more than a few hours and they could go sightseeing.

On the fourth day, for her fourth interview, Trey drove Lowry to Clayton County. Lowry liked Lost&Found's director, a World War II veteran with no legs. She liked the role he envisioned for her: "You're going to fight the city, the county, the landlords for us." She would be the sole attorney for an organization whose mission was to place disabled and homeless veterans in stable, permanent housing. Lowry even liked the office, a remodeled cigar store with a paint-faded wooden Indian still implanted into the concrete sidewalk out front.

"It's perfect," she gushed when Trey picked her up for the drive back to Atlanta.

"It's a hike," he said. "Or I guess I should say, it'll be a commute. A long one. My office has to be in Fulton County. You know that."

Lowry did know.

"Did they talk about salary?" Trey asked.

This was the biggest hitch. "Twelve thousand a year."

Both of them went quiet. Twelve thousand dollars was barely enough for two people to live in a large city like Atlanta. It might take several years for Trey to contribute an income.

"You still have one interview to go," Trey said kindly.

This last interview was with the firm of Matchison, Johnson, Locklear & Nowak. Lowry's first morning 'chat' was with two of the partners.

"We're looking to get more women in the firm," Mr. Nowak told her.

Mr. Locklear nodded agreement.

By mid-afternoon Lowry's mind was a slurry of names and faces. She couldn't remember who did what kind of work—except that everybody she talked to was involved in either commercial or residential real estate. "Let me take you and your fiancé out to dinner," Mr. Locklear invited, and of course she had to say yes. She had already sat through an interview lunch with a junior partner and two associates; this day promised to go on forever. At least she was allowed to return to the Hyatt to freshen up. And buy her first cocktail dress, ever, from the boutique store downstairs.

"Buck up," Trey said as she used a nail cutter to clip off the tags. "I'll be there with you. If you poop out, I'll take over. Go spend time in the ladies room, or something."

Mr. Locklear half rose when the maître-d' seated Lowry at the Midnight Sun restaurant. "You didn't see MJL&N at our fullest or best," he remarked genially.

"Tonight's New Year's Eve," Lowry said. Because it was. When the waiter handed out menus, she ordered what Trey did. It was easiest.

"I'm a great admirer of one of your professors, Al Guilford," Mr. Locklear mentioned.

Lowry perked up.

"I'm part Lumbee," Mr. Locklear revealed.

Lowry squinted: she hadn't wanted to wear her glasses with this dress. Mr. Locklear looked nothing like any Cherokee elder she had interviewed so far. But then, the Lumbee were a different tribe, living on the coastal side of North Carolina.

"My three times great-grandfather." He smiled at her amazement. "Locklear is a common Lumbee name. As is Lowry, spelled most often with an i-e." He regarded her questioningly. "Which made me wonder, ever since Clarence Chambliss called us about you, if you might be part Lumbee yourself?"

"I don't know!" Nobody in Lowry's family had ever mentioned this possibility. She glanced at Trey to share her doubt and wonder. He shot her a grin.

"I've got to tell you," Mr. Locklear warned, but with a touch of laughter, "that the Lowries were an outlaw gang during and after the civil war. I'm hoping you don't share their insurgent tendencies."

It was a joke. A partner from the firm of Matchison, Johnson, Locklear & Nowak was joking with her. Trey's foot gently kicked Lowry's. He didn't exactly wink—that wouldn't have been appropriate at a business dinner— but he narrowed his eyes just enough to convey his confidence in her.

⸺

A week later, once again in Durham, Lowry had the immense pleasure of phoning home.

"A job offer!" Dad was as excited as she had ever heard him. "Low, you'll be making as much as I did after *fifteen years* at Kaiser Permanente!"

"Mr. Locklear is part Indian. He says 'Lowry' is a family name in his tribe. Dad, could we be part Indian, too?"

"I don't think so." Dad was momentarily diverted. "Edith would have known for sure..." His voice trailed off, as if scouring memory.

"Oh, Low-Low." Mom used a name from way back, when Lowry had to reach up to tug at Mom's skirt. "You give us such joy."

CCCCC

In Crystal's house the Christmas decorations came down on the twenty-sixth. On the twenty-seventh, as usual, the family gathered in the foyer. Mother and Far were leaving for Far's annual dental convention in Maui. Mother's luggage—rich beige tweed and camel-colored leather—took up enough of the foyer floor so that Bee had to stand in the short hallway to the family room. Sean, centered beneath the open arch into the living room, sat on the floor. Crystal waited at the line of demarcation between foyer and bedroom hallway.

Mother was patting at her rose-gold hair in the foyer mirror. She was adjusting the rose-gold Christmas tree, set with semiprecious stones, pinned to her Chanel-like suit. She was turning to Crystal to say,

"Remember, Crystal. Lisa Snelling's engagement party is tomorrow."

Crystal had been hoping Mother would forget. Crystal had been planning to conveniently forget about Lisa Snelling's engagement party herself.

But Mother, perfectly erect and poised, maintained position in the foyer. She stared at Crystal with those blue eyes that hardly ever seemed to blink. Her tastefully rouged cheekbones were as stiff as Amazonian shields.

Far sighed. He looked at his watch. He opened the front door and began to carry luggage out to the car. From the corner of her eye, Crystal saw Sean settle himself more comfortably on the shag carpet. From behind her, Bee made no sound.

"I hardly know Lisa," Crystal began. That was her first shot.

"You've met Lisa at the club plenty of times," Mother rallied back.

"We're not friends," Crystal argued the truth.

"Her mother and I are friends."

Mother's was a more persuasive truth. She and Helen Snelling had been Tri Deltas together at the University of Southern California. Crystal had seen the pictures: Mother as a pretty blonde coed, Helen as a pretty brunette. Their faces bright with exaggerated squeals for the camera as they touched their toes to an incoming wave. Or, dressed for class in pleated skirts, white ankle socks, and saddle shoes—arms linked. Or, wearing corsaged strapless gowns for a double date.

Crystal approached from another angle. "Lisa won't care."

Mother lobbed a grenade. "Helen will."

As far as Crystal could figure, those years at USC had been the happiest of Mother's life: Delta Delta Delta sisterhood; a four year immersion into the etiquette of Emily Post.

"For me to accept, and you not to appear at a dinner dance, is exceptionally rude," Mother finished.

And there Mother had her: manners. Crystal had been drilled from birth. She could not escape such training. "Mother!" Crystal groaned in surrender.

Far had come back inside. He winked at Crystal, a commiseration that was no help at all. "Sandra, we've got to go."

Mother unbent enough to pick up her monogrammed cosmetic case. "Beatrice, Sean, while Crystal is in charge I expect you to behave exactly as if I were at home." The door shut behind her.

Sean rising from his spot, held out his wrist for Crystal to read the chronograph watch he had gotten for Christmas. "I think you went for a lot longer last year."

"Last year was about pizza," Bee remembered. "Mother didn't want us to eat at Beachy Pizza."

"Pizza." Sean nodded, acknowledging its importance.

Last year Crystal had been fighting for all three of them.

"We went to Beachy anyway." Sean picked up on the memories. "Even after Crystal promised."

This year Mother hadn't needed to extract a promise. This year there would be witnesses if Crystal cut herself free. An entire country club of witnesses.

"Oh, crap!" Crystal growled.

"Mother left you credit cards." Bee attempted to soothe. "She said if I couldn't get you out shopping, you could borrow her Christian Dior."

Crystal's anger froze. "Really?" The Dior wasn't even a year old. As far as Crystal knew, Mother had only worn it once. It was strips of silk chiffon, each tinted a different pastel, somehow fastened from shoulder to waist before falling to the floor like a descending rainbow.

"If it fits," Bee cautioned. "And if it's not too bare." Now she was reciting: "A naked back's okay, but only a floozy shows too much cleavage."

The following hour was lovely: Crystal and Bee played dress up. They safety-pinned the Dior bodice down until it almost fit, then stuffed the cups of an underwire bra so that it would indeed fit. While Crystal admired herself in Mother's triple mirror, Bee inventoried Mother's shoes. "These look the biggest." She held up a pair of gold sandals.

"They looked scuffed." Sean, who had finally allowed himself into their parents' bedroom now that Crystal was fully clothed, was critical. "But I can fix them. There's some gold paint in that model kit I got."

Bee handed the sandals over.

"Now…" Bee trailed the vowels, an anxious hesitation. Via the mirror, Crystal watched Bee puff out her cheeks as if preparing to blow. "You'll-need-a-date" burst forth as one word.

"A date?" Crystal had heard nothing about a date before.

"Because-Mother-accepted-for-two."

"She didn't."

"She did. And she's already asked Bob Griffin. He says he'll go." Bee was apologetic.

"*I can't believe her*!" Crystal yelled. This was Mother at her most Machiavellian. Mother at her most cowardly—leaving Bee to break such news.

"I know," Bee commiserated. "I told her you'd be angry." But in an instant, Bee's expression managed to segue into eagerness. "But I have a solution! I can go with you! I'll be your date. I'll wear my junior cotillion dress. Sean can spend one evening alone. I've thought it all through."

Crystal's heart almost broke, seeing the desire on Bee's face, the hope of attending an adult evening. An entirely Cinderella dream. Crystal had to step out of her own rage in order to figure out how to say 'no'. "It'll be all Mother's friends, Bee," she tried. "Lots of drunken old men. You don't need to be around drunken old men, not yet."

"Please?" Bee begged.

"No." And Crystal was firm. "It's really not what you think it's going to be. This dressing up part is the most fun. Boys who think a cigarette makes them cooler than God are enough for you to deal with for now. But I'm not taking Bob Griffin, either. Where's his phone number?"

Bee knew where to find it.

Crystal, sitting on her parents' bed, dispatched Bob with alacrity. "I'm sorry, Bob," she said. "But Mother lied."

"I told your Mom you'd never go for it." Bob sounded neither surprised nor offended.

Bee, who had been hanging around listening, followed up Crystal's phone call with a statement of the problem unsolved: "You still have to take someone."

Crystal could so easily see: the empty chair at one of the country club's round tables for ten; the other eight diners noticing; the server balancing an unneeded first-course plate on his tray. An expensive dinner going un-eaten.

"Shit!" Crystal conceded.

Because she hadn't brought her address book down from Stanford, she had to dial directory assistance in Fullerton seven times. She followed each directory assistance call with one to a 'Hanson'—'Adam' through 'Gregory'. Gregory F. Hanson turned out to be Scott's father. "Hi," Crystal said as soon as a female—a mother? a sister?—put Scott on.

"Crystal?" Scott sounded amazed. Probably because they hadn't com-municated—not a call, not a note—since graduation.

She started right in: "I have to go to an engagement party tomorrow night. A dinner dance at our country club. Formal. Will you go with me?"

"You want to go a party?" Scott was being slow to catch on.

"I don't have a choice," Crystal explained.

"What's making you?"

"The Tri Deltas," Crystal said bitterly.

"The what? No. I won't even ask. By the way, hello to you, too."

"Will you come?" Crystal demanded.

"Okay. I guess. I mean, sure." Like a true companion of The Table, Scott consented. "What time?"

"Seven o'clock." Crystal gave him directions to her house. She stood. She looked at the back of the Dior, which she had crushed during all the telephoning. She'd hang it in the bathroom tomorrow morning while she took her shower.

Bee, who had wandered off, came scooting down the hallway. "Did you find a date?" she asked.

"Yes," Crystal said wearily.

"I'll do your hair!"

⌒

Hair, in the hands of a fourteen-year-old, meant rollers, setting lotion, an hour beneath a bonnet hairdryer, and a final hour sitting before the vanity mirror in Crystal's bedroom. Crystal hadn't used the vanity itself— part of a matching bedroom suite—in years. While Bee fiddled—giving constant admonishments for Crystal to hold her head erect—Crystal searched through the vanity's side drawers with her fingertips. In the bottom right-hand drawer, Crystal touched a series of cardboard boxes. Each box was hand high, palm square. Why had she kept boxes? She pulled one out.

"Mom's!" Bee's busy hands paused against the back of Crystal's neck. "I wondered where she hid them!"

Crystal held the box up in front of her obediently erect head. She saw the airbrushed photo of a beautiful blonde. "Mom dyes her hair?"

"It's her big secret. Dad's not supposed to know. *I'm* not supposed to know."

Crystal had never imagined.

"She's not supposed to grow old." Bee stated as a matter of understood fact.

Crystal stared at the blonde, who couldn't have been much older than herself. Crystal's mind began to inscribe a poem over the blonde's sweetly smiling face:

If what you have is fleeting,
And too soon nearly gone,
Then...

Bee's hands stopped. "Look!"

Crystal lowered her own hands and looked. Hair, in the hands of a fourteen-year-old, meant waves that started at the crown and ended in fluffy curls at the shoulders.

"Do you like it?" Bee was eager.

"I look like a girl going to a party," Crystal temporized.

"Exactly." Bee was pleased. "Now, makeup." She selected products from a secret stash that she normally kept hidden in Sean's room.

"She pays rent," Sean informed Crystal from his off-and-on-again station just outside Crystal's door.

"Fifty cents a week. Close your eyes, Crystal."

Crystal closed her eyes. Then she opened them, wide. She turned her face to the side. To the other side. She acquired eyeliner, eye shadow, mascara, rouge, lipstick.

"Now, the dress!" Bee shut the door on Sean's face. She helped Crystal into the Dior. This was a slow and careful process because of the pins.

"It's a quarter 'till seven," Sean called from the hallway.

The doorbell rang promptly on the hour.

"I'll get it." Sean's feet pounded toward the foyer.

"You go, too," Crystal urged Bee. "Tell Scott I need a few minutes more."

Bee needed no persuasion. She sped away to see Crystal's date.

Crystal examined herself in the mirror. The image she saw was as close as Bee could get to a magazine cover. It wouldn't last because it wasn't real. Beauty was vulnerable.

Your choices, then, are numbered...

She didn't have time for this. She shook her head, too energetically, and so had to figure out how to repair Bee's work. With greater care, she reached to the floor to tug on the sandals—a half size too small. She minced down the hallway. She could hear Sean saying with solemn, adopted adult-ness, "I hear you play baseball," and Scott reply in the affirmative. She turned the corner to see Bee staring up at Scott with a wide-eyed, drunken expression on her face. Crystal let her eyes follow Bee's. Scott was tall, taller than Far. He wore a tux like he actually owned one. Which, as far as Crystal knew—and she didn't—he might. He was gripping an imaginary bat to show Sean something or other, and the stretch of black fabric from shoul-der to elbow displayed a finely sculpted arm.

Scott, like Crystal, looked different from himself. After a minute of star-ing, Crystal had the difference figured out: Scott had had his hair cut. For the first time, since that glimpse sophomore year, she could see the rising dome of his bare forehead. Scott was going the same direction as that actor who was so damned sexy—Yul Brynner. Bald. The kind of baldness that attracted a woman's fingers. No wonder Bee's mouth hung open.

"Wow." Crystal complimented her date, "Even your bald part is tanned."

Scott rolled his eyes in reply. "Nice to see you again too, Crystal."

"I'll get Mom's evening coat," Bee managed to gasp.

Getting outside to Scott's car was an interesting exercise in walking. Crystal stamped her feet, one after the other, sliding her toes down into a scrunch so she could more confidently navigate the paving stones leading to the driveway. When Scott offered her his arm with the comment, "Not used to heels, Crystal?", she realized that that was at least part of the prob-lem. She hadn't worn high heels since 1967.

She accepted his offer. How many times had she touched Scott? Not often. Not since... Crystal's heart caught. Scott had been a comfort then. Her only comfort. Right now, he was an easy firmness against which she could lean her weight while picking where to place her feet. Seated in his father's car, she sought to compose her thoughts. To her astonished relief, Emily Post came to the rescue. "How's Harvard?" she inquired, making ap-propriate evening-gown-and-tuxedo small talk. "Do you like the business school?"

Scott, occupied—gazing over his shoulder, backing out of the drive-way—said shortly, "Harvard's okay. How's Stanford?"

Okay; the same; never exactly right. Crystal fell back, again, on politesse. "Fine."

They were out on the street.

She got to the heart of it all: "I miss Kendall. A lot."

"Me, too." Scott nodded—one nod—at the windshield. He didn't look her way when he said, "Sometimes it feels like a long time ago. Sometimes it feels like yesterday."

"I write poems to him," Crystal divulged. "I write poems about Justa, too." That was harder to say.

Scott took a quick glance at her. His face was serious. "She's depressed. My dad gets depressed. There are days my mom has to shoehorn him out of bed, out the door. There are days she has to drive him to work. She says that once he gets there, routine holds him stable. Justa lost both Kendall and her routine at the same time: twice as hard for her as it is for us."

This was an insight, a sharing: Crystal hadn't so expected much. "Does Gil talk to you about Justa?" she asked. She hoped.

"No. I don't think they spend much time together, actually." Scott paused. "But then we don't talk much anymore, Gil and I. He's really busy. Like us." Scott's words were heavy with regret.

Which made Crystal wonder: could Scott be as lonely at Harvard as she was at Stanford?

The country club, from entry post onward, was still decorated for Christmas. A lighted Moravian star hung before the double front doors. Inside, the ballroom was exactly as Crystal expected: a confusion of voices; a blast of alcohol-fueled energy; the excess of clashing perfumes. Waiters, carrying trays of hors d'oeuvres, sidled to avoid gesticulating arms. Crystal snatched at the trays as if she were hungry —even though she wasn't—and ate for the sole purpose of having something to do.

She ate with one hand. She kept the other attached to Scott. She was glad, then gladder, then grateful she had brought him along. He knew exactly how to behave. While he paused for Mother's friends, he never lingered. While he let old men tell him about their Harvard days, he knew how to graciously detach himself. He was much better at this sort of thing than she was. He moved among the other guests with a courtesy and ease that made her think he probably did own his tux. He was proving to be an exceptionally satisfactory date.

It was Scott who found their table, their place cards, who introduced them to the four married couples. The husbands, leaning around the women and toward each other, began a conversation from which words like 'the Fed' and 'the prime' emerged. Scott entered into this vocabulary with alacrity. Crystal eventually understood they were talking about banking.

She surreptitiously unfastened and removed her sandals. She watched as course after course was set down before her—from which she hardly ate. She was too full from hors d'oeuvres. The chamber orchestra started a waltz for the engaged couple, and she prepared herself for doom. Her first three partners were exactly what she had wanted to protect Bee from: a hot breeze of bourbon down her neck; a nuzzling of her cheek; a hand slipping downward from her waist. Some things about the country club never changed.

But before a hand could cup her rear, Scott was tapping the owner's shoulder. "My turn," Scott said, with absolute friendliness.

And Crystal was released.

Scott led her in a foxtrot. He must have taken cotillion in junior high, too. "Do you always dance without shoes?" he asked.

"As much as I can."

Scott's super-polished shoes moved in safe concert with Crystal's exposed toes. He didn't hold her too close. He was the perfect height. And Crystal realized: for the first time in what felt like forever, she was dancing. *Really* dancing. She allowed her heart to float—until another would-be partner tapped Scott's shoulder.

"We're leaving," Crystal announced.

"We are?" Scott inquired.

"We are." Crystal let Scott fetch Mother's coat. Crystal didn't remember Mother's gold sandals until she realized the soles of her feet were hurting against cold pavement. She left the sandals behind.

All the way home, she studied Scott's profile. "Cut it out, Crystal," he said once. It didn't stop her.

By the time they drove up her driveway, she had made up her mind. "Why don't you come in?" she whispered, although there was no one else to hear in the car. "I want to show you something."

She unlocked the front door. She turned off the porch lights that Bee must have left on for her return. She made Scott remove his shoes in the darkness of the foyer. Then she led him by the hand down the bedroom hallway. She brought him into her room, and shut the door. She turned on her desk lamp before pointing to the bed. "Just for tonight," she hissed. "Can you be quiet?"

Scott raised his eyebrows. "Are you sure?" he hissed back.

"Why not?" Crystal said. "It's just the two of us, now."

Scott reached for her with equal need.

⌒

Hours later, as silent as could be, Crystal led Scott to the front door.

Afterward she stood for a minute in the foyer, the Dior wrapped around her like a towel. She weighed possibility against disappointment, decided for risk, and crept down the hallway to her parents' room. Once that door was secured, she carried the phone with its long cord into the attached bathroom's tiled shower. From behind two wooden doors and one of glass, she dialed. She awakened Gil, who complained before awakening Justa.

"Guess what?" Crystal began.

"What?" Justa spoke through the gust of a yawn.

"Scott just left. We did it."

"It?" Justa was awake now. "As in 'it', it?"

Crystal basked in the liveliness of Justa's voice. "Yep. Twice."

"Oh, Crystal!" And Justa actually giggled—almost like she used to do when they were roommates back in Lagunita. "How long has it been?"

Crystal had to think. "Since Freshman year. After three boys in that many weeks. I got tired of teaching them. Scott didn't need any teaching." She added that with some pride.

"What about you?" Justa asked. "Weren't you rusty?"

"It's like riding a bicycle." Crystal gave herself permission to relax. She was sharing a postmidnight chat with her ex-roommate. She unwound the Dior, settling her bare bottom on cold tiles. She began removing safety pins from silk, and hoped—with every fraction of her being—that Justa was also preparing herself for a long talk.

"Who made the first move?" Justa wanted details!

"I did." And Crystal continued the perfect ending to the best date of her life.

> *If what you have is fleeting,*
> *Too soon nearly gone,*
> *Your choices then, are numbered,*
> *Ephemeral as song.*
>
> *If what you have is precious,*
> *Soon to disappear,*
> *Choose it first, above all else.*
> *Humbly, hold it near.*

JJJJJ

Valentine's Day

At The Emporium, Justa was now wrapping gifts in special paper covered with hearts and the words 'I love you'. She offered each customer a choice of ribbon: pink, red or white. Mostly she was wrapping candy, jewelry, perfumes. Sometimes a cashmere sweater or fancy underwear. And most of her customers were men. Some of them wanted to talk: josh with her; or explain their romantic hopes, issues or successes in detail. Justa mostly said, "Uh–huh."

When she walked through the store on her way to or from the gift wrapping station, she couldn't help but see the decorations. Hearts, everywhere. She forced herself to endure: in the shape of every perfect heart she saw the clumsy attempts Crystal had cut out of construction paper last year. Justa's had said 'Gil'. Gil's had said 'Justa'. Kendall had drawn an atomic representation of quartz crystal.

It was a memory that pierced; it was a memory to hold on to. 'It is only through our response that we can find meaning.'

On Valentine's Day itself, after leaving the store, Justa went to the Berkeley Co-op where she bought ground lamb, onions, garlic, canned tomatoes, almonds and fruit. Those were the ingredients for a recipe that Gil especially liked from the Co-op's *Low Cost Cookbook*. The paper bag, returning to the apartment, was heavy in her arms. But its contents were a commitment: she was going to try.

In her kitchen, she browned the meat, added the other ingredients, and left the mixture to simmer. She would make the rice when Gil got home. But in the meantime... She looked over to where a Christmas gift lay on the floor, still boxed, still wrapped in 'Ho, Ho, Ho' paper. Justa knew what was inside. Mom had given her a blender.

Justa lifted the box up onto the card table. After she opened it, she had to look in the accompanying booklet to see how the blender pieces came apart. She washed and reassembled. There was a recipe for caramel pudding in the booklet. The ingredients were in her refrigerator, on her shelves.

The blender, when Justa got it working, sounded like birthdays.

Gil came home early that day. His gift to Justa, when he smelled the babootie, was an expression that had slowly been easing its way onto his face ever since Mrs. Soames: hope.

The Day After Valentine's

The day after Valentine's was especially hard. Gethsemane. Justa put the holiday wrapping paper in the storage room she shared with Books, Stationary and Sundries. She didn't have to help dismantle the hearts that decorated other departments. She only had to make it through her shift. It was a quiet shift. She was able to forget for long stretches of time because she was reading *The Group*, a book about friends who, after leaving Vassar in 1933, tried to find love in a broken world.

She finished the book only an hour after returning home.

She had six more hours of this day to get through.

She found herself on her knees in the stereo corner where Gil's LPs were still crammed in boxes. He hadn't organized them. He was rarely in the apartment long enough to do so. He had never even plugged in his components. Turntable, receiver, speakers. The last time Justa had touched any such equipment was the day she threw her own lot into the lake at Stanford.

This was a task she could do. She put her hand on top of one of the boxes and tried to wriggle a finger between two LPs. She couldn't get past her fingernail. But she could tip the heavy box to its side and cause the records to slide out. They came from the box with the swish of slick cardboard against slick cardboard. Each was a big twelve-by-twelve-inch picture: a posed photograph; an interpretive illustration; maybe swirls of psychedelic color. Duke Ellington, Pepe Romero, Fleetwood Mac.

Three boxes, several hundred records, and eventually Justa was sitting cross-legged amidst the silence of echoes: big band; classical guitar; and everything the Beatles ever sold in the United States—including an old 45 of 'I Want To Hold Your Hand'. Gil must have gotten that when he was in the fifth grade. He owned two performances of Beethoven's Ninth. The cover of one was a photograph of the Mormon Tabernacle Choir in red robes (the women) and black robes (the men). On the other LP, Beethoven glared out at the world. Justa passed her hand over the portrait that had come to represent him everywhere. How true to life was this painting? Beethoven looked so very ill. Well, he had been ill. And too deaf to hear his own creation. Justa set the portrait album aside.

Some hours later she had the three boxes—plus the blender box—pushed against the wall, open sides out. She filed the LPs first by genre, then by composer or artist. Her hands became filthy. Her jeans acquired black streaks where she absently wiped her hands before letting them become filthy again.

When she went into the bathroom to take a shower, her face in the drug cabinet mirror appeared mostly grief stricken, not so anguished.

She ate dinner by herself—leftovers. Gil got home around ten o'clock. She went to the stove to reheat what remained. Gil's anniversary-plagued eyes followed her movements as if he were asking a question of her entire body.

"What is it?" she asked.

"Am I Orpheus?" he asked in return. "If I turn around, are you going to disappear again?"

She didn't know. She couldn't promise. But she could show him what she had done. She held out her hand, and Gil followed her to where the Japanese futon was still folded up as a sofa. He sank onto it with a dispirited collapse. Justa sat beside him. But then—with a courage she had accumulated when? where?—she pitched forward until she was kneeling before Gil's components. She plugged them in. She settled Beethoven's Ninth on the turntable. She placed the needle before the first groove.

Her courage dissolved; fear took its place. As well as music, she was going to hear layers of memory: Mrs. Hudson choosing her to accompany the high school choir; riding the bus up to San Francisco with the Stanford Chorus; hearing that chorus in the soul-enlarging acoustics of the opera house. Riding home with Betsy, her friend, who then disappeared to the far end of the world.

Another friend sat beside Justa now. Gil was not gone. He had stuck with her through thick and thin.

She grasped the anchor of his arm.

She listened: the quiet approach of bows against strings; a tender punctuation by the double bass. Gradually, as the first movement progressed, Justa's grip loosened. She had been fearing an agony of the soul, but what she got was this: music no longer hurt, but it didn't expand her being, either. It possessed no reaches. In about thirty minutes the fourth movement would begin, and the chorus would start singing 'Ode to Joy' into an emptiness.

Her own.

May 6

The Day Before Lowry's Wedding

What Justa first noticed about Trey was his voice. In appearance he was merely nice-looking, although Mom tried to make him into something more. "Very good looking," Mom whispered to Justa. "Handsome, even." Much more.

He was the guy Lowry had said would be waiting for them on the verge of a road only a few minutes distant from their hotel, a road so thick with trees no buildings were visible. He held a magic-markered sign—'Lowry and Trey'—and he flagged down Dad's rental car with a shout, "Turn here."

That's when Justa heard: Trey's voice was more than ear-catching, it was resonant. Two Christmases ago, on the phone, she had automatically classed him as a pleasant baritone. Long-distance lines can so easily scrape the fullness of sound down to a thread.

"Here? It's a dirt road!" Dad muttered, as if not believing one of his daughters might choose to live without pavement. The car bumped into the woods, shuddering to a stop at a railroad tie barrier.

Trey instantly appeared at Mom's door. "Welcome, welcome!" he said while helping Mom out. "Finally, we meet!" His voice was sonorous, beguiling. He kissed Mom's cheek with a warmth of familiarity he couldn't possibly own. He turned to Justa, who was letting herself out. "Gorgeous!" he celebrated. "You look exactly like your sister."

It wasn't until hours later, back in the Brownestone Inn and seeing herself in a bureau mirror, that Justa recalled: she didn't resemble Lowry, not so very much.

But this was Lowry's day, Lowry's week. Yesterday, at the airport, Lowry had been a bouncing ball of eagerness, swooping up luggage, guiding Dad to the rental car counter, insisting that Justa accompany her to Durham in her own little car. After running Justa through a list of questions, to which Justa mostly answered, "Fine," Lowry had said, "You're going to love him!" meaning Trey. Lowry's voice was an odd mixture of slowness—that hint of the South she had picked up—and speed. The old level of excitement Justa remembered from other great events: proms, graduations, getting into Stanford.

But now, from the unpaved driveway, it was Trey who ushered Mom, Dad and Justa toward a small building that looked like two different centuries, stacked.

"Hi!" Lowry rushed down an outside stairway. "You don't have to do a thing!" Promising Mom. "I did it all!" With a salt shaker in hand, she gestured at a laden picnic table set in a green patch of fresh-mown weeds. "Go upstairs, take a quick look! The Chamblisses will be here any minute!" And she ran the salt shaker to the table.

Justa climbed the stairs behind her parents. Mom, entering Skywatch first, stopped to gaze around the little kitchen. Justa followed Dad into a room where the one chair was a bean bag atop the handmade rug from Lowry's Stanford dorm rooms. The only other furnishing was a brick and board bookcase.

"Where's her typewriter?" Dad wondered.

"Here, on the kitchen table," Mom called out.

Justa remained still. This room was all sunlight. Lowry's rug shone. Emi Yamada's wall hanging was paled, the photographed trees washed out. Other, living, *huge* trees blazed outside Lowry's windows.

Lowry shouted from down below, "Mom! Dad!"

The Chamblisses must have arrived.

Going down the stairs, Justa saw the Chamblisses before they noticed her: six people, aged old to very young. Trey began making introductions. Grandfather Chambliss was 'Clarence'. Trey's father was 'Chuck'. 'Trey' turned out to be short for 'Clarence Claude Chambliss the Third'. There was even the better part of a Fourth, ten-year-old Clarence Claude Grant, nicknamed 'Clarey'. Trey's sister's given name was 'CeeCee'. The brother-in law was 'Douglas'. Trey's mother was 'Elaine'.

"He has such beautiful manners!" Mom whispered to Justa.

With an apt word, with the judicious phrase, Trey stitched the families together. "Lowry said you were asking about that tobacco odor downtown," he mentioned to Dad. "Granddaddy knew some of the Dukes." And the two heads of family began discussing what happened when 'smoking' and 'non-smoking' were added to actuarial tables. "Mama's taking a Chinese cooking class," he told Mom. The two mothers compared woks.

He stitched Justa to CeeCee, who sang in a church choir. Justa prepared herself for a duet of politeness. But CeeCee was distracted by Clarey, who was peering through a downstairs window, previously hidden behind shutters. Real shutters made of roughly milled boards, not the decorative kind common in suburban California. Clarey had somehow managed to unlatch and swing the shutters open.

"Clarey!" CeeCee scolded.

"I just wanted to see if it really is a slave cabin," Clarey explained himself.

Justa would have liked to look, too.

But, "Absolutely not," CeeCee scolded, and Clarey dashed off to his father.

Justa again adjusted herself to discuss music. CeeCee, though, was frowning at Douglas and Chuck. The two men had wandered to the edge of the clearing where, in only a step or two, they would be hidden by the trees.

"Talking stocks," CeeCee disapproved.

For one confused moment Justa thought CeeCee meant 'stalks', as in those torso-wide tree trunks.

"A party isn't the place to discuss mo-o-ney." CeeCee, all the Chamblisses, added an extra half beat to every vowel. CeeCee caught her husband's eye; she tilted her head to make him understand he must return to the gathering. Not until her men were firmly reestablished on top of mown weeds, did CeeCee give her attention to Justa.

So Justa asked, "Does your choir sing Beethoven?" The question sounded inane to her ears. Every choir sang the 'Ode'.

But Clarey interrupted them again. He skidded to a halt before CeeCee, his arms forming a V from shoulders to hands, his hands cupped around the fragile disorder of a bird's nest. "Look!"

Justa leaned forward. Within the nest, three sky-blue eggs were cemented by old yolk to beak-curved straw. "Robins," she said. "It's been abandoned. They won't hatch." She reached to touch an egg, but before she could do so, CeeCee pushed Justa's hand aside.

"Dirty!" CeeCee chided. "Put it away, Clarey."

"Maa-maa," Clarey whined.

And CeeCee turned her full disapproval upon Justa. "We sing from the *Baptist Hymnal*," she said primly.

So later, back in the Brownstone Inn, Justa couldn't exactly say that she had enjoyed Lowry's luncheon. She could only respond—when Mom stated, "Such a nice family!"—with, "They're very strict." Preparing for bed, she tried to think of other adjectives with which to describe the Chamblisses: polite, well-spoken, self-assured. Southern manners, Southern speech, Southern certainty. Southern, not Western. Not Western, not warm.

Lowry's Wedding

The following afternoon Justa helped Lowry into a high-waisted gown: organdy lace over seashell white satin. The gown was beautiful, but the handmade mantilla—sent by Willow from Italy—was exquisite. Threads of real gold outlined the petals and stamen of white roses that aged from buds to fully open. "Stay still now." Justa carefully angled a gold, silver and abalone hair comb through the delicate, hand worked threads of the veil. She fastened the veil to a bobby-pinned swirl at the top of Lowry's head. She stepped back so that Lowry could stand and admire herself.

"Yes!" Lowry exhaled.

Somebody rapped at the door of the little dressing hut Duke Gardens provided to its brides. The rap was followed by the hindmost entry of one of Lowry's law school friends, bringing the bouquets. Lowry had chosen flowers in shades of purple for herself: iris, lilacs, heather. For Justa she had ordered a mixture of pink and lavender: peonies, larkspur, roses. Pamela handed each her bouquet and then said, while Lowry was turning back to the mirror to see the whole effect, "I didn't know you had a cousin who married an Asian woman."

"We don't have any cousins, not first cousins anyway," Lowry said absently.

"I mean Sam O'Brien," Pamela clarified.

"Sam married *into* the family." Lowry positioned her hands, the flowers, at her waist—just so. She didn't notice the confusion that settled over Pamela's face.

Justa did, but decided now was not the time to go into family history. "Is Dad ready?" she asked.

"Oh! Yes!" And Pamela held the door wide open.

Justa put up her hand to once again touch the bridal comb—first worn by Aito's wife, loaned to every Yamada bride since then. She touched the comb as a prayer for Lowry—that Lowry always possess hope, luck, love. "Are *you* ready?" she asked.

Lowry took a deep breath, let it go. "Yes."

Dad was waiting on a flagstone pathway, looking more nervous than Justa had ever seen him. Pamela dashed away, and a minute later the Bright Leaf String Quartet began playing Pachabel's *Canon in D*.

Justa knew the *Canon* as played by a chamber orchestra, as sung by a choir, as arranged for the piano. She took her place at the top of a series of flagstone steps, in front of Lowry and Dad—and her feet took over. They walked on an unevenness of stone, but soon organized themselves into a beat. One, two, three, four: beneath the now-sewn hem of her recital dress, Justa's feet tapped out common time.

Upon reaching flat ground, Justa's feet stopped. The string quartet still played, a lily pond at their backs.

"Justa," Trey hissed, and she remembered: she was supposed to face him.

The Canon's final chord. The wedding began. "I do," said Lowry. That was Justa's cue: she had been holding Trey's ring on her thumb. Trey kissed Lowry. The quartet started the celebration with the Beatles' 'All You Need Is Love'.

Lowry and Trey joined their guests—laughing, hugging, kissing—but Justa escaped onto a side terrace. A waiter chased after her, wanting the two bouquets she still held. He would put them on the cake table at the top of the garden steps, beneath a pergola roofed with purple wisteria. Justa found a bench beneath a crab apple tree.

She sat as the quartet played Vivaldi, lots of Bach, some Handel and Debussy. The quartet sounded like what they most resembled: a group of graduate students learning how to balance their instruments one against the others. Much as Justa and Crystal had done in the Lagunita dining room at Stanford. But better.

Justa's body jerked. Mari O'Brien was saying, "Scoot over." Mari, with a huge purse hanging over her elbow, held two plates of food.

Justa scooted.

"Just look at them," Mari sighed. Her twins lay, stomach down, with their heads hanging over the edge of the pond. Trey's nephew, smaller body and much shorter legs, lay between the twins. "Koi in there. Waiting for my boys to catch them. They'll be wet to their waists within minutes. I hope Clarey's mother doesn't mind."

Clarey's mother would mind. But instead Justa said, "I'm sorry about Hiro's leg."

"More fool he, washing cars at his age," Mari grumbled. "Broken fibulas don't mend so fast when you're older than them." She gestured her chin toward the twins. "We spent yesterday at Duke Homestead learning about tobacco. And slavery. Tomorrow we go to Colonial Williamsburg. More slavery. We brought the twins along for an immersion into American history, and what matters to them most is that they get a week out of school, and a day at an amusement park called Busch Gardens. Apparently, it has 'bitch'n' roller coasters. Grandad wanted you to have this. Today."

From her oversized purse, Mari extracted a faded cardboard box marked 'Kidshoes Plus'. "I had to hold it on my lap on the airplane," she complained. "You'll have to do the same, going home. Oh, no! Look at them now!" She handed the box over to Justa and, pulling a hand towel from her purse, hurried down to where one of the twins was vigorously shaking his head, like a dog, to get the water out of his hair.

Justa smiled. She lifted the box lid. Inside, beneath layers of tissue paper, there was a pink-lipped conch shell the size of her hand. She knew what she was supposed to do, what Hiro wanted her to do. What everybody did with conch shells. She waited until the quartet paused, then held the shell to her ear. For a moment, she was beside the Pacific: waves coming toward her, sand blowing against her face, the wind in her hair. From far away, a violin played two quarter notes before dropping a melodic third to a half note: 'little girl'. Justa heard it for what it was—the cadence of love.

LETTING GO

'Time Is On My Side'
as sung by The Rolling Stones in their early days.

Starting Autumn 1976

JJJJJ

One evening Justa left the Berkeley BART station to see the western sky streaked with orange and red and purple. Those colors—a shifting pattern, a sinking spectrum—made her stop and gaze and wonder. Could the sun's rays, traveling through the earth's atmosphere, also be creating sound?

Light waves, sound waves. Approaching her apartment, she began to hear the hiccups and bursts of a lone clarinet. Turning onto the path that led to her front door, she knew she had to be listening to Gil, tootling. She hadn't heard Gil tootle since senior year at Stanford. She had never thought to ask, after graduation, where his high school instrument ended up. But now she knew, because a large cardboard box lay tumbled on its side outside the door, waiting to be broken down. The box's return address said 'Idaho'. Gil must have taken his clarinet home, then asked his mother to send it back to him.

Justa took out her key, but didn't have to use it. The door was ajar. She only had to push, and there was Gil with his back to her, standing before the closed kitchen door. He had thumbtacked a length of white paper—a graph with bold ups and downs—against the wood. He took a deep breath and achieved a phrase, and then another. He was attempting Bach's 'Invention Number One in C Major', but with only one voice.

Justa found she couldn't tolerate the omission. It was like seeing a sunset stripped of red pigment. She tightened her throat, and for the first time since forever, she hummed. She set the counterpoint free into the air. She was no more practiced than Gil; they fit together.

Gil swung his clarinet away from the graph. He flashed a smile around his mouthpiece. Starting over again, he played face-on to Justa while she answered back. They only got through eleven phrases though. Gil became tangled up around a G sharp. Even so, he was happy. He lowered his instrument to say, "Do you know what we just did?"

"Bach," Justa answered. "Sort of." She could still feel the vibration in her throat.

"Fractals," Gil was immensely proud. "We played the sound of fractals." He went on to explain what fractals were: multiplications of reality; irrational numbers gone wild.

Justa blinked, attempting to understand. But within her mind shutters were popping open, their locks broken by her throat's vibration. Behind those shutters existed thoughts without words—a sheer vulnerability that was naked, raw...and compelling.

"Fractals map out the place where order ends and chaos begins." Gil had reached a conclusion. Almost. He tilted his head and frowned. "You know what, Justa? That's what you used to do. You could match rules to entropy and find harmony. That's why your music was so good. You had an instinct for balance." He studied her as if she had taken on a whole new dimension, as if her reality had suddenly multiplied. "Mandelbrotian fractals," he said, his voice soft with wonder. "That's you."

⌒

Justa went through the motions of dinner, washing up, preparing for bed. All the while she pulsed with something scary, but beguiling. She lay down beside Gil and, against her expectations, fell into sleep with uncommon ease. She dreamt incessantly, or so it seemed. Silent dreams of no story. Unpeopled dreams that followed one after the other, linked like movements in a composition for the deaf: an orgasmic dream, a kaleidoscopic dream, a dream of inchoate formlessness.

When she awoke into daylight she discovered her hands crossed over her face—as if she had tried to contain the dreams. She had to purposely ungrip her fingers. Afterward, her joints ached. Gil's side of the bed was smooth; the foam mattress no longer held the shape of his body's weight; he was long gone. Justa took her own body into the bathroom. In the mirror above the sink she watched the divots her fingertips had dug into her face rise like foam: eight red spots fading to pink, fading away.

When she eventually stepped outside, she stepped into sunlight, not fog. She accepted the sun's warmth as encouragement. She had plenty of time before work—she was scheduled for the afternoon-to-evening shift—

so she packed up both lunch and dinner before making her way to the public library. She entered the hallway that led to the restrooms, and stopped before the door with gold-stenciled words over opaque glass: 'Art and Music'. She closed her eyes and—with an effort that made her cheeks quiver—caused her throat to repeat that reverberation only she could hear, and only in the very depth of her ears. She tested the sensation for strength: it lasted as long as a breath. A breath was all she needed.

Justa pushed the door open.

And encountered an odor she would have known anywhere—the scent of music. She heard with her nose: the synthetic inks of colored titles on shiny covers; the yellow aging of paper.

She took another breath, a deep one.

Two elderly ladies, busy filing into adjacent cabinets, turned from their tasks. "May we help?" one inquired.

To speak, Justa had to force her nose, ears and mind to converge. "Bach?"

"Bach...?" The second lady added a pause so that Justa might fill it with specifics.

"The Inventions?"

It only took a minute for the ladies to pull a copy from their shelves. Justa sat at one of the tables. She arched her hands over oak and read with a silent tapping of her fingertips. C-D-E-F-D-E-C. Right hand, then left. Her hands were perfect friends. Bach had known everything that could be known about the twining of souls.

"Could I have a copy of the first movement? But with bigger notes?" she asked.

"Yes!" The ladies were pleased to agree—until they had to attack the complexities of their copy machine. With the aid of an instruction booklet—"Translated from the Japanese!"—and fifteen minutes of argument, they finally succeeded in converting Bach's six lines of music into three pages of enlarged notes. "Here you are, dear." The thin sheaf they handed Justa exuded the bitter taste of Xerox paper and toner.

"She'll need a folder." Together they searched the drawers of a big oaken desk.

Justa didn't allow her manila folder to bend all day—not while she was eating lunch on the BART, not when she was at work, not when she was eating dinner on the way back to the apartment. She spent the remainder of the evening alone. After preparing the bed for sleeping, she placed the folder on Gil's side, then lay awake, anxious, waiting to hear his step on the path, the creak as he opened the door.

She sat up as he came in.

"Justie?" Gil questioned. "It's so late."

"I have something for you." And Justa was shot through by a sudden fear: had she been silly? Dumb, even?

Gil dropped his knapsack on the floor. He knelt to open the folder.

"It's the sheet music," Justa told him all in a rush.

Gil's eyes were moist when he looked up at her. "Thank you," he said.

The next day he took down his graph and instead tacked the three sheets of music side by side on the kitchen door. They practiced together: Gil as the treble clef; Justa as the left hand, always.

One afternoon she returned from work to find the closed kitchen door denuded of paper—music or graph. She smelled cooking. She heard her share of notes turned into a solidly dry and flat "la la la"—a non-singer trying to accompany Gil's clarinet.

"Hello?" she called. She didn't remove her coat. She stepped in no further than the entry. These changes were so unexpected, too sudden.

The kitchen door opened and the space was immediately filled by a large young man: tall and bulky, but not fat. He was the color of ebony keys. "How do you do?" he said in a clearly French, vaguely British, accent.

"G sharp!" Gil sputtered, imperatively. Justa couldn't see him, but she could hear him take a deep, loud breath before he blew.

The strange young man nodded an apology to Justa before turning away. "La?" he tried.

Justa walked into the kitchen herself.

Gil stood before the stove stirring a pot with one hand, while holding his clarinet out of the steam with the other. Tomatoes and beef and onion. He was making a firehouse stew.

The stranger bent over the card table where the three pages of music lay. He penciled something in the space between treble and bass staves.

"Giant!" Gil announced happily, although incomprehensibly, upon seeing Justa.

The young man unbent from the table. He made a polite bow toward Justa. "I am Rémy Géants." His accent rendered his courtesy exquisite. "Known here, at Berkeley, as Giant. Perhaps you would tra-la while I write?"

"Okay," Justa agreed. Bemused, she draped her coat over the back of a folded chair. She gave Gil his G sharp. And there, within a vapor of firehouse stew, she joined the two boys and became the third voice in a trio: the cool shiver of Gil's clarinet; the graphite scratching of Giant's mechanical pencil; her own alto hum, sometimes transposed from the base. When Gil said, "Done!", about the stew and the music, she was damp both from steam and this reimmersion into sharing.

"What are you doing?" she finally had the chance to ask.

"Look." Giant flipped over one of the pages of music. He sketched an XY graph on the back. "Twelve notes in each octave. That's X. Each note occurs Y number of times. This is C." He put a dot at the top of the Y, a short distance within X, then drew a graceful undulation downward. "The Invention!"

Justa didn't understand. But she accepted. She had once thought that Gil heard into a different dimension. Now she saw he wasn't alone.

From that day onward she led a new life: Bach, Giant, and rice dinners. She bought fish and vegetables at the Berkeley Co-op; Giant seasoned the ingredients with spices his mother sent from Senegal. He insisted that fruit juice, as beverage, would cut down the heat. For further sweetness—desert—he spread sugar cookies with peanut butter and called them 'cinq centimes'. "Because that is how much they cost in the markets of Dakar."

"My mom makes incredible sugar cookies," Justa once mentioned. This was after an especially long session of tootling, humming and scratching. The library ladies' laboriously xeroxed Bach Invention was now pencil smudged.

"Yes, she does," Gil backed Justa up. And a week later, when she got home from work, the two boys were waiting for her outside the apartment, standing like palace guards on each side of a cardboard box that was too big to rest on the front step. "From your mom," Gil announced, as pleased with himself as if he were the giver. Because partially, he was—he had called Moraga to ask for Mom's cookie recipe. Along with the recipe, Mom had sent a Mixmaster—a wedding-present-quality appliance that, when unpacked, took up most of the kitchen's limited counter space.

"How do we begin?" Giant was intrigued by the machine.

"With butter. Which we don't have." Justa found only cream in the refrigerator. "Although you can make butter with the mixer."

Giant experimented, he played. He poured drip after drip of cream into the mixing bowl. He stared, trying to catch the exact moment when the liquid went solid. "A function of speed, time and volume," he muttered. "And maybe temperature?"

They baked enough for two dinner's worth of cinq centimes. Even so, returning home the following evening, Justa didn't expect to find more than a crumb left. Neither, though, did she expect to find the boys looking anxious, as if they had done something of which they were very, very unsure. This time, standing inside the apartment, they flanked a large, flat poster-sized object that leaned against the futon sofa/mattress. Cardboard, that's all the thing was. Thick, white artist's stock with Justa's name centered at the top. No, not just her name—a word equation. 'Justa=Bach=Mandelbrot.'

"Turn it around," Giant urged.

Carefully, Justa rotated the cardboard. The other side was a collage, a collection of musical notes cut from xeroxed paper and glued in a descending fall from top left corner to bottom right. From top to middle the notes were bunched, overlapping, covering each other up so as to give the cardboard a third dimension of texture. Descending from there, the notes had been set sparely. The shape was that of a narrow kite with a dotted tail. A kite that flew within the limits of an XY graph.

"Bach," Giant said simply.

Gil's face was strained.

"The first Invention," Giant supplied. "Fractals."

Justa touched. With a light hand, she traced the bunching, the fall, of notes.

"You can see how it approximates a line." Giant continued to be helpful. "A boundary. That's what fractals are."

A narrow section of time and space where all contradictions coexisted. That's what Gil had said weeks ago. This boundary wasn't the most comfortable place to be, but to her closest friend and lover it was Justa=Bach=Mandelbrot.

She looked past Giant, wanting to see only Gil. He awaited her word, his eyes glistening.

"Thank you," she whispered. "I love it."

LLLLL

Lowry Jeanne Matthews, Esquire

Nearing dinnertime, and Lowry—driving Trey's 240Z—flew like a bird. The Z felt infinitely lighter than the old, and borrowed, Corolla. Within the Z Lowry's spirit soared as if on high thermals. She was returning to Atlanta from the foothill town of Dahlonega.

And oh! was she ever bringing something special back with her! She rehearsed in her mind—easy to do when her only task was to stay in the far left lane on I-85—what she would tell Mr. Locklear.

After this morning's meeting in Dahlonega, she had invited the coordinators of the Gold Eagle Mobile Estates Protest Coalition to join her for lunch. They numbered three: Mr. Chattin, representing the Cherokee; Mrs. Thrasher, representing the Creek; and Mr. Brent, who had the thankless job of representing both White and Black residents of the trailer park. It was Mr. Brent who recommended one of those cinderblock restaurants that listed macaroni and cheese under the heading of 'Vegetable Sides'.

"Culpepper," Mr. Brent sneered, as he sat down.

Mr. Culpepper was the owner of Gold Eagle Mobile Estates. Lowry had not yet met him, only heard about him. She pictured Mr. Culpepper as being in the mold of a smart Atlanta businessman wearing a bespoke suit.

"Yep, Culpepper." Mr. Brent spat the name like a swear word.

Lowry kept silent. She had learned, while working with the Coalition, that if she dressed casually and didn't speak much, the Coalition members—fifteen to forty years years older than she—would begin to talk past and around her. They would open up, be frank. Lowry was just a kid.

"Back then"—Mr. Brent ignored the fried chicken set below his nose—"when I moved my trailer in, it was all 'Glad to have you, Mr. Brent. You're going to like it here, Mr. Brent. That pretty creek right down below. And nice neighbors, too.'" Mr. Brent nodded politely at Mr. Chattin and Mrs. Thrasher. "What Culpepper didn't say—which was what he ought've said—was, 'This here is a one-hundred-year flood plain.'"

The flood plain was the bedrock of the Coalition's case against their landlord. Mr. Culpepper was refusing to pay for damages to fifteen creek-side mobile homes. Gold Eagle creek had raged high after a hurricane-induced storm.

"Act of God," Mr. Brent groused. "Act of a cheapwad, if you ask me. And all along he knew. He knew because that previous owner, what was his name?"

"Thomas Keverell," Mr. Chattin supplied.

"Thomas Keverell." Mr. Brent stuck the new name into his narrative. "Keverell *told* him he oughta dam up that creek and redirect its flow. Keverell *told* him he wasn't supposed to bring in any new homes after the old ones moved out. That's gotta be why Culpepper got it so cheap. Culpepper sure didn't tell *me* I wasn't supposed to risk my home beside his creek. He tell you?"

"Nope." Mr. Chattin forked up some pulled pork.

Lowry was hearing new information. Nobody had ever mentioned Mr. Keverell's opinions before. Not at today's meeting, not at any previous. While she didn't want to stop this flow of reminiscence, she needed specifics. She risked drawing attention to herself. "Do you know who told Mr. Keverell about damming the creek? About no more new homes? Was it city engineers?" Lowry hoped, even though she doubted. She hadn't seen any such recommendation or restriction in her exhaustive search through city records.

"Don't remember." Mr. Brent finally picked up a piece of chicken.

"Where could I find Mr. Keverell?" Lowry pursued.

"He died not long after selling the property." Mrs. Thrasher dipped her spoon into Brunswick stew.

Lowry's hope dwindled.

"I heard it was Jacie Green what heard Mr. Keverell tell Mr. Culpepper all such." Mr. Chattin was Lowry's favorite of this trio. He sometimes smiled at her as if she were there.

Lowry hoped again. "Do you know where I could find Jacie?"

"Number thirty-seven," Mr. Chattin supplied.

Lowry spent the rest of the afternoon waiting for Jacie Green to return home from her weekly grocery shopping. Mrs. Green was a White lady, eighty years old if she was a day. "Call me Jacie, honey." Jacie remembered the conversation very well. "I still work part-time in that office. Can't retire, no ma'am." Jacie caused Lowry's heart to somersault when she said, "Mr. Keverell, he read to Mr. Culpepper off a letter."

"A letter?" Lowry squeaked. "Do you know where that letter is?"

"Might could find it," Jacie promised. "Let me put up my milk and cottage cheese."

Lowry helped Jacie unpack her groceries. Then s-l-o-w-l-y they walked up to where dirt road met paved. ("Love your silver 'L' pin, honey. Where'd you get something so nice? It was a friend what made it? My!") Jacie had a key with which to open the door of a small trailer-office. Jacie stood before a gray metal filing cabinet for a minute or two, talking her way through memories. "I would've filed it under...Drackner. Mr. Drackner was mayor at that time." The drawer she opened exuded dust like cough germs. "Hasn't anybody looked in here for a while." Eventually, she pulled out a yellowed sheet of paper with the Dahlonega town seal at the top. The carbon copy was still attached. "This do for you, honey."

It would! It absolutely, incredibly, wonderfully would!

So now Lowry had a xerox of that letter on the Z's shotgun seat. A county detective had made it for her, after seizing the original as evidence, and returning the carbon to city records.

Lowry soared at eighty miles per hour. These were the moments when she absolutely *loved* her job.

Trey sometimes kidded her, joshing that Mr. Locklear gave her too many pro bono cases, that she was being supported by overhead, that she wasn't bringing enough money into the firm to cover her salary. Lowry always protested back that she worked billable hours, too. That Mr. Locklear wasn't *only* a legal aid softie.

But Mr. Locklear's favorite cases, along with Lowry's, were always the ones in which she could slip like a spy into other people's lives—and end up making those lives better.

"This is going to cost Culpepper a lot," she gloated down the highway. She added a heavy gold University of Georgia class ring to her imaginary picture of the man. Her mind floated to Trey. "I just earned three months salary," she told the Z with smug satisfaction.

A Chambliss Christmas

It was Elaine who opened the double front doors to CeeCee's house. She welcomed Lowry and Trey with kisses. "So glad to see you, dear," she whispered into Lowry's ear. She ushered them into CeeCee's living room where the tree was a sparkling of silver: sterling balls and baubles; tiny white lights cupped in clear plastic flowers; crystal spheres, snowflakes and icicles that reflected and magnified until the tree blazed like the star of Bethlehem. No pipe cleaner giraffes or cutout snowflakes. No popcorn or cranberry strings. No carefully glued paper garlands. Nothing to remind Lowry of her own childhood tree in Moraga. The only possibly homemade decorations were the beautifully wrapped boxes—in white and silver—that circled the trunk.

Clarey bopped up from the ice blue—and impossibly clean—living room carpet when he saw Trey and Lowry. His kid presents—already opened, the debris cleared away—were arranged in a display that stretched from the tree to a far corner of the room. "Look!" He waved a doll about the size of Mattel's Ken, but much beefier, in front of Lowry's face. "Look through here!"

Lowry obediently peered into a tiny hole in the back of the little head.

"Whaddaya see?" Clarey's eagerness was a rush of words.

Through the doll's eye—which held some kind of wide-angle lens—CeeCee's silver tree burst into a nova. "An exploding star?" guessed Lowry.

"Wow!" Inspired, Clarey shoved his doll into a plastic rocket ship. He zoomed the rocket around the room. "Wu–u–u!" Clarey mimicked propulsion. "Br–r–r–wow!" He mimicked explosion.

Lowry laughed.

But then CeeCee's face appeared from around the archway leading into the dining room. Her arm reached out: she caught Clarey's shoulder in passing and grasped it in a full-handed pinch. Clarey flight stopped cold. "You're just in time," CeeCee said with faint criticism. "Dinner's all ready."

Which meant, Lowry knew, that they were late.

By now she was familiar with CeeCee's table. She saw it every Sunday when she and Trey joined the family for dinner. The place settings, water goblets and candelabra were all 'Lady Claire' by Kirk-Stieff. The wine glasses were Waterford's 'Clare'. CeeCee had ordered the china, 'Claremont', directly from the Hutschenreuther factory in Germany. Back last summer, when CeeCee gave Lowry a tour of the table, CeeCee had said, "Now that you're married to Trey, you can appreciate."

Lowry still couldn't. She only felt drowned in Clares.

During tonight's dinner, as always, she confined her conversation to compliments: about the food, the table—and today, of course, the tree. She had learned through trial: no politics, no religion—not ever. But when CeeCee delivered a condensed version of the Christmas morning sermon—"You should have been there," she admonished her brother and his wife—Lowry decided CeeCee's opinions had finally toppled from amazing-anybody-could-believe-that to ludicrous. Lowry couldn't help but speak out. "You cannot sit there and tell me the Virgin Mary wouldn't have supported the Equal Rights Amendment! How can anybody know? How can your preacher know? That's sticking an anachronism into holy history!"

CeeCee bristled. "Dr. Pollard was following a line of logic backward."

"Which makes no sense at all! The ERA is for *NOW!*" Lowry wondered if CeeCee would catch the pun: National Organization for Women. "If you want to hear an opinion about whether or not women should earn the same salaries as men, ask any of the women I work with. Ask any woman who works, period. Ask our new first lady."

"Mrs. Carter is a Democrat," CeeCee said conclusively—as if being a Democrat explained every lack of judgment and fault in taste.

"And you think Jesus' mother would have been a Republican? The early Christians were *socialists*." Lowry would pit her Stanford history degree against Dr. Pollard at any time.

"Now, now." Granddaddy Clarence interrupted them with a bluff chortle—his usual sound for settling down 'the womenfolk'. He spoke jovially: "Rosalynn Carter thinks she's one of those bionic women. Next, they'll be making her into a doll like Clarey has."

"Not doll. Action figure!" Clarey, insulted, was fierce.

"We need more wine." CeeCee's husband, Douglas, filled his own glass first.

"What we need," said Trey in his smoothest, most calming voice, "is to change the subject." And in front of the entire family, he put his arms around Lowry and kissed her—a long, lingering kiss, almost, but not quite, with tongue. He pulled away. "Yum-yum!" he celebrated, as if he had tasted something delicious.

CeeCee froze with disapproval.

Lowry, at first embarrassed, began to feel a tingling of success. Maybe Trey's kiss had been a clever ploy. Maybe, with Trey as her cocounsel, she had won. Sort of. She had gotten the last word.

Because she didn't want to risk losing that last word, she chose to not follow CeeCee and Elaine into the kitchen after cake ended the meal. Instead, she trailed the men into the living room. She sat on the floor with Clarey, whose action figure had three interchangeable arms – two with weapons, and the third with an oxygen mask. Lowry grabbed the laser arm and attacked, "Ps–s–s–s!" Clarey grabbed the pistol arm and retaliated, "Pop–pop–pop!" They had a very satisfying battle until CeeCee came wheeling in a butler's cart topped with her sterling tea and coffee service, 'Lady Claire'.

Clarey jumped up as though possessing bionic feet himself. "Can we open presents?" he begged.

Lowry and Trey had brought gifts wrapped in bright red and green papers printed with jolly Santas and prancing reindeer. Lowry had fastened all the packages with big, sloppy, bright-red bows. Not one package was white or silver; they looked like a misplaced pile on CeeCee's carpet, as if they should have gone to another home. But Clarey tore into them with abandon, with glee. And then he stopped.

To be from her, Lowry had combined a backyard bird feeder with bird whistles, bird books, and a tape of eastern bird songs. Clarey's reaction—at first thrilled—skidded down to confusion, then longing. His eyes sought out his mother.

And CeeCee shot down any hopes he might have had. "Bird seed can ruin a lawn," she pronounced. "Say thank you, Clarey."

"Thank you," Clarey mumbled.

Lowry tightened, deep inside.

For Trey's gift, Lowry had chosen a 'Little Professor' calculator that set math problems to its child owner. Dad had liked to give her similar gifts when she was in the sixth grade.

"I'm supposed to play with this?" Clarey asked doubtfully.

"Your aunt will teach you," Trey promised.

"I will." Lowry made her promise to both Clarey and herself.

She watched how Clarey set his gifts aside with resignation and good manners. She watched while he recharged, from wriggling feet up to a re-newed grin. Her innards didn't soften until he jumped into his next ex-pected role—that of playing elf for the adults.

And then Lowry got to see her other Christmas shortcomings exposed. She had bought every gift in one late-night spree at Rich's department store. Whizzing from the first floor upward, and then back down, she had selected French-milled soap for the men, and tiny samples of real perfume for the women. To be from Trey, she had picked out cashmere socks: black for Clarence, brown for Chuck, navy for Douglas, pink and lavender for Elaine, somber red and ecclesiastical purple for CeeCee. Lowry had done her best—given her time, given her money, given Trey's recommendation that she buy 'something nice'. But her gifts measured up as puny alongside what the Chamblisses gave her: a hand-loomed shawl in shades of green (from CeeCee); a full day's spa treatment (from Douglas, who was topping his coffee with Kahlua); a celadon silk robe with matching slippers (from

Chuck and Elaine); and a $500 treasury bill (from a genially beaming Clarence).

Lowry, sitting on one of CeeCee's perfectly white sofas, surrounded by Chambliss opulence, wanted to run away.

But Clarey was standing in front of her again, holding out the very last present. She had no choice but to take it from his hands. He stepped back, grinning knowingly. Everybody else—except for CeeCee—either grinned or smiled contentedly. CeeCee closed her eyes and exuded a sigh thick with layers of grief.

"It's old, it's fragile." Trey had come to stand behind Lowry. He rubbed her shoulders with tender excitement. "It belonged to my great-grandmother."

"My mama would be glad for you to have it." Clarence was a monument of ancestral pride.

Lowry, caught within this Chambliss spotlight, untied the white satin ribbon. She opened the carton. She lifted away silver-striped tissue paper. This last gift was a music box. As Trey had cautioned, it was old and fragile—a small wooden platform crowned with carved and painted figures. A black-maned horse lifted its forelegs into the air. A girl with long curly brown hair reached to calm the horse by putting a hand on its neck.

"You turn the little key on the bottom, and it will play!" Clarey revealed.

Lowry found the key; she turned it.

The tune was a mountain song, one Lowry had heard on the radio while driving. Sweet and lilting, it took the tiny charger and the little maiden around and around in an endless circle.

"Grandmama loved that music box," Chuck remembered.

"We hope you'll love it, too," Elaine said softly.

CeeCee began folding discarded wrapping paper into a bag for disposal. "I'll take this out." There was the slightest catch in her voice.

Lowry twisted to see. But her view of CeeCee's retreat was blocked by Trey, who had come to sit beside Lowry. He was smiling his mischievous smile, the one she loved most. "Great-Grandmama was born the last year of the War," he told her. "She never knew a slave. It was a freedman, an old coachman, who carved this for her."

A hundred years ago. This was a gift to meld Lowry into Chambliss family history. She held the music box reverently, both for what it had been and for what it was now. In her arms, it was a welcome. In her heart, it became an embrace.

CCCCC

Crystal had enclosed herself within a poem. She wrote as if the act of concentration might save her life. Despite such intensity, her touch on the typewriter keypads was light. Tap, tap. Crystal laid down words as though she were setting type of gossamer. This poem was about a girl who always listened inward, and a boy who spun melodies beside a lake. Crystal was working with great delicacy, sublime precision.

"Crystal!" The shout came from outside, from her landlady who lived in the house in front of Crystal's garage apartment.

Crystal ignored the call.

"Crystal!"

Crystal huffed in exasperation. With her next inhalation, she smelled smoke.

"Oh, God!" she yelled. "Shit!"

She grabbed two hot pads, and threw what was supposed to be her dinner out the window. For a half minute she couldn't see down onto the driveway for all the smoke—and steam. There was Mary, hose in hand, watering the blackened pot.

"Good one," Mary said. "I think this makes three. If I were your mother I'd stop giving you Revere Ware. I'd give you something nice and cheap that you can burn with impunity. Why didn't Scott's smoke detector go off?"

Crystal had to admit: "I haven't put it up yet."

"Christ, Crystal!" Mary scolded. "Sometimes I think you're the prototypical airhead."

"I love you too, Mary," Crystal said waspishly.

She pulled her head back into the apartment. The waspishness lingered. She resented having been pulled from her trance—despite it having been all her own fault. How many exact ideas, expressed by the only possible

words, had she lost? With a vicious tug, she pulled the paper from the typewriter platen, tearing a corner. She forced herself to slow down—which
created room for a more tempered regret. She had lost a much needed
distance from the exigencies of life.

She had might as well pack.

She walked listlessly into the bedroom. She couldn't help but see the
smoke detector box. It stood like a bright orange interloper in her bookcase. Scott had given her the smoke detector and three books for Christmas. Three different, sometimes conflicting, biographies of Emily Dickin-
son. Wonderful books. Crystal's original plan had been that Scott would
install the smoke detector when he came out for his—not her—spring
break.

That was before *Cyndi.*

Before Scott decided that, instead of coming out to California, he was
going up to Maine for some mid-March skiing. He went with one of his
housemates and that housemate's sister. Scott called Crystal during *her*
spring break to tell her: *Cyndi* knew how to cook, and often made dinner
for Scott's house; *Cyndi* was getting a PhD in German. Scott wanted Crystal
to know that he and *Cyndi* were getting close.

Crystal hated Cyndi, pure and simple.

Way back in January, she hadn't planned for this last job interview to be
at Simmons College, but now she was glad. It would give her a chance to
wage war. If need be. She pulled one of her old green suitcases from the
closet. Mother had wanted to buy a whole new set of luggage for Crystal's
first step into an adult career—teaching, since that's all Crystal's degrees
qualified her to do. Crystal, of course, had refused Mother's offer on principle. Right now she was glad she had been so stubborn. Because she
needed the past, for luck.

⌒

Her airplane breakfast, the next morning, arrived on a little tray and
consisted of reheated scrambled eggs, sausage, pancakes, and a sealed con-
tainer of make-believe maple syrup. Crystal was hungry. Last night's dinner had been two small containers of yogurt—peach and strawberry. She
ate everything the stewardess brought her. Then she opened up her old

green tote bag. She removed a notepad and pencil. And didn't write a word. Instead, she stared out the window at the empty sky. Overnight she had calmed, sadly reorienting herself toward the hard truths of reality. She and Scott had never had an exclusionary relationship.

"We'll always be friends," Crystal said.

The businessman sitting an empty seat away from her replied with a loud, "What?"

Crystal had to swivel. The man, peering at her from over his Wall Street Journal, had an expression of irritation on his face. She couldn't believe he had heard her over the airplane noise. She shook her head. He frowned.

Crystal returned to observing a blue void.

As *friends*, they had been seeing each other whenever they could. Like last summer, when Crystal was teaching gifted high schoolers at Stanford, and Scott was working at Fidelity Investments in Boston. Each had flown to the other's location for a long weekend. Well, Scott had flown three times and Crystal had flown once. It was her first trip to Boston, her first taste of raw oysters, which she would purposely avoid forever more. Too much alive.

She decided to forgo her airplane lunch.

When she finally disembarked at Logan Airport she hoped against hope that Scott would be at the gate. He wasn't. He had known she was being met by a contingent from Simmons. And there they were, over there—two fresh-faced girls flanking a young woman who held up a sign. 'Miss Crystal Kelsey.'

Crystal wet her lips with her tongue and prepared to smile.

The young woman was all teeth. "I'm Terry Sullivan! I started out as a lecturer, too. But I'm hoping I'll be an assistant professor next year." Out on the concourse, Terry revealed, "I'll be your escort during your visit. I don't know how many women's colleges you've seen, but Simmons is the *best*." While waiting for luggage, Terry confided, "I submitted my dissertation last week. *Currer, Ellis, Acton, and George: The Defeminization of 19th Century Literature.* If you'd like to read it, I'll be happy to loan you a copy." And on the way to the car, Terry confessed, "I've always wanted to write. Be a real writer, like you. But I didn't have the nerve. I went for a PhD at Rutgers instead."

Crystal had nerve? At the moment she was nervy, but in the 'anxious' meaning of the word. Terry's encroachment made her even more so. So much more so that, during the rainy ride from the airport to Simmons, Crystal found herself doing something she'd never done before: she began acting. She acted like the kind of person who might invert the 'y' and the 'i' in an otherwise perfectly normal name. She acted *cute*.

Her mouth opened to expel a limerick—which delighted Terry and the girls.

> *From coast to coast in six hours*
> *A plane is swift in its powers*
> *But it can't change the clock*
> *Time change is a shock*
> *Morning sun turned into night showers.*

It was if Crystal had been body-snatched and turned into a pod person.

That pod person gushed when Terry introduced her to the Dean, the English department Chair, and the retiring creative writing teacher, all gathered in the Dean's on-campus apartment. Crystal was to drink sherry with them before adjourning to the faculty dining room for a get-to-know-you supper. By adjourning time, she felt false to the core. "When I was here last summer I discovered Boston cream pie! It was heaven! I loved it!" The pod person rhapsodized.

The next day, Crystal was still body-snatched. She could see very well what the pod person was trying to do. Its end goal—a job offer—was the same as her own. But never before—not at Pepperdine, Northern Arizona, Colorado College, or the University of Puget Sound—had Crystal thought to be *charming*.

The pod person layered it on. During the individual interviews, it complimented the Dorothea Lange photograph hanging in the Dean's office, the Joan Miro lithograph owned by the Chair, and the minuscule Mary Cassatt painting that the retiring teacher had inherited from an aunt. The pod-person complimented art owned by lesser faculty: Escher's stair lithograph; a Grandma Moses print; even a Chez Panisse poster from the Berkeley restaurant.

Crystal really, really hoped that, when the faculty later met to assess and judge her, they would limit their discussion to what she, Crystal, had said about poetry and literature. She hoped they wouldn't compare notes about their wall art and catch on.

Thankfully, by late afternoon, the pod person was exhausted to death and melted away. Crystal was tired, too. When she entered the classroom where the airport students waited alongside six other English majors, she had no will to resurrect the same class she had already offered at four other schools. Instead she sighed, "Let's do a group poem." She plucked the subject matter right off the top of her mind. "About two-timing. Your boyfriend, another girl. Everybody write a sentence or phrase."

The girls, and Crystal, ended up shoving desks aside so they could position the eight slips of paper on the floor in one long list. The girls sat cross-legged on the floor. Crystal knelt and switched the slips around in experimental cut-and-pastes. They stopped with:

> *Deceit cuts you in half: love and anger.*
> *Assigning fault, I shove it her way.*
> *She isn't pretty,*
> > *only sexy,*
> > > *I wish I had her boobs.*
> *She would look prettier all covered with glue.*
> *And she was my best friend!*
> *My tears are solid gold.*
> *My name is Jane, but I am not an Eyre-head:*
> *My eyes can also swing.*

This end result satisfied everyone.

Late that evening, Crystal's last night in a Simmons guest room, somebody knocked on her door. The intruder was Terry, smile blazing. "I know I shouldn't show you"—Terry waved a sheaf of papers—"but look." Eight student evaluations, and Crystal never scored less than a nine. The comments were variations on a theme: 'Miss Kelsey is not only smart, she's nice, she's fun!'

—

Crystal stood in a hallway at the Harvard Business School, her green tote over her shoulder, her green suitcase at her feet. She was examining a wall display of book jackets—all with deadly boring, business-oriented titles—when she heard the brisk click of high heels against linoleum.

She turned and saw a young woman close to her own age.

"Hello," the young woman said, in a tone Crystal immediately disliked.

"How do you do? I'm Crystal Kelsey." Crystal's Mother-training kicked in.

The young woman didn't introduce herself. She instead said, "Pshaw"— as if suddenly ladened with an intolerable burden. She ignored Crystal by staring at the still-shut classroom door.

Crystal was taken aback. Cyndi—or whoever she was—was petite to the diminution of tiny. Which was probably why she wore heels. Her cuteness was accentuated by dark hair cut into a Dorothy Hamill Olympic-winner wedge. Maybe she was an ice skater, too. She looked the type with her cheerleader-muscular legs.

The door opened, and the tiny woman instantly concocted a smiley face.

It was mostly boys who came out, although a few girls—looking as tired as Crystal felt—also emerged. The tiny woman wasn't tired. She was peppy. She bounced on the balls of her impossibly small feet—click, click against the floor—until she chirped, "Brother!"

Crystal had never before heard a brother addressed as 'Brother'. Not in today's world. It was a conceit from the past.

But this brother obviously accepted the description as his name, because he reached out to pat the tiny woman on top of her head. "What are you doing here, Cyndi?" he asked.

Aha!

Right behind Brother, came Scott.

"I thought I'd take you home for lunch," Cyndi invited. "Hi, Scott!"

Scott, leaning forward as if to give Crystal a quick peck, stopped halfway. Instead of completing the kiss, he muttered, "Uh, yeah," and picked up Crystal's suitcase.

"I already got the groceries," Cyndi enticed. "We're going to have soufflé, salad and popovers."

For the briefest moment Crystal hoped 'home' meant Cyndi's place, that only Brother was invited. But her hope collapsed when Scott shrugged his shoulders in embarrassed resignation, and offered Cyndi the rote acceptance, "That'll be great."

What *wasn't* great was how Cyndi somehow paired everybody off on the sidewalk so that she got to walk ahead with Scott while Crystal had to tag behind with Brother. Brother kept up a polite conversation. Was Crystal liking Boston? How was Simmons? Was she applying to other Eastern schools? Her responses became monosyllabic: she watched her green suitcase, hanging from Scott's hand, bump against his leg, then Cyndi's, then his again. The sidewalk didn't force them to be that close.

Lunch, at the boys' house, was both delicious and excruciating. Brother continued to exercise his manners. Cyndi sought to monopolize Scott with topics in which Crystal could have no share, such as, "There's a great ski sale going on at Eastern Mountain Sports."

While Crystal ate, she spied. She looked for signs of Cyndi. Last summer, during her first visit, this house had been boy-messy with four tenants. It had smelled of stale pizza and dirty socks. Now the house was marginally organized; it smelled of air freshener. And when Crystal excused herself to use the bathroom, she found that the toilet seat lid had been put down.

Desert was homemade chocolate chip cookies.

"Crystal."

It took a moment for Crystal to snap away from inspecting what she could see of the living room. Cyndi was grinning at her, showing off her orthodontia.

"I should have washed Scott's sheets," Cyndi sweetly chastised herself. "Scott can show you where the machine is."

As an announcement of two-timing, it was perfectly done.

Scott's earlier embarrassment, now renewed and magnified, caused the balding dome of his head to glow. "I should have done it myself," he blurted. "I mean, Crystal, I will…" Making a fraught situation worse.

Crystal couldn't even stare Cyndi down. She lost her breath against such malice. When Cyndi finally departed for her own place—after having put leftover salad in the refrigerator for 'the boys' dinner'—Brother quickly excused himself to his private room. Only then did Crystal pull in enough air to say, "I don't know how you can stand her."

"She's not so bad, usually." Scott attempted an explanation. "She's okay. She's been really helpful. Generous, you know."

"Obviously." Crystal's mouth filled with the taste of bile. "Sheets."

"Not that. I mean, not just that." Scott halted, as if he knew he had no way to go but down, but still wanted to provide reasons. "She's cooked for us. She's cleaned sometimes. She supports two children in Tanzania." Finding something specific to say in Cyndi's favor seemed to steady Scott. It allowed him to continue earnestly: "She volunteers with a group that's trying to set up a charity relief fund for kids in East Boston." He finally found his way to the most important point. "She's here."

The simplicity of those last two words was another blow to Crystal's solar plexus. Feeling ill, she tagged along behind her suitcase to Scott's room. Along the way, she bumped her thigh against the couch. She was clumsy. Her body was a Crystal-shaped mass, oscillating between alarm and hopelessness. In the past, only Mother had been able to make her feel this miserable.

At the doorway, her feet stopped.

"Here we are," Scott said unnecessarily.

Crystal's body now had purpose. Her hands got to work. She stripped Scott's bed, trying hard to not see any potential stains. He attempted to help, but got in the way. Holding a bundle of red-orange-green plaid, Crystal wondered where the laundry was.

Scott took the bundle from her arms. "Cyndi may not have your straightforwardness or sense of loyalty. She may not have your grace or your depth. She may even be conniving sometimes." He shrugged, unhappily. "But business school can be really hard, Crystal."

Crystal didn't know how to respond. She let Scott help her remake the bed with sheets that, though wrinkled, smelled laundry detergent sterile. Scott, sounding defeated, said, "You can sleep in here. I'll use the couch." He smoothed out the bedspread. "I think I'll take a shower." He opened a drawer in the bureau that did not match his headboard, and pulled out a pair of boxer shorts. When he had been Crystal's boyfriend, alone, he had always worn briefs.

Crystal was left, deserted, in a room where—for a moment or two, back in Palo Alto—she had thought she might conquer Cyndi with sex. Now, she removed her shoes. She climbed up on the bedspread, depressing it with her feet, positioning herself exactly in the middle. She collected her body into one vertical line. And then she jumped. Jumping, she loosened. Her arms lifted and waved. Her head turned. Her torso twisted. She performed a dance in place, within a box confined to a double mattress and the limited height that she could touch.

She needed more. Space, yes. But also… She slowed, allowed her knees to buckle. She landed on her butt, and a conviction: she needed the enlargement of somebody else's opinion.

She had never called Justa at work, but she did so now. She used the phone on Scott's desk and asked Information for The Emporium.

"Gift wrapping," Justa eventually answered.

"I've met her," Crystal started right in. "She's *cute*," turning that descriptor into an insult. "And *mean*, at least to me."

"Wait a minute." Justa must have put her hand over the speaking part of her receiver, because Crystal heard a muffled, "Would you mind watching my desk? This is an emergency." Justa's voice came right back: "There must be something good about her if Scott likes her."

"She's peppy," Crystal said bitterly. "She's not like us."

"You and I and Gil have never been more than part of Scott's life," Justa said reasonably. "He always had another world, beyond ours."

"We were most important," Crystal stated, no other option allowed.

"Maybe, now, it's that other world that's most attractive to him." Justa's voice was gentle.

"It *can't* be," Crystal despaired.

"Oh, Crystal." Justa spoke with great kindness. "Have you ever thought that maybe it isn't Cyndi you want to chase away, but Scott you want to bring closer?" Justa must have put her hand over the phone again, because her "Okay, I'm coming" was muted. To Crystal she said, "I have to go."

Alone again—maybe always and forever—Crystal moved about Scott's room. She walked with her spine both straight and supple; with her head balanced over her shoulders; with her shoulders balanced over her hips. She was aware of each inch of contact her feet made with the floor. She opened Scott's closet door. She couldn't distinguish Harvard Crimson from Stanford Cardinal in the closet gloom. So she felt with her fingers until she touched the S of Scott's letter jacket. It wasn't pushed all the way back; it wasn't up front and easy to choose. It was simply there. In abeyance.

Crystal stepped away, closed the door, and continued to prowl. At the bureau, she stopped. She studied a cheaply framed snapshot from that day all five of them—Crystal, Scott, Justa, Gil, Kendall—went to Point Reyes in Crystal's car. They had wanted to see whales. Instead, after leaning against the cold damp wind—after enduring stinging sand in their faces—they had run to the ranger's station. The ranger took this photo. They were standing before a facsimile fluke in order of height, each leaning a left elbow against another. Scott, tallest, grinning hugely, leaned against the fluke as though he had discovered another best friend.

Somehow the snapshot had become crooked inside its frame. Crystal pried with her fingernails until she could separate picture from frame. She adjusted, she reassembled.

Somebody knocked at Scott's door.

"Come in," she said.

It was Scott. Wet hair, same clothes, bare feet. "I forgot clean socks," he apologized. "What happened to the bed?" He pointed to the tangle of bedspread, blankets and sheets.

"I jumped," Crystal admitted.

"Oh-kay." It was an accepting non-comment.

He was close enough for Crystal to inhale soap, shampoo. She had always liked the way he smelled. "I, personally, believe in monogamy." She heard the words slip from between her lips.

Scott's eyebrows shot up.

"I do." And Crystal discovered that, indeed, she did.

She knew that whatever she said next had to be absolutely true. Nothing easy. Nothing facile. Nothing cute. This time she picked out each word as if composing a poem. "And I want to be monogamous with you. Because you're a tie back to when life was its best, and I was my best. Because I want to be that person forever."

The expression on Scott's face shifted. It went from surprise, through thoughtfulness, to the openness of an amazed agreement. "Yes," he said slowly, carefully—as if he'd suddenly found himself in the most important moment of his life. "I think I want that, too."

"So now what?" Crystal's question was stuffed with desire, hope, even begging.

Scott's kiss was rich with the same.

❧

Returned to California, Palo Alto, her apartment, Crystal dropped the green suitcase just inside the front door. She frowned at the table until she realized what was different: somebody had stuck a pink index card against the platen of her Olivetti. Crystal plucked out the card and read, in Mary's handwriting, 'Look above your head.' Crystal looked up. She now had an installed smoke detector. She immediately forgot it. She carefully pulled a piece of paper, sheared of one corner, out of her tote. She had carried this poem all the way to Boston.

She sat. She wound the torn sheet into the typewriter. Her fingers began spinning her soul out like silk thread, delicately yet deftly. Tap, tap.

She walks a circle.
He loops her path
With ribbons of shimmering sound.

First gold, then silver, then
Melting copper, she
Turns leftward, always.
Always: per bend sinister.

While he waits for her
In perpetuity. Not dark,
But opening: infinity.

JJJJJ

Few people ever came into the public library's Art and Music room when Justa was there. Even so, the library ladies always whispered. Justa sometimes wondered if that was their only mode of speech: if habit had turned into a characteristic that couldn't be shaken off. Agnes, who specialized in art, was a quiet staccato—little beats that sometimes filled the air with excitement when she was researching a painting, statue or building that especially pleased her. Justa didn't know where her reports went. "To the public," was all Wanda said. Wanda gathered music and information for choral groups, soloists, instrumental trios, quartets, even a reed sextet. She seemed to know every music teacher in town. Her whisper never held a discordant note.

The ladies were always busy, but their patrons were always invisible. When Justa pushed open the Art and Music door, Agnes's staccato quickened, Wanda's whisper became a song.

It was lovely to be so welcomed.

Justa spent more and more time with the ladies: before work when she was on an evening shift; after work when her day was a normal nine-to-five. In private, incognito to the world, she sat at a library table and read. From the Bach Inventions, she moved on to other music she had studied: favorites from her times with Dr. Weber, Mrs. Hudson, Kath. She read with her fingers, hearing the mistakes they made—they were stiff and forgetful. They caused her to hear double: what the music should be; what she was doing. Gradually, the two interpretations began to merge.

One day, Wanda surprised Justa by asking her to look at a Gloria the Franciscan missionaries taught their converts way back in the late 1700s. It was unusual, even strange, music. Half plainsong, half not. Parishioners and priests alternated. While easy to sight read, it was almost impossible to hear. Justa thought she knew how the priests must have sounded—European, eighteenth century—but she knew nothing about the Indians. She asked the ladies for further information, and Agnes handed over a book on the rock art of the lost California tribes.

The only paints the Indians used were white, red and black. They depicted people, animals and creatures that might have been both. There were stars, wheels, ladders and intricate paths. It was a kaleidoscope of images that Justa began hearing on her BART trips. Beneath the whirr and buzz and metallic squeals of the train, she heard a rhythm with accents that felt possibly true.

Eventually, she was able to both read the Credo and sound it in her mind.

~

When that happened, she waited until her next day off, then took the bus into Oakland. After a long ride she stood before the front gate of Mills College. She felt like two Justas at once: what she had been; what she was now. The discord hurt her body, but her feet knew perfectly how to take her to Dr. Weber's office.

"Come in."

The voice both calmed and excited. But she entered.

"Ah, Justa!" He stood to greet her. He looked the same. He had always looked the same. Scarcely taller than she was, but far heavier. His hair a mixture of dark brown and gray. The same—or identical—hat and coat hung on the old coat rack near the door. "I was hoping you might someday come," he said with pleasure. "Sit, please." He pointed to the chair. He took the piano bench, his back to the keys. "Tell me, what have you been doing since I saw you last?"

Justa didn't have much to tell: "I'm living in Berkeley. I'm working at The Emporium."

Dr. Weber nodded. He considered. Then, "When I was a young man—about your age—I worked as a butcher," he revealed.

"You what?" Justa gazed at the hands that she, as a freshman, had admired for their reach. Still wide-knuckled, a strong muscle beneath the thumbs.

"Yes. I was at the conservatory in Vienna when the Nazis came. My father was a socialist. He was also a butcher, as his father had been before him. I, the student, was my family's pride—and then became their disappointment when, in Portugal, then Cincinnati, I cut meat for twelve years. The work suited my mood. I took care of my hands, though."

He had noticed her gaze.

He continued: "When my anger eased, and I touched a piano again, I discovered my reach, before a tenth, was now an octave plus four, a twelfth."

All this allowed Justa to ask what she had, *had,* to know. "When did you play again?"

"I did not really play until I had been at the Cleveland conservatory for a year or more. I was only accepted there because my professor had known me in Vienna. During that year I played Czerny." He turned to peruse his shelves of music. He pulled out a very battered, very old book. The cover might once have been yellow. He handed *100 Progressive Studies* to Justa. "Take this. For when you are ready. I regret to tell you that a student will soon arrive."

Justa was wrenched back into the quotidian. "Oh! I'm sorry! I didn't think!"

"Perhaps you have been thinking all along," Dr. Weber suggested.

Back in Berkeley, Justa hid the book beneath her winter sweaters. She wasn't yet ready for Gil to see.

∾

The library ladies never asked Justa any personal questions. The most she knew they knew about her was the hours she might come in, and that she usually carried her lunch in an Emporium bag.

It was this latter, Justa figured, that led to their polite ambushing on the first Monday in June.

"We have an idea," Agnes staccatoed, and Justa looked up. Agnes and Wanda had come to stand on the other side of the table. Agnes held a piece of paper.

"We want something different for you," Wanda contributed.

Agnes handed over the paper. The something different was a job announcement for 'Assistant to the Reference Librarian, Claremont Branch'.

"Give it a try," Wanda advised.

Justa allowed the ladies' idea to trail through her mind. In and out. Off and on. The ladies weren't advising something profound—nothing like starting the Czerny. Meanwhile, at The Emporium, Justa wrapped graduation gifts. She bought, and wrapped, a Cross pen and pencil set for Crystal. It was only then that she thought to call Crystal for advice.

"Do it." Crystal was exceptionally firm. "I'm finally leaving Stanford. This is our time of change."

⸺

The Claremont branch was a one-room neighborhood library. Above the reference desk, where Justa sat, hung a sign lettered 'Information'. Justa shared this desk with Connor Bridgeport, whom she had been hired to assist. Connor was a tall, thin young man, maybe ten years older than Justa. A dapper sort, with a narrow mustache and invariably pressed slacks. At first, Justa thought Connor was smart because he knew everything; then she learned he was smart because he knew where to find the answers.

During Justa's orientation he pointed to the 23-volume *World Book Encyclopedia,* also to the *World Almanac,* all in a low bookcase behind their desk. "Whenever you have time you should read these," he instructed. "They're the mother lode." He also directed her to atlases, legal and medical dictionaries, collectors' guides. After two weeks she knew how to find answers to the simpler questions, such as: 'How much should I ask for my '63 Oldsmobile?'; and 'What's the best way to get bubblegum out of shag carpet?'

One day an old woman with cataract-thick eyeglasses asked for an English trifle recipe. While Justa made a photocopy from *Joy of Cooking,* the old woman said, "You are much too thin, girl." Her accent was similar to Dr. Weber's. "What do you eat?"

Justa had never figured out what to say when customers got personal. At The Emporium, she had simply gone silent. So far at the library, people had asked her age, if she was married, and if her hair color was natural. Connor's counsel was 'Lie'— but Justa wasn't quick with deceit. To this woman she murmured, "Food?" Which was obviously an inadequate answer, because the next day the old lady appeared with a Tupperware bowl filled to the top with fresh fruit and whipped cream.

"For you," she said.

Justa carried the bowl to the break room. Connor was lingering over coffee. The sight of the Tupperware made him brighten. "Oh, good! Mrs. Appel. Great cook. Can I have some?" While his spoon sped through calories, he gave Justa a capsule biography: "Her husband was a professor at the University of Berlin. Mathematics, I think. They were both sent to Auschwitz. He died. She has family here."

At the end of the day Justa washed the bowl; she put a thank-you note inside; she set the bowl on top of the bookcase behind the reference desk. When she finally got to say thank-you, Justa caught herself glancing for a tattooed camp number on Mrs. Appel's arms. Mrs. Appel wore a cardigan. She had worn a cardigan before.

From then on, Justa couldn't help but notice things about other library patrons. Details about the man called Charlie, for instance. Up until Mrs. Appel's trifle, Justa had only seen Charlie from a distance—or peripherally. Justa kept her face turned to the side whenever she had to approach the fireplace nook where he spent his days. Charlie stank of sweat, ammonia and rotten food. Each day, as soon as the library opened, he beelined to the nook where he unpacked two items from a Safeway grocery bag: a mantelpiece-type ormolu clock that he never wound; and a large, heavy book. Charlie spent his days reading that book.

Connor didn't know what Charlie read. He, too, had never gotten close enough to find out. "Pornography," he guessed. "That, or the Bible."

The next time Justa was shelving near the nook, she held her breath; she snooped. Charlie's book was on the floor, having slid from his lap as he dozed. *The Complete Plays and Poems of William Shakespeare*. Justa had just enough oxygen to open the book to its frontispiece. 'To my beloved Charlie, on the occasion of his tenth birthday, from Mama, March 30, 1938.' Charlie was at least thirty years younger than Justa had imagined.

"Ah," Connor said wisely. "Charlie's one of those people who has too much story in their lives."

Connor had a story, too, which Justa only learned through a game he invented. One of his responsibilities was to recommend library purchases, and for that task he perused book reviews in various publications. *The New York Review of Books* was his favorite because it also carried personal ads. Right next to the stapler, on top of the reference desk, he kept a three-by-five card box with dividers marked according to the NYRB criteria: Single Jewish Female, Divorced White Male, Gay Black Female, etc. When Connor found an ad he liked, he cut it out and filed it. Upon discovering a match, he sent each party a preprinted postcard: 'Dear Box _____. Please contact Box _____ of (The New York Review of Books, The San Francisco Bay Guardian, The Mother Earth News). I am certain you will find him/her to be your perfect mate. Most sincerely, a well-wisher.'

One Tuesday, when Justa was working the evening shift alone, she found a personal ad in the NYRB that she couldn't wait to share: 'Gay White Male, Bay Area book lover, former altar boy turned fallen angel. Love is all around...' That was Connor's theme song: he refused to work on *The Mary Tyler Moore Show* nights.

But he didn't laugh when Justa showed him the ad next morning. Instead he looked sad—wasted actually—from his evening off. "That's me," he confessed. "I'm Box 22371. I thought I'd try. I'm tired of being alone. Having too many is just the same as being alone. What I want—call me an old-fashioned boy—is to settle down." He pretended to wipe a tear from his eye. The self-mockery only accentuated his despondency.

Justa didn't know how to counter his despair. She fell back upon platitudes: "You'll find someone. Until then, you've got your friends, your family—"

"Family!" The sad lines on Connor's face hardened into anger. "Connor Blakely Bridgeport the excommunicated, the disowned? No, Justa, my family has made it very clear: they don't want me. Not anymore. Not as I am."

On the bus that evening, going home from work, Justa had to sit near the back—the domain of the walnut shell man. This man's Afro was a mass of knots; his face was drug addict thin. When he set his shells and his tiny silver ball into the cut down cardboard box that guarded against wide turns and sudden stops, his hands shook enough to make the gamblers crowded around him raise their bets. Today, as on every day, no matter what the weather, the walnut shell man wore a jungle-camouflage flight jacket. On other men, that jacket might have looked like surplus from an Army Navy store. But Justa, recognizing the dead space in the walnut man's eyes, knew for certain the jacket was his own.

She arrived home to a steamy apartment, fragrant with minestrone soup. Giant was back in Senegal for six months, working up an idea for a dissertation that his government would fund. Gil was cooking by himself. "Hey," he called, not turning around from where he stood at the stove, one hand stirring while the other scratched numbers into a notebook. Gil had recently gotten a grant from the US Forest Service; his dissertation topic was to be 'The Fractal Geometry of Fire'. Gil hoped, the Forest Service hoped, that his research would lead to reduced destruction, fewer lives lost, lessened emergency.

Justa didn't advance any closer than the kitchen doorway. Instead she observed Gil exactly as she had the walnut shell man—as she had observed Connor and Charlie and Mrs. Appel. And she saw: Gil had experienced terrible things—flames reaching toward him from a burning building; the attempted resuscitation of a bludgeoned friend. But it was his nature to let things finish, to let things go. To build, even, from the past.

A pocket of energy Justa hadn't known she possessed suddenly opened, flooding her with wrath. She resented: the grief that had so emptied her life; the bleakness she had forced Gil to share; the excess of story that had so effectively silenced her heart, her soul, her hands.

CCCCC

Tableau Vivant: An Eminently Eligible Man
Directed (i.e. controlled) by Mrs. Sandra Kelsey

Part 1–Waiting for the Boyfriend

For as long as Crystal could remember, Mother had been a docent for the Festival of Arts of Laguna Beach. Every summer the festival staged elaborate *tableaux vivants* in which people were costumed and told to stand still long enough to represent a famous painting.

Today, the Kelsey's living room was Mother's set. Crystal, as one of the subjects, felt naked—even though she was wearing a sundress and sandals. She felt exposed. "Do I have to?" She found herself whining like a sulky teenager, like a kid who had no choices.

Mother took advantage of that momentary weakness to plop Crystal down on the sofa, at the end opposite to Far.

"Perfect!" Mother congratulated herself.

"You look pretty, sweetheart." Far reached to pat Crystal's knee.

"Two houses!" Sean crowed. Mother had arranged him and Bee at a Monopoly game on the floor, out of the way of traffic. It was a homey touch. Sean punched the air with his fist, pulling his starched shirt away from his belt. Mother was right there to tuck it back in.

"Mother!" Sean complained. His whine, a truncated version of Crystal's own, made Crystal smile. She was amused. No, she was anxious. No! She was angry! *Three A's*, Crystal thought wildly. And then, *Am I sort of hysterical?*

Far again patted her knee. "It'll be okay," he promised.

Crystal's problem was simple: she had stage fright. If she could manage to move, she would run.

But she couldn't manage to move.

Mother now stood in the foyer arch, examining her almost-completed portrait of happy family life. She looked perfect for her role: affluent suburban matron. Mother sometimes wore that dress for afternoon teas at the club. The dress provided a dark background against which she had tied a gauzy white cocktail apron. Ideal hostess.

A touch of sexy French maid, Crystal thought, inspired by the apron's frills. And then, *I can't do this*.

But Sean was bounding up from the floor. "That's Scott's car!" He must have heard what Crystal did not.

Mother's tableau fragmented.

Mother, herself, had already disappeared around the side of the archway, heading to the front door. Sean went racing behind. Far stood, took long strides to the foyer. Bee rose more decorously, smoothing the miniskirt she had taken from Crystal's closet over her derrière, her thighs, before scattering Monopoly money on her way after the others.

Crystal remained stuck to the sofa. This, Scott's arrival, was the most singular moment of her existence as a daughter.

The front door clicked open—even though Crystal was *certain* she hadn't heard the bell ring. Her hearing was suddenly remarkably acute. "Welcome, dear," Mother was speaking as if greeting an old, and well liked, acquaintance. Far said, "We're glad you could make it." Sean blurted out something about baseball, the Dodgers. Bee's silence provided an alleyway through which Crystal could make out Scott's responses: "Thank you," "I'm glad to finally meet you," "How ya doin', Sean?"

The foyer emptied back into the living room. Crystal could again see everybody. Scott was searching over heads to locate her. The smile he sent her was wry, kind.

Crystal interpreted that smile as meaning 'I can handle this'.

Her butt unglued from the cushioned seat. As she adjusted her body into a modicum of comfort, she remembered: tableaux weren't meant to last. That was their very nature.

Part 2–Interrogation

Mother had arranged for cocktails first. "What would you like, Scott?" He asked for wine. Mother sent Far to the wet bar in the family room, from where Far returned with two glasses of wine, two martinis, and two cans of coke. He gave the second glass of wine to Crystal, who hadn't asked for it, but who was grateful because holding the glass kept her hands occupied. She stayed out of the conversation, which was mostly chitchat about the route Scott had taken from Fullerton, about how he was only home for a long weekend, about his father's sixtieth birthday party which was the occasion for the trip. Through her fug of anxiety, Crystal heard Mother coo, "Oh, just call us Sandra and Roger," and Crystal's attention snapped alert.

She felt the burn of Bee's glance. Crystal met it. *Can you believe it?* Bee mouthed. Mother never cooed. Crystal jerked her head left, then right: *No.* She was discovering a fourth A in her vocabulary: she was addlepated.

The kitchen buzzer went off. "Hors d'oeuvres!" Mother enticed. She was only gone for moments before she was offering Scott a silver tray filled with hot cheese nips and tiny pastries filled with even tinier sausages. "Just a little something while the roast and baked potatoes finish," she said gaily.

Scott accepted a pastry. The entire family watched him swallow.

Mother said, "Tell us about your parents, Scott," and she was down to business.

Probing. That was what Crystal had been expecting. What she had been hoping was that Scott would pull out the same aplomb he had displayed at the country club two Christmases ago. Crystal listened as hard as any of the others—excepting Sean who became bored and built a neighborhood of houses and hotels, with streets paved with money, in the middle of the Monopoly game. Crystal heard things she already knew—Scott's father owned Hanson Frozen Foods, a wholesale business he'd built up himself. She learned things she didn't know—Hanson Frozen Foods supplied restaurants throughout Orange County, including the Disneyland Hotel. Scott's tone was an easy one, pleasant to hear—informative, matter of fact, utterly agreeable.

Crystal turned—Far and Bee turned—to witness Mother's reaction. Mother was holding her martini like an extension of her hand, her body tight. Crystal knew what that meant: a successful frozen food supplier was not socially equal to a dentist.

Scott continued to inform: "Mom's a docent at the LA County Art Museum." He spoke with entirely open friendliness. He could not know what the Kelsey's knew too well: Mother had applied, and been turned down, for a similar position some years ago. During the time of Mother's hope, she had said that the LA Art Museum was so far above the Festival of the Arts of Laguna Beach, it wasn't in the same universe.

Mother lifted her martini slowly toward her mouth. Perhaps she was in the need of alcohol. Crystal hoped so, because that meant the Kelsey-Hanson playing field was leveled.

Again the kitchen buzzer brought conversation to a pause.

"Dinner," Mother announced, her voice gone neutrally polite. Her family, then Scott, obediently rose. She gestured them into the dining room, where Far carved the meat. Mother passed around potatoes, peas and rolls. "I hope these peas are to your liking," she said to Scott—challengingly, Crystal thought.

He tasted. "They're perfect," he complimented.

Far tried to take charge—which he sometimes succeeded in doing. "Crystal says you've already started your new job. Do you like it?" he asked.

"I think I will," Scott answered. "It's early days, but I think so."

Crystal, still smarting from 'peas', interrupted with, "Scott only looked at jobs in Boston and New York. He thinks, and I agree, that Los Angeles is 'formless'." She stopped herself, aghast.

Scott promptly intervened: "I've liked Boston. But when I got the offer from Dreyfus, I realized I wanted to get to know New York."

Mother cleared her throat. Every Kelsey head, including Sean's, swung her way. "Well, Los Angeles has changed immensely since I was at USC," Mother conceded.

Crystal's mouth fell open, fully silent.

"We were disappointed that Crystal's only offer came from Simmons." Mother's tone, at first so critical, surprisingly softened: "But now that I'm certain *you'll* be nearby..." She ended her thought with a pause. She squared her shoulders, as if setting herself a task. "Well, let's just have a nice dinner for now. Then, Crystal, you can take Scott for a short walk. Roger, you'll help me in the kitchen. We'll have desert later."

"We don't have to help with dishes?" Bee asked for both herself and Sean.

"No, no." Mother said definitively. "You four can go outside."

Part 3–Out of the house!

"I think she likes him." Bee, exiting first, slid aside the glass door and stepped over a length of green hose Mother had carefully edged against the bottom rail. "I mean you, Scott."

"She isn't all that scary," Scott told Crystal.

"Anybody want to play ping-pong?" Sean hoped.

Crystal looked over to where the ping-pong table stood, subtly warped. It was supposed to spend the rainy season inside, but hadn't this past year. Sean, then Crystal, had learned how warpage enhanced the game: a player had to know exactly where to place the ball to win a point. Kelsey ping-pong could be undignified in the extreme.

"Scott?" Sean was obviously planning to conquer.

"Um..." Scott began.

"I'll play." Crystal could at least save Scott from this. She faced Sean across the expanse of green-painted plywood.

"We can sit on the edge of the barbecue pit," she heard Bee say.

"Ready?" asked Sean.

Sean slammed the ball to Crystal. She slammed it back. They sent each other flying. Crystal slid: the flat soles of her sandals weren't gripping the concrete pavers. She said, "Time out," and bent to unbuckle. Head down gave her a full frontal view of Scott's trousers from knees to shoes, and Bee's bare legs all the way up to the purple miniskirt.

"Sean's always been more like Crystal," Bee was saying.

"Hurry up!" Sean bounced in his shoes.

This time Crystal served so that the ball glanced away from the table and hit the fence. Fence ping-pong: a Kelsey variation, allowed. Sean returned; his ball skittered off an angled fence board. Crystal had to run into Mother's zinnias. On an ordinary day she would have rolled the ball in mud before throwing it to Sean. Today, however, she forbore. The score was nine to seven, in his favor, when he took a death spiral toward Bee. He landed on his side, the air pushing out of his body.

"Sean!" Crystal panicked.

But she needn't have worried, because Sean used his first breath to comment, "Your underpants are showing, Bee."

Bee clapped her knees together. She tilted her legs to the side. Crystal took stock. Bee's face shouldn't be so flushed beneath her tan, not even with embarrassment. Scott had loosened his tie and was dripping sweat onto his collar. Sean had popped open a seam of his Brooks Brothers Boys shirt, acquired a line of dirt and gravel along the leg of his good pants, and completely obliterated the shine of his BBB shoes. Crystal gazed down at herself. Her bare feet were caked in the mud that had also spattered her sundress. Belatedly, Crystal considered the fate of the zinnias. "Oh, no!"

"I can fix them." Bee, standing now, moved toward the flowers.

"I can help." Scott followed her.

"We have to change our clothes," Crystal told Sean. "Put your stuff at the very bottom of the laundry basket, okay? And hide your shoes for a while."

"Want me to spray your feet?" Scott was pointing the green hose, nozzle down, toward Crystal.

She stuck out one foot, then the other. Mud dripped onto the patio; Scott diluted it to invisibility.

Bee, carefully squatting beside the flowerbed, began bending leaves back into place, snapping away the worst of the flower damage, sticking almost-okay flowers back into soil.

Crystal issued more instructions: "We'll go through the garage, Sean. Bee, you stand guard."

"I'm decoy," she overheard Bee explaining as she led Sean away. "I've been decoy all my life."

Part 4—Just Deserts

Mother raised her eyebrows at Crystal's new attire, shorts and tennis shoes. And then her eyes narrowed at Sean's bare feet. "Shoes, young man," she ordered.

And that was all, maybe because they were having desert in the family room, which was where the Kelseys really lived. Far was already settled in his recliner. Bee, bringing out coffee, set everyday mugs—not china—on the coffee table.

Crystal pulled Bee to the side of the big TV. "Well?" Crystal whispered.

"She didn't say *anything* about him."

Mother gestured for Scott to take her special chair. This was a good sign. Enough so that Crystal decided to go for it. "Scott's offered to help me move across country next month. I've decided to take my car," was how she started.

"Dreyfus is giving me some time off," Scott contributed. "I thought I'd help Crystal drive. With your permission, of course."

"With our permission?" Mother's expression flicked through a gamut Crystal had never seen before: surprise, calculation, gratification.

"We had thought she would fly," Far demurred.

Mother interjected, "We'll pay for you to have separate rooms at your stops, of course." She was, astonishingly, inserting herself into Crystal's plans. No arguments about the non-necessity of having a car in Boston, the dangers of a cross-country drive, the lack of propriety in traveling with a boy. Although Mother attached a condition: "I will rely on you, Scott, to prevent Crystal from leaving important household goods behind at rest stops."

"Um," Scott, taken aback by this apparent non sequitur, agreed, "Sure."

"We're going to need a U-Haul." Crystal couldn't prevent that old whine from rising in her voice.

"Oh, I think one of those hard-shell carriers for the top of your car will do," Far automatically mediated.

"Is there any more cheesecake?" Sean asked.

"Yes, dear." Mother took Far's plate away before he had finished, and balanced it on top of her own. She picked up Sean's with her free hand. "Crystal, I want your help in the kitchen."

Once she had Crystal sequestered, Mother warned—in a low voice, with rapid-fire sentences—"Scott's patient. He has a sense of humor. He accepts you for what you are. That's what you need. That's what you should have. *Do not throw this away.*"

An instant later, and Mother was returned to her ideal hostess self. She called through the pass-through, "Scott, I didn't ask if you might like more desert."

"If you don't mind," Scott returned.

"Not at all." Mother gestured at Crystal to cut another slice of cheese-cake. "Put it on a clean plate," she ordered.

Crystal took a clean plate from the cupboard.

Mother sailed back into the family room carrying Sean's second help-ing. "Tell me, Scott, what did your mother major in at Smith?"

Before she cut Scott's second desert, Crystal spent a minute or two stud-ying how raspberry puree could be made to swirl so beautifully through cream cheese. She was feeling somewhat pureed herself. She angled her head so as to see into the family room. She couldn't see Far's face, or Sean's. But Scott was smiling, still easily polite. Bee was looking hopeful. And Mother—this was something Crystal could hardly believe—was beaming.

5 C's
Choosing Commitment,
Crystal
Causes Celebration.

I'm Dancing As Fast As I Can

is a searing memoir by Barbara Gordon about a life stolen
by prescription drugs.

Starting Autumn 1977

LLLLL

For Lowry's twenty-sixth birthday Trey gave her a beautiful brooch: a peach blossom fashioned of rose, white, and yellow gold, with tiny pearls delineating the pistils and stamens.

"To replace your silver L," he said. "Initial brooches are kind of high school, don't you think?"

So it was the brooch that Lowry expected would catch the receptionist's eye when Lowry stepped off the elevator. Lowry had chosen to wear a dark gray suit against which the three golds popped.

But the receptionist wasn't interested in fashion today. Instead she had something big to disclose, and she said it in a hushed tone, "Mr. Locklear's had a stroke."

"Will he be okay?" Lowry was afraid. Aunt Edith had died of a stroke.

"Nobody knows."

Lowry walked to her office dreading, then hoping. Aunt Edith had survived several strokes, little strokes, before the big one. And Aunt Edith had worked as a pharmacist up to the end.

Lowry's secretary handed over a handful of pink message slips. She consoled: "Patients respond best when they get attention right away. Mr. Locklear was with his wife when it happened."

Hope, then.

Lowry closed her door. She looked at her phone. Long-distance calls were allowed only for work. Aunt Edith had died when she was fifty-two. Dad turned forty-nine this year. It was six in the morning in Moraga. She called home.

Dad's answering voice was slurred.

"Are you okay?" Lowry worried.

"Yeah. Sure. Of course. Haven't had my coffee yet. Low?" Dad's enunciation improved with every word. He wasn't stroking out. He was waking up.

Lowry's panic settled. "Mr. Locklear's in the hospital. A stroke."

"A stroke," Dad told Mom, and Mom took over the phone. "Are visitors allowed?" she asked.

"I don't know." But a visit was something that Lowry could do. Help out.

"Take fruit he can offer other visitors," Mom advised. "Apples, oranges, something that will last several days. Something that will make him feel he can give, too."

"Okay." Lowry knew where to find fruit. "And Mom?"

"Yes?"

"Dad's healthy, right?"

"He's fine, dear. He doesn't have *any* of Edith's indicators," Mom promised.

Lowry could work, now. If she made progress on their current case, she could take news to the hospital that would please Mr. Locklear. So she put her mind into a brief that concerned a child, recently put into protective custody, who had adult cousins that wanted to take care of him. The cousins were Creek. The father was White. The White grandparents wanted nothing to do with the child. Lowry suspected the judge's decision would depend on where the parents were, which was a fact nobody knew. She built that uncertainty into a case that found stability within the welcoming arms of the tribe. She constructed a narrative for the judge that had a happy ending.

She was finished by mid-afternoon. She left work early and stopped by the curb market where she bought a basket; she filled it with apples and oranges. Riding the bus to Emory University, she held three layers on her lap: a briefcase, a purse, a basket. That's who she was: an attorney, a woman, a friend.

She got lost in the hospital, had to be guided, and eventually recognized Mrs. Locklear standing in a hallway. They had met twice before - at last year's Christmas party, and at a summer barbecue hosted on the lawn of the Locklear's Ansley Park home. Lowry smiled, and Mrs. Locklear asked hesitantly, "Mrs. Chambliss? Lowry?"

"Yes." Lowry offered the basket.

"Thank you, dear." Mrs. Locklear's acceptance of the gift was automatic. Her mind was clearly elsewhere.

"How is he?" Lowry asked.

"I wasn't ready for this." Mrs. Locklear's eyes filled. "*We* weren't ready for this."

"Of course not." Lowry found herself soothing, exactly as Mom would have done.

"He can't talk. Or move his arm."

Lowry's hope fractured. "Would he like to see me?"

Mrs. Locklear shook her head. "No, dear. He wouldn't want you to see him this way. But I'll tell him that you came."

Leaving the hospital, a pressure built in Lowry's chest. She felt she might explode. But she didn't: she had learned how to contain herself during the summer of Justa's collapse. She contained herself all the way home. To Trey, who said, "He'll be fine."

⌒

But Mr. Locklear did not become fine. Mr. Nowak became Lowry's new boss. The judge appointed the Creek cousins as foster parents in what became Lowry's last pro bono case. Mr. Nowak had plans.

"I'm pleased to have you on board, Mrs. Chambliss," he said. "I've wanted you on my team from the first, given your interest in real estate law."

This is what Trey had predicted Mr. Nowak would say. "You're a natural," was Trey's assessment.

Mr. Nowak continued. "I've told Kitty"—his secretary—"to give you the Cremfield files. I'll need a brief"—he checked his calendar—"November twenty-first. Tell Kitty to set an hour aside for us to talk that day."

Lowry spent the next month in her office and the firm library, reading and writing. She began by sketching out the case: Cremfield Development wanted to build a series of high-rise apartments on Jackson Street. The current owner of the property, Mr. Sam Bromley, was eager to sell. The wrinkle lay in the location—directly across the street from Ebenezer Baptist Church, where both Martin Luther King and his more famous son had been pastors. Only six months earlier, the church and its surroundings had been designated a National Historic Landmark District. Local preservation laws were in the works. Cremfield Development wanted its proposals to soar through the planning commission before such laws became a barrier.

It all looked very straightforward.

Lowry stopped by her own secretary's desk. "I'll be at the Fulton County Law Library," Lowry said, "in case Mr. Nowak asks."

But before walking to the library, Lowry chose to ride a bus to the property in question. She got off at the junction of Jackson Street and Auburn Avenue. She stood in front of the redbrick church: built with all practicality, it looked more like a factory than a cathedral. She turned 180 degrees. She and Trey rarely came into neighborhoods this modest, not even driving through. A beauty parlor, a fish restaurant, compact duplex houses far more confining than the one-bedroom apartment she shared with Trey. It was those homes, Lowry realized, that Cremfield would turn into a highrise.

Young girls dressed in dark plum and gray Catholic school uniforms passed by on the sidewalk. They were chewing gum and giggling—just as Lowry once did. Smaller girls, also in uniform, trailed after. This was a neighborhood of children. A neighborhood of people with little money and great practicality.

Cremfield Development would undoubtably advertise their apartments as being in an historic district of national importance and raise the rents to match.

At the law library, Lowry was duty bound to find cases that supported Cremfield's goals. She couldn't help but also keep track of those cases Cremfield's opponents—if they could afford legal representation—might cite. She somehow found the time to put together both cases. She assembled both arguments: the benefits of developing a neighborhood that was on the brink of becoming a city—no, a national—attraction; the necessity of maintaining the character of a site that, in the future, might become as important in explaining American history as was Williamsburg, Virginia.

To her regret, she saw how the one could be flipped into the other: 'cleaning up' the neighborhood—i.e. making it more White—would make it more attractive to White school groups and tourists. As an MJ&N employee—no longer with an L—Lowry couldn't withhold; she was required to flip. She had to find ways to paraphrase the word 'White'.

On November twenty-first, during her hour with Mr. Nowak, he expressed himself as being more than pleased. He was delighted. That evening, when Lowry reported to Trey, he was thrilled. "Legal eagle, Low!" he applauded her. "You've proven you're a whole lot more than a pro bono bimbo."

Lowry had heard that description before. Too often before.

"I'll open a bottle of wine," Trey celebrated. "There's that crate..."

"...in the basement," Lowry finished for him. "I'll go down." She was turning the door handle before her last word was out.

The basement garage also had a walk-in locker for every apartment. Once inside her own, Lowry sat on Willow's rug, rolled up around Emi's wall hanging. Trey hadn't wanted either in their apartment. Lowry had had them cleaned, then wrapped in brown paper. Now she picked off some of the tape at the end of the roll so she could place a finger on the rug's fabric. She imagined, rather than saw, the colors. She didn't have to imagine the comfort because, once freed, the colors encircled her like a friend's arms. Allowing her to finally indulge in private despair.

When Lowry complained of fatigue, CeeCee's affable family doctor recommended a multivitamin and tennis lessons. When Lowry fainted at work, after the inevitable pregnant-or-not excitement, a doctor who always seemed to be on call for MJ&N gave her a vial with twenty tablets of dextroamphetamine. This physician was a peppy little man who told Lowry he had retired from twenty-seven years of emergency room work, "To pamper myself with the nine-to-five mission of treating lawyerly nervous breakdowns."

Lowry wasn't having a nervous breakdown. She told him so.

"Of course not," was his reply. "You're not the associate who turned on a hot plate at three a.m., cut his carpet into pancake-sized discs at four a.m., and poured maple syrup into his telephone receiver at five a.m. Quite a breakfast that boy had."

The story was apocryphal, it had to be. But then Jeremy Crae, the Emory Law grad who shared Lowry's secretary, told Lowry that it was indeed true. The 'champion of breakfasts' now taught at Westminster high school, north of downtown and off of Highway 75.

"What a waste," Crae said. "The poor guy."

Lowry was in no danger of such a fate. Two dextroamphetamine refills later she was down to a size five and feeling better than she had in her whole life. She could do so much...and then so much more! Take this cram book sitting beside her in the shotgun seat of the 240Z. The partners at MJ&N had chosen her, not any of the other associates in the firm, to take the Illinois bar exam. She, not Crae, would be doing double duty, assisting the Chicago office. She wouldn't have to move, just travel, but as soon as she was bar certified she would be working out of both states.

Ah, here she was at the drive-up laundry. Damn, she would have to wait in line. HONK! Move it, people!

She was leaving Crae in the dust. He was her 'pacer', like one of those animals used for training race horses. Crae was Lowry's minimum speed. He didn't know this, of course. It was Trey's idea—and a good one. Trey said that by keeping Crae in her sights, Lowry would never lag behind her potential.

Her potential—*wow*! Who would ever have thought she could earn so much money? She still, sometimes, felt a pull toward that rainbow rug in the basement, but the truth was that she wouldn't be a real estate lawyer forever. Once Trey's solo practice netted her current income, she was going to switch careers. Trey was, as always, brilliant. She was going to take all her knowledge of the rich boys over to the nonprofit side of urban development and screw them where they sat.

She couldn't wait! HONK!

Another ten feet forward. Thank God for this laundry. Trey was dismal at housework. He couldn't cook, and the one time he washed their clothes he had stuffed as many as he could into the washer, packed it all down tight with a broom handle, and then put in so much dry powder that everything that wasn't already meant for painting a wall or polishing the car was ruined. Lowry had laughed while she cried, all the time on the phone ordering new jeans and T-shirts and socks from L.L. Bean. Her husband was hopeless; he was the smartest man she had ever known. Trey's potential was in the stratosphere! HONK!

She was almost up to the window now. After she picked up the clothes she would go straight home and study all afternoon. Then—a quick break to fry pork chops and toss a salad; she already had those ingredients in her refrigerator; she had discovered an all-night grocery where she could shop during the hours she used to sleep—she would make the required coconut cake for tomorrow's obligatory Sunday supper at CeeCee's. She would open out her cram book on the counter, and while she read and learned and memorized, her subconscious would create. Like that time she was working on *Gwendolyn Hannover v. Howard Development* and she didn't even remember spooning cocoa into the batter. She had lied and told CeeCee the cake was California-style German chocolate. It had tasted just fine. And Howard Development of the dangerously broken sidewalk, her client, won on the technicality that Lowry discovered—putting her that first big step ahead of Jeremy Crae.

Tonight's recipe would be a mix of Southern ingredients and Illinois law. She would call it 'The Lake Michigan'. She would let her hands choose whatever was easiest to grab in the refrigerator—orange juice, grape juice or ginger ale. Coconut cake didn't have to be made with milk. CeeCee would frown, but Trey would laugh. He would kiss Lowry and tell her what he always said—that she was one half of a marriage of like minds, partner in a timeline of success. HONK!

JJJJJ

Some days Justa woke up to darkness. More often, she woke up to light.

Light

Like the day she came home from work to find a letter from Mom in the mailbox. Mom was forwarding a postcard—a simple photograph of three red-orange persimmons in a row, black-markered with faces and hands in the classic 'see no evil', 'hear no evil', 'speak no evil' poses. The only clue to the sender was the circle of pasted stars on the back, below the stamp with its Saint Louis, Missouri, cancellation.

"Oh, my god!" Justa returned to examining the photograph. Once her eyes had been filled with this color. Once she had had a friend named Little Stars.

"Gil?" She went inside to where he was measuring a pinecone with calipers.

"Justie?" he looked up.

"Siu-Sing's alive." Aunt Edith's analysis of that terrible time, Justa's freshman year, had been absolutely right. Justa hadn't cried this hard since Stanford. Salt trickled into her mouth. Amazingly, all tears tasted the same.

Dark/Light

She couldn't wait to show the postcard to Lowry, who was picking her up on Sunday for a quick lunch in Moraga. Lowry was on a flying visit to San Francisco—legal business. Lowry had rented a car at the airport.

After getting into the car, Justa held out the postcard for Lowry to see.

Lowry gave one glance before pushing down the gas pedal.

Justa finished buckling in. "You never met Siu-Sing, but you remember, right?"

"Sure!" It was an automatic assent. At some time in her recent life, Lowry had learned to love speeding. She was oddly intent upon the street, the intersection, turning toward the direction of Caldecott Tunnel. She entered semidarkness, where the dim glow flicked by. There was a hunch in her shoulders Justa didn't remember. Lowry looked as though she were trying to push herself forward, bypassing a future second of time.

"Are you okay?" Justa worried.

"Sure!" Lowry's laugh was as brittle as thin sugar. "You gotta move on, past the past." She chuckled at her double use of the one word. "Trey says it's the future that counts."

The historian Lowry would never had made such a comment. This current Lowry began a stream of endless dictums, all beginning with, "Trey says..." Trey said that working in a library was perfect for someone like

Justa. "Quiet and healing, right?" Lowry pronounced, with the same endless, but achingly breakable, cheer.

Justa was suddenly afraid: "Are you happy?"

"Of course!" But Lowry's voice hardened. She drove in silence until, minutes later, finally in Moraga, pulling up into their driveway: "Trey says that suburbia is perfect for children." This was her real voice, her own self. A voice full of question.

Dad was opening the driver's door. "Low!" He tried to clutch Lowry in a hug before she was free of her seatbelt. Lowry's new laugh reemerged in full.

And Justa heard: Lowry had fallen out of tune.

⌒

Mom had prepared a lunch of Lowry's childhood favorites, modernized—which meant soy beans in the macaroni salad, and tofu in the brownies.

Lowry was the first to sit, the first to pick up her fork, the first to start talking. "I'm not even certified in California, but Mr. Bender wanted someone from MJ&N to come along and listen while he conferred with lawyers out here. Mr. Bender has a cousin who has a cousin who owns some property up in the Sierras. You know that saying, 'There's gold in them thar hills'? It comes from a *Georgia* gold rush! Trey says real estate is today's gold rush." And so on and so forth. When everybody finished eating, Lowry popped up from her chair. "Let's go for a walk! Trey says exercise is invaluable for the legal mind."

Justa had been watching Mom and Dad. They were utterly overwhelmed by the new Lowry. "Go ahead," Justa urged. "I'll clean up." With the family gone, she heard only a whoosh of air pushing through the dining room heat vent. She had grown up to this constant wind-chord in C major.

She knew: it wasn't all that hard to fall out of tune. So much depended on life's circumstances. Life's circumstances could change; a person might change. Over the first, that person might have no control. But she could shape the second with personal effort. Justa pulled Siu-Sing's postcard from her jeans pocket. Siu-Sing had figured out how to redefine a color.

Justa went to sit on her piano bench. Her bottom still fit perfectly. She lifted the fallboard to reveal the keys. She allowed her hands to curve, to position themselves for a C major scale. But her body wasn't flexible enough to play. It wasn't only her fingers and hands and wrists that were stiff—her elbows, shoulders, neck and back were stiff, too. Mrs. Hudson had prescribed Hanon exercises for everything from finger fatigue to backache. Justa stood to open the bench. Here it was, her old copy of *The Hanon Studies*. She placed the book on the stand. She pressed her right thumb down on middle C. The tone was sour. She hadn't played on this piano since college. It obviously hadn't been tuned. Out of tune, but not broken.

"Trey says…" Faint, but clear. Lowry's corruption of voice jangled Justa's heart.

But Justa could only fix what she understood. That's where she had to begin.

When the family got home, she was filling the dishwasher.

❧

She stole the Hanon. She didn't let anybody see her take it. She stuck the slender music book beneath her sweater and flattened it against her belly. She wore it out of the house and into Lowry's rental car. The trip back was a 'Trey says' litany. The book's not-so-subtle creaks bent into silence beneath Trey's wife's incessant chatter. Trey's wife regretted not seeing Hiro. Trey's wife couldn't linger in Moraga because Mr. Bender was attending a cocktail party at the San Francisco Yacht Club.

Hiro hadn't been able to schedule around lunch; he had hoped for dinner. Trey's wife didn't seem to care.

When Lowry halted, briefly, in Berkeley—"See you, Justie!"—Justa could escape.

She reminded herself: she could only fix one thing at a time.

She was alone in the apartment. Gil was up in Davis at a mathematics conference. She measured their card table with her hands—four octaves. She sat with her back erect but easy, her fingers arranged to tap. For a second, she wished laminated particle board could depress, but quickly gave up on the impossible. She would have to pull her taps, so as not to harm her joints. Now, with her mind in every part of her body, she began. In the old days she had played these exercises in a mental fugue, enjoying the mindlessness of repetition. Now she paid attention, feeling every physical change.

The next day she smuggled the book to the library.

There, Connor caught her at the reference desk with her fingers, her body, still working. "Justa?" he questioned.

And she confessed: "Once, I was a musician."

"Go for it," he said, bemused.

It was a freedom, of sorts. From then on, Justa's hands worked in-between questions: "Miss! I need to know about Brazil!"; "My goodness, are you doing Hanon? I played myself until I was twelve;" "If you wouldn't mind putting away your finger games and letting me know..." Justa worked until her back regained some of its old posture. As her body reformed and her muscles regrouped, she heard: the inaudible but endless chains of sound she created were reopening a path. If she chose, she could once again enter infinity.

She brought the Hanon back to the apartment. She laid the music book on the kitchen counter. She didn't speak: she waited for Gil to recognize the book's size, its shape, the title.

"Justie!" His face blazed with hope.

"Maybe." She had to caution him.

Light

For the first time, ever, she invited her own friend to dinner. Connor had never yet met Gil—who Connor sometimes referred to as 'Justa's elusive significant other'. He would also meet Giant: Giant had finally secured funding and, while he was forecasting Senegal's gross national product, was back in Justa's kitchen.

Giant had just begun to heat the oil for the fish when Connor rang the doorbell. Justa brought him in, and Giant, with his usual good manners, turned to hold out his hand. Giant froze. ("Did you know?" Justa later asked Gil. Gil questioned himself, "Me?" before realizing, "Not a clue!") Connor put his hand into Giant's. The two men stared at each other with the kind of recognition that had no history. The oil in the pan sputtered, then splattered and 'fwit!' became a fire.

"Giant!" Gil-the-fireman scolded.

But the dinner party had become something entirely unexpected: Giant's and Connor's first date. Gil ended up frying the fish. Justa served the food. Giant and Connor, sitting an acute angle away from each other at the card table, stared in silent communion. They didn't stay long; they refused desert. They paused at the door and attempted a graceful farewell. "How very nice..." Connor's glance wafted from Justa to Gil. "...to finally meet..." His glance kept going, landing on the futon couch where Justa had earlier dumped the Hanon "...your music."

It was, as Gil said, a fractalian slip.

LLLLL

A Sunday afternoon in March, and Lowry was doing four things at once: she was composing a motion for summary judgment in the case of *Friends of Howard School v. Stenworth Development*; she was tipping a can of plum tomatoes into a pot over the stove; she was ignoring the noise four men can make when they are watching a basketball game on television; she was trying not to cry. She had no reason to cry, none at all. But lately she had taken to tearing up at the smallest provocation—spilling tomato juice on her shoe, for example. She was embarrassed and puzzled by these occasional surprisings of sorrow. Trey was irritated and annoyed.

Lowry dropped a paper towel on the floor and toed it. There, all clean. She kicked the towel into a corner. She should probably sweep the floor. She had yet to clear the dining table where she had her stacks of photocopies arranged—not chronologically, but by a logical development of persuasive argument that she thought she could use to stop this issue from ever going to trial. A ruling favoring Stenworth Development would put her another big step above Jeremy Crae.

An eventual win for Stenworth Development would mean the demolishment of another historic site in Atlanta's Old Fourth Ward. Many Black luminaries had attended Howard School. Martin Luther King Jr. was one. The alum Lowry most admired—at the moment—was Mildred McDaniel, who in 1956 left segregated Atlanta, segregated America, to travel to the Summer Olympics in Australia and win the gold medal in the women's high jump.

Mildred McDaniel must have gotten her start on the school's playing fields. Perhaps she had lived in one of the small homes surrounding the school. Stenworth Development wanted to cover over Mildred's playing fields, tear down the school building, construct warehouses, and turn an historic neighborhood center into a mass of concrete.

Lowry's eyes began to leak again. She popped another pill. She glanced up at the top shelf of the bookcase nearest the dining table. She couldn't really see with such watery eyes, but she knew what she wanted to look at: two small photographs leaned against old law school textbooks. One photo was of Willow's three dark-haired children. Willow—now Guglielma—had become an Italian citizen. The more recent photo was of Justa, Gil, Victor and Emi Yamada, posed before the Peace Pagoda in San Francisco's Japantown. Emi was...what?...Victor's aunt? No, a sort of cousin. Everybody had written a hello to Lowry on the back.

Along with the photo, Justa had sent a Daruma doll, a small pot of sticky ink, and a hard-bristled paint brush. Trey had declared the Daruma doll ugly, which it was. But that was what it was supposed to be: the papier-mâché head of a stylized Japanese monk, painted bright red, with fierce features boldly stroked in black. The eyes were round spaces of white. The idea was that the recipient of such a doll, Lowry, would set a goal and mark the goal by painting a pupil in one eye. Once that goal was achieved, she was to paint in the second pupil.

Because Trey hadn't cared for the doll, Lowry took it to her office. There it sat on top of another bookcase, both eyes still blank. For some reason, Lowry had not yet been able to come up with a goal.

Ah! Emi was Victor's first cousin once removed! The drug had finally hit the targeted portion of her brain. Lowry blinked her attention down from the photos. With renewed concentration, she studied the notes she had scribbled last night. Her yellow legal pad was spattered tomato-red. She still had so much left to do.

The men in her living room—Trey, his father, grandfather and brother-in-law—all shouted. Something was happening with *Furman University v. Indiana*.

Lowry tuned them out.

She could tune out shouts, commentary, commercials, the cheery notes of Up With People during halftime. But she couldn't not-hear the wood-upon-wood scrape of the opening front door. Then a click, click, click. CeeCee must have worn high heels to her all-day Sunday School retreat. Lowry could blur off the sounds of the men greeting their family's alpha female. But she could not ignore CeeCee's approaching shoes.

Lowry narrowed her eyes until her vision was limited to her legal pad. But a drawer behind her was pulled open. Its tangle of utensils became a clash of metal chimes. One of those utensils clinked against the side of the sauce pot. "Too salty," CeeCee whispered.

An air horn would have been no more disturbing. Lowry's ears couldn't help but open. She gave up on *Friends of Howard School v. Stenworth Development*. "Hello, CeeCee," she sighed.

"Shall I put water on?" CeeCee bent, awkward in her high heels, to open a lower cabinet. She saw the paper towel, plucked it with her fingernails, and held it for Lowry to see.

Lowry grabbed, tossed the towel into the bin beneath the sink, and pointed. "Up there."

"I always keep my large pots low," CeeCee instructed. "Large, low"—as if it were a basic principle known to all but the incorrigibly ignorant. Standing, reaching, she came face-to-face with the cake Lowry had made yesterday, out-of-the-way and on top of the refrigerator. "My, how interesting," CeeCee commented, her usual opinion of one of Lowry's cakes.

"It's a Bourbon cake," Lowry said. She and CeeCee looked in unison over to where the men sat, drinking as well as refereeing the game. Trey had made a special trip to the liquor store so that Douglas would have plenty of bourbon.

"How many has he had?" CeeCee demanded to know.

"I don't keep count."

CeeCee sniffed her exasperation. She opened the refrigerator door, found a bottle of ginger ale, and took it to where the men were cheering. The testosterone-charged celebration slammed to a halt. CeeCee topped up Douglas's highball glass with ginger ale, left him that bottle to drink from, and carried the bourbon back to the kitchen. Cautiously, the men resumed their congratulation of their favorite forward. "Way to go, Jonathan!"

As CeeCee passed alongside Lowry's table, she paused. She set the bourbon down and began to tidy, gathering Lowry's carefully arranged cases into one hodgepodge pile. She disposed of the pile by putting it on top of the bookcase, where she lingered. Lowry guessed that CeeCee had found Willow's snapshot because CeeCee murmured, "Lovely." CeeCee would not have said the same about Justa, Gil, Victor and Emi.

CeeCee brought the bourbon into the kitchen. She placed Willow's photo where both she and Lowry could see it. "Whose are these?"

"My college roommate's."

Which led to the question CeeCee always asked—whenever, wherever. Once she had asked this question in the middle of a cocktail party. Lowry's boss, Mr. Nowak, had been nearby enough to hear. "Isn't it about time you got started?"

To which Lowry always answered, "When I'm ready."

CeeCee's usual counter was, "You're not getting any younger, you know." But today she hesitated. She turned the little carousel of spice jars, selected, and began pinching dried herbs into Lowry's sauce. "I wonder"— she began in a voice so low Lowry had to tilt her head to hear—"if you might be having marital problems?"

This was a new slant on the subject. "You're wondering *what*?"

CeeCee whispered: "This afternoon, at the retreat, we broke into selected groups to talk about personal things. About how we want to improve our lives. Some people in my group began talking about, well...pleasure." With oregano-basil-rosemary flecked fingers, CeeCee gestured at her abdomen. "Do you understand?" She obviously did not want to elucidate.

"You mean, like...?" Lowry was suddenly awash with glee.

Vaginal orgasms—CeeCee mouthed the words so that Lowry had to read her lips. CeeCee resumed whispering: "They increase the mothering hormone."

Lowry's glee fountained; it geysered. She whispered back, "Have you ever had a vaginal orgasm?"

CeeCee glanced to where the men were still engrossed in their game. "Of course," in merely a breath.

"Nonsense," and Lowry let her voice rise. "You're delusional, CeeCee," she announced in her attorney voice, her court voice, loud enough to make the men turn their heads. "Or you're lying. Because I know you're not a transsexual."

CeeCee gasped.

Cheers from the television audience.

"Three points!" Douglas attempted to swing his fellows back to the television.

"Look at that guy go!" Clarence seconded, waving the others around. Chuck and Trey complied.

Even though deprived of her jury, Lowry had no trouble providing herself as her own expert witness. "The vaginal orgasm is a myth," she preached. "That's been proven by Masters and Johnson. Surely you've heard of their book? *Human Sexual Response?*"

"I don't read filth!" CeeCee hissed fiercely.

"It's a text," Lowry expounded, "academic, you know. Dr. Masters being a gynecologist and Mrs. Johnson a research psychologist." She narrowed her aim: "But I know you read *Newsweek*—I've seen it at your house. So you must have seen that article about men who have themselves surgically altered to become women. About how the surgeon takes the skin from the former penis, and uses that skin—with all the nerve endings intact—to line the new vagina. So when another man's penis enters this 'vagina' there's stimulation. Pleasure. Orgasm."

CeeCee shuddered.

"People who are born female have penile-type skin, too, but it's limited to the clitoris," Lowry continued. "That's where a born female's orgasm comes from—her clitoris. It's only transsexuals who are ever 'blessed' by the vaginal variety." She let CeeCee absorb that fact, and then concluded with the preface which was also her summary. "So when you say you've had a vaginal orgasm I know you have to be either delusional or lying. Because I'm certain you're not a transsexual."

"God, Lowry!" CeeCee actually blasphemed. Her face was pink, her eyes damp. Without washing the oregano from her hands, she fled the kitchen. She circled the basketball fans to hover behind Douglas, leaving Lowry to put the pasta in the water with no comments about 'too many noodles,' or whether or not to put in salt, or how long the spaghetti should boil.

The doorbell rang: it was Elaine, bringing Clarey from a schoolmate's birthday party. The family sat down to eat. But after Elaine had commented on the meal, and Clarey had described his party, and the men had summarized the game, conversation faltered. During normal Sunday suppers, at CeeCee's house, CeeCee offered cues, established rules, provided direction. But tonight it seemed she couldn't inflate her lungs enough to speak. When Douglas asked, with careful interest, "How was the retreat, dear?" she looked like she might vomit.

"I'm full, Mama!" Clarey blared, taking advantage of his mother's extraordinary weakness to test the echoing quality of Lowry's apartment.

CeeCee rose. Click, click, click. She didn't say 'thank you', or even 'goodbye'. She led Clarey and Douglas out the front door and into the apartment hallway.

"What was that all about?" Trey asked after Clarence, Chuck and Elaine had also left.

"Sex," Lowry told him.

Much later that evening—after a clitoral orgasm, not a vaginal one – Lowry lay awake and reviewed her day. She had won the latest Lowry v. CeeCee skirmish, so she should feel successful. But she didn't. Instead, she felt empty. That was what all her victories felt like nowadays. Or now-a-nights, because these reviews always filled those hours during which she no longer slept. During the daytime she was alive with purpose, smart and insightful. But at night she chastised herself for being twisty and manipulative, for using her intellect to amplify what was only marginally honest. During the daytime she was productive and proud. But in the darkness she worried: was she becoming the kind of person who fought to win, no matter the cost? Was she was becoming the kind of person who sought to destroy, not to build?

Deep into Monday morning, she turned her face into her pillow. Very quietly, so as to not awaken Trey, she wept until her pillow was damp.

CCCCC

Crystal was in her office, grousing.

For twenty-one years she had been in school—two years of nursery school, thirteen of public school, four of college, and two of graduate school. Now she was out of school, finally, sort of, with a master's degree that had put her right back into school as a teacher. She was an instructor at Simmons College; she had a two year contract. It all sounded very grown-up and glamorous, and extremely impressive, but what it meant was that in return for interacting with undergraduates all day long, Crystal earned barely enough to cover her expenses. Her rent was $400 a month!

Crystal began to write 'stupid!' on a student paper, but stopped with the 's'. She ended up writing 'simplistic, go deeper' instead. She was trying: she knew that the trick was to keep her grousing out of her grading. But only last week the Chair of the English department had taken Crystal aside to recommend, firmly, that from now on Crystal articulate 'Think for yourself' with a certain degree of kindness. It was not the first time the Chair had made such a recommendation.

Crystal was failing at her first real job.

She was grateful when the phone rang—an almost-never interruption because Crystal's students never called.

"Hi," Bee announced herself, and Crystal knew exactly where Bee was standing. Crystal had once used those same pay phones at Corona del Mar High School. "We have to talk," Bee said crisply. Succinctly—as if she had a limited number of quarters to spend—she supplied the reason for her call. "Mother is driving me nuts. She followed me into the bathroom last night and talked for a solid hour while I sat in the tub. All about you."

"Tell her to stay out of my business," Crystal growled.

"She's afraid you'll lose Scott. She thinks you're not seeing him enough. She's getting desperate. She wants you to jump on it."

Crystal wrote 'Oh, shit' on her notepad, in red pen. She and Scott had been so naive, thinking a Boston-to-New York relationship would be easy. That was before Scott's average work day escalated to twelve hours, including weekends. That was before Crystal learned how much time and energy it took to prepare three new classes, three times a week. And the route between their two cities was horrible—nothing like Highway 5. Instead it was a complicated tangle of over 200 miles, with two toll booths. Crystal hated driving it.

"That will be one dollar for another two minutes," the operator interrupted.

Clunk, clunk, clunk, clunk. Bee inserted more coins. Her voice returned, now brightened: "Do it, Crystal! Jump his bones!"

Crystal's couldn't help herself. She snorted, spraying snot over the 'simplistic' student's paper.

"'If only Crystal were sweeter, kinder, more generous,'" Bee mimicked Mother. As herself, she commented, "You know, Crystal, sometimes I think Mother enjoys being upset about you. You give her something to think about. She's never bored when you're on her mind."

"Wonderful. I'm my mother's recreation." Crystal's bitterness flowed.

"No. You're the thumbtack on the velvet seat cushion of her life." Bee thought out loud: "She can't seem to get off you."

"Why, Bee, that's good!" Crystal was actually cheered. "That's really clever!"

Bee giggled from her end of the line. "It just came to me. Whoops! No more quarters."

For long minutes afterward, Crystal held onto her imagine of a phone booth beneath the California sun. Eventually, though, she had to return to Simmons: where she was a teacher; where she was alone; where winter's evening fell depressingly early in this cold, northern city.

Resolutely, she re-bent to her grading. From time to time she glanced out her office windows. When twilight blurred the outlines of students crossing the quad, she rose to pull on her drab-gray coat—bought here in Boston for its bulk, not its beauty. The Longwood MBTA was closest, most convenient for the ride back to her apartment. But the Fine Arts station attracted fewer Simmons people. Today, especially, Crystal hoped to avoid conversation.

She was out of luck. Terry Sullivan, her very first Simmons acquaintance, was occupying most of a bench, surrounded by all the paraphernalia Terry considered necessary to convey the image of an earnest assistant professor. Terry waved; "Crystal, come sit!"

Crystal had no choice. She had to squeeze herself between a lunch basket with a thermos poking out the top, and two canvas bags with angled bumps indicating books. Crystal balanced her own tote over her drab-gray lap.

"How are things going?" Terry inquired. She spoke with the kind of eager, hushed horror Mother's friends used when discussing an acquaintance's diagnosis of cancer.

"Okay," Crystal lied. Terry knew too much; Terry knew too little. Terry lived on hearsay; she didn't know Crystal at all.

"Nurture: from the Latin, *nutrire*, meaning 'to suckle'." Now Terry was being pedantic—but why, and about what? In response to Crystal's blankness, Terry explained: "Don't you remember? That's what the Dean said at the faculty meeting before Convocation. Our duty, as teachers, is to nurture our students."

"Suckle them?" Crystal was repelled by the image.

"Treat them like family," Terry said fiercely. And to Crystal's great relief, a train pulled in, drowning out anything else Terry might want to say.

It was a crowded train. Crystal ran to a car well behind the one Terry chose. Crystal actually found an empty seat. Once again she settled her tote on her lap. She had no trouble recalling the Dean's pep talk last autumn. The Dean was never pedantic. Her definition of 'nurture' had been an urge that her faculty behave in a parental, or avuncular, or aunt-like manner. 'Family.' The Dean had definitely used the word 'family'.

Crystal couldn't even be big-sisterly. She hadn't yet figured out how to relax with her students—they weren't Bee or Sean. She couldn't even laugh with them. And today she made a student cry. It had happened during Freshman Composition. Crystal's lesson was based on Amy Lowell's poem, 'Patterns'. One of the girls, another Amy, asked for the meaning of 'squills'.

"You should have looked it up," Crystal said shortly.

There was silence all around, and then the girl sitting behind Amy asked, as if for them all, "Miss Kelsey, are we really that different from Stanford students?"

Crystal had to think for a moment. She answered honestly: "No. But you're different from me."

That's when Amy cried. Crystal was so perplexed, upset – and angry at herself, above all else—that she could hardly watch the other girls comfort their friend. She could hardly wait for the class to be over, for that stretch of solitude during office hours. Now, on the train, she kept hearing Mother's opinion as a verdict: 'If only Crystal were sweeter, kinder, more generous.' Sweeter! Kinder! More generous! The words became wrecking balls, thudding, smashing, squashing, compressing every bit of self Crystal possessed. She clutched her tote to her chest so she wouldn't be reduced to dust and puddles. Her old green travel tote: once it had been her good luck tote; it had been where she gathered the poems for her master's project; it had been new on the day she met Justa.

Instead of continuing onward to her small and dingy—but with an included parking space—apartment, Crystal got off at the Longwood station. She returned to Simmons. She walked rapidly through the quad, stopping in her office to pick up her dance bag. She half-ran into the residential campus, where the dance studio was mercifully empty. There, the door shut, she turned her tape recorder on loud and let her body take over. Her limbs railed furiously to the beat of a Stones' album, *Out of Our Heads*. Her fists punched the air. Her feet kicked and leaped. She ran, she spun.

But still, she went nowhere but in a circle...even though she tried, and she tried, and she tried.

Her neck, her spine, sagged. Went limp.

With a desultory hand, she wiped at her shoulders with the towel from her dance bag. She could attempt another tape. Fleetwood Mac. But the studio door opened and an anxious face poked through the opening. "Miss Kelsey?"

Crystal looked at the clock. The Simmons Dance Company, represented by this face, was waiting to start their practice. Crystal knew the Dance Company's schedule well. Long ago, during those first weeks at Simmons, when she had still been hopeful, she had taken class with them.

"All right," she said. "I'm sorry. Come on in." She stuffed recorder, tapes and towel into her bag. She draped her drab-gray coat over her sweat-damp leotard. As the girls filed past, she left.

> *Life is like water.*
> *It flows through your hands.*
> *Grasping,*
> *You lose it.*
> *Cupping,*
> *You hold for*
> *Those short moments.*
> *My body is a sieve.*

LLLLL

Once upon a time—and in a place very, very far away from Atlanta—buying shoes had been fun. Back then and back there, Mom would take Lowry and Justa into Oakland for the afternoon, with a stop at Mrs. See's for chocolates. But right here and right now, on this particular Saturday, Lowry was annoyed. And angry at a shoe that had broken its heel. Because of that shoe, she would have to insert a trip to Rich's department store between the drive-up laundry and a stop at the grocery for the shredded coconut she needed for tomorrow's cake. She calculated: if she arrived at Rich's when the doors first opened, she'd lose no more than a half hour to shoe-buying.

Downstairs, in her basement garage, she took out some of her frustration on the Z. She started it up—it was overdue for an oil change, damnit!—and slammed the gears into reverse. The Z jerked backwards.

When she arrived at Rich's, most of the parking slots were already filled. She had forgotten. This was Founders Day; Rich's had opened an hour early, and the store was bursting with sales. Lowry's eyes instantly moistened. A discounted price wouldn't make up for the time she was going to lose waiting for someone to help her.

She ran inside anyway, grabbed a sample black pump from a display, and waved it purposefully each time one of the sales clerks happened to look her way. A woman standing behind her said, cheerfully, "Throw it at 'em. I'll throw mine, too," and Lowry turned. She recognized, then didn't, then recognized again. She knew this woman; how could she know somebody in a city where she hardly knew anybody? Her memory reached back and touched The Table at Stanford.

"Betsy?" she asked, disbelieving.

"Lowry?"

"Oh, my God!"

"My goodness!"

They hugged, sample shoes circling around each other's shoulders.

"You look so..." Lowry searched for the fair and fresh-faced girl beneath this almost-strange woman's veneer of grief and accumulated responsibility. Did Betsy also, some mornings, look into the mirror and not know who she saw? "...much the same. Except for the short hair." It was a white lie, the best Lowry could come up with.

"And you've become so thin! You look fabulous!" Betsy returned her own kind untruth. "What are you doing in Atlanta?"

"Married. Working." Lowry thought of what to say next: she had never known Betsy well; Betsy had always been Justa's friend. Justa! Lowry had good news about Justa! "Justie's getting back into music."

"Back? What do you mean: 'getting back'?"

And Lowry felt a binding string snap free in her heart. Here, at last, was someone with whom she could discuss Justa. Lowry continued to wave her shoe, her words pouring out, finishing with, "It was as if Justie had died inside. It was awful."

Betsy was appalled. "I'll call her. I didn't before because, well, I'm living with my mother. I'm divorced. What I mean is, I had to convince Farhad to divorce me. I couldn't do it myself, not in Iran. Women can't divorce there. But it's ever so easy for the men. All Farhad had to do was say 'talaq' three times before witnesses, and our marriage was over."

"And that's legal?" Lowry wanted to hear more, but a clerk was finally coming their way. Lowry bought her shoes. Betsy bought hers. Then Lowry did something totally unscheduled—she chose to give away an entire hour. Conversation with Betsy was satisfying so deep a hunger. "Do you have time for coffee?"

They took over a table in the Magnolia Room, upstairs. Betsy ordered sweetened ice tea. It was her turn to tell: "After the Shah's government fell, Iran became so dangerous." She touched her pixie hairdo. "One afternoon my little girl's nurse sneaked in while I was napping and cut off all my hair. The woman said I deserved to be stoned, that I was an American whore, that my child should be thrown into the streets."

Lowry hadn't followed international news for months. She couldn't comprehend. "Why?"

"War." Betsy's answer was simple. "That's what war does to people. We were in the midst of a civil war. And to make it worse, I couldn't just up and leave. In Iran, the father has all rights. Farhad only agreed to let us go after he understood the danger to Katty." Betsy took a photograph from her capacious purse so Lowry could admire the child. "He loves her. He loves us both."

"Do you still love him?" Suddenly that was the most important question Lowry could think to ask.

"Yes," said Betsy. "I do. But not enough to expose my daughter to such hatred."

Lowry's hour was up. She really, truly, had to get on with her day. She pulled a card case from her purse, extracted a Matchison, Johnson & Nowak business card, and wrote her home number on the back. "Call me," she begged.

"Chambliss," Betsy read. "You hadn't told me your married name."

And Lowry realized: for this last hour, she had been Lowry Matthews.

Adjacent to the Magnolia Room, she saw the Bake Shop. She could skip going to the grocery: she would *buy* a cake for tomorrow's mandatory supper at CeeCee's house!

And another of those strings binding Lowry's heart snapped free.

CeeCee was unflatteringly pleased to accept the Bake Shop box. "A real coconut cake!" she enthused. She put the Rich's specialty on a crystal cake stand—'Clare', by Waterford. Lowry's creations never sat on a cake stand.

The rest of the family also approved. At the end of the meal old Clarence even smacked his lips. "Um, um," he said. "That was a treat, Lowry." Then he cleared his throat as if to make an announcement. "Now that you two have made a good start"—he nodded down the table to Trey—"it's time you put down some roots."

Murmurs of agreement rose from Chuck, Elaine and Douglas—as if they were all in on a secret. Lowry looked to Trey. He was regarding his grandfather with the same enthusiasm with which the family had attacked their slices of Rich's cake. Lowry didn't understand.

"Whatever are you talking about, Great-Granddaddy?" Clarey asked.

"I was younger than you when I took on my first house." Clarence indulged in reminiscence, spinning out the suspense. "A wife, two children and a Studebaker." He chuckled. "Down payments are steeper now. Mrs. Martha Hunsford, she's a real estate professional, tells me that for you to live in the right kind of neighborhood you'll need close to twenty-five thousand dollars as a down payment. So...here it is." Removing a slip of paper from his breast pocket, he put the check on an empty bread and butter plate, and sent it down the table.

Lowry was still trying to sort: what Clarence wanted, what Clarence expected. But Trey grabbed. He threw his other arm around Lowry's shoulders, and hugged. "Thank you, Granddaddy!" he crowed. He kissed Lowry's cheek. "Isn't this great, honey?" He calculated out loud: "Right now we make enough for an eighty thousand dollar mortgage, easy. But with what Lowry should get for her next raise, and including her next bonus, I think we can go up to a hundred thousand."

That's when Lowry started to cry.

"Our first home!" Trey sang into her ear.

"Don't start too small," Chuck cautioned. "You need to start entertaining. You're building up a business, son. You need to start making more of your connections."

"Mrs. Hunsford can drive you around tomorrow." Clarence was beaming at Lowry's reaction. "Take the day off from work; give yourselves a holiday."

"I can't go, Granddaddy." Trey excused himself. "That arson case is coming up. I'll bet Lowry can manage a few hours, though—can't you, honey?"

Lowry didn't answer. She couldn't. She was sobbing now.

Trey hugged her tight while Clarence claimed, "It's not that much money, sweetheart."

But Lowry's tears were coming even faster. They were dropping from her face onto CeeCee's fine china.

"Lowry, dear?" Elaine questioned.

And suddenly CeeCee was at Lowry's side, pulling back Lowry's chair, helping Lowry to stand. With her arm across Lowry's back—so much lower than Trey's arm ever reached—she led Lowry out of the dining room, down the hallway, and into the guest bedroom. "Lie down," she ordered.

Lowry lay. She drew her knees up into a fetal position. Her tears now ran sideways down her face. There was the sound of water from the adjoining bathroom, the cool dampness of a cloth on her forehead. "You would think nobody has ever been nice to you before," CeeCee scolded.

"I don't..." Lowry tried, but her voice was thick. "I can't..."

She didn't finish because other people began to speak from a slight distance away—the doorway, perhaps. First Trey: "What's wrong?" Then Elaine: "Is she ill?"

CeeCee didn't reply. Instead, she commanded: "Trey, get me some brandy. Mama, get everybody else into the living room and give them their coffee."

"I don't want…" Lowry tried again.

But the washcloth was wiping at her nose, around her mouth. Small, strong hands lifted her into a semi-sitting position. The hard curve of a glass pushed against her lips. "Drink," CeeCee told her. And Lowry swallowed alcohol and salty tears.

"Is she ever going to stop?" Trey's concern was half complaint.

"Go home, Trey." CeeCee allowed no argument. "You can bring back whatever Lowry needs to spend the night. Now, go!"

The door to the guest bedroom susurred over carpet. Lowry's eyes opened: through a prism of tears, CeeCee's face appeared almost compassionate. The distortion of color made the clarity of CeeCee's eyes seem infinite.

"You don't want what?" CeeCee asked. She didn't pause for an answer; she disappeared into the bathroom. "What on earth is worth all these tears?" She returned with a box of tissues. "Get under the covers. You're probably shivering because you've dehydrated yourself. I'll go get you some tea."

Lowry never drank that cup of tea because, once she was under the covers, clutching a wad of tissues in her hand, she fell asleep—truly asleep, not a doze disturbed by remorse and guilt. Once, she was half-awakened by voices. CeeCee: "She's been taking these for how long?" And Trey: "She never says she's tired…" Another time she opened her eyes to find the room dark except for a little light over by the Parsons chair, a candle flame illuminating CeeCee who sat upright with her mouth slack. Perhaps in response to Lowry's stare, CeeCee snapped alert. "So," CeeCee said, and in four steps she was at Lowry's side, helping Lowry remove her blouse.

The blouse was silk: slippery. Lowry's slacks were linen: stiff. Underwires dug beneath her breasts. She removed each garment with CeeCee's assistance. When she was down to just panties—a tiny bikini, Trey's favorite—CeeCee dropped a nightgown over Lowry's head. "Drink this," CeeCee said. 'This' was milk, room temperature, but warmed with a good dollop of bourbon. "Good night." And CeeCee finally left, shutting the guest room door behind her.

She had forgotten, perhaps on purpose, the candle. Its warm yellow light flickered Lowry back into another sleep. Lowry slept so deeply, she didn't dream.

When she next awakened, daylight shone around the edges of CeeCee's guest room curtains. Lowry had to go to the bathroom. She couldn't bear the sight of her clothing, neatly folded on top of the bureau, so afterwards she returned to her nest beneath the covers. The sound of the toilet must have cued CeeCee, because minutes later CeeCee was entering the room with a tray and what smelled like breakfast. "I brought you herbal tea instead of coffee. I want you to drink the entire pot." CeeCee waited until Lowry had taken most of the tea, all of the orange juice, every bite of the muffin and egg, before asking, "You don't want what?"

And Lowry got to say what she hadn't been able to manage the evening before: "A house."

"Why not?"

"Because it'll all be on me. I'll have to pay for the mortgage, do the upkeep. There'll be a yard. I'll have to find time to entertain."

"In a few years Trey's practice will be a success," CeeCee reasoned. "He'll take over the payments, hire housekeepers, gardeners, caterers. He'll earn plenty—and more."

"But will it ever be enough?" Lowry's eyes were welling again.

CeeCee stood by, saying nothing for a moment. Then she pulled an amber vial from her apron pocket, and held it so Lowry could read the prescription label. "What are these for?"

"They help me," Lowry explained.

"How?"

"They keep me on track."

"Who's track?" But CeeCee answered her own question: "Trey's. It's the Triple C Railroad all over again." She grimaced. "That's what Mama calls it when someone gets run over by a Chambliss. It's mostly people like Mama and you who get flattened. But sometimes it's another Chambliss. Did anybody ever tell you how Clarey got his name?"

"No."

"I wanted natural childbirth. I took Lamaze classes. But Daddy and Granddaddy thought natural childbirth was a primitive idea. They convinced the doctor to give me drugs. *My* doctor. They took it upon themselves to talk to *my* doctor. They didn't bother to consult Douglas. When I woke up, Granddaddy was holding the baby and Daddy was grinning so wide. The first male of the new generation—they were ever so proud of themselves. I decided right then and there to name my son Clarence Claude so Trey couldn't name his child—your child—the same. No more C.C.C.'s."

Lowry gawked.

"You can be ruthless, too," CeeCee remarked. "You certainly are when you're arguing with me. You've learned how to hit me head on."

"I have." Lowry discovered she could still smile.

"What happens when you and Trey disagree?"

"We don't." Lowry told the truth.

"Then I'd say your fights with me are practice for a discussion you should have very soon with your husband. It's your time to do some derailing. No more Triple C Railroad. No more of these." CeeCee stuck the vial back in her pocket. "You'll stay here for the rest of the day. I'll tell Trey to come to supper." CeeCee picked up the tray and maneuvered the door shut as she left.

Lowry lay back. Her body felt so heavy, and her mind was so slow. Without the focusing agent of dextroamphetamine, her thoughts wandered. When was the last time she and Trey had argued? Not since law school. Why? Because Trey was so smart and she was proud of that fact. Why? Because Trey always won. Why? Because he was invincible. Really? And with that question Lowry's thoughts shattered into so many shards, flashing so many colors of possibility, that she was amazed by—of all things—herself.

In 'What I Did For Love'

the dancers of A *Chorus Line* sing their sadness and their hope.

Starting Autumn 1978

LLLLL

In September, when CeeCee decided that she and Lowry would visit a spa, the family protested. CeeCee overrode them all—Trey's, "Lowry will lose three days of work!"; Clarence's, "I don't know if the little lady is well enough to travel"; even Elaine's gentle, "What if Lowry has another episode?" 'Episode' was family code for Lowry's breakdown. CeeCee was perfectly acquainted with Lowry's episode and potential for future episodes. What CeeCee wanted to work on now was the fact that Lowry and Trey had still not had 'the talk'.

CeeCee should have known—even better than Lowry—that Southerners had a million ways of delaying. *Not now, honey. Later.*

Which—all of this—was why Lowry now stood at the windows of a double room in a renovated plantation house, the Liquidamber Inn. The long driveway down below was hidden by a tunnel of crepe myrtles, only partially flowered now. This was the trees' green time of year; this was when they shed pink, lavender, and purple petals. The same colors Lowry had chosen for her bridal bouquet. She hadn't stopped loving those colors.

"Your turn," CeeCee called out, which meant Lowry could use the bathroom. But Lowry simply walked to her suitcase. She didn't mind stripping down in front of CeeCee. CeeCee had seen Lowry naked plenty of times before. Those first two weeks in CeeCee's house, when Lowry was so exhausted—but agitated to the extent of shaking—CeeCee had had to guide Lowry into the shower. Those first two weeks, Lowry had felt as if cleaved by a sword: her one half continually reciting, "I have to go to work," while her other half couldn't move.

Standing before her suitcase, Lowry pulled off her T-shirt. She slid down her jeans. She felt CeeCee clap a heavy terry robe over her shoulders. In this modicum of a cave, Lowry unfastened her bra.

"I hope all that hot mud will ease these knots in my shoulders," CeeCee commented.

Lowry had so many knots throughout her body, they felt more real to her than her muscles.

Wearing the inn's white robe and slippers, she followed CeeCee to a floor lower than the antebellum lobby they had entered earlier. This lower floor had its own lobby—one that opened to a garden surrounded by more crepe myrtles, all white petals this time. Every flower in the garden was white. The woman who greeted them wore a white duster that was almost a doctor's coat. She searched for their names on a list, and then told them, "Martha May will be taking care of you."

Martha May—first and middle name? first and last name?—took them to a room with three tanks, lined-up sarcophagi filled with steaming red-gray clay. "Now, just let yourself down easy," Martha May instructed. Lowry paused at the rim of her tank and stuck in a toe. Not too hot. Not too cold. She handed her robe to Martha May, who continued instructing: "Try to let yourself float a little. If you want to dab it on your face, fine. But remember, you're scheduled for facials later."

Not now, honey, later, Lowry mouthed as she sank into the mud. It supported her with the firmness of Pacific Coast beach sand. It lay over her torso with the weight and warmth of an East Coast winter blanket. It relaxed her into the drowsiness of almost-sleep. During her third week at CeeCee's house Lowry had tried to not sleep—her nightmares were so intense. She had dreamed the fantastical—ugly gardens filled with human-sized pitcher plants that cried out like cats and wept like broken babies. She had dreamed the too-real—her old boyfriend, Stillman, bloated to three times his usual size, sticking pins into his flesh to watch a hideous red gas pollute the air. So many pictures, and they stuck in Lowry's brain like a memory of an Hieronymus Bosch painting.

To counter this, CeeCee prescribed movies, sometimes double features. They saw *Revenge of the Pink Panther, Hooper, Foul Play*—mostly comedies. When Lowry exclaimed at a preview of *Sergeant Pepper's Lonely Hearts Club Band*—a film she was certain CeeCee would never have chosen for herself alone—they went. At the theaters they ate enough popcorn, raisinets and chocolate-covered ice cream bites to substitute for supper. Lowry drank paper cup after paper cup of Coca-Cola. Between the cola, which kept her awake, and the movies, which established galleries of silly portraits in her mind, she survived the second week of withdrawal.

"Ma'am?" Someone was speaking to her now, gently calling her up from the mud-induced slumber. "Mrs. Chambliss?"

My name is Lowry Matthews. That's what it says on my law school diploma. Lowry heard her own voice, but only in her mind. She reached for the towel Martha May was holding—the color of weathered redwood. She obediently rose and wrapped, and then trailed CeeCee to a shower room. She shut herself into a teak-paneled shower and turned the water on full blast so she wouldn't hear CeeCee and Martha May chatting. She had a choice of two soaps: White Magnolia or Holly Berry. She chose White Magnolia because it smelled like pink lemonade. There was a time when Lowry had loved pink lemonade.

After showering, she and CeeCee were scheduled for massage. They lay side by side, each beneath an almost weightless covering of smooth-as-silk cotton sheet. "Um," CeeCee groaned, "this is nice." Their two masseuses kept up a lively conversation in a language Lowry couldn't identify. Jamaican? Haitian? Lowry's masseuse rubbed oil into her shoulders; beneath the strong, gentle pushing, Lowry drifted off again—to ruminate about, for some reason, Dad. She remembered him back when she had thought him the most important man in the world—when she was about twelve, when he entertained them both by teaching her the rudiments of double entry accounting.

She had been such a smart little girl.

Her college years were years of estrangement. Why? Because of Stillman? Partially. But mostly, Lowry now thought—lazily and with the extreme comfort of the muscles in her back sliding upward—because of anger. Lowry's anger. She had needed anger in order to break loose.

Anger was an interesting emotion. It was fire in the belly, a ball of incipient energy, holding tight and unreleased even beneath the kneading of expert hands.

"Mrs. Chambliss?"

I was Lowry Matthews at Stanford, too.

She was next led to a deeply reclining chair. Here, other hands pushed her cheeks in circles. Here, she was lulled by an incense that smelled of fir trees and plums. Dad once mentioned, during a Christmas long ago, that Aunt Edith was 'too independent' for marriage. Code for Lesbian; Lowry had been too young to understand. Now, beneath the facial specialist's clever touch, she wondered if she, Lowry, might also be 'too independent' for marriage. She wasn't a Lesbian. But maybe being too much like Aunt Edith explained her failures. Lowry's eyes popped open. They teared, but not because of drugs. The incense stung.

By the time she and CeeCee were back up in their room, Lowry was fully alert. In the dining room, waiting for their dinner to be served, Lowry held her tongue while CeeCee lectured on the sanctity of marriage, the importance of balancing a couple's needs, the trials and tribulations of holding on. Only when CeeCee launched into the topic of family '*above all*' did Lowry interrupt the flow of opinions. Then Lowry stated simply, not unkindly, "You have all that Claire stuff in your house because you always wanted a name, not initials. Because you should have been 'Claire'."

CeeCee's lecture skidded to a stop. "Yes," she admitted.

Anger could take so many forms.

They ate an excellent meal of shrimp and grits with fried green tomatoes. They ate together silently—not like family, not as friends. But rather with the ease and understanding of allies. They split a piece of chocolate bourbon pecan pie for desert.

CCCCC

'Events can be like stepping stones'

Crystal sat in the antechamber of the Dean's office, watching the Dean's secretary work at her bright red Selectric typewriter. That red was the only brightness in Crystal's moment, in her day. November was cold and gray outside the window. Crystal's heart was cold and gray, too. She had come here for a performance review that would determine whether or not her contract as an instructor would be renewed. She suspected in a matter of minutes she was going be fired from her first professional position.

She thought it must be true that the dying review their lives during the seconds preceding death, because she was doing that now. She was sitting here, on this dull green upholstered sofa, not only because she was failing at being a teacher, but because facts from her past had linked together to lead her to this point.

Number One: Kendall died. When that door closed, Crystal's soul shrank to a pinpoint...

Number Two: ...so she began a master's degree in Creative Writing...

Number Three: ...where she got experience, first as a teaching assistant and then as a section leader for 'Reading and Writing Poetry'—a big introductory course for mostly Freshmen and Sophomores. During two summers she taught at a pre-college prep program where talented high schoolers dropped onto the Stanford campus like manna, stirring everything up with their brightness, naiveté, hilarity and sheer stupidity. For them, Crystal had been more of a troop leader. She led them through a book titled *Sound and Sense*, because that's what poetry was—you created sound that made sense. High schoolers understood that. Undergraduates spent too much time mining their psyches to have fun.

All of which led Crystal to Number Four: She began working as an instructor here at Simmons.

No, go backwards.

What led Crystal to a teaching job was the master's program into which she had fallen because she didn't know what else to do. The reason she had been so lost, was because she lost Kendall. She was lost, still.

"Miss Kelsey?" The Dean's secretary stood before her. The secretary had left her desk and walked this way without Crystal noticing any movements. The secretary stood as if she had been waiting for some while.

"Yes?" Crystal's spine stiffened up, as if held against the kind of Victorian backboard of which Mother would have approved.

"The Dean will see you now."

'Only in Maine did I feel free'

The Dean was at her desk. The Chair of the English Department sat in a wing chair beside a reading lamp. The Dean motioned Crystal to one of those hardwood academic souvenirs with a university seal applied to the upper frame. Crystal read enough of the seal before turning her bottom around. The Dean had attended the University of Michigan.

"Miss Kelsey," the Dean began, and Crystal's heart thudded to the depths. She was not going to be 'Crystal' at this meeting. "Miss Kelsey, Professor Gleason and I have had many consultations about you during your short tenure here at Simmons. We brought you in with all the expectations that accompanied your having Stanford undergraduate and graduate degrees. Your recommendations were somewhat guarded: as a section leader you were, apparently, known for doling out sometimes trenchant criticism. Accurate criticism, but"—the Dean picked up a paper from her desk—"'those students with tougher egos were able to jolly the more sensitive into taking a humorous view of Miss Kelsey's sharpness. Her more egregious adjectives were soon known as 'Crystalisms'." The Dean paused, as if making room for Crystal to reply.

Crystal didn't know what to say. Her back was straight. Her Stanford students had taken to shouting 'Crystalism' whenever she said something they didn't like. At first she was cowed because she thought they were ganging up against her. Then she thought *Well, they're right,* and laughed with them. It became a joke in class, something that kept students in constant attendance because they wanted to be the first to shout out. The suspense and laughter kept the students *listening*. They left the course as—if not accomplished poets—very acceptable poetry readers. Crystal had been proud of her success.

"We should have paid more attention to that comment," the Chair mused.

"The student evaluations from Miss Kelsey's sample class here were so very positive," the Dean countered. She addressed Crystal, "What happened between then and now?" and her voice was almost kind.

Crystal might have melted at that kindness if her back hadn't been so erect. Instead, she opened her mouth—and then closed it again. The Dean's question was so open-ended. How should Crystal start? Tell these women that Simmons was her only job offer? That she hadn't had any idea what working at a real job would entail? She played for time. "Umm..."

"Crystal." The Dean had dropped 'Miss Kelsey'; she leaned over her hands. "Are you happy here?"

Crystal could give a simple, single answer to that. "No."

"Do you know why?"

Again Crystal had to think. Again she said, "No," because she didn't, not truly. She had her complaints, of course. But did those, even in the aggregate, sufficiently explain her degree of unhappiness?

"We don't understand why it has been so difficult for you to fit in."

This time when Crystal thought, she probed deep: what was it that made her life here at Simmons so hard? There had to be something more than weather or distance to New York City. Or having to create so many new classes. She drilled into that idea: the possibility of more. At Stanford she had been a student/writer first, a teacher second. At Simmons she was expected to be an instructor first, and fit whatever else around her teaching duties. But it was the whatever else that meant the most to her, that was infinitely more important. In order to be a teacher, Crystal had had to pour her entire existence into a sideline. She raised her eyes to the Dean, in horror at the trajectory her life had taken.

The Dean was exchanging a glance with the Chair.

Crystal admired these women. They were accomplished in so many directions: teaching; administration; the Dean was an expert in economic history; and the Chair was finishing up a psychoanalytical biography of Charlotte Perkins Gilman. They were multifaceted in a way Crystal had never been. They succeeded in spreading their attention, throwing it wide. Crystal only ever spread her attention wide in order to later pull it in close, to create a poem—or a dance.

"I'm not like you," Crystal mourned.

"We know that." The Dean was gentle.

"But we decided we'd take a chance," the Chair supplied. "Enlarge the department by bringing in a working poet. Unfortunately, our experiment wasn't a success."

Not with Crystal, anyway. She hadn't written a poem since being in Maine last summer. "I'm sorry." Her upright posture allowed her to apologize with all the honesty and frankness she could pull from her spine. "I shouldn't have taken this job, but I didn't know what else to do."

"There is a bias in university culture..." The Chair seemed ready to lecture. "Academics beget images of themselves. No matter what the discipline. Our graduate programs are designed to swell professorial ranks. I've said this time and again. I've *written* about it time and again."

"What Dorothy is saying, is that while going through your master's program you were probably offered no other path than to pursue a teaching career," the Dean translated.

Not exactly. While a teaching profession hadn't been pushed on Crystal, she was certainly made aware that it protected an artist from having to scramble to earn a living. "It's what our professors did," Crystal observed.

"Exactly!" the Chair emphasized.

"So what will you do now?" the Dean asked with concern.

That was the moment Crystal knew for certain her contract would not be renewed for the following autumn. She was being 'let go' in the most nurturing manner possible.

'Time can be its own event'

A year and some months ago, when Crystal had chosen her Boston apartment, its most important attribute had been the parking space for her Nova. That's what she had been thinking about when she signed the lease—not what it would be like to come home to a space that was always shadowed by taller buildings, darkened even further by winter's short days.

She keyed her way into the entry hall, trudged up the stairs, and unlocked her front door. Before taking off her coat, she picked up her phone and dialed. "Scott Hanson," she told the Dreyfus operator. She had to wait, which was no surprise—Scott could be sucked into his work just as she got sucked into the composition of a poem.

"Crystal?"

"I've been fired."

"Oh, Crys," Scott sighed. He wasn't surprised—but he wasn't disappointed in her, either. That was important. "I'll call you tonight. Remember: you can always live with me here in New York. I'd like that."

"Okay." She felt better. Not good, but better. Scott's few words were comforting. He was her best friend in this time zone.

Waiting for evening, she wandered about her apartment, disliking everything she saw. Somehow Mother had been able to impose her taste even on those items she hadn't been able to load into Crystal's car. That loveseat looked kind of Motherish. That was a Mother-style lamp. Had the discount furniture store been an eerie extension of Mother's brain? Crystal stood in the exact middle of the sitting room. She turned in a slow pirouette, only to see Mother, Mother, Mother. Her rotation brought her back to the phone. She could call Justa. There was always a chance Justa might be home.

Crystal hoped and dialed. The phone rang far too many times. She was about to give up when she heard Justa's voice—dim, abstracted. "Yes?" Justa floated out the word.

"Justa?"

"Crystal!" The voice came alive. "I almost didn't answer! Listen."

The sound of Justa's phone being carried about was a comfort all on its own. Crystal had heard those noises so often before. But this time the phone knocked against something different. And from the bottom of Crystal's ears—or so it seemed—rose an arpeggio. A piano? Couldn't be. Crystal listened to the matching descent.

And then Justa was back on line: "Gil bought it for me! The music department was selling off used keyboards! This one only has seventy-three keys, but I can turn it up louder or down quieter. I can even plug in headphones. It came in a *suitcase*."

"Wow!" Crystal celebrated. "Play something for me." Which Justa did, although Crystal couldn't tell if the piece was classical, modern, or in between because of how the sound came up from the bottom of her ears with some notes too loud and others disappearing.

"That's Czerny!" Justa's voice popped back into Crystal's earpiece. "Do you want to hear more?"

Crystal heard more, and when Justa was ready to talk Crystal told her, "I've been fired." Crystal plucked a tissue from the box on the coffee table—which could also have been chosen by Mother—and blew. "What am I going to do?"

Justa knew, immediately. "Write poems," she said firmly.

When evening finally came, Scott seconded Justa's advise. "I'll put up some shelves for your books," he offered, because there was no room in his apartment to add a desk.

After hanging up, Crystal tried out her friends' advisement on her furnishings. "No, I won't be earning any money," she asserted to the loveseat. "Yes, I'll be living off a boyfriend," she defiantly informed the lamp. Only to the little television, which had once been a friend, did she provide an explanation. Hesitatingly, "I'll be being myself."

The next morning, stepping foot on campus, she felt like a stranger—embarrassed. Just inside the Main College Building, she had the great misfortune to meet up with Terry Armstrong.

"I've heard," Terry said with an eager, soliciting, sorrow.

And Crystal was suddenly swept with the kind of sweetness that could dig cavities in chickens. "I'm sure you have," she cooed. "So, Terry, I'm resigning from all my committees and working groups. I imagine that will mean more assignments for you, but I'm certain you'll be willing." The sweetness expelled, Crystal turned her back and climbed the stairs in a fury.

She clicked her office door shut. She shrugged off her coat, letting it and her green tote drop. She walked into the middle of this room, and she performed another slow, circling, inventory: she liked the window that looked out over the quad; she didn't much care for the institutional desk or hard-seated chairs; she loved the aged wood floor. As her feet shifted in rotation, it was as if the floor whispered a four count beat up through her soles. The floor was friendly.

It encouraged her to remove her typewriter from the desk, to set her typewriter down on its wooden planks.

Crystal spent every free hour throughout the next several months sitting on that floor. She sat on a loveseat cushion brought from her apartment—so she wouldn't shiver—and she typed and she sorted. She wrote fresh poems; she revised old poems from her thesis. She created twenty-one piles, arranged in thematic progression. She diminished each pile until it was down to three poems. She then stacked the poems, in order, as a possible chapbook.

She went to stand at her office window. She saw spots of purple and gold. Crocuses? She had one last task before packaging her manuscript, before taking it to the Simmons post office. She needed a title. The title she had given her thesis was *Emerging Empathy*.

That would do.

'And bring me back to me'

On spring equinox morning, Crystal exploded. She drove the two hundred plus miles to New York City in under three hours. She stopped cold in front of the Dreyfus building, ignoring all the honking behind her. She burst out of her Nova and ran inside. She punched the elevator button eleven times, once for every floor she would have to ascend. At last, she flew around an irate receptionist and into the cavernous hall where Scott and his fellows labored in cubicles. She scanned for Scott. He stood halfway down the room, talking to a much older man in a much finer suit. Crystal launched herself. The older man, bemused, watched Scott absorb the full impact of her hug.

"We'll talk later," the older man said.

Scott nodded, smiled goodbye, and whispered in Crystal's ear, "What?"

"Look!"

She unfolded a piece of paper in his face. It was a letter from Ravenswood Press.

"Mr. Hanson!" The receptionist was panting, out of breath from her own sprint.

"It's okay. I'll take care of everything." Scott put an arm around Crystal's shoulders. He led her out of the cubicle corral and back into the much smaller, professionally decorated—and now distinctly Crystal-unfriendly—domain of the receptionist. He sat Crystal down on a visitor's sofa and put himself close beside her. He read the letter. Crystal reread, from around his shoulder:

Dear Miss Kelsey. We will be pleased to publish Emerging Empathy. *While we offer no payment, we will be sending you twelve free copies.*

"Wonderful!" In total disregard of the receptionist, Scott kissed Crystal. "Congratulations!" He hugged her, kissed her again, and then—with sudden apprehension—he asked, "Where did you park?"

"I kind of didn't," was Crystal's reply.

He rushed her back down the elevator. Her car had gathered a policeman, a very expensive ticket, and a long harangue from a cabbie—all of which Scott managed while Crystal said, "Sorry!" to everybody. She drove back to Boston with an occasional glance at the roadside: trees were gently highlighted with a tinge of green. Green, her heart sang, for glorious.

She arrived on the Simmons campus barely in time for her Advanced Poetry Writing class. She only had three students, so hardly anybody would have been disappointed had she failed to appear. But she wanted to be in class today. She wanted to show. To tell.

Her three students were all thrilled by her success. That's when Crystal became aware: she liked them. She had, in fact, been liking her students all winter. Three girls, one of some talent, two of middling ability. She'd grown to like them as people.

Leaving Simmons late that day, Crystal took notice: almost every girl she passed nodded at her, or smiled, or said, "Hi, Miss Kelsey." Crystal acknowledged everyone back. This friendliness had been creeping up on her ever since the day she was fired. Simmons girls were what she and Justa—also Betsy and Lowry—had once been. They were the robins, goldfinches, bluebirds and cardinals that burst color into the world every spring.

> *Flight Path*
> *I never saw a Bird of Paradise,*
> *But I have seen*
> *Young dancers*
> *All lined up,*

Barre ready.
And the instructor
Preparing them for life—
And good posture—
With the admonition,
'Tuck in your tail feathers, girls,
(Bottoms down)
Before you try to fly.'

LLLLL

According to Trey, Lowry had lost her advantage at Matchison, Johnson & Nowak for three reasons: her 'illness' last summer; the ensuing, and inevitable, gossip; and her ongoing malaise. He could do nothing about the first two, but he was being incredibly patient about the third. He pampered Lowry, often bringing home take-out dinners; hiring an occasional maid service to clean their apartment. He was looking forward, he told Lowry— so many times, and in so many ways—to when she began to feel 'more like herself'. That's when they would talk.

Which left Lowry to ponder the question: which self did she want to return to?

Today at work, Lowry was tapping a desultory pen against a brief she was supposed to be editing. But in fact she was staring at her Daruma doll, wishing she had a window to look out of. Her phone rang and her secretary announced, "A Mr. Victor Yamada on line two?" Definitely a question mark at the end there. Lowry swallowed her surprise and, using her pleasantest potential-new-client voice, replied, "Oh, of course. Please put him through."

"Lowry?" Victor sounded exactly the same as he had four years ago.

A wave of homesickness and fear, strong enough to make Lowry gasp, flooded her entire frame. She had to know: "Is Justie okay?"

"Doing well," Victor assured her. "Wanna come out to lunch?"

The question was so unexpected—such an ordinary/extraordinary invitation— it made Lowry laugh. "Where are you?"

"Downstairs, around the corner, in a telephone booth at…" Victor paused. "Auburn and Peachtree Center Avenue."

So near! "Really?"

"Truly," said Victor. "I'm in town for an AMA convention. I've escaped from a totally boring presentation."

"I'm bored, too!" What a relief it was to say so out loud. "Give me ten minutes and I'll meet you at the phone booth." Lowry put her own phone down; she rapidly strategized. She put an expression of extreme tension on her face—not hard to do, she'd had lots of practice—grabbed her coat and purse, and scooted from her office as though there were fire at her heels. "I'll be at County Administration," she called in passing, specifying no further. In moments she was at the elevator, pushing the button and hopping on her heels until the doors slid open.

Victor was exactly where he had said he would be, looking in all the wrong directions with the air of somebody who needed a map. Coming closer, Lowry saw the changes: his hair was shorter, so he no longer had the habit of absently pushing it aside; there were tiny creases on his face. He no longer looked like a guy who was interminably in school. He had to be in his early thirties now.

"Dr. Yamada?" Lowry said before he saw her.

He swung around, grinned, and hugged her tight. "The very same!" he caroled.

"You told my secretary, 'Mr'."

"Disguise." Victor wriggled his eyebrows. "I didn't want to bring my white coat, either. Where do you want to go?"

Lowry had thought about this in her dash outside. She, too, was in disguise—acting like a person who actually took off time to eat instead of ordering a sandwich for her desk. Like a person who sometimes saw the sun. "There's a deli near here, and a pocket park about two blocks away. Is that okay?"

"Fine." Victor was all agreement. "Show me the way."

They both chose ham and cheese sandwiches with extra large pickles. "And brownies!" Victor insisted, leaning over the three varieties displayed: with nuts; without nuts; only two left with extra chocolate chips. He bought those two. He wanted a coke, since Coca Cola was a true Atlanta drink, invented for health purposes a hundred years ago. Lowry, who had already drunk enough colas for a lifetime, asked for a take-away cup filled with tap water.

The pocket park was a triangle of green near the Georgia State campus. Lowry had found it by accident the first time she tried to walk to the county courthouse, and got lost. Victor's head swiveled while they walked there. "What kind of museum is that?" he asked, and, "Is that a hospital?"

By the time they sat down on a bench he was thoroughly, and happily, confused. "You'll get me back to the convention center, won't you?"

"Sure." Lowry's pleasure was immense. She had never played hooky before—not in high school, not in college, not in law school. And here she was playing fugitive with someone who, by his surname, was one of her oldest friends. "How is everybody? Tell me all the news."

"Everybody?" Victor questioned. "The entire Yamada countdown?"

"Hiro, then," Lowry amended.

"Old and intractable," Victor began. "Can't stop bossing the world around, being the senior Yamada now—Great-grandfather being gone." He continued with Ike's generation, then Mari's. So many people, so many stories. He paused after telling Lowry that Fort's little girl was in the fourth grade. "More?"

"I'll bet you're up to date on Matthews news." Lowry doubted she had anything to contribute.

Victor scrunched his nose. "Well... It was Justa who told me how to get in contact with you. She told me to call your office, not your home. She suggested I use 'Mr.' She didn't tell me much else—only that your husband has never come to California to see your family. Is that true?"

"Yes," Lowry had to admit.

Victor's face was no longer open, blithe, investigating the world. Instead his expression inhabited those recently acquired creases. "I know you had a bad flu last summer. Justa's worried about that. They all are—your parents, Great-Uncle Hiro. And Lowry, I've gotta say, as a doctor, they have reason. You don't look so good."

"It's just taking a while." Lowry waved her hand in the air, trying to blow the subject away.

Victor frowned. But he didn't press. Instead he studied her face. He offered an off-the-wall prescription: "Fun. That's what you need. Can you give me another hour or two?"

Lowry's answer was most assuredly, 'No', but she was intrigued. "Yes."

Victor nodded. "Okay. Get me back to the Convention Center and we'll find where the vendors have their booths."

It did't *sound* like fun, but Lowry complied.

⌒

She walked Victor the mile or so, again as his tour guide. At the Convention Center he took over. He looked for signs, asked for help, and somehow procured a badge for Lowry to wear in the vendors' hall. There he ushered her past displays of medical instruments, technological devices, and big gory photographs Lowry didn't want to examine too closely. When they came upon a globe-sized model of an eyeball, Victor slowed down. "Here we are!" he exclaimed. "You'll need a bag."

Lowry dutifully accepted the canvas bag a contact solution vendor handed her. She also accepted a sample bottle and a contact lens case. "Is this all free?" she whispered to Victor.

"You bet! You're with a doctor now!"

They fell into a spree of freebie shopping. Lowry picked up two rival brands of contact solution, another lens case, and some eyedrops. She also allowed a vendor to press a model eyeball into her hand. It was the size of a Ping-Pong ball, and cunningly engineered so as to come apart and then be put back together—like a Visible Man. She would give it to Clarey. No, she would keep it for herself. Victor picked up items alongside her. He said, "Look at this!" And she said, "What do you think of that?" They were like best friends in a toy store.

"Over there's the girl stuff." Victor was proud to point, continuing his role as vendor hall guide.

'Girl stuff' meant dermatology, more gory pictures Lowry didn't want to see, but also racks and arrangements of creams and lotions. There were even makeup counters. Victor steered her toward the first, a booth with products from a Swiss manufacturer Lowry had never heard of. And Lowry used to work in a department store: she knew makeup counters. She could identify a makeup professional at a glance.

"Do sit, please," one such woman invited. So Lowry perched on a stool before a mirror. Victor pointed at colors, the woman overrode him, and Lowry got a makeover. The artist/saleswoman chatted: she was a specialist normally sent to aesthetic centers and plastic surgeons in private practice. When she, Lowry and Victor were all satisfied with Lowry's beauty, the woman gave Lowry every product used. Full-sized, not samples.

"You wanna try another booth?" Victor offered.

"No," Lowry regretted. "I've been gone for"—she glanced at her watch and felt immediately, but not fully, guilty—"almost three hours."

"Ah." That doctor look was returning to his face.

"But I've had so much fun," Lowry thanked him. "I haven't had this much fun in years." Which was the truth. This afternoon had been better, had made her feel better, than CeeCee's spa.

∽

That's what Lowry thought about while she walked, by herself, from the Convention Center back to her office building. She enjoyed her new face as long as she could, then washed it off in a lobby bathroom before taking the elevator up. She didn't bother giving anybody any explanation for her long absence. She even cut her day short by adopting secretary hours and riding the bus home with the commute crowd. At her apartment building, she first went down to the garage and the storage area behind the Z. She hid her booty there, tucking the canvas bag behind Willow's rug. She stared at the rug for a moment and then sat, denting the roll with her weight.

She had cousins. She had forgotten about that. The Yamadas weren't *exactly* cousins because of the cultural/racial thing, and because they held themselves apart with their constant awareness of what they had once owed Aunt Edith. But Lowry loved them with the same class of love she held for Mom and Dad and Justa. She had fifty-plus cousins who were watching her back.

JJJJJ

When the rains ended Justa began commuting by bike across the Berkeley campus. Today, as on every day, her feet slowed; her hands touched the brakes; she stopped in front of Giannini Hall's famous ginkgo. For weeks she had been watching the tree green: buds breaking open to allow one, three, maybe five tiny stems emerge; the stems unfurling at their tips into perfectly shaped, if miniature, leaves. Those bright green fans enlarged until now they were big enough to catch the breeze, to rustle a concert of innumerable breaths. Justa waited, listening. She, and the tree, were caught within a rare ray of morning sunlight.

Six musical notes belled in Justa's mind. Where had that earworm come from?

From an autumn memory when the ginkgo tree had shone gold, when every leaf was a variation upon ten carat brightness, when each shivered its own whisper. And from a much older memory: Justa had once seen a golden tree in a film, around the time she started kindergarten. Mom and Dad had taken her and Lowry to a drive-in movie. The idea was that the girls would sleep while the adults enjoyed the show. But Lowry chattered: "Mom! Why are the ladies wearing such big dresses? Mom!" And Justa listened to instruments she had never heard before. Was that her first time to experience a harmonica? Yes. And the banjo had been new for her, too. The use of bells made her shiver. Why? Those bells had been part of the theme which reprised soft and loud and angry and hopeful, and sometimes filled with love.

Now she sang the six notes again and again into the wind that she and her bike created, passing through the air. Entering the library, she must have been smiling because Charlie grinned back at her. Charlie, whose every feature revealed a history of hurt and pain. Whose common expression was one of distance and defeat. What memories did Charlie carry in his book and his clock?

⌒

Going home, she detoured to downtown. She hadn't visited the ladies in the Art and Music room for months; they were thrilled to see her. She sang her notes aloud and their response was immediate.

"Such a sad movie," said Agnes.

"But happy," countered Wanda.

"Sad but happy," Agnes agreed.

They got to work. Eventually they gave Justa a record album and a piano book. She carried both home on her handlebars. Sitting at her keyboard, she absorbed the notes into her hands. She was still playing when Gil came in. He touched her shoulder. "Have you eaten?" She shook her head. She sight-read her way through the abridged movie score, discovering all the emotions she remembered: hopeful exploration, romantic promise, puzzled wistfulness, joyful surprise, unexpected horror, mature effort, confused half-success, frustrating setbacks, hard toil, resolution of a new reality.

When finally she lifted her hands away from the keys, and straightened her back, her joints were kinked. "Hungry yet?" Gil called from the kitchen. She didn't answer. Instead she placed the LP on Gil's record player. She gently dropped the needle and Nat King Cole's velvet voice filled their apartment.

"Wow." Gil had come to stand at the kitchen door. "I mean, *wow*."

"'Raintree County'." Justa read from her book. "'Which Had No Boundaries in Time and Space, Where Lurked Musical and Strange Names and Mythical and Lost Peoples, and Which Was Itself Only a Name Musical and Strange'." She raised her eyes to Gil. "The movie ends with the shot of a golden tree that is lost in a swamp."

Gil came to put his arms around her.

⸻

The next morning at work, when Charlie smiled back at her, Justa took special notice of his face. His eyes were a pale, washed-out blue. The skin above his ragged beard was the grayish color of the soil up in Strawberry Canyon. His beard, brows and hair were tinged with the same color, and Justa wondered if what she had thought to be age might instead be the dirt in which he lived. She did a quick calculation: according to the inscription she remembered from his Shakespeare book—'To Charlie on his tenth birthday, March 30, 1938'—he was almost fifty-one years old. The same age as Dad.

"Charlie," she said, and didn't know how to continue.

Charlie's smile widened. His teeth were a sticky brown, blackened in spots. Justa took an involuntary step forward, to better ascertain, and entered the miasma of his odor. She immediately pulled back. She had seen enough, though. Charlie's teeth were straight, not crooked or tangled. He still had them all. He needed a dentist. He needed... And Justa encountered an idea that, like the memory of a golden tree, had been waiting ages for her to notice. Charlie needed a bath.

"A bath!" She took her idea to Connor.

Connor listened, then asked the salient question: "Where?"

Justa had an idea for that, too. "Hearst Gym. The university. If we take that raincoat from lost and found, and wrap Charlie up in it, we can smuggle him in."

"His head."

"Put a hat on him."

"His smell."

"Dowse him with aftershave."

Connor considered. "We'll have to Lysol my car, afterward."

"You'll do it?"

Connor looked over to where Charlie sat, always alone. "You bet."

To convince Charlie meant entering his solitude. "Charlie," Justa whispered. One step away she had been at work, but within his Charlie-defined circumference she was an intruder.

Charlie looked a 'what?'

"If Connor took you to a place where there's a shower, would you let him wash you?"

It wasn't until Charlie spoke that Justa realized: she had never heard his voice before. She had heard Charlie cough and sneeze and sigh. But she had never heard him utter a word.

"Will it be my birthday party?" Charlie asked, and his query was the barest wheeze, as if his lungs were too cracked and old to be of much use.

"Absolutely," Justa promised, as her heart absorbed his grief.

For the birthday party, she went to Woolworth's and bought paper plates and decorated napkins and silly hats. She commissioned Giant to make a layer cake, which was an unknown experience for him until she checked out the library's copy of *Joy of Cooking* and showed him a recipe. "Ah," he mused, "un gateau." He built a cake dotted with banana and pineapple and toasted pecans. He put freshly whipped cream between the layers.

"How many candles?" Gil wondered.

Justa bought five packets of ten and one special candle that burned a green flame. She coordinated everybody's schedules—hers, Connor's, Gil's and Giant's—for a Friday after work. On the last day of March, she and Connor bundled Charlie into Connor's car. Connor opened his front windows. Justa, sitting with Charlie in the back, reached across the Safeway bag to open Charlie's. Charlie lifted his face, much as a dog does, his lost and found hat flying from his head onto the shelf behind. "Charlie," Justa alerted him. But her attempts to correct were stopped by the smile that he turned to her. Blackened teeth—but even so, Charlie's smile was beatific.

At the end of the short journey, after Charlie stepped from the car, Justa took his hand. She had never touched him before, but now contact felt natural. "We'll have to walk across the street." She waited for a signal light to change. She led Charlie to the steps of the gymnasium where Gil and Giant and the party makings waited.

"I'll guard the goodies," Justa volunteered. She couldn't do anything else—she wasn't allowed in the men's locker room. She could only watch: three young men and one pretzel-bent, shuffling character—draped in a woman's raincoat and an Hasidic fedora—entering a gym filled with twenty-year-old students.

She set up for the party. She chose the shelter of a California live oak because its leaves never changed color, because its always mature greenness was now spangled with bright yellow catkins. Beneath this exuberance of green and yellow she spread a paper tablecloth that repeated 'Happy Birthday!' in crayon colors. She laid out the matching plates and napkins. She did not uncover the cake. This was Charlie's cake; exposed food would attract panhandlers; only Charlie could cut the first slice.

When he finally emerged from the gym he was a clean version of himself. Justa realized she had been wishing for a transformation. Or at the very least a straightening of his back. This scrubbed Charlie was neither reborn nor renewed. His old expressions remained intact. The greatest change was to the color of his inexpertly trimmed hair and beard—a light brown. He was a Goodwill dressed figure who walked up to Justa and stood waiting. Justa hoped he waited with hope. She couldn't tell.

"Charlie, you look so handsome!" she cried.

Charlie blushed: that was actual color moving across his face.

She had pleased him. "Sit down!" Justa bubbled. "Cut your cake! You've earned it!"

Charlie sat. He cut. He ate. He bobbed his head in time to Giant's Frenchified version of the happy birthday song. "Joyeux anniversaire, joyeux anniversaire…"

When the sun began to drop bayward, Connor offered to drive Charlie wherever he chose. Charlie refused, whispering, "Thank you"—his only speech of that day. He removed his Shakespeare and his clock from his Safeway bag. He padded the bottom of the bag with the tablecloth and leftover napkins. He repacked his clock and book. He sheltered the remaining cake with paper plates, under and over. That became the top layer in his bag. Then he stood and simply left.

The others watched his slow progress up Bancroft Way, toward the hills.

"Did you know he was a soldier?" Gil said into the air.

"Is that what those tattoos were about?" Connor asked.

"Korean war," Gil answered. "He was a Ranger. They saw the worst of the fighting. When I was working in that logging camp in Idaho, I got to know men with similar tattoos. All of them—and I mean all—woke up the bunkhouses with their nightmares."

"But they could work." Connor continued to watch Charlie diminish. "Hold down a job."

"Hold down a job, out there in the wilderness, where they were mostly left alone."

Charlie finally disappeared. They all busied themselves, each with a separate task. Justa gathered up the Woolworth's bag and her purse.

"There but for the grace of God," Connor murmured.

Justa turned westward to where the sun was being swallowed by a Golden Gate fog. There would be no sunset. Nightfall's beauty was hidden—for now. Justa changed Connor's invocation silently, privately, to one of her own. *There but for love go I.*

LLLLL

Lowry always paid bills on the tenth day of the month. On April tenth, her alarm clock rang an hour early, which caused Trey to groan and push his face into his pillow. But Lowry rose immediately. She grabbed her bathrobe and, with a cup of tea and a bowl of cold cereal, sat at the dining table and began opening envelopes.

She was well into the process of writing out checks when Trey finally emerged, dressed and groomed for work. Instead of saying good morning, he ruffled the hair on top of Lowry's head—something he had started to do after Lowry's 'episode'. Lowry supposed Trey thought the gesture was tender. It made her feel like she was six years old.

"I'll be in court all morning," Trey said. "I'll pick up Chinese on the way home." He left without breakfast. He rarely ate breakfast. He would stop at a Dunkin' Donuts on the way to his office.

By the time Lowry got to the water bill she had almost emptied out their checking account. Damn. She would have to move money from savings into checking, which meant going to the bank. She looked at the clock. She didn't have time. She should make the time.

She stood up from the table, half revving and half reining back: a physical contrariness that was left over from her 'episode'. She squeezed her eyes tightly shut and planned: she could take the savings book to work, skip out to the bank during a quiet moment in the day, and finish the checks this evening. She opened her eyes, consciously sighing herself into almost-relaxation. She went to the kitchen junk drawer, which was where the savings book normally stayed. But it wasn't there. Lowry hadn't withdrawn money for months. Trey had done so more recently to pay for the Z's 100,000 miles servicing. Where had he put it?

Her search became a treasure hunt. She picked up papers from on top Trey's desk. She investigated the desk's one drawer. She scanned the bookcase, left to right, from up to down. Because she had to squat to see the lowest shelf, she shuffled around 360 degrees to spy out spaces beneath furniture. Upright again, she stuck her hands behind and beneath chair and sofa cushions. She emptied pockets in hall closet coats, and passed her hands beneath hats. She even went through the other kitchen drawers on the off chance that Trey might have aimed incorrectly.

In the bedroom she had drawers, closet, and under the bed to examine. Under the bed was where Trey kept his 'red box', an imitation of the Queen of England's big briefcase in which she held important missives. Trey used his, a Christmas gift from his parents, to hold copies of those files and records he deemed crucial for the rebuilding of his practice, should his premises ever be burgled or torched. His red box was locked, but Lowry knew where to find the key. In the kitchen, in the junk drawer, in an envelope marked 'Miscellaneous'. She had found it there during a speed-charged cleaning spree, before her 'episode'.

Within the red box she found their savings book, and immediately beneath it another one from another bank. She and Trey had never had an account at SunTrust. They still didn't, because this account was held by Clarence Claude Chambliss III alone. It contained $27,720. Lowry immediately understood: Trey had held onto his grandfather's down payment gift from last year; interest rates were historically high this year; Trey was letting the money grow. For himself?

Or for that house he so wanted?

Lowry felt sick, so sick she sat down on the floor and dropped her head onto the unmade bed. She smelled sex from last night; Trey's scent mingling with her own. She jumped up and ran to the bathroom where she vomited cereal and tea.

Then she carried Trey's savings book to her place of work at the dining table. She shoved the bills aside and stared at the opened savings book until her eyes were gritty. With the final amount imprinted on her retinas, she first called her office: "I don't know when I'll make it to work. I'm at the dentist. They're going to have to fit me in. "

Second, she dialed Justa.

"Huh?" Gil answered. It was five thirty, their time.

"Justie," Lowry required.

"Justa." Gil spoke with the phone away from his face.

Justa's oh-so-familiar voice fell over Lowry like a balm. "Low?"

                    ✐

"It could be—you don't know—the money is for something else. Maybe a secret for you!"

Lowry only briefly considered the possibility. "No."

Justa pressed: "You have to make him tell you. You have to give him that chance."

"The thing is, I don't think he cares what I want." When Lowry spoke those words out loud, they tasted of anger. Something built up in her breast. She had known, hadn't she? Almost always?

"You can only live with the truth," Justa said sadly.

                    ✐

Lowry started by lying. She called work to say, with a novocaine mouth, "I won't make it in at all today."

Then, instead of finishing the bills, she marched to a branch of the bank she shared with Trey and withdrew half their savings. She carried the cashier's check to SunTrust, only a block away, and opened a checking account for herself alone.

But on her walk home her pace slowed, her step became less determined: Trey would say she was over-reacting; Trey would say she was being unfair. Lowry put her hand to her chest. She wished she had something to hold onto. Like Bilba's L brooch, which was now pinned to the brown paper protecting the Stanford rug from dust. All of Bilba's love and skill had been consigned to the basement.

Before leaving home, Lowry had slipped the basement locker key into her purse; she had planned to hide her new bank book inside the bag from Victor's AMA convention, which was hidden behind the rug, which was rolled around Emi's wall hanging. She pinned the L to her T-shirt while standing among these reminders of her past. Her excised past. The only elements of her past that had been allowed were her Stanford and Duke diplomas. If she had to, she would pry them from her office wall.

Riding up to her apartment, she was Lowry Jeanne Mathews, Esquire. Trey should be in his office now. Before calling, she drank a glass of milk for sustenance. She told him only, "Come home. Now. Please." Not allowing him to launch into questions—or protests, or excuses—she hung up. About the time she thought he might be arriving, she positioned herself behind the table, behind *his* savings book.

"Lowry!" he exclaimed, obviously—and truly—worried. He blinked at the L on her chest; his vision dropped to the table top. "Oh."

"What is this for?" Lowry asked.

"You okay, honey?" He reverted to, and solidly remained on, his initial reaction. "I assumed the apartment was on fire." His tone had become as warm and cozy as a comforter on a winter night. Lowry heard: he was manipulating with his voice, exactly as he did in court.

"Why have you held onto this money?" Lowry persisted.

"You scared me something awful—like that bad time last year when you weren't yourself."

For the barest flick of an instant, Lowry wondered if her remaining 'ill' for so long had somehow suited Trey. But what she said was, "I was more myself then, than I had been for years."

"You were irrational," Trey pointed out with sympathetic concern.

"I needed help!" Lowry spoke the truth.

"Which is what we've been giving you. I'm picking up Chinese tonight. CeeCee and Mama send casseroles home with us every week."

He had taken Lowry off topic. She refound her purpose: "The savings book."

Trey sighed. With infinite reason, as if enunciating to a six year old, he said, "Granddaddy told me, 'Hold onto the money, your wife's a reasonable girl, she'll come around, she knows what's best for her'."

"And what's best for me is...?" Lowry gritted her soul and body, readying herself to hear Trey's truth.

"For us to get back to our original plan." Trey was earnest—so very, very earnest. "To get back to what's best for us both. We were on a 'timeline of success'. Remember?"

Lowry remembered.

"It's not too late." An eagerness darted into Trey's voice that sounded genuine. "We can still get back on that timeline. You haven't entirely lost your status at MJ&N. I know. I've asked around. I've talked to Ted Nowak. He says you've been doing your work well enough. The partners know that you're steady. Ted is concerned about you, but he expects you to 'rise like a phoenix.' That's what he said. That's what you can do, Lowry! You've had your period of ashes; now is the time for feathers. Show yourself off! A bit of drama will not only make you more interesting—it will make the partners sit up and watch for what you will do next."

Lowry was horrified. "What I want"—it was her turn to enunciate—"is to change jobs."

"This isn't a good time for that, honey. I just explained."

There had been a time when Lowry had thought this man to be her lodestone. Seen through the rushing glow of dextroamphetamine, he had appeared to be her hope. Now she saw that she had married her despair. "You think it's your right, don't you?" She was careful to say precisely what she meant. "That I should make lots of money, take on a mortgage, entertain in order to advance your career. Cook and clean your house."

"Yes," said Trey. And with equal care, because he was a most accurate and brilliant attorney, he chose words from their wedding ceremony to enforce his claim. "I do."

CCCCC

Crossing campus, her sweat-soaked hair drying and lifting from her neck, Crystal headed to the only place she really liked in the state of Massachusetts: her office. She entered the Main College Building and had her office keys in hand before she was halfway up the stairs. When she unlocked the door, she sighed. *This* was home.

She closed her eyes and yearned: if she knew how to pull up floorboards and take down walls, she would steal this room. If she could fit a purloined section of a nineteenth century building into the trunk of a Chevy Nova, she would commit larceny. Daydreaming, her mind eventually bumped up against reality. Where would she take her stolen office? The only place she had to go to, for now, was a small apartment in New York City.

She sat down upon her floor.

In a month she was leaving Simmons to go live with Scott.

If she hadn't come back east, she would never have gotten to know the real Scott. She wouldn't have learned that he loved thinking about money almost as much as she loved thinking about words. Or that he was adorable when he worked, running his hand through what was left of his hair, making it stand out in little tufts. If Crystal was behind him in his minuscule kitchen—getting a glass of water, say—he sometimes initiated the oddest conversations. "Liechtenstein," might be the beginning, and now Crystal knew enough to answer, "Currency?" "Down," Scott would mutter. "Potential?" Crystal might ask. "Some leverage," was one possible response. What they were talking about, she never knew—it was like chatting with a sleepwalker who was living inside an invisible dream.

In this way, they fit.

⌒

After arriving at her apartment, Crystal called Justa. She began with: "I want to talk about living with Scott. How to do it."

"Okay." Justa was willing, but sounded puzzled.

"How do *you* do it?" Crystal needed to know.

"It wasn't easy at first," Justa said slowly. "Nothing was. My dad wanted me to get married. But after...Kendall...I couldn't bear the thought of making myself so vulnerable. Magnifying an even greater loss. Now, what I want is to be free to choose to be with Gil—and he with me—every day."

Crystal had never heard anything more romantic.

"I think it's different for everybody," Justa mused. "Look what happened with Lowry. I don't know what will happen with you."

That, of course, was Crystal's true question.

The next day, a Saturday, she carried her uncertainties to Simmons, to the dance studio. She soared with Stevie Nick's 'Rhiannon'. Afterward, she wrote a poem:

Black skirt, black jacket, black shawl,
Black stockings, and a pointed hat.
She hums as she arranges:
Utter darkness against a pattern
Of red and green and blue and purple.
Grandma had such careful fingers -
Placing each color like a note,
Arranging patches like music.
Bequeathing to her daughter's daughter
A talent, a gift -
Of how best to express her soul.

And by Monday morning, she had figured out what felt right—something that fit almost like a leotard. Emily Post had, sort of, defined the netherworld between living off a boyfriend and getting married. An existence that could explain a possibly protracted sojourn in New York City—with no reference to having been fired with no place else to go.

That evening Crystal called the Stanford Bookstore; she ordered a man's class ring. "Baseball player hand size," she said, confusing the clerk. "No. Not engraved. I don't have the time." She made reservations at Scott's favorite New York City restaurant. While she waited for the ring to arrive, she bought a new dress—which she would also wear at Simmons' upcoming graduation ceremony. On the day of her special dinner, she drove down to New York with her heart, mind and soul jittery from anticipation and anxiety. She waited until Scott arrived at the restaurant, until they were seated, until Scott had ordered wine to go with stuffed eggplant, before she posed her idea.

Scott blinked. "What?"

"I said, I want us to become engaged. Not married—don't worry about that. But engaged as a couple. I got you a ring." Crystal pushed the little box across the table.

Scott opened it. He gazed. "For me?"

"Of course." Crystal became alarmed: "Don't you like it?"

"Sure. I mean, yes. I mean, Crystal, what are you doing?" With one hand, Scott held the ring box. With the other he plowed those little rows through his remaining hair.

So Crystal told him her deepest reason: "I want to think of myself as being something more than just a girlfriend."

"Oh." Scott let go of his hair. He plucked the ring out of the box and experimented with twirling it around the tip of his finger. The red stone made the balance uneven. "Okay. But aren't you forgetting something?"

"What?" This was proving so hard to do.

"Like, maybe how you feel," Scott prompted.

In reply Crystal said something she'd never said before, not to her high school boyfriends, not to her freshman year flames, not even—back then—to Kendall. Not with this meaning: "I think I love you."

Scott's eyes crinkled into a grin. He shook his head. "You are something else, Crystal. Sometimes you take my breath away."

"Is that okay?" Crystal's anxiety was killing her now.

"Actually, it's kind of wonderful."

"So you accept?" Crystal was desperate.

Scott laughed. He laughed until he choked, and then he cried, and then he laughed some more. Finally he inhaled all the air Crystal had stolen from him, and slid the ring down to the base of his finger.

"Just for the record, Crystal," he said, "I think I love you, too."

> *Now I know what it was like*
> *For all those boys*
> *Standing at the edge of my life*
> *Waiting, waiting*
> *For me to say, "Hello."*

LETTING BE

'The Long and Winding Road'

is the sixth track on the second side of *Let It Be*,
the Beatles' last album.

Starting Autumn 1979

LLLLL

How could divorce be so easy? Perhaps to make up for marriage being so hard.

When Trey discovered Lowry had already divided their savings, he offered to be the one to move out—thus allowing Lowry to remain in their apartment (and continue to pay the rent). He would take the lonely road to his parents' home where Elaine would provide food/laundry/cleaning services. Trey made this offer in the street-level coffee shop of Lowry's office building. Lowry watched his face—which she had once loved to the extent of blindness—and saw a honed self-interest moving beneath the silky manners. How had she not seen those hints of the Triple C Railroad before? How could she *not* have seen them?

She regarded his hands, the touch for which she had once trembled. Trey's hands were calm, in control, accustomed to getting what Trey wanted. Unlike Lowry's own, which she twisted and rung with anxiety while she and Trey agreed on what would next unfold.

Their divorce.

As lawyers, they both retained attorneys—even though theirs was a no-fault divorce with little to split up. In exchange for the furniture, Lowry took possession of the 240Z, now seven years old. All else she wanted were the gifts that had come from 'her' people: Willow's rug; Emi's wall hanging; Justa's Daruma doll; the twelve place settings of silver flatware from her parents. And the exquisitely painted fan the Yamada family had sent east, via Mari, only three years ago.

Three years and four months. By the end of August 1979 she was no longer—legally, officially or personally—Mrs. Chambliss. Once again she was Lowry Matthews.

Now she stood on the thirty-seventh floor of Chicago's First National Bank Building, looking out the window of her new office. She had visited MJ&N's Chicago branch before, but today she was a permanent employee, a senior associate. She had achieved Trey's anticipated promotion, which meant an increase in salary—but more importantly, her own window. When she put her hand on the glass, she could feel a pulse of wind. Chicago was the 'Windy City'—just like Atlanta was sweltering heat and San Francisco was earthquakes. Only yesterday Lowry had overheard someone say, "The wind's coming up from the South." Like her.

She gazed downward. People in the street below wore sweaters and lightweight jackets. This morning, when Lowry pulled clothing from her closet, she ended up with what she had worn that last week in August: a short-sleeved business dress, cool, smart and modest. No jacket. Linen, not Italian wool. She hadn't put on a career suit since her marriage spiraled into nothing last April.

She leaned her forehead against the glass. Was this how she was going to calendar her life from now on? Before and after splitting from Trey? From childhood onward, the year had been renewed every autumn when school began. The expected turning points—graduations, a wedding— didn't change time. A failed marriage did.

∾

When she reported to work last Wednesday, her new boss, Mr. Mazur, showed her around. Those first three days aggregated into fleeting impressions, a mismatch of names and faces. She needed to think as well as smile and nod, so she came in on Saturday to take a more considered view of what her new work place—and work life—were to be.

She wasn't the only employee to give up a precious day off. She had to be discrete as she went about pushing at doors and examining secretarial desks. Most of the doors didn't open. The secretarial desks were more productive. As a female attorney, Lowry would have to be almost a man while not being a secretary. She knew that role well by now. She also knew how much easier her work life would be with secretarial good will. Her own secretary—not shared—Mrs. Andersson, displayed photos of two children who were as blond as Crystal. Grandchildren, no doubt. These were descendants of the Scandinavian immigration—not the great-grandchildren of slaves. Their ages appeared to be around ten and twelve.

Clarey was thirteen. For his birthday, Lowry had given him a subscription to *Monster Trucks* magazine.

One hour and forty-three minutes. That's how long she had left to focus on the file Mr. Mazur had given her for this afternoon's meeting. It was enough. When the knock came, she stood as Mrs. Andersson entered.

"Your car is waiting," Mrs. Andersson said.

Following Mrs. Andersson into the secretarial hallway, Lowry met a gauntlet of female eyes. She paused at Mrs. Andersson's desk, leaning so as to better regard Mrs. Andersson's photos. "The bigger boy, he must be in junior high," Lowry remarked.

"Seventh grade." Mrs. Andersson appeared gratified to have her family so mentioned. "And Eric, the little guy, is in fifth grade."

Lowry knew the news would follow her down the hall—the new woman attorney was fond of children. Lowry would become almost female.

"Could you give me a large envelope, and may I buy stamps from you?" Lowry asked. "I have a friend who is moving to Chicago, and I've been collecting information for him."

This new woman attorney was a person who had friends.

"Of course." Mrs. Andersson quickly produced both envelope and stamps. "How many?"

Lowry attempted to figure: "Enough to send a ten-page contract? That weight?"

Mrs. Andersson knew exactly which stamps Lowry needed. She refused cash. "I keep a little account here, for when you send out for sandwiches and such." Mrs. Andersson was more than accommodating, she was warm—"Have a good drive, now"—as if she was accepting Lowry to be her own.

Going down in the elevator, Lowry shivered. Why? Because she had been almost Trey-like just now? Insinuating? Manipulative?

No. She was chilled because of the weather. Autumn arrived earlier here in Chicago. She would have to buy a heavier coat for the winter. Maybe one of those long down coats she had seen in the windows of Marshall Fields. Marshall Fields, her new Rich's.

When the elevator doors opened, she hesitated before stepping out. The air was too cool to be humid, not cold enough to be crisp. It was a discomfort that rasped against her bones.

"Ms. Matthews?" The man addressing her wore a chauffeurs' cap. "I'm Jim Carlson." He held open the back door to a Lincoln town car.

"Thank you." Lowry slid into the quiet, dim interior. She had known a car like this. She knew that when the tires began to roll, she would feel a gentle bump as rubber met street; that during the journey her body would lean into buffered turns; that she would gradually sink into the leather cushions. This car was a twin to Hiro's best.

"Mr. Carlson?" She had to tap his shoulder to get his attention. "How long will it take to get there?"

"'Bout half hour." Within the car, his voice was loud, like that of the partially deaf.

Lowry settled back. She had time. She opened her briefcase to remove what little it currently held—a lease, a Chicago map, a public transit guide. She slipped those items into Mrs. Andersson's envelope. She frowned at her spiral-bound notebook—the same kind she had used in college—and uncapped a pen.

'Dear Victor', she wrote. She could write easily in this Hiro-like car.

> I've gone ahead, as you asked, and reserved that apartment
> for you, starting January. I hope you will like it. It's two floors
> above mine, same view, overlooking the Chicago River. Alt-
> hough you don't see much water. I'm about a half mile walk
> from work, crossing over the Clark Street bridge. You'll be
> about the same distance to Northwestern Memorial Hospital,
> except you'll be heading east, toward the lake. I haven't walked

the route for you yet, but you'll have to cross Michigan Avenue,
which could be hairy. You can always take a bus.

Lowry stopped to consider: her apartment, so near to the Loop, wasn't cheap. She didn't know how much medical fellows earned. So she added, 'If you decide my building is too far from the hospital, or if it is too expensive, let me know and I'll look for another place'. She paused again before ending, 'I'm glad you are coming'.

She was more than glad—she would be grateful to have a friend in Chicago. She was not yet ready to call Nancy Salinsky, her old study group partner in law school.

Lowry tore the page out of her notebook and stuck it into the envelope with everything else. With expert hands, she weighed her package—only about half the heft of a ten-page contract. She had more than enough stamps. She pasted them all on anyway, as insurance that Victor would get the information. She wrote out his address and set the envelope on the seat beside her. She would carry a briefcase empty of everything but notebook and pen into this coming meeting. When she left, her briefcase would be stuffed with papers that she would be expected to read like a novel.

"Dead prose to be read by a numb attorney," she muttered.

Mr. Carlson didn't appear to have heard.

She turned her gaze to the car window. This was a struggling neighborhood of mostly Black residents, whose parents and grandparents had probably come up here as part of the Great Migration—that enormous diaspora from the South. A movement of hope that, for too many, had turned into despair and anger.

⌒

Anger and despair.

"Ms. Matthews?"

Lowry had lost track of the time. At some point she had curled her body into the upholstered corner, with her knees on the seat and one shoulder tucked over her chest.

"We're here." Mr. Carlson was parking the car in a redbrick manufacturing district undergoing gentrification.

Lowry's face was damp. She fished for a tissue in her purse. She dabbed, then peered in a compact mirror to make certain her makeup wasn't smeared. "How do I look?" she asked Mr. Carlson, because there was sympathy in his eyes.

"Fine," he said. "Just fine."

She left the car and paused to peruse her surroundings, to take note. The old factory buildings, while neglected and battered by time, had inherently graceful lines and cathedral windows: definitely condominium potential, as this client had said. Mr. Mazur had asked the client to arrive early for a private discussion during which Mr. Mazur planned to assure the client of MJ&N's invested interest. Lowry's entrance was set to follow. In a few minutes Mr. Mazur would perform an introduction, handing her over as the client's point person. Handing her over with the same bonhomie with which her Atlanta boss had effected her transfer up north—similar smiles meant to underline stories of Lowry's successes.

Then it would be the client's turn to tell the attorneys—at length—everything he wanted them to do. This was the period during which Lowry would figure out what he *needed* them to do. These minutes were crucial, the key to the law firm's success. After a final handshake, Lowry would leave with her briefcase filled with memos, letters, typescript and ephemera. Mr. Mazur would remain reassure, to re-extoll Lowry's virtues, before winding up the meeting.

Lowry stiffened her back and began to walk. She could do this. She was still a real estate lawyer—for now.

⌒

When she left the factory, it was already dark outside.

"I'll take you home before I return the car," Mr. Carlson assured her.

"Thank you."

He was a man of kindness. This time, in the Hiro-like car, Lowry dozed.

Entering her apartment building, she first went to the mail center where she inserted Victor's envelope into a slot. Her box was empty. But upstairs, on the seventh floor, a cardboard carton blocked her door. With the side of her shoe she pushed the box inside. She set her purse and briefcase on the kitchen counter before hunting for a sharp knife. She had rented this apartment 'fully furnished', which meant a deceptively comfortable décor with mostly empty kitchen drawers. She ended up opening the carton with the edge of her door key, sawing through strips of tape. The tape obscured the return address, a shipping store from…somewhere. Beneath the cardboard flaps, beneath crumpled newspaper, on top of layered tissue, sat a letter. 'Dear Lowry.'

Lowry well knew how CeeCee wrote her name.

> I expect you are surprised. You probably didn't think you would ever hear from me. Perhaps you don't want to. But I had to write, I had to tell you. For three years you were part of my family. You were part of my life.
>
> This is yours. I took it from Trey. I told him he had given it away, and what you give away you cannot keep. He doesn't remember Great-Grandmama, but I do. She was the strongest woman I ever knew. She took care of Great-Grandpa Chambliss during the years of his decline. After the tuberculosis killed him, she raised three children all on her own. Most people thought her stern and forbidding, but I knew that she was a good person, deep in her soul. She loved her family, and she loved her church. What she always told me was, 'You have to do what's right, CeeCee. What's right isn't always easy to perceive. Right and wrong get awfully muddled in this world. But you, CeeCee, you do what's right."
>
> I hope I've done what's right.

Lowry sank to her haunches. Carefully, she shifted sheet after weightless sheet of tissue paper. A curve of black-painted wood; a horse's head; the top of Great-Grandmama Chambliss's music box. Gently, as befitting something old and fragile, Lowry lifted the music box from the carton. She set it on the rented glass-and-chrome coffee table. The music box looked different here than it had back in Atlanta. Back then, back there, Lowry had never taken special note of how only one figure stood beside the horse. One, not two. Female, not male. It was the maiden, all alone, who reached to touch the charger and calm its great energy. It was her small hand that held all the power.

Lowry turned the golden key. The tune that Great-Grandmama Chambliss had chosen was an old Appalachian song, 'Over the Waterfall', a metaphor for Great-Grandmama's life and now perhaps for Lowry's life, too. They had each tumbled into the new and laborious.

The tune repeated. From the wall entertainment unit that lacked television or stereo, Lowry removed three folders—one each from the University of Chicago, the University of Illinois at Chicago, and Northwestern. She arranged the folders beside the music box, then curled herself up on the sofa. She and Justa had come up with a plan: Lowry would audit a graduate course in policy, planning or public administration—something that would switch her mind back to the nonprofit sector. First a course, then a new job...and maybe another city.

One step at a time—that had been Justa's advice.

This class at UIC not only looked interesting, UIC was closest by. Lowry unfolded the application to begin filling out the form. The music and maiden slowed to a halt. Lowry turned the key again. She spelled out her old/new name, 'Lowry Matthews', and the music tinkled on.

CCCCC

Scott found a part-time job for Crystal. "Some guys from Saudi Arabia came to work with us for a year," he told her. "One of them was asking about finding an English tutor for his wife. A female tutor, of course. I suggested you." In the immediate days following, other men added their wives. Crystal ended up with a class list. She wouldn't be earning enough to pay her share of the rent. But it was a start.

She met her new students on a clear, crisp autumn day when the leaves were just beginning to turn. The apartment she entered had endless windows overlooking Central Park. Crystal's amazement was torn between the view, and the appearance of her new acquaintances. Six women, aged from the mid-twenties to maybe fifty. They all wore makeup—lots and lots of makeup—and fashions taken from designer shop windows. Crystal's hostess, Fatima, performed introductions, and since Crystal couldn't keep the women straight by names—there were two other Fatimas—she classified them by jewelry: some jewelry; lots of jewelry; loads of jewelry. Because

British accents were mixed with American, she inadvertently went formal, and addressed each one as 'Ma'am'.

She was asked to sit on a sofa that could seat twelve, facing the windows. With the women arrayed alongside her—three to the left, three to the right—she didn't know in which direction to look. "A conversation club?" she echoed Fatima One, her hostess. "Okay." She was too bowled over by the excesses of Saudi life to add anything more.

"This is what we will do." Fatima One proved both the oldest and the group leader. "We will go outside, what American children call a 'field trip', on Wednesday afternoons. On Friday afternoons we will meet here to discuss our experience and learnings. Are all agreed?"

Of course all agreed. Towed by Fatima One's leadership, six Saudi and one American couldn't do anything but.

"We will begin by attending the theater." Fatima One had already purchased tickets, including Crystal's. "We will be seeing *Children of a Lesser God.*"

~

Crystal was excited. This was her first Broadway play. She waited for 'my ladies', as she had begun to think of them, on the sidewalk outside the Longacre Theatre. She was dressed in her best. Her add-a-pearl necklace didn't add up to much, but it was what she owned. She waited as two limos bullied their way exactly in front of the theatre. The people the limos disgorged were not her ladies. These women wore long dark coats, and scarves that covered their heads and necks. One wore a veil across the bottom half of her face.

"Crystal!" That was Fatima One's voice from behind the veil.

Crystal was gobsmacked into silence. She hadn't anticipated that her Fifth Avenue habitués would be religiously observant.

Fatima One gestured for an elderly gentleman in a perfectly tailored suit to step forward from their midst. "This is Uncle Khalid," she informed Crystal. "He accompanies us today, and will do so from now on."

Uncle Khalid nodded his head, silent.

His role, Crystal came to understand, was simply to be male, to be present, and to sit at one end of their row of seats. Crystal at the other end, presumed that she also was protection against infidels. Fatima Two, beside her, and Reema, who sat one beyond, whispered throughout the play to Crystal in English, and to each other in Arabic. "Do all deaf children attend such schools?" they inquired. "What work do such people perform as adults?"

Crystal couldn't answer. She was ignorant. She was a tutor who was ignorant about, above all things, her students.

"Did you like the play?" Scott asked her that evening.

"I don't know," Crystal answered honestly. "I hardly know what it was all about." But that night, lying at Scott's side, awake while he blew out the occasional snore, she reconstructed in her mind what she had seen on the stage and came up with a few questions herself. Had she ever experienced total silence? No. For a silent person who can sign, learning how to speak was more than creating sound—it was learning a new use of the body. A mouth—and Crystal opened and twisted her own in consideration—could simply be for eating and biting and breathing. Or it could learn to move in the shapes of a language. "Je suis une etudiante Américaine en France," she whispered in her college French. Each language had its own shapes.

When she arrived at Fatima's One's apartment two days later, she was prepared. She had researched answers to Fatima Two's and Reema's questions. She was ready to say 'Every state has a school for the deaf', and 'Deaf people frequently work as laboratory technicians, bookkeepers, electricians, photographers'.

She was not prepared to hear Fatima One start the discussion with,

"In the Anglophone world we are as the deaf."

"What?" Crystal was completely thrown off track.

"In the Anglophone world there is only one language," Fatima One amplified.

"Yes," murmured the women gathered in the expansive living room with its great windows and expensive view. They were dressed as they had been at the first meeting—haute couture perfection with Diamond District gleam.

"Those who do not speak English may as well be nonexistent out there," Fatima Two gestured toward the windows.

"Until we open our purses!" one of the younger ladies exclaimed. Her accent was heavy. Her purse was large and bright orange. Crystal remembered seeing orange at the play. Had this woman been carrying her orange purse and wearing orange shoes? Yes.

"In the play, when James insists that he loves Sarah, she tells him that hearing people who think they know her, don't," said a strong, quiet, British-accented voice. "When hearing people 'translate', they see only a reflection of their own minds. Sarah doubts whether she and James can ever truly come together."

"Ayesha remembers everything," Reema disclosed in admiration.

"Oh!" Fatima Two bounced with inspiration. "Crystal must come to visit us in Saudi Arabia! She and her husband!"

"Scott and I aren't married," Crystal mentioned.

At once, the surrounding chatter stopped—as if turned off by volume control.

"Not married?" Fatima One was concerned. "Yet your phone number is the same. Your address, too."

"We live together," Crystal explained.

That explanation caused consternation all around, in Arabic. "Enough!" Fatima One quelled the rest. To Crystal, she said, "You share a home, but you are not related—except by friendship?"

Fatima One had summed Crystal's situation up perfectly. "Yes," she agreed.

Fatima One then spoke with regret—great regret—"You must be married, to be with us."

"And to travel to see us when we are back home." Reema was wistful.

"What if she intends to be married?" Ayesha asked. They all looked to Fatima One.

"Intends..." Fatima One considered. "Yes. But it must be done soon."

Crystal didn't want to make the phone call. She knew what would happen. But she had to let her family know they shouldn't plan to see her at Christmas.

"Why forever not?" Mother's response was a swift challenge.

"Scott has to go to Turkey, and he asked me to come, and…since-it'll-be-easier-for-traveling-we-got-married." Crystal appended this corollary in a fading whisper.

As she expected, Mother went ballistic—Mother's reactions practically followed a script. Since Crystal had been hearing these opinions since birth, she could push their meanings to the background. Instead, she paid attention to the words' shapes, their modulations. And what she encountered, puzzled her deeply. She encountered a profound relief that was tempered by heartache.

She called Bee, who was now in college at Pomona.

"You got married by a magistrate?" Bee was exasperated. "Why? How could you? Mother's been planning your wedding ever since you drove off to Boston with Scott."

"What?" Crystal yelped.

"Didn't you ever wonder why she never griped about you moving in with him?" Bee asked this with incredulity.

"She wanted me to jump his bones," Crystal defended herself.

"She'd already bought you a dress." Bee spoke so as to drive this fact into Crystal's brain.

Crystal was furious/curious. "What does it look like?"

"What does it matter?" Now Bee was impatient. "All Sean says is, 'It's white and has stuff on it'. He can't sit on the pot without Mother coming to the bathroom door to tell him all the details."

"Well, I can't do anything about it." Crystal heard the old whine rise in her voice; she cut it short.

"Oh-yes-you-can!" Bee had become teeth-clenchingly firm. "You can promise to come out here and let her give you a reception. As big and fancy as she wants. Second best, but it'll have to do. You can come out here, and you can wear whatever damn dress she buys for you, and you can smile at all her damn friends, and you can make my damn life livable again. Not to speak of Sean's. And Far's."

"My, Bee!" Crystal sought to deflect Bee's force. "You do have a damn way with words."

"Promise!" Bee demanded. "If I'd known you were going to pull a stunt like this, I wouldn't have chosen a school so close to home. You owe me. You owe all of us. Promise!"

Crystal carried her phone to a window. She saw the city through a veil of snow. Suddenly, the West beckoned: sunsets over the ocean, desert hills turning pink with dawn. Bee, Sean, Far. And Mother: an eternal storm sheltering incomprehensible sorrow.

"What would I have to do?" she cautiously inquired.

∾

She had to give Mother a list of those friends she wanted to invite. The only friend she could think of was Justa. When she called Justa, she unloaded.

"Wait. Wait. Slow down," Justa begged. And at the end of Crystal's verbal scree: "If your mother wants a party, we'll come. June seventh? I'll ask for a long weekend off. And I'll let Gil know. Why don't you invite Lowry? I think she'll come, too. She seems lonely out there in Chicago."

Lowry answered on the first ring.

"This is Crystal," Crystal said. "Do you want to come to my not-a-wedding? It's next June."

Lowry's laughter was a welcome insert of merriment into Crystal's day. Lowry accepted, then suggested, "Why not invite Betsy? Did you know she's back in the States again?"

Betsy! Another friend!

Crystal called Atlanta to hear a very Southern accent—Betsy's mother's maid—followed by a Southern-quickened-by-Stanford voice: "Crystal! I can't believe it!"

Crystal talked to Betsy for two hours. Betsy had such amazing stories to tell about armed street battles, and a disgruntled Iranian mother-in-law.

"So there I was," said Betsy. "I would have walked out on the woman. Really, I would have. I wasn't going to hear one more time about how Far-had hadn't married her choice of a wife. But there were tear gas bombs outside. Tear gas, Crystal! Talk about a rock and a hard place. So I said to her, 'I can cry in here, or I can cry out there. And I'll just show you what I prefer!' So I opened the door, and went out into the courtyard, and pushed open the gate—and she came running after me. 'Don't you dare,' she said in that posh British accent she picked up in boarding school. 'That's my grandchild you're carrying in your belly.' By then we were both coughing and choking and crying—but not because we cared anything about each other, but because we both loved this child. That's the one thing I'm sorry for: Katayoun will probably never know but one half of her family. Even if the people aren't ideal, they're still yours."

When Crystal hung up, she had acquired two more guests for her party—Betsy and her little daughter, Katayoun—and an entirely odd and unanticipated appreciation. Her own un-ideal mother had never sunk to the level of tear gas.

❧

Crystal's final six guests invited themselves. Crystal hadn't thought to consider her ladies as friends, but—apparently—that was how they saw it. "We will come," Fatima One announced. "But first, we will give you a bridal shower."

"Oh, yes!" The younger women applauded Fatima One's idea.

To Crystal's horror, the ladies planned their next field trip as an expedition to the lingerie department at Saks. On that Wednesday, they settled Uncle Khalid a discrete distance away—on a chair in Better Dresses. They pushed Crystal into a mirrored cubicle, sending a saleslady in to assist. Then the Saudi women—a birds' chorus of giggles—dropped bras, panties, slips, nightgowns, peignoirs over the top of the door. "She'll need a 34B," the saleslady would announce, and the giggles would crescendo.

Crystal's 'shower' became a rainfall of silk and lace.

She ended up with six big bags that were almost weightless. She took a cab home, surrounded by exquisite finery. Arrived at her building, she had to crush the bags together so as to get them out of the cab, through the door, and into the elevator. The other elevator riders squished together to give her extra room. Crystal was embarrassed by the inconvenience of her opulence. She began adding up numbers in her head: she couldn't have that final sum right. Could she? In the apartment, she found Scott's old Stanford calculator and performed some electronic math. $776.91. Her new underwear had cost more than a month's rent.

Layers
I can count my layers -
I've watched them all put on
By myself and others.
The next's a wedding gown.

I can't always see my mother's.
My memory is too short:
She has layers that precede me,
That encase her like a fort.

But I've absorbed her layers -
Or at least a shadow of.
To what extent does who-I-am
Reflect her tortured love?

JJJJJ

Charlie had pneumonia. Justa learned this after worrying for three days—no Charlie at the library door at opening time, no Charlie settled in the fireplace nook. She got the information from a Veterans Administration Hospital volunteer who called the library because: "That's what he wrote for next of kin on his admission form. Your library." The woman was laughing. "Are you all members of the Albert family?"

"Albert?" Justa had to have it made clear: "Our homeless Charlie is really Charlie Albert?"

"That's what it says on my paperwork." The volunteer seemed a cheerful sort of woman.

"Thank you for calling." Justa was honestly grateful. "How ill is he?"

"So-so," was the reply. "But we're watchful. He's no longer young, and hasn't had the easiest time of it." This last was an understatement. It turned out the police had gathered Charlie up, fevered and hallucinating, after one of Berkeley's few remaining middle-class citizens called to complain that a man was having nightmares in her garden shed.

Justa hung up. "Connor!" She shouted across the library, and all the quiet patrons looked up to stare at her.

Connor hurried close. He listened to her report. "What should we do?" He properly used their library voice, a crisp sotto voce.

Justa thought. She answered, using the same: "They'll already have him clean. He'll be well fed. What do you think he'd like?"

"His clock? His book?" Connor checked the nook to make certain they hadn't been left there. They had not.

"Shakespeare!" Justa was inspired. And the following Sunday, she ushered Giant and Gil into Connor's car for a trip to the VA hospital in San Francisco.

The hospital was in Lands End, not far from where sea lions barked. Charlie was in a respiratory unit. The volunteer from that initial phone call met them. "What a family!" she sparkled. She had the air and bearing of a person who went through life with gusto. Her energy was sufficient to overrule the objections of the nurse at the front desk, who had taken one look at Giant and said,

"They're not family."

"They're family enough!" The volunteer's definition was victorious. She led Justa's party to Charlie's room, saying cheerfully, "I can't decide which of you he most favors." She stayed to watch while the group arrayed themselves around Charlie's bed.

"We brought you a surprise," Justa told him.

Charlie smiled his most holy smile. Somebody kind had draped his birthday tablecloth over his bedside stand. His clock sat behind the hospital-issued jug of water.

"Okay," Justa directed her boys. Each opened a library copy of *Twelfth Night* that she had marked, lightly, with pencil. *Twelfth Night* was one of the few Shakespeare plays she had actually seen performed. She couldn't guess which was Charlie's favorite, so she picked what she almost knew. She nodded at Gil to start.

Gil did so, embarrassedly. "'Approach, Sir Andrew'," he read as a very stiff and un-inebriated Sir Belch. "'Not to be abed after midnight is to be up betimes...'"

Charlie's excitement could scarcely be contained in his eyes. He gazed at Gil as if this most-unrepresentative Sir Belch were speaking the words of truest life, of permanent dreams. Then it was Giant's turn, and his Britishized Frenchy English was perfect for Sir Andrew Aguecheek. When Connor opened his mouth, Feste the clown became a drag queen of extreme dimensions. The others broke whatever little character they had assumed, and bent over their bellies in laughter. Connor sang the fool's song in a wavering falsetto, and the volunteer gasped, "I'm going to wet my pants!"

"Again," Charlie whispered.

"'What is love?'" Connor warbled. "''Tis not hereafter; present mirth hath present laughter.'"

Charlie's roommates applauded.

∾

The next day, Monday, being a work day, Justa started preparing a second scene for her little troop of actors. She angled work-time permission to go downtown on the pretext of picking up some forms. She spent the better part of an hour in the Art and Music room.

"Music for Shakespeare!" Wanda enthused.

"Sibelius!" Agnes suggested.

"No, no!" Wanda disagreed. "Ralph Vaughn Williams!"

The two ladies had a lovely time.

Going home that evening, Justa carried Korngold's *Songs of the Clown*. She didn't know if Connor would be able to hit all the notes. But even if he couldn't, she knew he had enough showmanship to sing them incorrectly with pizzazz.

"I can hardly wait," she laughed with Gil.

But then, two days later, the volunteer phoned the library, asked to speak with Justa, and said, "I'm so sorry. So very, very sorry."

Justa had heard those same words, spoken the same way, before. Aunt Edith. Kendall.

"Charlie took a sudden turn for the worse," the woman continued. "Last night, or rather very early this morning, a nurse taking routine vital signs found him...passed away."

"Passed away," Justa repeated. Such a gentle euphemism: it only skimmed the surface of a brutal truth. She didn't return to the cart of books she had been shelving. She didn't ask permission from anybody, or even say goodby. She simply walked out the door that Charlie would never enter again. She contained herself like a statue, waiting for a bus. She remained tight until she could finally get herself into her apartment, until she stood before her keyboard. Then, all bonds released, she crashed her hands down into a chord that should have shouted a horrendous, ear-mauling, shearing of beauty. The instrument teetered forward and back, side to side; its spindly folding legs couldn't take the force with which Justa needed to play. The dissonance came out as something weak, flabby. This ersatz piano couldn't handle the anger and loss flowing upward from Justa's toes, downward from her skull, viscerally from her gut. It couldn't hold the weight of anything heavier than a euphemism.

Justa bowed her head over the shallow plastic keys and wept.

When Gil came home, he phoned Connor. Connor contacted the VA hospital.

"There'll be a funeral," Gil told Justa. "We can say goodbye."

☙

The VA would make all the arrangements, the volunteer had told Connor. Charlie's 'next of kin' must only choose what to wear.

For Justa, the decision was easy: her most formal outfit, the navy blue dress and pumps she had last worn five years ago, to Mark Cunningham's hearing at the Old Courthouse in San Jose. She tried the dress on, in front of the bathroom mirror. It fit better now. She stared at her reflection, trying to see how the person she was now had overlain the person she used to be. The phone rang and—in eerie coincidence to the dress—a woman's voice said, "Justa, I thought you would want to know: Mark Cunningham is dead."

"Mrs. Soames." That voice was one of the layers in Justa's soul.

"I'm flying out," said Kendall's mother. "He'll be buried tomorrow afternoon in San Jose."

Justa waited for the old horror to swallow her up. But it didn't. Instead, noiseless music latched itself to remembered words: 'The rain it raineth every day'. The refrain from a *Twelfth Night* song.

"At the old Jewish cemetery there," Mrs. Soames continued.

'With hey, ho, the wind and the rain.' The music matched the words perfectly.

"At three p.m.," Mrs. Soames said.

This music wasn't anything the ladies had shown Justa—it was nobody but Justa herself. When had she begun to interpret Shakespeare? Shakespeare—like Beethoven, like Bach—had been one of the few human beings who understood the ineffable.

"Will you meet me there?" Mrs. Soames asked.

"Yes," Justa told her.

The following morning she dressed for two funerals. Connor drove them—her, Gil, Giant—all the way across the Bay Bridge, through San Francisco, and into San Bruno. Endless rows of identical white headstones—acres and acres of uniformity—marked the Golden Gate National Cemetery. "We're going to send Charlie off with full military honors," the VA volunteer had promised. The volunteer was waiting at the gate with a map so they could find the right plot. They, plus she, were the only civilian attendees. The other 'mourners' were not: a funeral director in dress uniform; a trumpeter who would play 'Taps'; an honors team from the National Guard. The trumpeter performed with the skill of bored repetition. The one female soldier walked around the polished walnut casket to hand Justa a tightly folded flag.

"Lieutenant Albert's last insignia," the volunteer smiled.

But, "What about Charlie's book?" Justa asked. "What happened to his clock?"

The volunteer didn't know.

"Will you find out?" Justa begged.

"Of course, if you want me to." But the volunteer, previously so helpful, appeared inconvenienced by Justa's request. She looked at her watch; she was moving on to other demands of the day. Justa had nothing but a birthday hat to lay at the place where Charlie's stone would eventually rest.

"Okay?" Gil asked her worriedly.

"Okay," she had to tell him.

She took over the driver's seat of Connor's car. She drove the boys to the Daly City BART station so they could catch a train across the Bay. Each protested in his own way. Gil: "I don't have to teach today, Justie. I can come with you." Connor: "I can call in sick." Giant: "I also will go to San Jose, if you wish."

Justa did not wish. What came next was for her and Mrs. Soames.

She drove down a freeway that edged the San Andreas fault, passing by towns to her left and long narrow lakes to her right. Fault lakes, breach lakes, reservoirs of water covering land that had once before, and would someday again, break in two. She glanced in the rearview mirror and saw the line that had centered her brow ever since college—the breach mark of her own life.

After forty miles she arrived at a cemetery where unmatching tombstones meandered in uneven, shaded rows; where Christians lay sheltered by live oaks; where Jews rested beneath Old Testament trees. Mrs. Soames stood beneath a fan palm. A man wearing a yarmulke was speaking to her, and only to her. There were no other people present. Justa went to take Mrs. Soames's hand, a resumption of their courtroom closeness.

"For He will give His angels charge over thee, to keep thee in all thy ways," the rabbi concluded his prayer. "You're late," he said to Justa, but he wasn't scolding. "You can still put dirt in the grave."

Cunningham's casket already lay in its deep hole: a plain pine box—nothing like Charlie's USA government issue. Ashes to ashes: Justa stooped to clutch up soil from the neatly heaped pile. The earth was dark, heavy, mixed with sand. Dust to dust: Justa didn't just drop her handful, she aimed for and struck the boards over Mark Cunningham's heart. What should have been a gentle pattering became a firing of shot.

The rabbi's eyebrows popped. "Wow!" he said. And then, with kind concern, "Would you ladies like to chat? We can go into the chapel, it's nondenominational." He smiled, and Justa realized that this last was supposed to be the sort of joke that would ease them into conversation.

But, "No," said Mrs. Soames. "Thank you. If you don't mind, I think Justa and I will sit here for a while, by ourselves."

They sat on a stone bench, their hands again joined. "I got here this morning," Mrs. Soames said. "Six o'clock your time, three o'clock mine. I took a red-eye. So little advance notice. Did you know that Jewish law requires a body to be buried the same day, or the next? I didn't. Cunningham had converted—or more likely chosen from a background of nothing. He used to write and tell me how sorry he was, how he wished he could exchange his own life for Kendall's. He was reading through the great books of religion. He eventually chose from among the monotheistic faiths. He felt that the god of the Old Testament suited him best, knew better how to punish."

Mrs. Soames paused. For a moment she appeared drained of words. Then she continued: "I never answered. But I read his letters. Sometimes all he'd send would be a clipping from the newspaper—a photo or depiction of a butterfly, a moth, a bird. Anything that flew, always accompanied by his own sketch of an angel. I think he was telling me, perhaps telling himself, that Kendall's spirit had flown away and become an angel. That in some manner, Kendall still exists."

Justa had never allowed herself to consider that possibility. Her breath caught. She asked: "Do you think he does?"

"No. I can't go down that route. I know that Kendall is gone, just as Mark Cunningham is gone. Just as that part of my life is gone. Loss demands acceptance. That's why I needed to put dirt into Cunningham's grave. I had to finish."

Justa wondered if she, herself, were finished. No, not yet.

"Kendall's father is holding onto his anger. He's holding onto his grief—he won't allow it to grow and change. He thinks that I'm heartless, unloving, insane. We're separated now."

"I'm sorry."

"Don't be." For the first time, Mrs. Soames smiled. Oh, how she looked like Kendall! "It frees me to go on." She leaned close to kiss Justa's cheek. Then she stood and stretched her arms way up, and then way out to the sides. "I must leave you now. I'm on standby for another red-eye."

Justa stayed put. All the while that Mrs. Soames had been talking, cemetery workers had been filling in Mark Cunningham's grave. One man rode atop a little backhoe, another wielded a shovel, a third operated a tamping device. The men worked within a choreography of long-set practice—fill, smooth, tamp. They took no notice of the women. They didn't acknowledge Mrs. Soames' departure. They simply completed the job. Then the tamper attached his tool to the backhoe, before balancing his buttocks on the narrow ridge behind the driver's seat. The shoveler clung to the roll bars. "*Vámanos,*" he said.

Justa was left with Mark Cunningham's finished grave. She made herself stand and go inspect the oblong of bare ground. No marker, no flowers— not even a paper hat. This space of earth possessed nothing but the emptiness of grief, something Justa hadn't observed when she was throwing dirt at the coffin. Now she was aware of a rawness—not the opportunity of turned soil, but rather the exposure of pain.

"Did you truly change?" She found herself whispering. "Did you grow?" She expected no reply.

But if there had been one, would she stay to listen?

Maybe.

CCCCC

Deplaning at LAX, Crystal—as always—looked for Far. As the tallest of the family, he was easiest to locate. Today the expression on his face was muted, quiet—until he saw Crystal beyond the gate, and then he lit up with pleasure. Crystal grinned at him before taking in the rest. Sean was bouncing on his Nikes, trying to see over heads. Bee had her bottom lip caught between her teeth: she was anxious. Mother was postural perfect with rose-gold hair.

Past the gate, Mother pressed her own cheek against Crystal's, then let go.

"Hi, Crystal!" Sean shouted happily.

Far got his chance to hug Crystal, and he did so, tightly.

As a cluster, the Kelseys moved through the terminal to baggage, and from baggage to the parking garage. Far settled Crystal's suitcase into the trunk, and then it was Highway 405 all the way, with the ocean visible after Long Beach. When they finally turned off the highway, Crystal rolled down her window to suck in the air. Her first taste of Pacific salt.

Home.

Up their own driveway.

"We have things to show you, Crystal." Mother swung her legs from the car, knees together.

"Wait 'til you see it!" Sean teased. Bee pinched him. "Well, I like it," he defended himself hotly.

Mother, then Sean, then Bee, then Crystal crowded into Crystal's old room. There it was, laid out on the bed, the dress Mother had bought last year. The dress was beautiful. More than beautiful, gorgeous. Much of the dress was lace—but not the filmy lace Crystal had expected. Rather, this was a crocheted lace in grayish beige that draped from the elbows, belted the waist, and marked the skirt tiers of creamy crinkled cotton.

"It's a Mexican wedding dress," Mother said crisply. The dress wasn't crisp at all. It was soft to the eyes, and—when Crystal reached to touch—soft in her fingers.

"Do you like it?" Bee asked, and Crystal swung around, suddenly aware. Bee was afraid of the inevitable argument that normally started off Crystal's visits. This could have been a huge one.

"I love it, Bee," Crystal told her.

Mother sighed, perhaps with relief. Crystal couldn't tell.

⌒

After dinner she heard and saw Mother's plans: everything from how Mother had auditioned musicians, to the bulletin board on which Mother had thumbtacked circles and squares representing tables and chairs—including a booster seat for Betsy's child. The following morning, when Crystal wandered into breakfast, Mother and Bee sat waiting for her at the kitchen table. Crystal took one look at the meaningful silence on Bee's face, and put herself at Mother's disposal. "What do you want for me to do to-day?"

Bee beamed.

"I want you to see the Gardens," Mother said promptly. "Since there will be no rehearsal tomorrow." Was there a hint of blame in that phrase? "I want you to become familiar with the layout so that on Saturday you'll be able to walk among the flowerbeds and tables, to chat with our guests."

"Okay." Crystal pictured herself in that dress, performing the kind of smooth sidling that normally belonged to restaurant waiters.

"I'm giving Sean a driving lesson," Bee put in—which Crystal understood was a ploy to engage Sean's energies and keep him out of the way.

"If you could just dress up a little for the Gardens?" Mother hinted/insisted.

Crystal looked down at the old shorts and T-shirt she had found in her room. "I brought a skirt," she admitted.

"Good!" Mother approved.

An hour later, wearing the skirt, Crystal entered the Sherman Gardens. She stepped into a glory of fuchsias, and stood still. Blossoms covered bushes, they hung from baskets. The petals were a medley of pinks to purples, with every red in between. There were other flowers in the Gardens, too, but it was the fuchsias that made Crystal feel as though she were in the midst of a sunstorm.

"Lovely, isn't it?" Mother oozed satisfaction.

'Lovely' was an insufficient adjective.

Mother was not satisfied with: the fact that the Gardens only had nine round tables waiting, when Mother had specifically asked for ten; the laundry guy who was in the process of delivering white linens instead of the blush pink Mother preferred; the many champagne bottles still standing in their crates, instead of in one of the restaurant's glass-fronted coolers. Mother—a Garden patron, now client—magisterially expected the staff to accommodate both her intrusion and her complaints.

Which they did, until a waiter—carrying a tray with a plate of sugar cookies and two tall glasses of iced tea—ushered Mother and Crystal out into the sunlight so as to seat them at a patio table for two.

Crystal tried to recall: had she and Mother ever sat like this, alone, together, in a restaurant? She didn't know where to put her legs, her feet, so as to not bump into Mother's.

Mother showed no such discomfort. She knew exactly what this social situation required. She began to gossip as if Crystal were a friend, not a daughter. "I don't know if Bee has told you..." Mother said, and went on to divulge that Lisa Snelling was getting a divorce. Bob Griffin had taken the late Harvey Milk's advice and declared himself gay. The scandal! "And to think I thought he might be right for you." Mother shook her head

Crystal couldn't resist. "You can be so wrong."

"Yes," Mother, surprisingly, agreed. She looked directly into Crystal's eyes: "But I can admit it."

Crystal felt as though a hand had pushed her, hard, against the back of her chair. Did Mother's claim hold some truth? Or was this the beginning of what Bee had always dreaded: the fight that had been brewing ever since Crystal's 'thoughtless' marriage, ever since she was fired from Simmons, ever since the day she was born? Crystal opened her mouth to speak, but couldn't formulate a rebuttal. She was caught in a quandary of memories she was being forced to rethink.

Mother suffered no such discomposure. She went on to another story: one of her friends had been caught shoplifting at Robinson's department store. Scarves, this woman only stole scarves. "It turned out," Mother said with honest amazement and undisguised glee, "that she had three thousand scarves in her attic, most of the silk ruined by heat. Can you believe it!"

Crystal couldn't. She wouldn't be able to understand anything until she succeeded in translating this unsettling occasion into a poem. Or poems. 'Broiled Hermès'—what a great title! But what might it mean? Crystal allowed Mother to carry on the conversation, unimpeded. Crystal's brain was much too crowded with contradictions.

∽

Friday was airport day. Crystal had her assignment: she was to pick up Justa, Gil, and Justa's parents at the Orange County Airport. Then she was to take them to the Marriott where Mother had reserved rooms. Crystal was to make her guests comfortable. (Crystal's only guideline, here, was an aside from Bee that it would be best if Mother didn't have to be bothered with *anything*, because of a crisis concerning centerpieces.) Crystal decided, all on her own, that she needn't return home until dinnertime. That left her free to take Justa to the beach!

Crystal was as bouncy as Sean, waiting at airport windows. She saw Gil leave the airplane, descend the moveable staircase. Crystal waved until Justa, following Gil, noticed whatever visible disturbance Crystal was making behind the glass, and waved back. Mr. and Mrs. Matthews stepped onto tarmac, and Crystal bopped impatiently on her toes until everybody finally entered the terminal.

Crystal hugged and kissed, and was hugged and kissed back, until she lost track of where all the hugs and kisses were coming from. "Come on!" She led her group to collect their baggage, and then outside. At Far's car, she politely offered Mrs. Matthews the front passenger seat.

"Let Justie sit there," Mrs. Matthews said.

So Crystal got to drive with her best friend at her side—like in college. From the corner of her eye, she examined Justa as best she could. Justa looked better than she had last year, and it wasn't only because her hair was shorter, which was nice. Justa looked rested. Reassured, Crystal glanced at her other passengers through the rearview mirror. She should sort out what would make them comfortable for the remainder of the day. She asked.

Gil: "I told Scott I'd wait around the hotel for him." Scott, whose parents had picked him up at LAX yesterday, was busy ferrying cousins from the two airports to the Marriott. Crystal might get the chance to wave at him across the lobby.

Mr. Matthews: "And we'll wait for Lowry," who was renting a car at LAX, and driving Betsy, Katayoun, and one of the Yamadas—named Victor— down to Newport Beach. Crystal didn't know Victor at all, but when Lowry asked, Crystal had been more than happy to add another person to her friends list.

"Do you want to go to the beach?" she asked Justa, hoping. "I brought one of Bee's swim suits for you."

To Crystal's joy, Justa agreed immediately: "Okay!"

Crystal, very properly, got the Matthewses to the Marriott, helped them carry their luggage and find their rooms. She and Justa took over a bathroom so they could change into the bathing suits.

They were free to go.

It was a freedom the like of which Crystal hadn't felt since...well, since before Kendall died. She felt young, and wondered if Justa did, too. Riding in the elevator, she showed off the white-gold band she and Scott bought at Tiffany's the morning they got married.

Justa took Crystal's hand in her own. "A ring to match your hair," Justa remarked. She pressed Crystal's hand, looked up, and glinted amusement into Crystal's eyes. "If Kendall were here, he'd give us its exact chemical formulation."

⌒

Fast forward, and Crystal stood in the Sherman Gardens next to her parents, with Scott and his parents on her other side. Her Mexican wedding dress swirled marvelously, and helped her alleviate that special tension caused by a mixture of anxiety and boredom. She slowly twisted her body so she could feel a touch of lace, and a breath of air, over her toes.

"Thank you, so much," she said to Helen Snelling and her daughter, Lisa. They had come without husbands. Crystal allowed Helen to airbrush her cheek with a kiss.

Thank you, so much," she said to somebody she didn't know, but who knew Scott's parents.

Sean, hovering between the Garden entrance and the parking lot, shouted, "They're here, Crystal," which she heard easily over the continuing congratulations. From where she stood, she could see something of what was going on in the parking lot. And right now a lot was happening because the Saudi ladies were arrived. Fatima One had decided that the Sherman Gardens was an extension of Crystal's home, not a public venue—for this one afternoon—and Crystal expected to see them dressed to kill.

Which they were. The people in line, instead of looking forward, toward her and Scott, were instead gaping backward. Crystal leaned so she herself could better watch a catwalk from New York, Paris and London extend into her party. Mother stood frozen, her right hand hanging alone in the air, ready to shake. She had gone silent during the phone call when Crystal said the Saudi ladies, and Uncle Khalid, were coming as friends; that they were staying at the Beverley Hills Hotel, not the Marriott; that they would secure their own transportation by instructing somebody or other to hire a limo service. Within a week, Mother had found three people—distant sorority connections—to successfully fill out the Saudi table: the haute couture buyer for I. Magnin (flying down from San Francisco); and a Foreign Services couple (flying in from DC). Crystal was always amazed at how far the power of the Tri Deltas reached into the world.

"Thank you," she said, because Mother was back to welcoming, her hand back to shaking. People remembered where they were and what they were supposed to be doing. The line resumed movement.

Crystal had to remain standing until the line dwindled, until most guests found their place cards, until Mother decided the few latecomers would have to enter ungreeted. Only then could Crystal relax. The people assigned to Scott's and her table—Justa, Gil, Lowry, Victor, Betsy, Katayoun, Bee and Sean—had already served themselves from the buffet. Bee—under age—was sipping wine.

"Ask her," Katayoun poked Betsy's ribs.

"Katty wants to know if she can have the rose on the top of the cake," Betsy obediently requested.

Crystal looked over to where a wedding cake sat in all its glory: three layers for today, and a top layer that would be set aside for a reason Crystal couldn't remember. "It's real," she said of the rose. "You can't eat it."

"I know," Katayoun whispered.

"She knows," Betsy repeated.

"Fine with me," Crystal agreed.

Betsy helped Katayoun down from her chair. Mother and daughter walked hand in hand to the cake table. Betsy bent across the top to speak to the caterer; little Katayoun put her hands on the edge, pulling herself close, listening in anticipation. Only now did Crystal see, only now could she appreciate: while little Katayoun was dark and Betsy was fair, their profiles were two renditions of the same.

All I can do
Is try
And work in
Small ways
On Kindness.

CODA

"There's no place like nowhere."

John Lennon, a few months before he and Yoko Ono began recording
their album, *Double Fantasy*.

Autumn 1980

Somewhere near Seattle

Justa's new home was a winterized summer cottage on top of a hill in Washington State—Gil's find. He was still inordinately pleased with himself for having seen the notice on a kiosk. Up until then, he and Justa had been crossing off rentals in *The Seattle Times*. As a beginning assistant professor at the University of Washington, Gil couldn't afford to rent even a closet near campus.

And then he discovered the cottage, only fifteen miles away, on top of a hill and surrounded by Douglas firs, mist and rain.

'The rain it raineth every day.'

It was the rain that made Justa feel so far away from her previous life. She had never before lived in so little sunlight. The interior of this cottage was dark even by Berkeley standards, with the windows facing mostly north and east. But she liked the fireplace with its rough wooden mantel. And she loved the tiny bit of stained glass above the door in the entry hall. She absolutely loved the hill: mountain quail that announced her approach with tiny foghorn calls; the click-squish of squirrels pattering along fallen timber that was turning to mulch; the wind combing through standing firs until the trees sounded like rainsticks, or invisible hail.

On this Saturday of unceasing rain, she was studying a composition titled 'Les Jours Pluvieux' that she had borrowed from the university's music collection. She wasn't playing the piece yet, only reading. She thought she may have finally found a composer who matched her soul: the unknown, obscure, utterly truthful-to-sound, Marie Jaëll.

Gil, coming inside after checking the mailbox, broke her concentration.

"Anything?" she hoped.

Gil held a postcard in his hand. His face was trying to hide a smile. "I have to go out," he said, "to the bottom of the hill. I may have to wait a long time."

"Why?"

He wouldn't tell her.

Once again alone, Justa dragged her cushion down the room to where her keyboard rested on the floor. She and Gil had moved with only what they could carry in Gil's dilapidated new/old Mustang; they owned no chairs. Sitting cross-legged, she bent over keys.

Her hands stuttered. The rain's patter complicated her tempo. Justa adjusted until she was in concert with the rain. And then she stopped. The truth was, even rain on the roof could gather a chord better than did an electronic keyboard. Justa scooted away from electronic music and over to the sliding glass door. There she listened to a symphony of percussion with no obvious form; there she picked out the possibility of themes that someday she might play.

Outside, a car door slammed. The rain was now playing against twilight: Justa had listened away most of the afternoon. She heard another—then a second—slam of a much heavier vehicle door.

She went into the entry hall to see Gil partly inside, but mostly on the front step, shaking himself like a dog. His head and torso were sheathed in waterproof nylon. He appeared a very self-satisfied purple tent. Beyond him, two identical young men with auburn ponytails were pulling on rain jackets. They looked familiar, almost Asian. One went around to open the back of an unmarked van while the other waved cheerfully at Justa. Bemused, she returned the wave.

"We're Matt and Mike," the waver called to her. "O'Brien. Remember us?"

Justa did, now. The last time she saw them was at Lowry's wedding, sticking their heads into a koi pond. Now they must be at least eighteen years old. With their long legs, they hardly had to jump to disappear into the van. Gil rushed to help them do whatever it was they had come here to do, but stopped before disappearing. He lingered on the ground while the boys lowered a ramp. Gil, more sedately, ascended.

"We'll get in front of it," Justa heard Matt, or Mike, say. "All you have to do is guide it. Okay?"

"Okay." The van was too full of people and things for Gil's voice to echo much.

The twins emerged, side by side, controlling the descent of a large something that was obviously very heavy. It was tarped and padded; its casters bumped irregularly against the ramp's corrugated metal.

Justa's breath caught in her throat.

The large something reached driveway cement. The twins separated. "Okay," said one. "We'll push, Gil. You guide it from the front."

Gil flashed a smile at Justa, and put himself in place.

The boys pushed.

"Greatdad says hello." This boy could push and talk without losing breath. Justa remembered to exhale. "And so does everybody else."

Justa counted back generations. 'Greatdad' was Hiro.

"This will be our last job before starting at Davis," the same twin told her. They were on the front path, now.

Gil stopped before the two door steps. "What should I do?" he asked the experts.

"We've got a portable ramp," the voluble twin told him, while the other loped back to the van.

"We've been working for Greatdad all summer." The talking twin, his brother and Gil, got the something into the house. "Greatdad wants to cut off our ponytails. Says he won't give us our last paycheck 'til we do." The three rolled their burden into the cottage's living room. "Where do you want it?"

Instead of speaking, Justa went over to her keyboard, unplugged it, picked it up, and pointed.

"I'll get the bench," the silent twin offered. He left the cottage through the still open front door.

"We're gonna sic Mom on him." The talker was cheerful. He and Gil began untying. Gil folded the tarp carefully, so as to minimize the amount of water dripping onto the fir-planked floor. "Greatdad doesn't stand a chance." The twin pulled away the last blankets, and Justa's spinet stood before her. "Ta-da! Your dad says it's gonna be out of tune."

Justa never doubted that for a moment. She let Gil and the twin push the piano against the wall.

"So he sent a check to pay for the tuning. We have it. Somewhere."

Gil lifted the keyboard cover. He touched middle C. To Justa, and Justa alone, he gently said, "It still works."

"Here's your bench." The talky twin announced his brother's arrival. "Oh, yeah. The envelope's taped underneath." The two boys unwrapped the bench.

Justa stopped hearing Hiro's great-grandson. Instead, she listened to the voice of this piano in her mind, so distinct from any other piano she had ever played. It possessed a particular tonal quality that meant home, that meant herself, that meant who she was from way back...well, forever.

"Would you guys like something hot to drink? Coffee, tea, apple cider?" Gil's voice had a music of its own.

Justa sat. She allowed her fingers to run up and down a C scale. She tried out a few chords. The piano—even with its chords jangled, its notes turned to oddities—responded to her fingers like a lover. Beneath the temporary aberrations, its acoustical soul sang Justa's songs in a way that tingled her toes. She experimented: Jaëll, the rain. Then her right hand started a phrase that her left hand echoed—treble and bass coming together in an interweaving of two equals. She strung the notes of Beethoven's Invention Number One along the chain of a rainy day rhythm. "It's our song," Gil's words, clarinet-clear, came to her from the kitchen. "Justie calls it 'The Fractal Melody'.

You will eventually lose everything you love, but in the end, the love will always return in new forms.

From a story about Franz Kafka, as told by Vipassanā meditation teacher, Tara Brach.

Permissions, Acknowledgments and Notes

Front Matter

Henry Adams, from *The Education of Henry Adams*, The Massachusetts Historical Society, 1918.

Prelude

Duck and Cover, Official Civil Defense Film produced in cooperation with the Federal Civil Defense Administration and in consultation with the Safety Commission of the National Education Association, 1951

Chapter 1 Starting Autumn, 1969

Spiro Agnew. Citizens Testimonial Dinner, New Orleans, Louisiana, October 19, 1969; Spiro T. Agnew papers; Special Collections and University Archives; University of Maryland Libraries.

The Moratorium to End the War in Vietnam, organized by a small, ad hoc committee, brought people together in communities and colleges throughout the world. Eight thousand students and citizens participated at Stanford.

Linus Pauling. Courtesy Ava Helen and Linus Pauling Papers, Special Collections & Archives Research Center, Oregon State University Libraries, Published Papers and Official Documents. 1969s.13: Manuscript, Typescripts [English and Spanish], Correspondence, Notes, Background Material: *Stop the War!*, Vietnam Moratorium Meeting, Stanford University, Palo Alto, California, October 15, 1969. Permission granted May 22, 2024.

The nationwide student strike of Spring 1970 was a spontaneous eruption. Because there was no central organizing committee, each campus planned its own response. At Stanford, the strike lasted for about a week.

The Holy Scriptures According to the Masoretic Text, a new translation with the aid of previous versions and with constant consultation of Jewish authorities, The Jewish Publication Society of America, Philadelphia, 1917.

Karl Marx, *Critique of Hegel's Philosophy of Right*, 1843.

Mahatma Gandhi. *Harijan*, Nov. 19, 1938, Volume 6, p. 343. Digitized by the Gandhi Heritage Portal,
https://www.gandhiheritageportal.org/journals-by-gandhiji/harijan

Chapter 2 Starting Autumn, 1970

Sing a Battle Song: The Revolutionary Poetry, Statements, and Communiques of the Weather Underground 1970-1974; edited by Bernardine Dohrn, Bill Ayers, Jeff Jones; Seven Stories Press, First Edition (September

15, 2006).

Virginia Woolf, *A Room of One's Own*, Hogarth Press, 1929.

'Girls Say Yes to boys who say No', Smithsonian, National Museum of American History, CC0.

Chapter 3 Starting Autumn, 1971

Janis Joplin and The Full Tilt Boogie Band, *Pearl*, Columbia Records, 1971. 'Buried Alive In The Blues' was written by Nick Gravenites.

Chapter 4 Starting Autumn, 1972

Our Bodies, Ourselves, A Book By and For Women, The Boston Women's Health Book Collective, Simon & Schuster, 1973.

Tillie Olsen. Crystal's Tillieism is paraphrased from *Tell Me A Riddle*, Tillie Olsen, Rutgers University Press, 1995. Permission granted May 23, 2024.

Henry Kissinger, October 26, 1972. https://www.archives.gov/exhibits/remembering-vietnam-online-exhibit-episodes-9-12

Phi Delts. While the raffling scandal really happened, the women's march happened, and the university's response happened, I have fictionalized much of the story. I condensed four weeks into three days. I moved up the scandal by several months to make it fit better into the Lowry timeline. I made up a headline, an ad, and an article quote. My historical sources were articles from *The Stanford Daily* archives, dating from April 26, 1973 to May 31, 1973.
P.S. I marched, too. The Phi Delts were suspended for two years.

Chapter 5 Starting Autumn, 1973

Judy Collins #3, Elektra Records, 1963. 'To Everything There Is a Season' was written by Pete Seegar in 1959, based on a verse from Ecclesiastes.

Only 30 Black students in Lowry's Stanford class? That's the number I found by counting faces in the 1969 Froshbook.

Guilty, Guilty, Guilty! by Gary Trudeau, Holt, Rinehart & Winston, 1973.

Student firefighters? Amazing but true. The Encina Hall fire actually happened in June 1972, but I moved it to Autumn 1973 for this story. https://stanfordmag.org/contents/when-students-fought-fires

Lorin Hollander graciously provided me with the information—and wording—I needed, in a January 14, 2013 email exchange.

Pelé was one of the greatest soccer players of all time. He grew up in poverty in Brazil, and in 2018 founded the Pelé Foundation to help impoverished children everywhere. While the incident described by Kendall is imaginary, I believe it fits Pelé's personality.

Chapter 6 Starting Autumn, 1974

I read about the Night Rider Program in Duke Law School's 1975-1976 *Bulletin*.

Kingfish, a legendary Bay Area band, was founded in 1973. Their first album, *Kingfish*, was released in 1976.

Chapter 7 Starting Autumn, 1975

Gerald R. Ford, 'Statement and Responses to Questions From Members of the House Judiciary Committee Concerning the Pardon of Richard Nixon'. *The American Presidency Project*, https://www.presidency.ucsb.edu/node/256137

The Brothers Karamazov, by Fyodor Dostoevsky, as translated by Constance Garnett, Modern Library, 1929.

Chapter 8 Starting Autumn, 1976

'Time Is On My Side', written by Jerry Ragovoy, and covered by The Rolling Stones in their 12x5 album, ABKCO Records, 1964.

Chapter 9 Starting Autumn, 1977

Barbara Gordon, *I'm Dancing As Fast As I Can*, Harper Collins, 1979.

Human Sexual Response, by William H. Masters and Virginia E. Johnson. Published by Little, Brown and Company in 1966.

'The Transsexuals', *Newsweek*, Nov. 22, 1976, page 104.

Chapter 10 Starting Autumn, 1978

A Chorus Line, music by Marvin Hamlisch, lyrics by Edward Kleban, book by James Kirkwood Jr. and Nicholas Dante, opened on Broadway in 1975, directed by Michael Bennett.

Raintree County...which had no boundaries in time and space, where lurked musical and strange names and mythical and lost peoples, and which was itself only a name musical and strange; by Ross Lockridge Jr; Riverside Press; 1948. The MGM movie released in 1957, *Raintree County* was based on the book. Directed by Edward Dmytryk, it received four Academy Award nominations. Nat King Cole sang the theme song.

Chapter 11 Starting Autumn, 1979

'The Long and Winding Road', The Beatles, *Let It Be*, Apple Records, 1970.

Children of a Lesser God, by Mark Medoff, Westmark Productions, 1980.

Songs of the Clown, Erich Korngold, Op. 29, 1937.

The Holy Scriptures According to the Masoretic Text, a new translation with the aid of previous versions and with constant consultation of Jewish authorities, The Jewish Publication Society of America, Philadelphia, 1917.

Chapter 12 Autumn 1980

John Lennon, 'There's No Place Like Nowhere', article by Brian R. San Souci, *Rhode Island Monthly*, June 2010,Vol. 23, No. 2, pages 52-55, 87-92. Permission granted May 24, 2024.

Tara Brach. From a talk given on May 20, 2015, 'Impermanence—Awakening Through Insecurity, Part 2'. Permission granted November 18, 2024. You can find the talk at
https://www.tarabrach.com/part-2-impermanence-awakening-through-insecurity/

And also...

The type fonts I used are all open source. The titles are in *Lora*, by Cyreal Fonts. The text is in *Libre Baskerville*, designed by Pablo Impallari. And the glyph is from the *Nymphette* font designed by Lauren Thompson. Thank you, all!